This Side of the Divide

Stories of the American West

This Side of the Divide

Stories of the American West

Foreword by Claire Vaye Watkins

Edited by Danilo John Thomas

with the University of Nevada, Reno
MFA Program in Creative Writing

BAOBAB PRESS
RENO, NV

First Printing

ISBN-13: 978-1-936097-24-1
ISBN-10: 1-93609-724-9

Library of Congress Control Number: 2018960515

Baobab Press
121 California Avenue
Reno, Nevada 89509
www.baobabpress.com

Printed in the United States

waters parting . . .

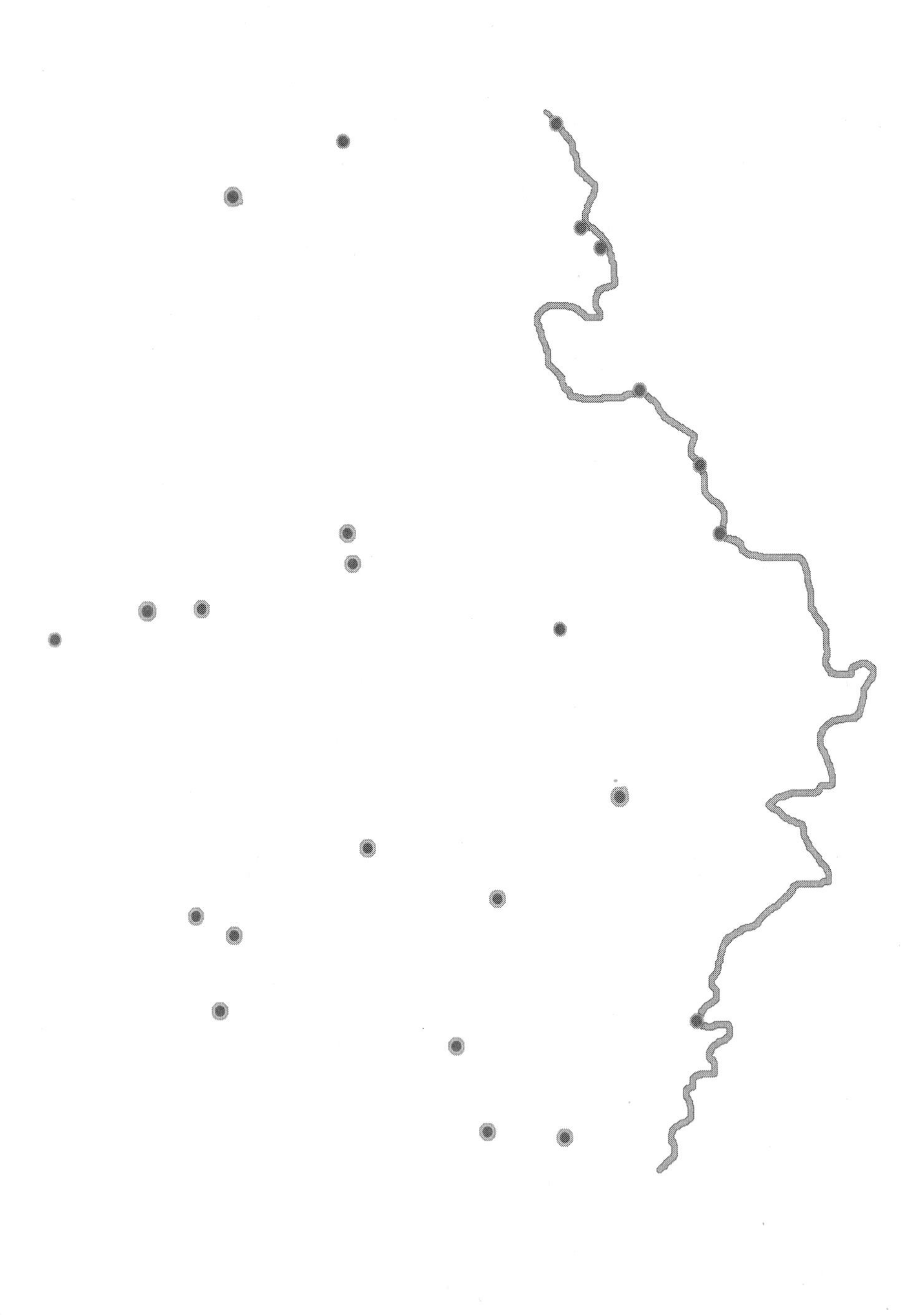

Contents

This Side of the Divide

Stories of the American West

Foreword

Claire Vaye Watkins

I like place in fiction. I like my stories to happen somewhere to people who are from somewhere. More than like, I need place. I don't know how to start a piece without a long meditation on its setting, pages and pages about its geology, ecology, and culture that a reader will never see. My writing process is deeply dependent on place, and my reading process too. The fiction that has stayed with me often has a dynamic and deeply resonant sense of place. If I have an aesthetic flag to run up a pole, it's this: if we're not somewhere, count me out.

Let me amend that. Let me bring down my flag and scribble an asterisk on it with a Sharpie. There are plenty of good reasons to set a story in a vacuum. Maybe you're working in an absurdist minimalism like Samuel Beckett or Etgar Keret. Maybe you're working in the realm of myth or fable like the fantastic Aimee Bender. But when I'm reading what we call realism, regional or otherwise, set somewhere as glancing as "the city," I have to ask: Which city? Which neighborhood? And how can they afford it?

These are impolite questions, I admit. But asking impolite questions is basically the writer's job. And if she asks impolite questions about where we are, she notices how quickly these scratch the surface of polite society, how a serious consideration of place gives way to all we'd rather avoid. What's in the air, the soil, the water? How does a person survive here? Who are the architects of its buildings, its laws and customs? When a story's place is seriously considered by the fiction writer, it becomes more difficult for her to dodge those aspects of American life that mainstream culture would rather she ignore.

What does a character see when she looks out a window? In the hands of bold writers of regionalism, this common writing prompt can be a radical exercise. To write place deeply is to admit that, contrary to the dominant American mythology, so much of who we are is determined by where we are, where we were born and to whom. From school districts to nuclear test sites, increasingly in America where you are determines what kind of an education you'll have, how the nation's laws might be enforced, what chemicals might be in your soil, in your walls, in your water.

The literary tradition of regionalism is a tunneling. It is a recursive body, tethered in space and rising from a given landscape by boring deep into it. Its subject may be shared terrain–here, the western half of America–yet each story mapping that territory is made singular, the writer hopes, by her specific alchemy of style, structure, voice, and gaze. The stories in this anthology, carefully assembled by the editors of Baobab Press, display regionalism's inherent eccentricities and the American West's particular polyphonic palimpsest. This anthology runs no stylistic or political flag up the pole. Instead, *This Side of the Divide* offers readers the chance to embrace the subjectivity of the human experience as it unfolds across the American West. Its inquiry is circular. It tunnels down, which is to say back, and in this tunneling expands.

Critics have put a lot of energy into making a distinction between Literature of the American West, and its genre counterpart, the Western. It's a comforting partition, but writers of the American West seem to prefer this root ball tangled, perhaps sensing that this tradition is as inspired by the Western as it is by the landscape of the American West itself. The Western was a reactionary and nostalgic camp from the get-go, emerging after the collapse of open-range agriculture and in the immediate wake of Frederick Jackson Turner's "Frontier Thesis," in which Turner fretted for America's dynamism and democratic ideals now that our frontier was officially closed. Concurrently, some Americans of the Progressive Era feared that industrial society was creeping upon them and devouring their lives. We do not ride upon the railroad; the railroad rides upon us, as Henry David Thoreau put it in *Walden*. The West, though recently belted by rail, beckoned as the last bastion of America's pristine and primitive past.

This is the climate in which Philadelphia-born and Harvard-educated Owen Wister began his travels west. Wister was a close friend of Theodore Roosevelt, and according to Wister scholar Richard Etulain, together the two men conceived the Western novel "as a setting for displaying the greatness of the Anglo-Saxon past." Wister's novel, *The Virginian*, is widely credited as the first Western, though Wister himself called it a historical novel.

If *The Virginian* was based on history, it was a Roosevelt-approved version of history gleaned from widely popular political theater. *The Virginian* harnessed the nation's frontier nostalgia by capturing the fervor that audiences had for "Wild West" shows, which considerably warped the image of the cowboy even as he was being elevated to the status of national folk hero. Cowboys in these open-air melodramas, and later in Westerns, bore little resemblance to the actual riders of the open range, most of whom were southern European immigrants, free slaves, Mexicans, and Indians. Gone from this new genre were the cows the cowboys had driven, replaced by guns, which actual *vaqueros* seldom carried. But historical accuracy was of little use to the emergent genre, which gleefully festooned its cowboy as a reluctant lawman, a handy extension of the state into territory freshly stolen. In the manner of *The Virginian,* most Westerns were written about a way of life that was decades past by people who had never experienced it.

Recalling that the Western emerged not from a literary tradition but rather from political theater and propaganda, it should be unsurprising that the genre has been wielded as a cudgel for American white supremacy. Writing in the *New Yorker* in 2017, Alex Ross called Wister a "repulsive racist who halted his narrative to praise the superiority of Anglo-Saxon stock and declare the Declaration of Independence enshrined 'the eternal inequality of man.'" The Western was firstly a propaganda tool to make heroes out of the pioneers, to exalt westward expansion, to justify—and celebrate—killing Native Americans.

That the Western was a foot soldier in the march of Manifest Destiny (well after that actual physical endeavor of crossing the continent was ostensibly complete) are well-documented. If there is any useful distinction between what we call genre fiction and literature it is that one reaffirms our idea of the world as we know it and another challenges everything we think we know. Wister's endeavor was not the artist's mirror-tunnel but the shallow reflection of the dominant culture's brutality back to itself in a flattering light. As Literature of the American West continues to distinguish itself from its genre cousin, its practitioners resist the bloody boosterism that characterized the Western. Narrowly defined, regionalism of the American West is macho, rugged, individualistic, and violent. But as Willa Cather put it in a 1915 letter, the "cow-puncher's experience of the West was not the only experience possible there." This anthology lets post-frontier literature range as far and wide and deep as the West itself, from melting mountain glaciers to the plastic-strewn sea and all the vexed microclimates in between. *This Side of the Divide* welcomes readers into the vast landscape of worries and wonders dogging some of the most gifted writers of today's American West, themselves a whitecap on a wave of writers contesting the propaganda and writing against American amnesia.

In these pages we encounter a spiritual idiom indebted to the Transcendentalists by way of the Beats. We see lyricism married to noir, experimentalism making happy home with sentiment. We see a guarded curiosity about the Romantic sense of the sublime, attempts to replicate with mere ink and papyrus that feeling of grand smallness one gets from gazing upon the Tetons or the Sierras. In these stories, wonder often gives way to bewilderment and eventually elegy.

We see the tradition of local color morphed into a desperate search for transcendental euphoria, a search oft thwarted in these stories. The narrator of Miranda Schmidt's "Aquarium" dreams her city flooded, crosses bridges fearing earthquakes, and finds a familiar waking anguish in her morning coffee: "feeling guilty for the plastic, the lid, the wasteful sleeve, the cup that couldn't be recycled. Guilty but also silly for being guilty. Because what did one cup matter, really in the grand scheme of things." Schmidt's Susan wants frantically to comprehend this grand scheme, "the shape of a world in decline. She tried to trace its boundaries. She tried to find its edges but no edges were there." The contours of the future resist

Jeffersonian cartography, leaving us groping across "a place where the land that seemed friendly and fertile and yielding could at any moment rise up and swallow you whole."

Writers preoccupied with climate change and its ravages in the West find that the future tense doesn't work anymore. In "and drop" by David Gillette, a boy and his family are on a "pollution tour of the American West" that culminates at a Flintstones theme park outside of Flagstaff, Arizona. Here the narrator and his father encounter a buffalo wearing a necklace of bones, an image both lasting and inscrutable as the boy comes of age: "I see the buffalo gazing at me that afternoon while scratching its message in the dust." The message, the meaning, never comes. Instead we are left with "the emptiness that drifted through me hours later as we drifted home in a bus filled with strangers."

Again and again, we feel profound grief radiating from these chroniclers of the American West. In "A Thirteenth Apostle's Star" by Douglas W. Milliken, a free-wheeling road trip has ended in a crash on a "crumbling county road (numbered, not named)." Zane Grey's purple sage has gone grey in this story of a slow-motion spiritual emergency. The pastoral boosterism of yore is supplanted by devastation and grief. Death touches everything. Sunflowers are "horrible things, hairy stalked and drooping heads of curling, parched yellow." The sense of divine purpose assured by Manifest Destiny has withered along with that ideology in this suicidal post-frontier where train and car—twin gleaming emblems of man's mastery of nature, one for the nineteenth century, one for the twentieth—collide. At the site of this ghastly late-capitalist accident, the "first responders are not the first to respond," and "given no other choice, the observers become involved." It must be asked, of the man driving the Ford pickup, of the God who demanded mountains of buffalo skulls from America: "Do you think he knew what he was doing?"

What a relief to finally admit: "I don't think he knew much of anything."

A Thirteenth Apostle's Star

Douglas W. Milliken

There's no exact measure to the emptiness of the desert between one barely extant town and another. Miles opening unto greater miles of flat brown shovel-breaking earth. Ringed in far-off mountains. Oppressed by the never- ending downward press of sky.

Yet still: there are birds, circling. There are occasional crippled trees. Wicked thorns and arthritic habits. Sagebrush and weeds that give nothing back to the land. There's an arrow-straight line of railroad tracks cutting from one set of mountains to another, and there's a crumbling county road (numbered, not named) and where the two meet to form an X, a Ford pickup is jammed into the side of a ten-car commuter train. Engine tipped over and derailed in the hardpan. A black plume of smoke marking where all these things meet. Funneling straight into the great blue palm above.

As of yet, no one's begun to scream. The silence that followed the tearing of metal—the woofing and flaring of fuel devouring—is almost more shocking than the preceding throttle and violence. The living don't know yet if they're dead. The dead don't need to know. No one has begun yet to scream.

It's from this silence and swelling black smoke that Al emerges. Grey suit torn at the elbows. Right eye blood-blind from the gash tracing his fading hairline. He holds his head to keep the whole world from spinning away. He has no idea where he is. He sees the road and he sees the rail-line but neither means a thing. But the sun is a seething smirk. The unmoving air is a smirk, but the crippled- tree shade is a kiss blown to him through the dead air, through the deathly light. Al stumbles away from the wreckage into the shade.

SOMEWHERE FAR AWAY, a sheriff's dispatcher gets a call. Someone somewhere sees smoke. Soon another call, and another: smoke in the desert. The dispatcher sends a cruiser out to investigate, though the poor kid has no idea where he's going. Head east until you see smoke. Head for the smoke. Finally, a call comes in from one of the train's passengers. Total hysterics. Insisting that everyone is dead. The dispatcher hangs up and sends out many more cars. Find the tracks. Look for smoke on the tracks. No one knows yet where they're going.

BEFORE THE SIRENS can be heard above the cries of the wounded and distressed, Al has wandered some distance from the wreck. Shambling from one pool of darkness to the next. Weaving between grey humps of sage. Stepping on tiny, tightly thorned cacti. Following the shadow-trail cast by the trees.

A quarter mile from the wreck, the trees lump into a tangled copse. Invitingly dark yet taunting in density. Al pushes through the lattice of deadwood and stems, discovers the trees' bright thorns. Softly sinking in. Only resisting when he tries to pull away. When he emerges on the other side, he no longer cares about cool or darkness. Only to escape the bite and sting.

It's in this state that he discovers the old woman. Hunching near her wheel-robbed caravan, kneeling in her pitiful garden. What are those horrible things, hairy-stalked and drooping heavy heads of curling, parched yellow? Sunflowers. She's kneeling among her sunflowers when he finds her. Sun shining off the fairly bald dome of her scalp. Shapeless dress like a sun-bleached curtain, almost floral, cinched around her waist with a man's leather belt.

Baring her teeth, the old woman raises one skeletal hand. Turns it at the wrist. Makes some parched and ancient sound with her throat.

Dumbstruck, Al takes his bloody hand from his head and waves back.

ONCE WHEN HE wasn't much younger, Al learned amazement at the swift changes a body can undergo, often in such short periods of time. How could something so helpless and small develop strong arms, a broad chest? How could blind, blinking eyes ease into seeing? The infant in the pictures could not possibly be the man he'd become. In high school, he could swim faster than any of the other boys. He could dance with girls and make them want to touch him. How could he have once been something else?

Yet even after all possible advantages have been attained, the body continues to change. His hair began to fall out. His waist took on a shape that made his legs somehow birdlike and gawky in comparison. The flesh of his neck thickened in unintended ways. There was nothing he could do about any of this. He could still make women want to touch him, and the women did touch him still, but they were changed too. It depressed him to realize that he and everyone was helpless and had been from the start. And if he could look at his own life as a series of incomprehensible and uncontrolled physical changes leading to his disappointing yet still capable middle-age, then what must this old woman feel as she rises and strides like some paralytic stork out from the dead or dying sunflowers and through the weeds to him, where her withered bone-trap hand takes his spotty and blood-smeared hand, where her myopic eyes squint at his bleeding brow as she asks him if he has something to do with that train wreck back over there?

Glancing over his shoulder, Al watches the black smoke billow and plume into the vapid blue. Blinks as the black expands, as the blue expands. Finally turns away.

"What train wreck?"

"DO YOU THINK he knew what he was doing?"

"I don't think he knew much of anything."

Calmly the father helps his teenage daughter out their train-car's window. Behind her, a pack of bodies waits to get out. But they're going to have to fend for themselves.

"I mean, maybe he thought he could beat the train." The language spoken between father and daughter is not the language of the other people on the train. "You know? Maybe get across the tracks before we did."

"Yeah, maybe." Taking his daughter's hand, the father leads her running to the shade of a nearby tree. "Or maybe he was drunk or on drugs or asleep."

"Maybe," she says as behind them, the first of countless strangers falls out of the window, landing badly on his shoulder, crying out among the other cries. "I guess he could have been asleep." Neither father nor daughter turns back.

THE OLD WOMAN'S voice is high and reedy and incredibly dry sounding. Like two dead trees leaning against one another, groaning in night wind. Looking out toward the horizon, Al sees the entire world glimmering through a hazy screen. Shimmering sunflowers. Shimmering mountains. No matter how he tries, he cannot understand what she says. Finally, she tips her hand toward her mouth, and he gets it.

"Yes. A drink. Wonderful. Please. God bless you. God."

THE FIRST RESPONDERS are not the first to respond. A miniscule stream of traffic backs up on either side of the wreck. Some people wait in their cars. Because there's air-conditioning there, and satellite radio too. A few get out to look, standing on the roadside, leaning at the waist as they stare. As if bending forward might give them a better view. After some time, a broken voice rises through a shattered window–

"Are you *doing* anything?"

–and given no other choice, the observers become involved. First a farmer and his young grandson. Then a truck driver on his way from Missoula to Sacramento. Yet even these people hesitate in their steps as alone with her two sleeping children in a sleek and spacious hatchback, a cow-eyed mother gradually comes to the conclusion that maybe the police should be involved. She finds her phone and dials 911. Plainly states where she is and what she sees. And now the dispatcher knows where all the cops and EMTs scattered seekingly throughout the desert should now, finally, be sent.

"WHAT'S YOUR NAME, son?"

"Name?"

Somehow, now–finally–he can understand her. Her withered mouth-sounds finally resolving into words. On paint-flaking chairs around a paint-flaking table, they're sitting in the caravan's shade, beneath the limp boughs of a tree. Leaves like long tickling fingers. Barely swaying. Al can't remember how he got here from the garden. Like time remained constant while space folded, erasing the gap between here and there. But wasn't that in a children's book?

"You know. What your mother called you."

Awfully technical for a children's book. On the small table between them, a glass sweats coolly between his hands, riding in a small pool of its own creation. He wipes a fingerful of moisture from the glass and rubs it into his eyes.

"Honestly, ma'am, I don't rightly recall at the moment."

"Then you shall be Laban." And she smiles. "You present yourself like a Laban."

"Great." Al sips and deduces his drink to be ice afloat in some sort of bourbon. On the table before the woman rests a can densely scripted in medical jargon. "Thank you." Unopened. "You going to join me? Or am I drinking by myself out here?" Somehow, the words feel familiar and welcome on his tongue. Like some holiday ritual. Repeated many times before.

Rearranging the lines of her face into some deathly sort of web, the old woman grins and checks her watch. "Give me ten minutes, okay?"

From far away, maybe one or both of them hears someone scream.

AT THE VERY rear of the train, there's a certain question among the passengers about what, exactly, is going on. Not long ago, they were drifting like fired bullets through the world. Now they're stopped. This is all they know. From their angle, they cannot see the smoke of the flaming pickup or the engine overturned on the ground. Large rocks block their view, and hunchback trees. Throughout the final car, there are whispered conversations as to what, if anything, they or someone else should do. The air conditioning has stalled along with their forward progress, and the automatic doors between cars have sealed shut. Something, obviously, must be done. People groan and throw their hands, wipe the sweat from their brows while near the back of the car, a couple in their mid-forties–a used-car salesman and the secretary to a used-car salesman (a friendly competitor at the lot up the street)–quietly argue. She thinks that, if he gets off the train, they'll begin moving again and he'll be left behind. He's convinced (rightly, though for the wrong reasons) that this will not happen. They're each trying to use the narrow armrest between them. Neither seems to think that the other is sharing enough.

"Trust me, babe," and smiling, he leans in to kiss her cheek. "It's going to be fine." And in the moment when their two fleshes touch, the salesman's wife hopes he's wrong. She hopes the train will pull away and leave him out here. She hopes the sun mercilessly cooks him into a pretentious, condescending cinder.

Pulling the emergency latch and slipping out through the opened window (it's not as easy as he thinks it should be), the secretary's husband starts to walk alongside the train, trying to match his step to the creosote-soaked ties. But his stride is unnatural and awkward. And above the scent of the sun-hot ties, something bad hangs in the air. And in the passing windows, pale faces look out at him, imploring, needing. So he jogs down the talus embankment, away from the tracks and into the hardpan and weeds. And now he sees the black finger of smoke accusing the open sky. And just past these hunchback trees bowing like leprous beggars, he can see the tipped engine and see the burning truck.

The secretary's husband likes to brag about his time in the service. He thinks this will endear him to his customers and maybe solidify a sale. But he was only ever a weekend reservist. Our war then was cold and if our enemy had ever struck, we'd all have died at once anyway: the battle would have been everywhere in a sterilizing flash, then just as quickly, not been anywhere. The only mortal combat in which he ever engaged was with a thirty-pack in the back of a troop carrier, roving the peripheries of the SAC base in the ink-and-blotter mist before dawn. Nothing he'd done or claimed to know has prepared him for the flames and torn metal, the crying figures dragging themselves out of broken windows, the still bodies spread out on the ground. He stands and watches while his insides turn into a cold and syrupy fluid. Then he rushes back to his wife. It's imperative: he must return to his wife.

BEFORE THE FLAMES boiled to peel its paint away, the pickup was a pale baby blue. Fenders rusted to a coxcomb orange. A red and black NRA decal crooked in the rear window. The train an industrial grey with a blue stripe running its length. The windows all tinted black.

Cracked desert clay the same faded ochre as a desiccated orange rind. Baked beyond life in the sun. The sagebrush is grey. The leaves of the track-side trees all silvery green.

The tracks are gunmetal black, the ties a deep tar-stained brown. The smoke is an opaque ashy smudge.

And amid the dead grey weeds and deadly greying sunflowers, the caravan is a washed-out red and gold. The windows are aged with fly-shit and dust. Over the door, a punched tin star hangs by an eight-penny nail.

And the old woman's skin is a burnt and leathery red. Wisps of hair fishing- line white. Her eyes a clear piercing blue. From her neck by a shining gold chain, an ornate crucifix is poised and for Al—all pale skin and blonde hair and torn-up slate-grey seersucker—this last detail is a strange revelation. He had not noticed the cross before. The colors of the world come together into a broken vision of dirty stained glass, Dead Sea lost, and at its center, a golden dead man hangs in suspended tribulation from a polished golden cross.

Al sips amber off the melting ice in his glass. The old woman checks the black ticking hands of her watch, and sighs.

BACK BEFORE HIS body continued past the apex of its progression, Al spent a summer on a recently abandoned farm. The sun-stained shapes of missing pictures burned in the wallpaper. Clothes still scattered in drawers, on the floor. The water and electric still ran, at least at first, and the fields were still orderly yet totally gone to seed, an occasional stray and lost-eyed cow wandering through.

It was the summer between semesters, and he lived in a ghost farm with a woman whose body was a candle flame eating up the wick of his heart. Did he meet her here in this big empty place? Did she follow him here from school? Perhaps he was the one who followed her. They spent their days reading books in the sun, in the wind, on the porch or in the soft susurrus of bending wild grass. He remembers the sound of her laugher as her body opened like praying hands. He remembers a wind-chime on the corner of the porch. Tolling three notes like the suggestion of a beginning or end. Tolling one note three times. Tolling one note just once.

But really what he remembers is the night they pushed a mattress out of the extra bedroom's second-story window. How it bounced and cartwheeled across the yard. It was the longest day of the year, or anyway, the latest the sun would set. They dragged the mattress into the tall grass and spread out a soft moth-holed quilt over top. The nodding wheat heads formed a frame above them: in all the world, there was only the mattress and the grass and the box of sky overhead, slowly turning from deep pink to purple to black, filling impossibly with an unending wash of stars, brightly winking planets, an eventual godlike slice of sterling, blinding moon. There was nothing else in the whole world. Not even the two of them, watching. Least of all the two of them.

Whatever happened to that girl, he wonders now in the shade beside the caravan. He can't even recall her face. Just her long blonde hair. The arc of her hips. Her voice like the first sip of cold beer on a hot night. He wonders if maybe he married her or if maybe she got away. He looks at his hand for evidence of a ring—a faint indentation, a discolored band—but the blood he now wears obscures whatever proof he might seek.

For a moment, he wonders where the blood came from. Then he remembers. Somewhere far behind him, a siren faintly sounds. Watching him observe his own hands, the old woman smiles silently to herself, then after a moment digs around inside her dress to produce a leather-bound book. Deep red and no bigger than a cigarette pack. Creased and worn as if by centuries of earth-dirty callused hands.

"Let me read to you something, Laban," she says, thumbing through the nearly translucent pages. "I think to you this might somehow apply."

The sight and sound of the open book fills Al with a sick sense of unease. Like a snake all curled up in the dank cave of his belly. Ready to unfurl.

And she reads:

After these things, the Autogenes said, "Let the twelve angels come into being so that they might rule over the chaos and the oblivion." And behold an angel appeared from the cloud whose face was pouring forth fire, while his likeness was defiled with blood. And he had one name, "Nebro," which is interpreted as "apostate," but some others call him "Ialdaboath" . . . . Nebro then created six angels to attend him. And these produced twelve angels in the heavens, and each of them received an allotted portion of the heavens. And the twelve rulers, along with the twelve angels said, "Let each one of you . . ."

"But the rest of the scripture," she says, pausing to clear her throat, "is lost."

"Well," Al says, "isn't that something." But this idea—angels creating angels to give shape and dominion to and over the earth and heaven—does not click with Al's understanding of the world. For there are beautiful coastal mountains plunging headlong into the sea. There are towering trees and hills teeming with life. Birds in the sky and fish in the rivers. Everywhere all at once. Yet there's also this: an empty dead expanse of nothing at the center of the world. Every inch identical to the inch before and after. The whole middle of the country, he knows, is like this: unshaped and unformed, a flat and undifferentiated plain. Just like Russia. Just like Australia. Where is there any evidence to prove that God did not simply give up? An entire infinite system of burning gases spinning around burning gases, and our tiny blue planet enthroned with the universe revolving worshipfully around it. But God gave up. Moved the center somewhere else. Left His failure behind. For every ounce of His divine soul He poured into our creation—every mountain and every forest, each tree and antelope and butterfly and monkey—every last detail His attempt at perfection, and each one a monument to failure. The overspecialization of the giraffe and koala or any other marsupial. The obscene vulnerability of the manatee and every human male's exposed and flaccid genitals. Unable to make real what His mind envisioned, the Great and

Unknowable Failure turned away from His unfinished and dismal masterwork, abandoning His failed creations to cope in their failed, imperfect home.

The old woman closes her book and grins. "So many busy hands!" and laughs. A singularly horrible sound.

WHEN THE POLICE and ambulances and fire trucks finally arrive, the evacuation is already well underway. Once the shock of having survived set in, people began leaking out of the wreck, automatically knowing only to save themselves. When the secretary's husband returned from his scouting, the other passengers in the rear-most car—rattled but generally unscathed—poured out the windows, kicked open the emergency exits, rushed to the front to help the other survivors free. Near the front, where the flames of impact were spreading—eager and fierce as cannibals to consume—an elderly man cradles the ruined body of his wife of fifty-three years. They were enjoying a late-morning bagel with cream cheese, some coffee. Then the engine tipped over and she was dashed into their café car table. Now her body's like a limp sack holding the splintered dust of her bones. He presses her bloodied brow to his mouth, to his cheek, holds what's left of her close. The flames dance and lick around him and someone shouts through an open door for him move, c'mon, let's go. But eventually, the shouting stops. The old man closes his eyes and waits for his chance to let go while outside, a pregnant woman in a pretty blue dress squats down with her back against a stone and wails into the dead air, hugging her belly above the blood staining the ground beneath her. Children wander and cry out to their parents who may or may not hear or respond. Men and women seek out their partners, their children, their friends. Red Cross volunteers hand out blankets, uselessly. A helicopter arrives and dumps a spray of retardant chemicals on everyone. And in his pickup, the man responsible for all of this curls more tightly around the steering wheel, blackened and growing blacker. Somehow all of this Al knows without seeing. The fluid through which all light must pass. In the superheated sky, the rising plume finally succeeds in eclipsing the sun, leaving the survivors to toil in the apocalyptic shade while a quarter-mile away–in a waste of sunflowers and locusts and olives, at the very end of the line–Al finishes his drink as the old woman slowly unbuttons her shirt to reveal a plastic tube and funnel stretching out from a bandage on her softly distended belly. Breasts like deflated honeydew. Funnel and tube cloud-stained dirty with use. Opening the can on the table before her with one long and yellowed fingernail, the old woman holds it up with her pinky daintily jutting–

"Bless this bounty."

–and pours her breakfast directly inside. And for a moment, Al has to wonder–in the absence of all other knowledge, his family and past, his own pitiful and meaningless name–if maybe he's the man inside the burning pickup, hands clutching tight the mechanism of his mistake as his eyes melt out from the grottoes of his skull, as his mouth falls open to shatter and split like driftwood, like glass, as the flames lovingly lick as the most delicate lover the ringed knuckles of his spine.

and drop

David Gillette

I fell into the Grand Canyon the year we took our pollution tour of the American West. My father often said Nixon paid for the trip, implying that Tricky Dick had personally signed and mailed checks directly to my father in compensation for his government mission. We took the trip in 1972 in our dark-blue, Monday-made Ford station wagon that rattled from every joint starting the day he drove it off the lot. My father refused to hear anything negative about the station wagon, which he believed to be an unsurpassed deal he had finagled through guile and his appreciation for fine machines. Our mother hated the thing, calling it the Broken Beast when he was out of earshot.

The year of my Grand Canyon plummet, our father was enlisted by the EPA to join one hundred of the nation's top photographers for the Documerica program. Their assignment was to photograph natural landscapes and small-town America beset by smog, oil slicks, and burning garbage dumps. The goal was to show the country what it was doing to itself. The EPA and Documerica were the only two goddamned things Nixon ever did right, according to my father.

"Even though he's a total sonofabitch," my father would say, "the bastard should still get credit where credit is due."

My father was assigned to the Four Corners team, which he believed made him responsible for documenting all four states and required the entire family to hit the road. This would be his largest and best-paid assignment in over a year, with an actual salary for every day he was shooting. Every photo selected for use in D.C. meant national exposure and possibly more work. The photographer who sent in the most compelling, widely published images would take home the most cash. My father talked about it as a sports competition, a physical battle, especially against Michelson and Crane, two photographers from New York also assigned to the Four Corners. My father insisted on taking us out of school at the end of January to get on the road ahead of the New Yorkers. He said they would be frightened by the thin mountain roads, black ice, and the snow. He needed children in his shots of smokestacks, junked cars, and tailings ponds to introduce conflict and character into the images. This trip would be a life lesson for us, education on the road, he claimed.

My mother did not buy any of this, and they argued for a week at breakfast, at dinner, and loudly in their bedroom, late into the night. My parents' main form of communication was argument, which my mother won most of the time. Their central topic in my childhood was my father's photography. My mother called it a habit. My father insisted photography was a career. By the end of the week she relented, saying it would be acceptable only if our teachers found a way for us to make up for school. She also knew we needed the money.

With her best sales voice and ingratiating smile, my mother convinced my sixth-grade teacher, Mrs. Roof, and my sister's fourth-grade teacher, Mrs. Peterson, that this road trip would be the educational opportunity of a lifetime. She explained that our entire family would learn about American history by driving right through it. Then, while gazing at the flag on the wall, she claimed (in a quiet, solemn tone) that this was our patriotic duty. Our teachers assigned us readings on American history with a bag of books from the library. We were required to write two-hundred-word essays every week that our mother graded and marked with a red pen. I spent the whole time writing about Lewis and Clark. My sister wrote about the history of horses and the Cheyenne. We favored illustration over writing, however. I drew canoes between my paragraphs, my sister drew horses everywhere and sketched elaborate feather headdresses in the corners.

On the day we left, our father sat two huge Styrofoam coolers squeaking between us in the back seat, stuffed to their brims with sealed bundles of slide film. My sister and I were responsible for keeping the lids in place. To buy all that film he hocked his precious stereo system, our new color television, and most of the tools in the garage. Without my mother's permission he also sold the washer and dryer, and the fancy couch her parents had given us the Christmas before. This was not the first time we came home to missing furniture that had been transformed into film. Once again, our life had been reduced to yellow boxes of Kodachrome. We would drive and shoot until there was no film remaining. Our mother studied the coolers like a ticking clock, counting down as film disappeared day by day.

Once we were on the road and the Beast hit sixty-one, a nervous quiver swept back to front. My father accelerated, undaunted as the quivering increased. Exactly at seventy-five the Beast's uneasiness dissipated, transforming into a blue missile, surging swift and sure down the freeway. The back of the car emitted a slithering scent of burning rubber and musty socks intermingled with the acidic undertone from my father's Salems up front. When he was smoking, my mother blasted the vents at her face. In back, my sister and I sat at opposite ends, cheeks pressed to the windows, sipping from the stream of fresh air whistling through gaps in the frame.

FOR TWO MONTHS we lived out of the station wagon and our musty army surplus tent, eating mostly canned beans, apples, creamed corn, and Spam-Velveeta sandwiches. Once a week we splurged on a meal at a truck stop or a lonely highway café where we lingered as long as possible to bathe in the kitchen heat and greasy aroma of hot food. Through it all, my mother said nothing. Not a word of complaint. She had never been so quiet and compliant. It was unnerving because we knew she was simmering, especially when she stopped talking entirely after one long, cold week of Spam and tomato sandwiches with Tang at every meal. My sister and I knew something was coming. By the end of March we had circled back toward Flagstaff and were on the Grand Canyon rim, tossing snowballs, thrilled that home was only a few hours away. My father kept telling me to back up so he could get a better shot.

That's when I fell. My mother believed her son had just plunged to his death directly before her and she erupted with a terrified and angry scream so loud it echoed from the nearest canyon walls.

I wasn't dead. I had fallen about ten feet onto a ledge (mostly dirt, some snow, a few pointed rocks) where I lay on my back, staring at the sky, trying not to move because I was certain my spine or something important around my head was probably broken. The Scouts always instructed us not to move people after a bad fall because that would make things worse. That's what the evangelical EMT reminded us at camp one night, when telling us about a gruesome climbing accident in Montana.

"It would have been fine, but they rushed in and moved him without a brace," he said. "Snapped his spinal cord like a stalk of cold celery. Now he's a C4 in a wheelchair and needs a machine to breathe, Lord bless him. Remember, boys: until help arrives, they stay where they lay."

So I lay there, moving my fingers and toes a bit, cautiously checking things out. I turned my head slightly just in time to see a row of camera bulbs flashing my direction like silver plates flipping in the sun. Pressed against the viewing fence were hundreds of tourists from Vegas buses, jostling one another, holding cameras high to snap photos of the boy who had just fallen off the Grand Canyon–every one of them beating my father to the punch with plastic Instamatics and fold-open Polaroids.

My mother was shouting louder than I had ever heard her.

"You fucking, goddamned, self-centered bastard. What do you have to say for yourself now? Go ahead. Take my goddamned picture. Do it! Take my fucking picture! Kill me too! Come on. Do it! Kill me!"

Snow slipped off the ledge, hitting me on the forehead. I saw my sister peering down at me. She was lying on her stomach, mittens gripping the edge.

"You okay? You didn't scream. I don't think you should move. Why didn't you scream?"

"I don't know. It wasn't that far. I think I'm okay. I can wiggle my toes."

"Everybody screams on TV when they fall."

"This isn't TV."

"You should stay down there. Momma's not happy."

"Yeah, I hear that."

"Come on, you fucking bastard." She was thumping against something up there, probably hitting him. We were all wearing dingy silver ski parkas from Goodwill, with yellow gloves clipped at the wrists. Every time we moved, a few goose feathers escaped the loose seams. It sounded like she was having a pillow fight, landing a soft thud between every sentence. "Take my goddamned picture. Go ahead. It's so important. You're the big government man now. Getting paid. Come on. Take. My. Fucking. Picture."

"You bleeding?" my sister asked.

"No. I don't think so. Maybe. My pants feel wet."

"Stay there," she said, sounding older. "You shouldn't move. Okay? Don't move."

"Oh, Jesus! Get away from the edge. Not you, too... Jesus. Don't stand up. Just slide back, honey. Come on. I'm so sorry. You shouldn't look. Come on, slide back to Momma."

My sister's head slipped behind the snow and I saw only sky again. Blue sky. And a large bird. Circling.

"Put down the goddamned camera and comfort your daughter."

"He's right there, Momma."

"I know, darling, I know. It's terrible. I know..."

"He's not dead. He's right there. He's fine."

More snow dropped on me, then my parents' faces tipped over the edge and my sister's face appeared again, sliding from between her yellow gloves.

"I'm not dead," I told them.

"Is anything broken?" my father asked.

"No. I don't think so."

"His pants are wet," my sister explained.

"Can you move your toes?" my mother asked. I wiggled them again inside my boots just to be sure.

"They work."

We all looked at each other for a moment.

"Well, then, get up," my father said. My mother hit him on the shoulder. Feathers popped out.

"No. We find help. Nobody touches him until we find help. You okay down there, sweetie? You okay?"

"Yeah, I guess so."

"His pants are wet," my sister said again.

"Yes, sweetie, we know that. Thank you." She turned to my father, "Go get help. Do something useful for a change."

He looked down at me, nodded, put his hand before him like he was holding me there against the ledge, nodded again, then left.

"I'm going to stay right here with you until help arrives. Are you cold?"

"No, Mom, I'm fine."

"Don't move. Just stay there. We're going to stay with you while your father finds help. He had no business taking you kids over here. It's much too dangerous. You could have fallen right to the bottom. I should have said something. The both of you could've . . ."

"I did fall."

"Well, yes, I know, but it could have been much worse. I mean, it's a straight drop right there. Oh, Christ... Don't move. I can't believe how close . . . I don't know how we're going to get you back up."

"Momma?"

"What, darling? Don't worry, your brother will be okay."

"I have to pee."

"Here? Now?"

"I gotta go, Momma. I'm sorry."

My mother pulled my sister away from the edge, then leaned over again to see me. "We'll be right back. Don't try to stand. It's not safe. Ignore your father. Just lie there. Don't look down."

"Okay."

Then it was only sky again. The bird was gone. I thought about what had just happened, how lucky I was to land on my back, how far I could fall if I moved. I thought, carefully, about death.

My mother was right, we had no business being there. At the end of the parking lot for the viewing area, we had deliberately stepped over the small fence marked in three places with safety-orange warning signs saying: Do Not Cross. He knew better. We all knew better–this was something tourists would have done.

Flagstaff was only ninety minutes away. We were here all the time for Scouts and on weekends. Among his many jobs to support his photography, my father had served, briefly, as a park ranger in Colorado. He liked to talk shop with the Canyon's rangers every chance he got, mostly soaking in their complaints about the latest fool from Vegas, Europe, or somewhere East-like the woman from New Jersey who decided to hike down Bright Angel Trail wearing heels, a dress, no hat, and no water in July. She had to be brought up by mule hours later, dehydrated and delirious after twisting both ankles at the bottom of the ninth switchback. "Idiot," they'd concluded together. "Useless tourist."

He told us to throw snowballs at each other on the rim. The orange afternoon light cut into the Canyon to our right, highlighting each century of sediment as the Colorado snaked along the bottom. The river was black in the shade but shone brown-blue under a bright finger of sunlight stretching from the opposite ridge. He loved the contrast of snow and desert, past and present with two children frolicking at the center in futuristic apparel. It was too good to pass up. After I threw the first few snowballs he asked me to step back while he kept shooting, then a bit more, then once more. I felt air under my back foot and dropped over the side.

The bird was back, with a friend. Both circling.

More snow fell on my head, and I saw a man with a beard and a park ranger's cap squinting down at me.

"Hello. You okay, son?"

"Yeah, I think so."

"Don't move. We're sending someone to get you. Listen to what he tells you to do. Can you do that for me?"

"Yes, I can."

"You're a very lucky young man."

"I know that, sir. Thank you."

"Just wait for him to tell you what to do. We'll do this slowly, so be patient."

"Yes, sir. I can wait."

A ranger in a climbing harness and helmet leaned backward over the side, glanced at me, smiled, then fiddled with ropes as he rappelled. It took a long time to lift me with a lot of checking and more rangers asking for my attention, being professionally jocular. I heard my mother talking with someone and my sister asking about food, but nothing from my father. The sun was setting by the time they pulled me over the side, patting me everywhere to be sure I was fine. I sat in the back of an ambulance so the paramedic could check some more, and my mother stood outside the open doors talking to a woman who clutched a large green notebook against her chest. My sister hid behind my mother's legs as she did when smaller. I knew the ambulance spooked her. When they first pulled me onto my feet, my mother and sister rushed over to hug me. After everyone cleared away, I was able to see my father, smoking and leaning against the Broken Beast in the far corner of the lot. He met my eyes for a moment, stubbed out his cigarette, tried to smile reassuringly, then turned to sort things in the car.

By the time I left the ambulance it was dark. He was sitting in the driver's seat, hands on the wheel, staring forward, his face lit blue by the instrument lights and radio. He had started the engine to warm the car. One of the rangers shook my hand, and the woman gave my mother a stack of papers from her notebook. No one looked at my father except me, but I knew what they were thinking: useless tourist.

On my mother's insistence (with only a slight nod of acceptance from my father) we ate at a restaurant that night with real tablecloths and too much silverware. My mother paid for the dinner with the emergency money she kept in an envelope in her purse. We had seen her envelope a few times during the trip but she had never used it, even during the week of Spam, tomatoes, and Tang. We checked into one of the expensive log-cabin rooms at the Rim, using more envelope money. The restaurant was filled with Germans who laughed loudly while they ate. My mother talked all through dinner and finished three large glasses of wine while explaining what we would do when we got home, how we would catch up with school, the friends we would see when we arrived. At the hotel room she turned on the TV and asked us to cuddle along both sides of her in bed to watch a cowboy movie. As soon as we climbed in and pulled the blankets to our chins, my father grabbed the ice bucket and left. He didn't return.

THE NEXT MORNING my father didn't roust us at sunrise as he usually did by tugging off sleeping bag covers or shaking the end of our cots. He didn't shout his morning greetings in his mock drill-sergeant voice (Up and at 'em, people! Things to do, places to go! Clock's a-ticking!), or complain about how slowly we were getting dressed, or point out the spectacular morning sunlight while measuring it at arm's length with his light meter, calling for his cameras. My father was, instead, not there. It was quiet and calm. His shaving gear and small evening bag were gone, as were most of our things—already packed away, we supposed. Our clothes for the day were stacked, neat and prim, on a chair by the front door, something he liked to do, so we knew he must have returned at some point.

My mother insisted we sleep until noon and for the first time ever ordered room service. She showed us how to use the menu and gave us permission to order anything. My sister and mother ordered huge breakfasts with extra bananas. I ordered a hamburger, fries, two different kinds of pop and a strawberry milk shake. My mother gave me a ten-dollar bill to hand to the waiter after he set the table. The waiter called me Sir as he left, and my mother threw the curtains open across the sliding glass doors, revealing a stone tile balcony with stained glass and iron railings proudly framing the continuous expanse of the South Rim. The rich canyon light flooded the room, making everything appear slick and expensive. My father would have commented on it and taken a photo. My sister found a classical station on the FM radio built into the TV, turned it up loud, and we dined like movie stars in our pajamas.

We left the room a mess, towels everywhere, tissues on the floor, even a few dishes on the bed, but our mother also put a stack of ones and a ten under the ashtray by the TV and left a thank-you note on the table. When we came out of the room, our father was sitting on a bench by the stairs, reading a magazine as if on vacation, alone and unattached. "Let's go," he said to no one in particular, then strode ahead of us to the car.

Every day of the trip my father lectured on the terrible state of all things: the decline of democratic government; the dangers of ignorant southern racists and snake-charming Christians; the collapsing economy and inadequate school systems; bankers; Mormons; Nixon and his brood. He especially went on about how we were filling our rivers with sludge, our air with poison, and our ground water with radiation. These were occasionally interesting lectures, and he sometimes explained things in a funny way when we had questions from the back, but mostly it was an insistent station of complaint that my mother ignored and my sister and I learned to not hear. So, when we drove away from the Canyon with all the windows open to the high desert air, it took me a while to realize he wasn't talking. He was just staring ahead, listening to my mother as she eagerly tripped through a list of responsibilities to be settled in the coming months. The evergreens fell away and we flew onto the desert floor for a straight run at Flagstaff, the Beast humming steadily in missile mode.

We were settling in for the last stretch of the trip when my sister and I fixated on the head of the big green dinosaur gazing at us from the distance. It was a few hundred feet away, closer than we'd ever been. My sister squeezed my hand.

Construction had started on the Flintstones Park the year before with digging machines, dump trucks, and graders shoving dirt around the desert. For a while, we thought they were building a road, then maybe a hotel. Every time we drove past on the way to the Canyon, my father shook his head, locked his eyes forward and sped up.

The first thing to rise from the dust and commotion was a brontosaurus that could be seen for miles in every direction. It was a giant white sculpture for a few months then finally was painted cartoon green with white saucer eyes and black freckles clustered on his sides. Around him arose a number of fake rock houses, stone cars, hatching dinosaur eggs, a barber shop, log benches and stone bus stops—everything modeled from the show. The last piece to appear was a fake stone wall that hid the park from the highway, except for the dinosaur's long green neck and head that rose above it all, tilted toward the road as if suddenly noticing the cars screaming along.

Every time we approached Bedrock City on the way to the Canyon, my sister and I scrambled to that side of the car and watched the park zip away, shouting out additions since last time: I see a stone bicycle! Candy store! Train! Pterodactyl on the roof! My father never stopped, and we never asked him to do so until he nearly killed me at the Grand Canyon.

"Ask him," my sister said.

I saw my mother looking at me in the rearview mirror. She knew what we were thinking.

"Dad," I said. "Do we need to go home right away?"

"Yes. I have another shipment deadline before the weekend, and we need to clean the car. Why?"

"I was thinking that maybe, because we're right here, maybe we could go to Bedrock City."

He slowed the Beast and three large tour buses thundered by.

"Please," my sister said, "just this time. I want to pet Dino."

"It might be fun," my mother said. "You could shoot the park, or shoot the whole family. All of us, like tourists. Make it an assignment. You have two rolls left. Just this once. It's a kind of landscape. And it's God-awful blight, you've said so. I bet they'll use it in D.C. Michelson and Crane wouldn't stop here. I promise you that."

"Please, Daddy, please," my sister pleaded, tapping the back of his seat with her feet.

The Beast rattled from every joint as he pulled onto a dirt lane leading to a long, nearly empty parking lot. We stopped just beyond the entrance, which was a gateway of tall, bright white dinosaur bones. A flat stone hung from the bone over the entrance with Bedrock City spelled in huge letters using curvy fake logs. To the right, a freshly painted Wilma statue stood on her toes, waving hello, ready to take a step forward. To the left stood Fred, leaning forward slightly, his arm thrust out as he pointed directly at us with his thick, knobby finger, just like Uncle Sam. My sister tightened her grip on my hand as she stared at Fred and the park. I couldn't tell if she was excited or scared. A sign on the wall next to Fred said, "Yabba Dabba Doo Means Welcome to You."

My father parked and told us not to wait for him since he needed time with his cameras. My mother paid the woman in the ticket booth tucked behind the big bone entrance, then asked about bathrooms.

"Oh, ma'am, I'm so sorry," the woman told her. "They're out of order. Problem with the septic. We closed them hours ago."

My mother looked into the park, down at my sister, at the little red tickets in her hands, then back at the park.

"Go ahead, honey. It's okay, I'll catch up." My sister took off toward the nearest stone car. My mother turned to me. "Go tell your father. We'll need the seat." My sister had already climbed in, steering the rock wheel, running her feet into a blur under the seat like the show.

"Momma, look at me. I'm driving. Hop in. I wanna go to the bowling alley."

As I walked back outside, two tourist buses pulled into the lot, stopping with a sigh of brakes. A cloud of dust and diesel wrapped around me. The doors opened, and tourists cautiously stepped into the sunlight, muttering in Italian and German. I watched for a moment as they blinked madly and fumbled for sunglasses. A few snapped photos of each other with cameras dangling from their necks and a small group gathered at the back of the buses to stretch and count through sloppy calisthenics. Most of them were older, my grandparents' age perhaps, with white hair and walking sticks, but there were a few families with teenagers, younger kids chasing each other, a few babies. The tour guide–a trim, officious young woman in a grey business suit with a blue badge for EB Tours on the suit pocket–began calling the tourists together, shouting in German, Italian, then thickly accented English. As they shuffled into a single group she turned to me and asked something in German. I shook my head. She tried again in English, "Where are your parents, young man?"

Confused, I pointed at the park behind me.

"No, no, no, that is no good. Collect them back here. No time for outside pictures. No wandering. We have a set schedule. That's a good boy."

She waved me away, then began calling names from a sheet in her hands, pointing to different locations in the parking lot where the tourists rearranged themselves into small groups. When I arrived at the side of the buses, our station wagon was gone. It should have been right there. I walked the length of the wall, finally spotting the Beast poking from where the wall stopped. The tailgate was open. Two camera bags rested on the hood. When I came around front, I found my father crouched over his large tripod, locking down a camera. His longest lens was attached to the front with an additional support arm.

"We need the seat," I told him.

He kept fiddling with the camera. When he was composing a shot, he often didn't hear anything. I tapped him on the back.

"I need the seat."

He didn't turn. "Oh, fine. You know where it is."

I looked where he was shooting.

From this perspective the park appeared like a scattering of discarded toys in a sandbox. The green dinosaur rose from the center, and beside it stood a small, pointed volcano that was supposed to be a gas station, but from here it was identical to the concrete-teepee tourist shops my father had photographed throughout Arizona and Utah. To our immediate right was the back side of the stone wall, revealing the bent chicken wire shaping the plaster, and the wood beams propping it up. The sun cast long shadows from the volcano and the dinosaur, pointing in tandem toward the blurred, dusty horizon. But what he focused on was an animal pen about fifty feet away, designed like a miniature Stonehenge of white plaster and concrete pillars forming a ring with a black metal gate facing us. A few hay bales were stacked next to the gate. In the middle of the pen stood a large, dark-brown buffalo wearing a plastic bone necklace, studying us with wet, black eyes while it chewed. Beside the pen was an arrow-shaped sign pointing at the buffalo. The sign said, "Buffalosaurus."

My father changed settings, took a reading with the meter, then clicked off the first few frames. He shifted the tripod and took more photos.

"That's a real buffalo," I said finally.

"Yes, that's a real buffalo."

"I've never seen a real buffalo," I said. "I don't think he should be here."

"No, he shouldn't be here." My father clicked off more frames.

"*Scheisse*!" I turned around. The tour guide was right behind me. "That is a buffalo. A-one American buffalo," she said.

"Yes," my father whispered, moving his tripod closer.

"We are not to be here. We need to go to the front," the tour guide told us, not looking away from the pen.

"I'm with my family. I'm sorry, we're not on your tour. We're not tourists," I said. "We live here."

"Oh, Americans." She realized her mistake. "Not with us. I am sorry. My error. This is your home."

We all looked at the buffalo which kicked its back foot a number of times and continued staring at us.

"*Scheisse*," she said again.

"Exactly," my father said. "It's perfect."

The tour guide apologized again and walked into the park, giving the pen wide berth. I retrieved the toilet seat from the car, collected toilet supplies into a paper shopping bag, then followed her. When I glanced back, my father had left his camera on the tripod and returned to the car. He had just taken the photo that would soon appear everywhere in America: in magazine articles, public-service announcements, high-school textbooks, posters and teeshirts. Photo editors loved to use it for stories about social decline and the American West. If you close your eyes, you will recall seeing a buffalo in the desert with white bones around its neck—everyone has seen this photo somewhere, at some time. This buffalo made my father and Documerica temporarily famous.

Now, when this photo finds its way to me, I see the buffalo gazing at me that afternoon while scratching its message in the dust, and I remember the emptiness that drifted through me hours later as we traveled home in a bus filled with strangers. I think about my father clicking that shutter release, and I step right back into what happened next.

I passed a stone mailbox with thick stone envelopes stacked beside it, then saw my sister waving to me atop the back of the brontosaurus. She was up there with my mother, in a yellow, thatched-roof cab. That's when I realized the animal was supposed to be from the show's opening, with Fred working at the quarry, driving his dinosaur as crane and bulldozer. When a whistle blew at day's end, Fred slid down the tail directly into his car and raced through Bedrock City to his stone tract house where Wilma was cooking dinner. I could now see long straps swinging from a bit in the dinosaur's mouth, draped down into the cab. There was a set of black metal stairs on the side of the dinosaur, away from the road, allowing visitors to climb up. When I reached the base of the tail I found it was actually a steep metal slide. My sister slid from the top, giggling with her arms in the air, landing at my feet.

"That's so fast." She popped up and brushed off. "I've been down nine times. You can see a lot up there." She was excited and out of breath. I rested the toilet seat against the tail with the bag next to it. My sister ran ahead, up the stairs to the cab. "Beat you! I beat you!"

At the top I did see everything. The highway was perfectly straight, as if drawn across the desert with a black felt pen against a ruler. My mother stood in the corner of the cab, holding the railing, looking toward the Canyon. "Where's your father?"

"He's taking pictures over there." I pointed. She turned.

"That's good. Where?" She bridged her hand over her eyes. "I can't see."

"He's by the wall. At the end." The Stonehenge pen was visible, but I didn't see the car, or my father. "He was right there."

A veil of dust blew over from the parking lot and a blue station wagon drove onto the dirt lane toward the highway. "That's the Beast."

My mother lowered her hand from her eyes to grab the railing again. "That's your father," she said.

"Where's he going?"

My sister ran past us, swung on the bars along the side of the slide then shot down the tail, arms aloft like taking a roller-coaster ride, giggling the entire way.

"I have no idea," my mother said.

Our station wagon pulled onto the lip of the highway then paused. There was no traffic for miles in either direction. He was deciding which way to go.

"Maybe he has to get gas. Or mail some film," I said.

"Could be."

The right blinker started, he pulled onto the road then accelerated straight to seventy-five.

"He's going to Flagstaff," I said.

"Looks like it."

"When's he coming back?"

My mother watched him drive away then stepped from the railing, dusting off her hands while our car shrank smaller and smaller. "I do not know," she said. "He's done this before."

"He has? When?"

"A few times. For a few days, when you were much younger."

"Oh," I said, staring at the road, waiting for the Beast to stop, turn around, come back for us. It didn't.

"That's something you'll learn about your father," my mother said. "He likes to disappear."

"He must be getting gas. Or toilet paper," I explained, mostly to myself. "He'll be back."

"Maybe. Maybe not."

We watched for a while as our car became a dot then merged with the horizon. "Well, shit. That's not good," my mother said, looking for my sister. "Where'd she go?"

We began scanning the park for clues. The tourists had made their way toward the entrance and were already climbing into buses.

"Hello, there!" Down by the dinosaur's front foot, the tour guide waved at us. "Buffalo boy!"

I waved back. She held up her Instamatic with her other hand and pointed at it. We both nodded. My mother pulled me tight against her and out of habit we stood tall, chests puffed, chins tilted, peering at the sky in the contemplative pose my father recommended for his subjects. My mother called it the Noble Adventurer. She thought it was hokey as hell, and she told him that many times. He kept asking for it anyway.

"That's good," the tour guide said as she took her photo. She turned her camera sideways and took another. "Thank you!"

We waved and she headed for the entrance.

"Buffalo boy?" my mother asked.

"Yeah, there's a real live buffalo over there." I pointed where my father had been.

"You don't say."

I nodded and pointed again, shaking my finger for emphasis. My mother didn't look, she was searching for my sister. The park was empty. My sister was out there somewhere among the cartoons.

"Is he coming back?" I asked.

"We can't wait to find out. You think those buses are going to Flagstaff?"

I nodded firmly, as if I actually knew.

"Tell you what. Why don't you make sure. Go talk with your buffalo buddy."

"About going to Flagstaff?"

"Yes, we need a way home. I'll find your sister. You check with your friend. All right?"

I looked toward the tourist buses, wanting to be useful, and thought what I would say, how I would explain our situation. I could call it an emergency and say my father had raced ahead to collect someone important. Or claim there was an explosion. Maybe a flood. I sorted through the disasters they talked about in Scouts, certain that one would work. I imagined climbing aboard the bus with my mother and sister, holding our portable toilet for luggage. The bus would smell of strange cheese and sausages. All the tourists would wave their hands in greeting, eager to help these refugees from whatever disaster I concocted. "Hello, Americans!" they would shout in unison, so happy to see us.

The story I finally settled upon involved forest fires and a celebrity. It was an obvious bundle of lies but did win us a ride to Flagstaff with the tourists and their guide.

"This place will be closing soon," my mother said, rubbing my shoulders, moving me toward the slide. She scanned our surroundings, talking to herself, "Where'd she go to? Oh, there she is."

My sister skipped toward us across the desert, kicking and spinning in the dust like splashing through a wading pool, overcome with delight. She stopped at the bottom of the slide. "Come down and play," she said, jumping with each word. "Come. Play. With. Me."

The bus engines rumbled to life. "We need to get moving," my mother said with urgency.

I stared down the dinosaur's tail. The metal was shiny and smooth like the surface of a deep river in the shade. It was a sudden descent, the biggest slide I'd ever been on. My stomach felt hollow and skittish as I imagined taking that first step over the edge. My sister had done it, no problem, but it frightened me. My mother gave my shoulder a slight shove, "It will be just fine. Close your eyes. It'll be fun. Go on. It's our adventure now. I'm right behind you."

I grabbed the edges of the tail, swung my legs over and down, closed my eyes and dropped.

Aquarium

Miranda Schmidt

The separation, when it happened, was simple. So simple it almost seemed easy. They filed the papers. They divided the things. They both found new apartments on opposite sides of the city. Neither wanted to stay in the old one. Neither wanted to make any trouble. John took the car. Susan took the kitchen things. Neither wanted the plants, so John left them by the dumpster in the alley. Susan tried not to notice them as she packed her last box into the U-Haul, her things looking small and desolate piled tidily along the back wall. Someone would take them, the plants, someone who could care for them better, someone who could love them more clearly.

Susan had chosen for her new place of residence one of those modern apartments on the east side of the river. It was the opposite of the two-bedroom she had shared with John in one of the city's old red-brick buildings, quaint and historic as anything, but surely not safe in an earthquake. This new place was sturdy and small, just a studio, but it had a dishwasher and a washer/dryer and plenty of electrical outlets. Its crowning glory, the reason Susan had decided to take it in the first place, despite the exorbitant rent and the fact that it was on one of the busiest sections of Hawthorne–former hippie/hipster paradise, now the domain of rich mothers with fancy baby carriages and expensive exercise wear–were the windows. The apartment had an entire wall full of windows that looked out onto a large maple tree. It reminded Susan of the view from Lily's room back in college, of the old tall maple that stretched its leaves across the yard. For one whole summer, Susan would wake to that view every morning. She'd watch the sun glance off the deep green of the leaves until Lily woke beside her. It seemed fitting, she thought, at the end of a marriage, to go back to a place that felt like the beginning of things.

Aquarium

The windowsills were wide and white and empty. When she'd seen the apartment, she'd imagined them filled up with plants: potted violets and ferns and succulents. But now, moving in, the prospect of foliage made her nervous with its needing, its wanting for water and sunlight and care. She couldn't imagine, alone in this place, not killing any living thing through sheer neglect.

When she had wrestled her boxes upstairs, blocking the elevator for long enough that her neighbors began giving her dirty looks as they led their dogs to the stairwell, she sat on one of her two folding chairs, the only pieces of furniture—besides the card table and the futon—she now owned. In her almost empty new apartment she felt heady and exhausted. She closed her eyes and felt herself floating, untethered, away from her life, lost in the immensity of the possible that simply struck her, now, as claustrophobic. She was trapped in a keen sense of lightness.

THAT FIRST NIGHT, she dreamed that the city had flooded, that every building and bridge and tree was submerged. The Portland she knew had turned to an underwater metropolis. It was a deep sunken grey. Turned upside down by haphazard currents, cars floated through the deluge, tires rotating freely. She was tumbling through water. The waves wound her into them until she could not tell which way was up and which down, until she did not know which way to swim to surface. In the dream she felt a strange sense of calm in the face of her predicament. Even as she felt her lungs filling up with water, with that burning sensation you get when you breathe in a pool, she felt placid. It wasn't safety, precisely. It was more like the relief that comes when, for a moment, you forget to be afraid.

YEARS AGO, ON graduation weekend at the University of Oregon—not hers, hers was still a whole year away—she saw the girl sitting in the campus coffee shop. The girl was curling into the couch at the back corner of the café, knees pulled to her chest, sketchpad balanced on the sofa's arm.

Susan was never sure where she found the courage. She was usually so full of midwestern reserve, of the shyness that comes to a particular kind of person from a particular kind of conservative upbringing. She'd seen, the week before, on that same couch, two women sitting with a baby between them, minding the child as if their little family were the most normal thing in the world. It might have had to do with the shock of relief Susan felt at the sight of them, that moment of recognition.

It was that new, temporary courage that allowed Susan to do a thing she had never done, not even at parties, not with boys or girls: it allowed her to walk over to this stranger, to this girl in this coffee shop, and strike up a conversation.

"What are you sketching?" Susan asked.

The girl looked up. Her eyes were grey like water. She shrugged.

"Not sure yet," she said.

"You don't know before you start it?"

"Not always," the girl said, "I usually just let the pencil sort it out with the paper."

By the end of their conversation, Susan knew the girl's name—Lily—knew that she was originally from Seattle, knew she had just finished her art degree, that her parents were divorced, that she'd once had a dog named Rascal, that her favorite color was umber, and that she was going to a party that night that she thought Susan might enjoy.

By the end of that night, they had shared their first kiss.

By the end of that week, they had taken to seeing each other almost every day, and Susan was surprised by the ease of it, by the way she almost didn't seem to have to try, by the way they both seemed to be caught, for a time, in the same current.

JOHN CALLED AT ten in the morning.

Susan woke to the buzz of the phone. She winced at the tightness in her neck, surprised she had fallen asleep for so long in her chair. Her shoulders ached too, her back and her head, as if her dreams had battered her in the night. She moved herself cautiously, stretching a thirty-nine-year-old body that felt too worn for chair sleep. She answered the phone with the hoarse and whispery "Hello?" of a still-dreaming voice.

"How did the move in go?" John asked her from the other side of the city, his voice sounding friendly and concerned as if nothing had changed, as if he would see her again, after a long day, at dinner.

"Fine," she said. "Not hard at all."

"Good, good. I'm settling in pretty well over here. The water pressure's better than at our old place, but the heating doesn't work as well."

She tried to stop herself from imagining John in his new apartment, opening his eyes to the grey of the day, calling first thing from the bed they'd once shared that she didn't want, not now, not anymore, but that he hadn't seemed to mind taking. She'd been astonished by that. How, she wondered, did that bed not hold the same shadow of failure for him as it held for her?

"Everything work okay at your place?" John asked. "Let me know if you need anything fixed. I'm happy to help out."

"All fine," Susan said. "All perfectly fine so far."

He was quiet then, as if he were trying to listen to the meaning between her words or waiting, as he always did these days, for her to say what she was thinking. She could hear the sound of his breathing. It was as if, for a moment, he was in the apartment with her, standing right next to her, so close they could almost touch.

Outside her window, the maple's leaves cast a soft green glow through droplets of rainwater. She wondered how old it was, how much the neighborhood had changed since it put down its roots. She imagined the tree as a sapling, the buildings rising around it, the people scurrying below, while it stood alone, growing, flowering, bearing its seeds, as if its surroundings were nothing but noise in a dream.

"I have to go," she lied, "I'm meeting a friend for coffee."

She spent the next hour unpacking boxes before deciding to make the lie a half-truth by venturing out for her coffee alone.

THE WALLS OF Lily's room were covered with paintings of women changing shape: women half enclosed inside sealskins, women with antlers, women baring the faces of wolves. She'd made them all herself, conjured them all out of her own imagination. Susan found them astonishing and terrifying and beautiful. With Lily, she found herself to be astonishing and terrifying and beautiful. With Lily, she felt she could almost be anything.

She spent that whole summer in the same heightened state that comes with knowing the ending of a thing is contained in the beginning. It was like an impending death, that awareness of coming catastrophe. Lily was moving to New York at the end of the summer. Susan was staying to finish the last year of her teaching degree.

"Why do you paint them?" Susan asked one morning, wanting to know everything all at once, wanting to shove a lifetime of knowing into that handful of months.

Lily laughed at her questions, "Why do I do anything?"

"I don't know," Susan said.

Lily's brows drew together. It gave her face an air of surprising seriousness, as if she had grown up twenty years in a moment. Susan had already learned to identify this as the expression Lily used when considering something quite deeply.

"Maybe I want to be a different shape," she said finally.

"Why?" Susan asked. She loved Lily's shape, her long gangly limbs, her angular face, her spiky short hair that turned to soft tufts in the night.

"I don't know," Lily said, "Humans are just so . . ."

"What?"

Lily shrugged, "Heavy. I guess."

"What would you be instead?"

"What do you think I'd be?" Lily asked, meeting her curiosity with a mischievous grin that felt to Susan more like an infuriating mask held up between them. It felt like elusiveness put on for show.

Susan looked at the paintings instead, at the one of the seal girl. She liked the in-between-ness of her, the way she was partway to water and partway to land.

"That's the one I'd be," she said.

"Really?" Lily asked and Susan felt a little thrill at the surprise in her voice. "Why?"

"Probably because I'm scared of drowning," Susan said, the blush creeping into her cheeks.

"Susan the selkie," Lily mused, studying her face and seeming to see some kind of newness there. "Where'd they hide your skin?"

SHE SET HER coffee on the empty countertop, feeling guilty for the plastic lid, the wasteful sleeve, the cup that couldn't be recycled. Guilty but also silly for feeling guilty. Because what did one cup matter, really, in the grand scheme of all of it?

She turned to unpacking. She had boxes of books and kitchenware to put away. She had old mementos that could lurk in the back of a closet. She had the painting she needed to hang or to hide, but she couldn't decide, not yet, what to do with it. She had a shoebox of pictures and clippings and quotes she'd been collecting for over a year now. Inside the box were stories about melting glaciers. Inside the box were photographs of endangered birds and sea turtles swimming through plastic. The box held towns in Alaska plagued by starving polar bears wandering in from dying habitats. It held the coastlines of Louisiana as they sank into the Gulf. It held islands devastated by climate change-strengthened hurricanes. It held the drought-fed wildfires that darkened the summer, raining ash all along the West Coast.

It hadn't been a box at first. At first, she'd tacked the clippings on the wall above her desk. At first, she'd looked at them every morning and seen the shape of a world in decline. She'd tried to trace its boundaries. She'd tried to find the edges but no edges were there. Nowhere was right right now. Always, some disaster was coming. She, herself, was a part of that disaster. They all were, each and every human. They were all the disaster. And they were all trapped inside it.

John had taken to calling it her "Wall of Destruction." At first, he'd been amused. "My wife, the bleeding heart," he'd said with a shake of his head.

Then, as the collection grew to cover more of the wall, moving past the boundaries of her desk and over toward his, he turned from impatient to plaintive. "Why obsess over things that you can't control?" he asked her. "You're a good person. You recycle. You take the bus. You're a vegetarian, for God's sake. There's nothing more you can do."

"But it's all still there," she said. "It won't just go away. I have to understand the shape of it."

But he hadn't understood what she meant and she couldn't explain it any better.

LILY WOULDN'T LET her see the painting until it was finished.

"You need the complete vision," Lily said. "It won't make sense if you only see a part of it."

So Susan waited, wondering what animal Lily would turn her into. Would she be a creature of water or land or air? Would she seem fierce or kind or shy or free?

When Lily finally revealed the painting, pulling back the scarf she'd kept covering it whenever Susan came over, the scarf Susan had not touched, not once, despite the temptation, when that scarf was pulled back and Susan caught that glimpse of herself, she couldn't tell, at first, what she was looking at. It didn't look the same as the other transformation paintings. It didn't look like magic transformation. It didn't look beautiful. It looked like a woman consumed. There, staring back at her were arms trapped in a constriction of wood, held down tight, skin turned to a pale peel of bark, toes curled to immovable roots stuck in place. And the leaves, dry and autumnal and falling where her hair should have been.

Lily was talking excitedly about mythical figures, about folkloric associations of women and plant life, about the story of Daphne turning into a tree to escape from Apollo, about Celtic lovers taking root side by side.

"It's so ecofeminist," Lily said. She'd been looking at the painting as she spoke, but then she turned her gaze to Susan. Susan tried to rearrange her face, to give a smile, or at least a bland expression for Lily to imagine a smile on.

"You do like it, right?" Lily asked. There was nervousness in her voice but there was also an edge, like a dare. "I mean, you get it?"

Susan nodded. "Of course."

For days she woke from dreams of leaf hair crumbling into her pillow. For weeks, she'd touch her chapped lips and think of that pale peeling bark.

IT WAS WHEN she crossed the bridges that Susan thought of the earthquake. She'd read about it the year before, how the Cascadia subduction zone was long overdue for disaster. Everyone had read about it. When the article came out, no one had talked about anything else for a week. But John had not been worried.

"We have an emergency kit," he said. "We have extra batteries. We'll be fine"

"But what if the building falls in on us when we're sleeping?" Susan asked. "Or what if the bridges collapse? What if we get stuck on opposite sides of the river?"

"If the building falls down, then we'll die nice and quick in our sleep and we won't have to worry about it," he said, giving her a smile that said he was trying to be reassuring.

"But what if–"

"Don't worry about it, Susan. It's not likely to happen. They've been talking about this earthquake since I was a kid. We'll probably be long gone by the time it comes around."

"But it was in the *New York Times,*" Susan protested, which is when John burst out laughing.

She hadn't mentioned it again, but she'd thought about it. Some nights, while she was trying to fall asleep, she would worry she could feel the ground shaking beneath their bed beneath their building, rumbling to life.

She hadn't grown up with it, as John had, that murmuring threat just under the surface of things, half real and half child-imaginings. There would be, they said, buildings that crumbled as if they were made of nothing stronger than sand. There would be, they said, liquefaction of seemingly solid ground. There would be the tsunami, water rising to engulf the coast, sending the inland rivers and streams up and out of their banks.

On the bridges, she imagined what it would mean to be caught over water, suspended above the seemingly friendly Willamette, when the disaster came. Would the tremors throw her from the sidewalk, sail her over the railing as if gravity itself had been shaken? Would the bridge even hold? Or would it crumble, all its oblivious cars and pedestrians sent tumbling into the waves?

Susan had grown up with the threat of tornadoes, with the school drills that sent you away from the windows, crowded you into the hallways, side by side with your classmates, holding your hands over your neck to protect it from glass shards. Those drills had terrified her, sending her childhood dreams, on those drill nights, into a strange, fevered mix of *The Wizard of Oz* and *Twister*. But tornados were local anomalies: they hit lines of towns, sometimes destroyed them, but they didn't take on whole regions. Tornados gave warnings, made time for you to hide in basements and bathtubs. Earthquakes were another beast entirely. They were greater and vaster and quicker than her mind could contain. She found, when she tried, that she couldn't imagine being a child in Oregon, growing up in a place where the land that seemed friendly and fertile and yielding could at any moment rise up and swallow you whole.

ALL THAT SUMMER on most afternoons, they would go out to the McKenzie, throwing their inner tubes over their shoulders to scramble down the river's banks and set themselves afloat. Tubing was a favorite summer pastime among the college set, but somehow Susan had managed to spend three summers in Eugene without ever trying it. As she drifted down the river with Lily, she imagined they were leaves borne away by the current, escaped from the trees. Some days, when the weather was cloudy, they were the only ones out: two girls caught between grey sky and grey water.

The day Lily fell in was just such a day. It had rained the night before and the river ran high and fast. They went out on it anyway, laughing. Susan was aware of the strange tone her laughter took, the terrified tensing of it. As they waded in, her laugh was a high-pitching creature escaping her mouth. But Lily's eyes were sparkling, so Susan convinced herself, in the face of that high-running water, that she had to be brave.

There was a moment, just before Lily tipped into the water, losing hold of her inner tube in the grip of the current as the water tugged her under more quickly than Susan thought possible, when she did not feel fear. In that moment, she was watching Lily's face. It looked triumphant, having conquered a river with nothing but rubber and air. Susan could feel the water move beneath her. She was perfectly balanced atop it, pulled along by its momentum. She watched the trees blurring by on the shore. She felt a heady sense of peace, as if she was nothing but a drop of clear water.

Then Lily's expression changed. It was a flash so brief Susan couldn't be sure that she hadn't imagined it. The triumph shifted into something else, something harder, determined.

When Lily went under, disappearing, just for a moment, beneath that surface, Susan felt her body moving without her. Diving in, she did not feel the cold. She will never remember quite how she did it, how her arm found Lily and wrapped itself around her while the rest of her somehow managed to drag them both to shore. She'll remember forever how still Lily felt, how, at first, she would not move to help her. She'll remember her own grip, how her arm transformed into something strong and clinging—a vine, a vise—how she could not have let go if she'd wanted to.

They crawled up the river's bank together, exhausted. They lay on their backs looking up through the leaves, listening to the river run by them. It was drizzling, just a little, but they hardly noticed. Lily reached for her but Susan crossed her arms over her chest, trying to conceal the shaking of her hands.

EARLY SUNDAY MORNING, she walked downtown across the Hawthorne Bridge to see John's new apartment. She'd awoken to his voicemail, left the night before, asking her to stop by. It sounded casual and friendly, but she could hear the loneliness rising up just under his usual tone, and that made her guilty. It was misty that morning and the clouds threatened rain. She felt, as she walked suspended over the Willamette, like the only person left in the world.

She imagined herself diving over the rail, shifting shape as she fell through the air, hitting the water in an entirely different form. She imagined herself vanishing beneath the waves of the river, hiding just below the surface.

John's apartment was furnished in deep greens and dark browns. It was still their furniture—the couch from the living room, the table and chairs from the kitchen—but without her light-blue curtains, without the cream-colored tablecloth she'd picked up at a garage sale, without her plants, the furniture looked darker than it ever had before. It was, she saw now, his furniture. It always had been. He'd chosen the deep earth tones. He'd brought them home. Here, now, the furniture was in its natural element: western hunting lodge-inspired bachelor pad. She could see it already, what the apartment would become in the months to follow. Slowly, John would accumulate dishes (probably the wooden kind: smooth bowls and plates and cups shaped from the whirls of wood grain). Next would come new blankets bearing the images of bears and wolves. A fake bearskin rug might come after. Eventually, at one vintage store or another, he'd come upon an old dusty stag's head he could hang on the wall. Just the one. A conversation piece. The women he brought home would be impressed. They'd be the outdoorsy kind, the ones who loved camping, who climbed mountains on the weekends and knew how to start fires with sticks. They'd be the kinds of people John, the perfectionist city kid with only basic Boy Scout skills, aspired to be himself. They'd fill in the spaces he lacked.

He offered her coffee. He'd bought a new coffee maker, he explained, one of those fancy espresso machines. He could even steam milk with it.

"That's alright," she said, "I don't need anything."

"You sure?" he asked and it suddenly felt like a conversation was moving under their words, an undertow of silent meaning they were only half aware of, pulling them along.

"I'm sure."

"What about a muffin?" he asked, gesturing to a box on the counter. They looked healthy and grainy and seed-filled. "Can I tempt you with a muffin?"

She shook her head.

"So, the apartment still okay?"

She nodded.

"Living alone not too lonely for you?"

There was an edge to the question, an accusation she tried to ignore.

"Not too lonely," she said.

John let out a sigh and turned toward the coffee maker, pouring grounds with his back to her.

"I just wanted to see you," he said.

If she were a good wife, she knew, she would go to him and put her arm on his shoulder and say, "I know," and maybe even, "I wanted to see you too." If she were a good wife, she'd accept the coffee and the muffins and she'd sit with him in his bachelor apartment and talk about all the good times they'd had in their marriage: the road trip to California; their wedding; that first week after they'd first moved in together; their meeting, just in time, in that last year of college. She would have stayed all day and maybe even the night. But she wasn't a good wife. She was another creature entirely. She was the kind who wouldn't eat muffins, who didn't want to talk, who'd stayed in a marriage for years after she'd already left it. She couldn't love her husband in the ways that she should. She couldn't hold herself here in this moment.

"I have to go," she said. "I have an appointment."

She was lying again and he knew it. Still, he didn't say anything but, "Okay."

When she got back to her apartment, she unpacked Lily's painting. She hung the tree woman up above her desk.

"OH, LOOK, IT'S Lily's bi-curious girlfriend," one of Lily's housemates said one afternoon, toward the end of summer, when Susan knocked on the door.

A trickle of laughter sounded from the living room. Susan bristled at the word and the laughter, but she gave a smile anyway as she asked for Lily, explained, unnecessarily, their plans to get lunch.

The housemate raised an eyebrow. At first, Susan thought the expression had to do with lunch plans, that the housemate disapproved of such a traditional college date, so lacking in creativity or rebellion or vision. Then she saw the housemate's eyes shift, communicating not derision, but concern.

"Lily's gone. She left for New York this morning. She didn't tell you?"

"Oh," was the only sound Susan could muster.

The housemate seemed, for a moment, to be at a loss for words before they came tumbling forth in a tone that was uncharacteristically soft.

"She left a painting behind. You can have it if you want. She might have meant it for you. She didn't say."

Susan found herself ushered upstairs and left alone in Lily's almost empty room, staring at a painting of herself turning into a tree. The painting had grown. It seemed Lily hadn't stopped working on it. There was more bark. There were more leaves now. You couldn't even see the human face anymore. You could only just make out the eyes.

THAT SUNDAY EVENING, Susan didn't decide to enter the pet shop so much as she found herself standing inside it. One moment, she was on the street and the next, she was through the sliding doors and standing between the dog food and the kittens sleeping in glass cages.

She passed the kittens by, leaving them to their toothsome dreams of hunting with tiny paws. She walked to the back of the store, toward the glow of aquariums and the soft hum of filters. Here the fish floated through water, flipping their translucent fins, rolling their bright bodies to propel themselves forward. She watched them, some swimming together, whole schools full of back-and-forth pacers, some swimming apart, meandering circles alone. She wondered if they felt trapped in their tanks, in their tiny allotments of water, their little lives bounded by glass they could not break through.

She found herself watching a tank of silvery blue ones with long slim whiskers.

Blue Gourami, the card said, labyrinth fish, changes color with mood.

"What does labyrinth fish mean?" she asked when the store clerk came by to ask her if she needed anything.

"They rise to the air to breathe," he told her.

"How do they do that?"

"They have a special labyrinth organ that lets them survive out of water, at least for a little bit."

"So if it jumped out of the tank?"

"Yeah, as long as you found it before it got too dry, it could be fine."

She left the pet store with a small aquarium and a bag of green gravel, a water filter and two blue gourami in a little bag full of water. They circled the plastic looking perturbed

Back home, she followed the pet shop's instructions to take care with the water temperature, to set the bag inside the full tank before releasing the fish from it. The bag floated toward the surface, the two fish bumping up against the plastic edges. She put the tank by the window so she could see the maple's leaves warping through water. That night, she imagined the maple submerged, sinking, floating, weaving its branches through waves.

The Casita on Flower Street

L.L. Madrid

The ad called the house a casita. My sister sniffed and said, "That's a euphemism for small and in the barrio." When I pull up to the address, I know she's right. The old house is tiny, and in walking distance of a bar, a pawn shop, and two 7/11s. These are not deal breakers. Max is starting kindergarten in the fall, and 640 Flower Street Unit D is on the outskirts of the good school district—the one with the best developmental program in the state. It's the only place I can afford in the area. That's what matters now.

I park in the dirt courtyard that's flanked by four identical units. A saguaro looming over twenty feet high stands sentry. The cactus is pocked with holes from birds and its numerous arms point at odd angles, like it fell from some great distance and broke all its bones.

"Max, did you know that it takes a saguaro seventy years to grow its first arm?"

No answer. He's white-knuckling the edges of his booster seat.

"I saw a Gila wren poke her head out. I bet she built a nest in the cactus. Let's go peek."

"I like our basement. I don't want to move."

It's not our basement. It's my sister's, and three years living in her "exercise studio" hasn't been a blast. Still, it's hard for Max when something as small as a chair gets relocated. The idea of moving is weighing on him. "Change doesn't have to be scary. It can be an adventure."

Max folds his arms and stares out of his window. He ignores me when I open his door. That's nothing unusual. He sits motionless, watching the saguaro until an old VW bug pulls in beside our Accord. A little woman steps out. She wears layers of linen and is wrapped in silver and turquoise.

Her fire-red hair is stuffed and fluffed in typical old-lady style. She grins and waves an arthritic hand; her multiple rings gleam in the sunlight.

"You must be Sabrina! I'm Bernadette."

"Hello." I try to smile back. I'm terrified that this place will be a dump. The only other in-budget place I've found is an apartment complex that lights up with red dots when you check the sex-offender map. There are only two dots in this neighborhood. I tap Max's shoulder and gesture to the house. He climbs out, refusing to make eye contact with Bernadette.

"Hi, there!" She squawks and gives Max's back a pat. He recoils. Unfazed, Bernadette shakes a key ring at me and says, "Shall we?" She struggles with the front door. It sticks even as she slams her shoulder against the peeling green paint. "Needs a little TLC." Obedient at last, the door sighs and swings open. "Well, young man, why don't you run ahead and explore?"

"There are no flowers on this street," he says.

"Pardon me?"

"Why would they call the street Flower if there aren't any?"

"You're quite the character, aren't you?" Bernadette shakes her head, the feathery curls quivering. Max steps in and leans against the wall grim-faced.

I decide against explaining Max. Usually, people nod sympathetically and add that they know someone whose child is on the spectrum, or that he seems normal to them. I don't feel like fielding any unwelcome comments today.

The house is small and square. From the front entrance you can see into the bedroom through a series of cut-outs in the dividing wall. The lack of privacy is annoying, but I could block the view with books. Besides, I've been sharing rooms with Max since he was two.

If I'd known that I'd be celibate for three years I would have had sex with Jake more often at the end. I was resentful. I didn't want to fuck my then-husband. Now, given the chance and a bit of privacy, I don't think I'd turn anyone down. There's a deep pang, like hunger, when you go too long without intimacy. I get chills when someone brushes by me and I feel a bit of skin, if only for a moment.

I look out the front window on the dirt courtyard and giant cactus. Set back far enough from the crumbling street, the view isn't bad. Thick tiles adorned with blooming blue and yellow flowers line the windowsill.

"Those are the originals. Hand-painted in Mexico. Frank wanted to tear them out, but I think they're lovely. There's more over the stove." I follow her into the kitchen.

It's the size of a bathtub. I'm thankful that all our dishes, including pots and pans, fit into one box. Besides, there's something to cramped living; it's womblike. Safe. The cupboards are clear-sky blue. The yellow back door stands next to the counter. This looks like a place where we could be happy.

The windows over the sink and dining area show every angle of the fenced-in yard. That's a bonus. I glance over the bar that divides the kitchen and living room. Max hasn't moved.

Following my gaze, Bernadette chimes in, "Young man, why don't you explore the yard? There's plenty of dirt and bugs. Things little boys like."

Arms straight at his side, Max's fingers twitch and tap. It's his tell. When he gets excited he can't help but hold his hands together and let his fingers waggle and fly. I smile; I love when he does his happy hands. "Go on, Max. I can see you through the window." He nods and walks with monklike solemnity to the door. Once he's outside he starts running laps.

"Let me show you the rest of the place."

Heart tight in my chest I peek out the window. I don't like having Max out of my sight.

"Sabrina, this house is bite-sized and the walls are thin. Your boy will be fine. If he wasn't, you'd know that instant."

I don't know if I like Bernadette, but I know she's right. So I follow. Black mold huddles in the upper corner of the bedroom. She catches me looking up. "That'll be gone before you move in." I don't say anything. There are two doors at the end of the bedroom. Bernadette opens one and shows me the bathroom.

"What's this?" I point to the other door.

"Storage closet. I always mean to have it fitted with shelves . . . You can cram a lot in here." She flings the door open and a warm golden glow pours out.

My breath catches. "I love the skylight."

Bernadette's thin fuchsia lips suppress a smile as I step past her into the miniature room. The storage closet represents an old dream of mine, back when I had flights of fancy. I received my fine-arts degree eight years ago. I never made a penny from drawing, and I owe thousands in student loans. Still, I was happiest in my art school days.

I believed I'd be an illustrator and live in a house with a studio brimming with natural light. I haven't done more than napkin doodles in years, but here is the perfect little studio. I think of the Rubbermaid tub of art supplies I've been carting around for years. When the bank foreclosed on the house I jettisoned almost everything but that tub–I dragged that piece of my dreams from marital home to childhood home and then to my sister's. A warm sigh escapes me; the closet has enough room for a small drawing table. I breathe in with certainty that I'll bring the tub here and at last unpack its contents.

"Time to see how Max is doing," I say and we walk back through the house. Bernadette tells me about the laundromat her cousin owns a few blocks down. I nod. There's a quiver of excitement deep in my core. I want this place. We can make it work, Max will go to the good school, and I'll have a little space to myself. My own studio.

We step out into the blaring sunlight. The yard is little more than a dirt lot wrapped with a worn and deteriorating wood fence. Still, it's huge, and a pomegranate tree in a neighbor's yard drapes the fence. It's loaded with fruit begging to be pilfered. In the opposite corner, Max is looking at something on the ground.

"Whatcha doing, Max?" I walk over and he holds a finger to his lips. He's sitting by a cracked slab of concrete. Gingerly he selects a pebble and locks eyes with me before pressing it through the fissure. I open my mouth but he holds his finger to his lips once again. After a few seconds, there's a soft plunk.

"Clever boy, you found the well." Bernadette squints at us. "I'd almost forgotten it. It's been there longer than any of the houses on this street. It's from the time of the cowboys."

"Is it safe?" My studio dream slips a bit.

"Of course, it's been covered for decades, never a problem."

Max drops a larger pebble and claps when there's an audible splash.

"When can we move in?"

THE WINDOWS ARE open, and rocks prop the doors. The smell of bleach clings to the walls like the layers of paint concealing the original lead coat. Which is worse? The toxins buried beneath the eggshell white, or the black mold plotting a return? I shake the negative thoughts away. The lead is buried, and the mold banished. The chlorine scent can't linger forever.

Six years ago I would have never moved into a house this rundown. Of course, back then I was pregnant with Max and didn't even eat soft cheese or sushi or drink coffee. I took those gritty prenatals with devotion. In the end, none of that mattered. Mommy blogs failed to prepare me for a baby that never stopped crying. Pediatricians were useless when two-year-old Max started slamming his head into walls–over and over–without reason. It's a little easier now. I accept the jealousy that resides tumorlike in my gut when I see small children covering their parents with kisses while mine only looks at me blankly.

Best intentions can't keep your world from falling apart. Research, counseling, and prayer were all mere distractions while my husband drifted into depression before drinking himself out of a job. I've gotten over my love not being enough to save my marriage, but I'll never accept that it won't be enough for my son.

"How you doing, Maxie?"

Busy lining his trains along the grout, he doesn't look up. I walk over and ruffle his hair. His shoulders hunch, and he stiffens. The flinching will always hurt. Sometimes Max gets bad ear infections, and while I feel terrible for him, I delight in the change. Those are the only times when he allows me to hold him, to stroke those black curls and touch his sweet dimpled face.

"You hungry, buddy?"

Max shakes his head at his trains.

"I'm going to unpack stuff in my studio." My studio. The phrase makes my heart flutter. My fingers tremble as I remove the lid from the Rubbermaid tub. I prepare myself for dried-out paint, or books ruined by leaks. I pull out brushes and tubes of acrylics and set them aside. The sheaves of unused archival paper and small canvas squares get neatly stacked. There are twelve sketchbooks, full and dusty with abandonment. Pausing my sorting, I flip through the pages of one. My sketches were good. Better than good. My stomach twists as I wonder if talent can rot and dry out like the accumulating detritus in the garbage bag.

"Whose doll is this?" Max is standing behind me. He's ninja quiet.

"That's my artist model. Your grandpa gave it to me when I graduated from college."

"Before he died?"

"Yes," I say placing the sketchbook on a small bookcase nestled in the studio's corner.

Max pulls the wooden figure from the box and looks at it closely. The model hits the wall so fast and with such force that I don't register what's happened. Max is screaming.

"What's wrong?" I grip his shoulders trying to calm him. I drop my voice low. "It's okay, Max." My eyes drift from his red bellowing face to the figure on the floor. Realizing I'm more worried about an object than my child, I cringe and focus on Max. "Deep breaths, buddy. What happened?"

"It hurts!" His left hand is tucked protectively under his right arm.

"Let me see." I force his fingers open. His palm is red and swollen. Not a splinter. I scan the room and spot it. Nickel-sized and near-transparent, the scorpion presses against the baseboard. Its spiked tail twitches. I grab a Dadaist textbook from the bin. I lunge and flatten the scorpion, smacking it three times to be certain.

Max is sobbing.

"I'm sorry, baby."

He lets me wrap my arms around him and soothe him with the promise of a Popsicle from the 7/11.

"Why did it do that?"

"It was probably scared because you're so big and it's so small."

"But why did it hurt me?"

"That's what scorpions do."

"The bug didn't do it. Your doll did."

"The scorpion was in the box. They like wood. Maybe he was sleeping on the doll."

Max shakes his head. "It was the doll. You killed the bug for no reason."

After settling Max on the couch with an icepack and Thomas the Train, I examine the figure model. A crack splinters down the spine, but the doll is still functional. I hate myself for feeling almost as much relief as I did when the nurse hotline told me not to worry, that the scorpion sting wasn't serious. I place the doll on my drawing desk and whisper, "Everything is going to be fine."

MONSOON SEASON BEGINS in the middle of our second week on Flower Street. In late afternoons, black clouds form to hurl lightning bolts and release enough water to transform the once-dry washes into powerful streams. Meteorologists predict record-setting rainstorms, and each night the news features dramatic rescues. We watch people stranded on tops of cars staring dumbly from underpasses that held inches of water before transforming into rivers.

Transfixed by the footage, Max sits with his nose almost against our old box television. "How come that big truck got stuck in the water, but the little car made it through okay?"

"The water changes everything in an instant." I position a sauce pan by the front door. The casita leaks. When the storms come, we rush around placing mixing bowls and pans in the spots I've marked with masking tape. Bernadette hasn't returned my calls. I worry about the wood-beam ceiling. What if it rots and the house falls down around us?

Max is miserable. Our basement was soundproof. Here, the thunder causes dishes to rattle and the whip-crack snaps make us both jump. Now, Max can't sleep. He lets me burrito him in blankets. The compression makes him feel safe. I wish he'd let me lie down with him. I'd squeeze until he fell asleep. When I offer, he says, "I don't like to be touched."

The lightning flashes outside of our house, setting our little world to strobe. When the thunder rocks the walls, I give Max his headphones and play calming binaural beats until he falls asleep. Even after the rain stops, the lingering anxiety jolts him awake throughout the night. It's like having a newborn. I'm exhausted. I remind myself that this is all for the greater good. I met with Max's new teacher; she seems nice and is very understanding of his quirks and needs. He's going to like school. I promise Max this, and myself. The monsoons will move on in a few weeks, and life will get easier. This is my mantra.

When I wake at dawn, I creep to fill my coffee cup and then slip into my closet studio and draw. These moments of solitude when I create are some of the happiest I've had in years.

A screech jolts me from concentration. I knock my mug over and it drenches a week's worth of illustrations. The screaming continues as I rush from the closet without righting the cup. I think of the scorpion. What other creatures could come for my boy?

He's sitting up on his bed, red-faced and wailing like a toddler. I take him in my arms and squeeze and rock. "Sssshhhhh . . ." I whisper rhythmically until the cries stop and Max peels my arms from around him. He shoves me. Hard.

"You were gone."

"I wasn't. I was drawing in the closet."

"I didn't see you. I don't like when I can't see you."

"Maxie, I would never leave you. I promise."

He wipes his nose with his pajama sleeve and stares at the closet. "Were you playing with the doll?"

"I told you, it's for drawing figures." I go to the closet and gather the sodden sheets. Heavy with fluid, some tear when I lift them. I shut my eyes and inhale. Exhale. I get the garbage can from the kitchen and crumple the pages together and shove the wad into the trash. I try not to think of the sleepy hours of early-morning work that the now-junked drawings represent. I don't tally up the cost of supplies as I tie a knot in the full garbage bag. I don't cry when I hurl it into the dumpster.

Don't cry. This is what you do when everything goes wrong. You start over. You've done it before and will surely have to again. Don't cry. My chin quivers as I go to make more coffee. The tin is near empty, only enough to make a cup. It's two days until my food stamps card refills. I decide to save the remaining coffee for tomorrow. Don't cry.

"Momma?"

Don't cry.

I don't turn from the sink. "Yes?"

"Sorry I yelled. I don't like you to be gone."

The tears slip out, one by one. I swipe my thumb at them. Beyond the window, the new day's sky is full of pinks and reds. "I wasn't gone." Forcing a smile I turn around. "You hungry?"

THE NEXT MORNING I sip at my ration of coffee, trying to clear my head of all the things I have to do in the coming hours. Get Max up, drop him off at Miss Thandie's, go to work, get school supplies, and on and on. I take a gulp and set the mug on the floor, away from my drawings. I close my eyes and think about what I want to draw. A robot for Max. Smiling, I sharpen the charcoal pencil. When I set the sharpener down, I see that my figure model is missing from its stand.

As I check the floor and behind the boxes of supplies I know I won't find it here. I tiptoe out of the closet; Max is in his bed, angelic in his slumber with his thick eyelashes resting on his baby-fat cheeks and a halo of black curls on his pillow. I check under both twin beds and in the dresser drawers. The figure isn't in the clothing closet.

I sigh. I'll ask him when he wakes if he's in an okay mood. Mornings are hard. Max needs his routines and there's an obsessive element to them. A slight alteration, and the entire day can go by the wayside. I sit to draw, but I'm too tired. I put away the pencil and paper and find Max sitting on his bed staring at me.

"Morning, kiddo."

He shuffles to the bathroom. When he comes out I ask if he knows where the figure model is.

"No."

"Only two of us live here, and I didn't do it. I'm not mad. It's special to me. My daddy gave it to me."

"I don't have a dad."

"Max . . ." I bite my lip. We've had this conversation hundreds of time. I try to answer his questions as best–and as honestly–as I can, but he's never satisfied. I don't blame him, but there isn't much more I can say. "You have a dad. He went away."

Max slumps into the living room and sits on the floor by his crate of trains. Carefully, he sets each engine and car on the tile, in a straight line, always in the same order. This is how Max shuts down. He won't answer me when he's in train mode, and if I try to break the spell he goes ballistic.

Two days later, I find the art figure wrapped in a dish towel and shoved under the kitchen sink. When I ask Max about it, he only shrugs.

The boom and subsequent crash are so powerful that it shakes my glasses off the nightstand. Max cries and I go to him, holding his body to mine. It's been a while since I've carried him, and with a bittersweet sorrow, I realize this may be the last time I do. He's getting so big. "It's only thunder, baby."

The storm is fierce. Gusts of wind hurl branches and garbage against the casita. Car alarms blare, and Max screams and doesn't stop until the storm settles, his hoarse cries turning into whimpers as the downpour depletes into trickles. The sun is sneaking into the sky when at last; Max falls into a deep slumber.

THE NEXT DAY we survey the storm's damage to our yard. I shift my weight and the mud oozes under my shoes. Max mutters, counting the puddles. When he finishes, he points to one and asks, "Can I?"

I nod. Arms flapping and fingers dancing, Max clicks the yellow rubber heels of his rain boots together and dashes away. I watch him systematically pounce from puddle to puddle while squealing.

"Momma! Look, there's a really, really big hole!"

I see where he's standing, and my heart claws into my throat. "Don't go near it!" I run to him and grasp his arms. It is a really, really big hole. The massive rainfall has destroyed the concrete slab. I lean over carefully. All I see is an endless dark pit.

Max throws a stone down. I count the seconds until I hear the plop.

One.

Two.

Three.

Four.

Five.

Six.

Seven.

Splash. I recall a long-ago word problem involving a well and figuring its depth in some physics class. I don't remember the equation, but I know this well is dangerously deep.

"Let's go inside."

"I'm not done splashing!"

"We gotta get the well covered before you can play back here."

"Why?"

"Anything that falls down there will never come back up."

BERNADETTE STILL DOESN'T return my calls. Her voicemail says that she's gone to California for the summer. Rent's low for a reason. I place a couple of rotting two-by-fours over the top of the well. They don't offer much protection from falling in, but X marks the spot. I warn—beg—Max to stay far, far away from that X.

The ground is supple from weeks of rain. I sit outside with a sketchbook across my knees observing my son. We've been out here for hours with Max constructing an elaborate railway system. His pink tongue pokes from the corner of his mouth as he works. Using an old serving spoon, he shapes hills and hollows out tunnels.

The sun offers perfect light today. With great care, I draw Max at play. I want to capture that elusive flicker of imagination, the way a long lock curls just beneath his left eye. I pause to sharpen my pencil, and when I glance at what I've made I feel a tingling at the back of my head, and I know that this will be my best work to date.

"Max, I love you forever and always."

He looks up, meeting my gaze before his dark lashes nearly kiss his cheeks as he squints against the sun. "Forever and always, I love you too." He goes back to his trains. The loamy earth squishes as Max clicks and clucks, making the sounds of the rolling locomotives. In these seconds we are truly happy. I want to hold on to this muddy moment for as long as possible.

WHEN MAX IS asleep and his little snores harmonize with the hum of the swamp cooler, I slip into the bathroom and fill the tub. I pour a glass of the wine I've been saving for a good day and grab a paperback. Inspiration strikes, and I grab the bottle as well. I want fun. Today was good, and I'm keen to celebrate. Saying a tiny prayer that Max won't wake, I sink into the hot water. Ignoring the lines of mildew creeping along the grout, I take a sip of the earthy wine, swallowing my worries down. The water turns tepid by the third glass and the words of the book start to swim. I let the novel fall to the damp floor and shut my eyes.

A strobe of lightning wakes me. My neck is sore and my skin has gone pruny from the long soak. Thunder claps, and I slam my elbow against the porcelain tub. Groaning, I pull myself up. The long day in the sun is doing wonders for Max's sleep. I'm surprised he isn't calling for me. I dry off and put on a teeshirt and panties and tiptoe into the bedroom.

The room lights with another flash from outside. Icy fear pecks at my chest. A vulture gnawing and clawing until it burrows down to the juicy red heart. "No," I whisper. I tell myself it was a trick of the light or the wine sloshing in my belly. I walk to Max's bed. Another flash. My hands tear across the sheets. I throw the pillow and a balding stuffed bear to the floor. I slam the light switch. "Max!"

I hit the floor and check under both beds. It takes only seconds to run through the house. Gone. Gone. GONE. "Max! Where are you!" Panic consumes me. I haven't checked the bathroom. I dash in, arms failing, and knock over the wine bottle from the edge of the tub as I spin. Red and glass pool on the tile. No Max.

I don't know where I put my cell. I check the studio. Rain spatters against the skylight and when the night illuminates with electricity I see that my art model is gone.

I don't wait to find the phone or dig for the flashlight under the sink. I run outside into the rain, screaming for Max. In the yard, I slip on the wet ground and scramble in the mud. I don't see him. Oh God, I don't see him.

Then I see something. I crawl forward. A board has been dragged from the well. I try to scream. To call his name again but I can only utter a strangled cry.

In the desert, the raindrops are as warm as fresh blood. The water changes everything in an instant: dry washes turn into wild rivers, roads crumble, cars are swallowed. The monsoon cultivates new life while it carries away old remains. On hands and knees, I inch closer and closer to the well whispering, "Max... Max... Max." When I'm at the edge I hear a sound soft as a mouse.

"Max?"

"Momma." The cry comes from behind me. I manage to stand. I rush forward, slipping and sliding along the wet earth.

"Max, where are you?" I hear him crying. I find my boy huddled beside the water heater. I scoop him up and kiss his muddy face. I squeeze him tightly, vowing the impossible–to never let go.

"Momma, I'm sorry."

"I was so scared."

"I got rid of the doll. It worked. You came back."

"Oh, Max." Yards away a bolt of lightning hits, turning everything electric white before the return of dark. I gather him up and walk him through the storm.

In the house, we puddle to the floor. I kiss his forehead and he doesn't shudder. Rain patters against the roof. The vast pit is so close. I count Max's hot exhalations against my cheek until I drift off to dream of painting in the rain, Max coloring at my feet, each of us creating our own imperfect art.

Confluence

Andrea Lani

Emily did not want to go to the desert. She had built a dome of safety around her and Andy's and Jacob's lives—the four walls of their little house, the tall oaks and pines that sheltered it, the familiar routes she followed to work and daycare. Danger, of course, lurked everywhere—ticks, the neighbors' pond, other people's germ-infested children—but Emily had come to grips with these hazards and forged comfort from routine. The parched desert, a land of death, two thousand miles from their mossy green hollow in Maine, would blast her dome of safety off its foundations.

But Andy had talked about Canyonlands for as long as Emily had known him. In college, he and his brother, Steve, had taken a road trip out west and landed in Moab, where they spent the fall hiking, mountain biking, and camping. When winter came, Steve stayed, but Andy returned to Maine to finish school. Emily met him four years later, while waiting tables in a brew pub where Andy stopped for dinner after a weekend rafting trip. Every Sunday for the rest of the summer, he made his way to the pub, more than an hour out of his way, and always made sure he was seated in Emily's section. When the brewery closed for the season, Emily moved into Andy's timber-frame cabin in the woods. She loved the green cocoon of trees that cradled their home, but she knew Andy longed for red sandstone and open sky.

"I want to take you to redrock country," he used to tell her in moments of quiet intimacy. But since Jacob's birth, nearly ten years after Andy returned to Maine, Emily thought he'd stopped thinking about sand and rock and sky. Then Jacob turned three and Andy said, "We need to take this boy to the desert."

THE FIRST FEW days of their trip she had managed to hang onto the protective dome—at her brother-in-law's ranch house in Flagstaff, in the orderly Park Service developments at the Grand Canyon. But as they drove through endless miles of hard rock, bright colors, sharp edges, she yearned for the soft, mossy green of home. Green meant life, and the desert was short on green.

The land frightened her. Not the creatures that inhabited it, but the land itself. She'd never been outside of New England, where a green mantle swathed the land. Here the earth's bones were laid bare, with no fleshy cloak of vegetation to soften the edges, like something she wasn't meant to see. The naked desert brought to mind images of Jacob's bones showing through his transparent flesh after he was born. Andy had led her, wincing in pain from her incision, to the neonatal intensive-care unit, a space-age room of clear plastic boxes with babies inside, looking more like laboratory specimens than anything human. In his isolette Jacob lay curled, no bigger than a kitten, wearing only a miniature diaper and knit hat, gauze covering his eyes and wires and hoses connecting parts of his body to blinking monitors and IV bags. His vertebrae showed through his waxy skin like a row of pearls draped with translucent silk.

"You can touch him," Andy had said, and reached his hand into an opening in the isolette. The tiny foot disappeared between Andy's thumb and forefinger. After a moment, he stepped aside. Emily slid a trembling hand in and tentatively stroked the sole of her baby's foot. The skin was so soft, so unmarked by time, that it almost felt like touching nothing at all. His toes curled and she snatched back her hand.

ANDY HOISTED HIS pack. "You're going to love Canyonlands. I mean, the Grand Canyon is grand and all." He laughed at this joke he'd made a dozen times in the last week. "But the confluence is incredible. There's nothing like it."

Emily fumbled with the straps on her pack, shifted it from side to side, trying to find a comfortable place for the weight. Andy had taken the heavy stuff, but even with only sleeping bags, a change of clothes, and water in it, her pack felt like a large boulder settled onto her narrow shoulders.

"Are you sure this is a good idea?" She looked around at the landscape, bare but for a handful of dusty shrubs. "Backpacking with a three-year-old?"

"I've never been more sure of anything in my life. It's only five miles, and Jake's a little trooper, aren't you, buddy?" He reached down and fluffed his son's white-blond hair. The boy gazed up at him with shining eyes and a wide smile, and the two of them turned and strode down the trail, hand in hand. They looked like creatures born to the desert–Andy, a cinnamon-colored bear, large and powerful with a stride that devoured the trail, Jacob a tiny pale lizard, scurrying beside him over parched ground.

The two had been inseparable since Jacob's early, horrific birth. When he had become stable enough to be taken out of his isolette for short periods of time, Andy would sit with him cradled on his bare chest. Emily had never felt comfortable with what the hospital called "kangaroo care."

"Skin-to-skin contact helps preemies grow," the nurse said as she placed Jacob on Emily's bare chest. "Like a joey in its mother's pouch."

Emily's hand covered Jacob's entire body. He looked at her with muddy blue eyes and made mewling sounds, his nails clawing her skin like needles. She felt like her fingers would crush his eggshell ribs.

"I-I can't," she stammered.

Without a word, the nurse scooped Jacob back into his isolette and rearranged his wires and tubes. Emily buttoned her blouse with trembling hands and got up to leave without looking at the nurse, afraid of what she would see in her eyes. Disappointment? Disgust?

"I'm sorry," she whispered, brushing past the outstretched hand.

When Jacob came home from the hospital, Andy's chest was the only place he wanted to sleep. Winter was the slow season in Andy's business, and he stayed home with Jacob, quarantined from germs that would invade the baby's delicate immune system. Emily went to work and pumped milk for Andy to feed Jacob from tiny bottles. Father and son grew closer while a small voice inside Emily warned her to keep her distance, to not grow too attached to something so fragile, so easily lost.

WITH ONE LAST, wistful look at the rental car sitting by itself in the parking lot, Emily followed them down the trail. Half an hour later, thirsty and sweaty, she caught up with them on the canyon floor. Jacob and Andy sat on a rock, playing a game in which Jacob called out the names of things around them and hooted with laughter every time Andy said, "Nope, not that either." They looked cool and rested. Andy handed Emily a water bottle, stood and held his arms out to Jacob, catching the boy as he leapt off the rock.

"Here we go up the other side." He started toward the steep tumble of boulders that made up the other wall of the canyon.

"That?" Emily stared up at the red wall. "We're going up that? No, Andy, this is crazy."

"Relax. It's no problem. This first mile in and out of Big Spring Canyon is the hardest part. Once we get to the top, it's easy going all the way to the confluence." He tugged on Jacob's hand. "See those piles of rocks, buddy? Those are cairns. We follow them up that big hill so we won't get lost. I'm going to stay right behind you on the steep parts, okay?"

"Okay, Daddy. Let's go."

He scrambled ahead up the trail that wound between boulders and scrubby bushes. Andy winked at Emily and set off after Jacob. Emily followed the cairns with her eyes, straight uphill to the piercing blue sky.

THE NIGHT BEFORE, they had camped on the rim of a much larger canyon. The river below was nothing like rivers back home in Maine. There they flow broad and straight and muddy brown, crowded on both banks by sheltering trees. This one wound in big, looping twists between bare rock walls a thousand feet high. The setting sun colored the water a bruised purple and it looked, in color, shape, and glistening wetness, all the world like the coil of umbilical cord that had prolapsed eight weeks before Jacob's due date.

Emily clutched the narrow railing that edged the cliff, the bloody river a time machine spinning her back to the ambulance race, the emergency

C-section, the months of waiting through infections, scares, and close calls for Jacob to come home. The hours chained to the breast pump, its painful, sucking cones drawing from her body the only thing she had to give a creature too fragile to be her baby. The inescapable suspicion, despite the doctors' reassurances, that she was to blame.

"NEARLY THERE." ANDY pulled Emily in for a sweaty hug. They had been hiking for less than an hour and already she was exhausted. "After we get to the top, it's smooth sailing for the next four miles." Waves of fleshy sandstone rolled down from the rim to the ledge they stood on. At the back of the ledge, the stone curled back in on itself in a deep recess. A short, rusted ladder spanned the gap, and on the top rung, at the height of Andy's head, perched Jacob.

Emily pulled back from Andy's embrace. "Jacob, be careful."

"He's fine. Hang on there, buddy. Here we come."

Andy swung himself up the ladder, took Jacob's hand and the two of them bounded up the slope, Emily plodding after them. At the top of the climb, they emerged through a keyhole in a fin of pink stone. Beyond lay a plateau dotted with scrubby trees and fat columns of rock sporting domed caps.

Jacob's eyes grew wide at the sight of the rocks. "Castles!"

"Yeah, buddy, castles," Andy said. "Where do you think the knights are?"

"Defending the king!" He and Andy trotted down the gentle slope. With his strawberry-blond hair and beard and sun-pinked skin, Andy looked molded from the red earth. He seemed even taller and broader here, under the big sky, while the open space made Emily feel small.

Andy stopped and looked up. "The sky. I've missed this sky." He scooped Jacob into his arms and spun. Jacob leaned back and shrieked with laughter, his pale hair rising from his head.

"Sky, sky, sky!"

Emily pulled her hat low over her forehead. The sky made her uneasy. It was too big. She missed the shelter of tall trees, of being held safely to the earth by their spreading branches. All this openness gave her a dizzy feeling that gravity might let loose.

"Stop!" she cried, holding her hands over her ears. Andy wound down and lurched to sit on a rock, with Jacob on his lap gazing up at him.

"Whew," he said and Jacob imitated him, his eyes mirroring his father's, the exact blue of the sky. Andy looked at Emily. His forehead creased in concern, and she turned away.

THROUGHOUT THE AFTERNOON, Jacob alternated between marching hand in hand with Andy and riding on the crook of his father's arm. Just over two pounds at birth, Jacob had never caught up in size, and now, at nearly four, people mistook him for a toddler. Cradled in Andy's arm, he looked like a bird perched on the branch of an oak.

They had been hiking for three hours–long enough, Emily thought, to cover five and a half miles–when Andy stopped and pulled the map out of his pack. He studied it, taking off his hat and rubbing the thinning red hair at the back of his head. Jacob settled on a rock and kicked at loose pebbles. Emily dropped her pack on the ground, dug out two water bottles, handed one to Jacob, and guzzled from the other.

"Seems like we should have crossed this jeep road by now." Andy showed her the map. She glanced at it and looked back over the way they had come, the bare sandstone and hard-beaten soil less a trail than a gap between rocks and shrubs.

"You mean we're lost?"

"No, not lost." Andy squinted at the map. "Just turned around a bit."

Emily looked at the sun, its colorless orb maybe six or eight fingers above the horizon, and down at Jacob, sitting on the rock and fiddling with the lid of his water bottle.

"What are we going to do?" Tears pricked at the corners of her eyes.

"We're having an adventure, right, Jakey?" Andy's voice was cheerful.

The boy looked at his father with eyes that said he would follow him off the edge of the earth and nodded. "An adventure."

Andy smoothed the map's creases. "This is just part of the adventure."

Emily turned and walked away, brushing tears from her eyes as she went. She told herself everything would be fine. They were just a few hours' hike from the road. They had food for a night and a day and Andy's pack bulged with water. This was a national park, for goodness' sake. It was probably crawling with rangers and other hikers. She pushed aside the memory of their rental car alone in the lot. Andy was smart and capable and could read a map. Hell, she could read a map. She'd been in worse situations than this. But not with Jacob.

She heard Andy's footsteps behind her, felt his arm slide over her shoulders. She shrugged him off and walked faster.

"C'mon, Em. We used to have adventures all the time."

"This isn't an adventure, Andy. We're lost." She waved at endless desert landscape. Her pep talk to herself hadn't worked. Her hands were shaking and her breath came in short, shallow gasps.

"I'm pretty sure I know where we went wrong, and if we retrace our steps we'll find the right trail in fifteen, twenty minutes. It's not a big deal."

"People die in the desert, Andy. Like those two college kids a few years ago, lost a few hundred feet from the trail." She pushed her hair back from her face. "One of them stabbed his friend because he was dying of dehydration."

"They were idiots. We're not. Don't be afraid, sweetie."

"I'm not afraid." Andy took her hand in his. She pulled it free and stormed away, past shrubs and boulders. He caught up with her and reached for her hand again. She whirled to face him.

"You're right. I am afraid. I've been afraid every single moment for the last four years. Afraid I caused Jacob to be born too soon. Afraid to get close to him. Afraid of losing him. Every moment of his life has been so tenuous, and now, just when we were getting to the point where I was sure he was going to be okay, that I wasn't going to have to worry every second of every day, you bring us here, to the middle of nowhere and get us lost."

"There will always be something to worry about, Em. A year from now he'll start school. He'll learn to ride a bike. Someday he'll be driving the car. Every moment is fraught with danger, but also full of possibility. You think

I don't worry? You don't think I've been afraid? Jesus, if we lost Jacob, it would be like having my beating heart ripped out of my chest. But I don't let that stop me from living."

"Well, I guess you're just a better person, a better parent. It was so easy for you. You and Jacob just . . . fit together. And I didn't. What kind of mother can't love her child?"

"What do you mean? Of course you love Jacob. You've been there for him every second."

"He was so fragile. I couldn't keep him safe inside me, how could I keep him safe outside? And look, I was right. We're lost in the desert. We should never have come." Tears she'd been holding back streamed down her face, and her breath came in short, choking gasps.

Andy wrapped his arms around Emily and stroked her hair. "You know what? Jacob's an awesome little dude, and that's as much on you as it is on me. Those first months were tough as shit, but we made it through. And we're going to make it through this too. I promise."

Emily pressed her wet face into Andy's teeshirt, breathing in his sweet, sweaty smell. When her sobs died down, she wiped her face and took a deep, ragged breath. Her arms were still shaking, but Andy was right. Everything was going to be okay. They weren't clueless like those two dumb college kids. No one was going to stab anyone with a pocket knife.

She smiled up at him and nodded. "Okay. Let's go get Jake and find our way back to the trail."

They walked hand in hand back toward the place where they'd stopped. Coming around a fat juniper bush, she saw their two packs lying on the ground, next to a bare rock.

"Where's Jakey?" Emily dropped Andy's hand and turned in place, scanning the rough landscape. The plateau that had seemed barren to her ten minutes ago was now a morass of boulders and trees, every one big enough to conceal a small boy. "Jacob? Jacob, where are you?"

Her eyes came to rest on Andy's face, white under his sunburn. "Oh, Jesus, oh, Jesus," he whispered. He clasped her hands and looked into her eyes. For the first time, she saw real fear there. "You stay here. He can't have gone far. I'm sure I'll see a footprint or something before long. We'll find him." He clung to her hands a moment longer, then walked away, spiraling out from the rock where Jacob had perched, calling "Jacob! Jake-eee!"

Emily looked around. The only ground soft enough to take a footprint was the dust around the base of the bushes and trees. Everything else was bare stone or hardpan. She tried to push out of her mind all of the stories she'd read of children lost after a moment's inattention, wandering alone in the mountains or desert, found days later, bloody and emaciated—or worse.

She called his name again, but her voice came out in a hoarse croak.

She crouched and picked up his water bottle where he'd left it beside the rock, her shaking hands fumbling with the lid. As she tipped the bottle back, she noticed one of the massive mushroom-capped rocks looming a few hundred yards away. Hoodoos, the ranger in the visitors' center had called them, formed when soft rock had eroded away beneath hard caps, leaving behind strange, lifelike formations. This one did sort of look like a castle.

Castle! She sprang to her feet and ran, bounding over rocks and dodging around bushes. Her teeth rattled with each step. Her knees and shins ached. Her hat flew off and the searing blue sky jittered in her peripheral vision. She stopped at the base of the rock and leaned over, hands on knees, gasping for air. When her breathing calmed, she looked up along a crack that angled diagonally to the top of the hoodoo. It towered over her, as high as the peak of their house. Just below the heavy mushroom-cap dome, she saw a patch of green, too bright to be piñon or juniper. Jacob's teeshirt.

"Jacob?" she called. A white-blond head leaned out of the crevice.

"Mom?" Jacob sounded small and far away, but not afraid.

"Stay right there, honey." Emily willed her voice to stay casual. "Mama's coming up to you. Don't move a muscle. Please."

She placed a hand on rough sandstone. The crack angled back, wedge-like into the wall of stone. Grasping knobs of rock and propping her feet against the uneven surface, she worked her way toward Jacob. About halfway up, the crack angled more steeply. She crammed her hand and foot into the narrow space at the back of the fissure and heaved herself to where the more gradual angle resumed. How had Jacob surmounted that section?

When she reached a juniper growing near the top of the crack, she wrapped her arm around its trunk, pressing her cheek into the coarse bark. Jacob crouched on the other side of the tree, among its tough roots, which were anchored to bare rock without, as far as Emily could see, the benefit of soil. From his perch, Jacob gazed out at the desert, calm as a monk.

"Look." Jacob turned and handed her a feather, its exquisite shade of ocean blue incongruous in this parched red land. She held it up to the bright sky and the blue vanished, leaving only a network of translucent brown barbs.

"It's beautiful, buddy." She held it out to him.

"It's for you."

Emily smiled down at the feather, then pressed her eyes closed.

"Thank you." She tucked the quill into her ponytail and looked over the dusty red earth, at the scrub trees and boulders and hoodoos, the smudge of distant blue mountains. What bird had flown across this brittle land and paused to rest on this twisted little tree?

"Wow, what a view." The calm in her voice surprised her.

"Do you like my castle?"

"I love your castle. But we should go down now and find Daddy, so he doesn't worry about us. Ready?"

"Ready."

Emily turned and lowered herself backward. "Come on, Jacob. See if you can come down backward like this. Like a ladder. I'll go first and be right below you if you need me."

They picked their way down, Emily searching out hand- and footholds, and Jacob shimmying after her agile as a lizard. When they reached the steep place, she lowered herself as far as she could with her arms and let go, scraping her knee as she slid the last few feet to a ledge. Before she could think how to get Jacob down this section, he turned and slid on his bottom, face alight with a wild thrill. She caught him and held him close, then they scrambled the rest of the way down and jogged toward the place they'd left the packs, intercepting Andy on the way. He lifted Jacob into his arms and pulled Emily to him. His broad shoulders quivered as he clung to her, Jacob squirming between them.

"I climbed the castle." Jacob pointed to the hoodoo that towered behind them. Andy turned wide eyes on Emily, and she described how she had found Jacob and climbed to get him.

"And then we slided down," Jacob said.

"What?"

Emily laughed. "I'll explain later."

"I found that jeep road." Andy pointed over the rock-strewn ground. "It's just a little distance that way. There's a parking lot and an outhouse. We can camp there tonight and head back first thing in the morning."

"Isn't that really close to the overlook?"

"Yeah, the confluence is another half mile beyond the parking area."

"Then we should at least hike the rest of the way tomorrow and see what you brought us here to see."

Andy looked at her with one raised eyebrow, then smiled and pulled her in for another hug before they walked back to their packs.

IN THE GRAY light of early morning, Emily crept from the tent, leaving Andy and Jacob asleep in their bags, and hiked the last half mile to the Confluence Overlook. She sat at the rim of the canyon and looked out over two rivers merging far below. One river flowed dark and coffee-colored, the other a milky tea. Where the rivers met, the two colors flowed side by side, mixing in a narrow, swirling band down the center of the stream. Along each bank grew a narrow band of living green. Emily pulled Jacob's feather from her hair and, brushing it against her cheek, closed her eyes and listened to the flow of water deep in the canyon. The gravel behind her crunched, and she turned to see Andy coming up the trail, Jacob perched on his arm.

"I thought we'd find you here." Andy squatted beside her and handed her a mug of coffee.

Jacob rubbed his eyes and reached for the feather. She handed it to him and he strained out of Andy's arms and into her lap. A Stellar's jay rasped from a nearby piñon pine. Was this the bird who lost its feather? What did it live on out here, air and dust and sunshine? Perhaps love and faith and courage. The jay made a harsh, throaty sound and lifted off from the branch. Emily watched it flap across the canyon and looked down at Jacob, curled on her lap, his eyes the color of the sky, his face pale as the half-moon that hung in the west. He was here, and whole. Tiny, but tough as a juniper berry. She pulled him to her chest and held him until he squirmed to be let free.

Desert Rats

Leah Griesmann

I had been trying to dump Jerry for three weeks. The first neighbor I'd met at the Desert Rose, he'd introduced himself as a "nice Jewish boy," though he was in fact forty-three. We started sleeping together because I was new in Vegas and had been lonely before I arrived, and he was chubby and impossible to anger because even the harshest criticism he met with choked laughter.

"Hi, hon," he said when I opened the door.

"Don't call me hon," I said, and he laughed.

"I need your help for a second. I was trying to feed Millicent and the rat got away. I need you to hold this bag while I chase the rat into it."

He handed me a torn plastic sack from the nearest chain supermarket. A smile parted his chubby cheeks, which were framed by sharp Elvis sideburns. He doted on his ball python, and he had dealt blackjack and craps at second-rate off-Strip casinos for over ten years.

"You want me to hold a bag while you chase a rat into it?"

He laughed. "You make it sound so unpleasant."

I closed the door. He knocked and I held my breath.

"Hon?"

"I hate rats. I'm working. Please don't knock on my door anymore."

"Okay, bye," he said to the peephole, adding in a hopeful sing-song. "Talk to you later."

I had moved into the Desert Rose my first day in Las Vegas, lured by a teaching position at one of the city's understaffed schools. My latest relationship had ended badly, and I was fed up with the packed SEPTA buses and Philadelphia snow. In August, I retrieved my dented Celica from my brother's backyard in upstate New York and drove for four days, windows down, sweltering as I crossed the Mojave.

The tangle of highways and midmorning glare obscured my view of the pyramids and skyscrapers that rose from the Strip as I cruised off Frank Sinatra. In a palm-lined neighborhood close to the Wynn I had met the apartment manager Ruby at the end of a 110-degree day when all of my Internet leads on apartments proved sleazy or over my budget.

Tucked away on a sleepy cul-de-sac, the Desert Rose with its Spanish tile roofs, manicured palm trees, and turquoise pools evoked Las Vegas's heyday, an image that Ruby, with her magenta hair and shell earrings, was eager to foster.

"Sammy Davis Jr. stayed right next door," she told me with pride, adding, more equivocally, "the rest of the Rat Pack were ... you know ... on the Strip. This was back in the sixties."

The rent on a roomy one-bedroom was half what I'd paid for my studio in Philly with a view of a snow-covered dumpster. That first desert evening, the air thick with night-blooming jasmine, I lay on a lounge chair next to the kidney-shaped pool, watching the sun drop over the rust-colored mountains.

In the four months since I'd moved in to the Desert Rose, my license plates had been stolen, my back window busted, and bullets had punctured my tires. I'd learned that the lounge chairs next to the pool were treadmills for cockroaches, the Laundromat up the street a campground for crackheads. My brief stay in the city had taught me what my fellow teachers knew all too well—that Vegas could be a stopping point on the road to ignominy or despair, with one clear exit—escape.

The minute of talking with Jerry had filled my apartment with heat. I turned on the AC and hunched at my desk with my folder of essays. A rattling noise startled me out of my chair.

"Hello?" I jumped. I still wasn't used to my cell phone, which jangled and throbbed like a wounded ferret each time it rang.

"Amy?"

I recognized the quavering tone of Olivia Jones, the first teacher I'd met at the school. With her mousy brown hair, sloped gait, and faded skirts she resembled a potted plant that had gone too long without water. I gave her a lift home from school after watching her hobble and squint in the harsh desert sun. Since then she'd become an unwelcome attachment, persistently copping rides to the grocery store and Walgreen's with unending stories of woe.

"I'm so glad I got you. I didn't know who else to call."

"What's up?"

Her voice was more strained than normal. "I have an emergency. Everett is really sick. I think he might be in a coma."

I swallowed, a bilious feeling crawling up my throat, wondering if she had a child or a partner she hadn't mentioned. "I'm so sorry," I said.

"I really need a ride to the vet. It isn't far from your place."

"Oh," I said, relieved, but still apprehensive. "Everett's your dog?"

There was a moment of silence followed by a tight, "No."

"He's your cat?"

"No."

"He isn't . . . a snake?"

"He's a rat," she said, with a tone of defiance.

"A rat?" My jaw clenched.

"He's very tame." Her voice became shrill, choked by muffled tears. "He's on his back. I think he's in a coma. I can see his tail twitch."

"Oh. I've been kind of . . . um . . . I'm not . . . um . . ." It was no use. I was out of practice with women like Olivia–if they'd existed in Philadelphia they'd never entered my orbit.

"I don't want him to die! Can you please come quick?"

"All right," I said, grabbing my purse and double-locking my door. On my way down I saw Jerry bent into a cactus, still scooping with his plastic bag.

The drive to Olivia's apartment was less than a mile but took fifteen minutes. Built on a grid, Vegas' blocks were controlled by traffic lights set on uneven timers. Each block I drove I slowed for yellow as neighboring drivers pressed on their gas, speeding through red lights as jaywalkers ran for their lives.

When I arrived at the Palm 3 Apartments near the corner of Maryland Parkway, I saw Olivia, wire-rim glasses reflecting the sun, clutching a small metal cage.

"You're my angel," she said as I opened the door.

"I can drop you off at the vet's and then I have to run."

"Thank you so much." She sat with the cage in her lap. "You're really my angel."

On the drive to the vet, past the ninety-nine-cent stores, gas stations, and off-Strip casinos, I did my best to ignore the cage, but Olivia's anxious prattle didn't let me forget it was there.

"I noticed two days ago that he wasn't eating as much. Then he had diarrhea and I figured it was just a stomach virus. Then his tail, which is normally pink, started to look gray and it kind of had these tiny bald spots . . ."

"Up here on the right?"

"Yes. Then I noticed he was sleeping more, not just napping but really passed out. And then when he turned on his side I just knew. The last rat I had got liver cancer but it started out really differently. His eyes kind of glazed and he developed this vomiting reflex . . ."

"It must be this street?"

"That's it."

I pulled to a stop.

"My angel."

It took Olivia several minutes to get out of the car while a man in a pick-up truck held down his horn and sped around, yelling "cunt" at my window.

"It's hard to get this cage out," Olivia said, struggling to raise herself onto the oil-stained asphalt, "with my serrated disc."

"Good luck," I said as she hobbled onto the curb.

On my drive back toward my apartment my cell phone erupted into its jangling screed, startling me so much I nearly sideswiped a Chrysler. I fumbled for it at the first yellow light.

"Hi, Amy, it's me."

Jonathan was my best friend in Las Vegas. He had dated my roommate

Luciana in college, who'd moved to France, studied block printing, and married a timpanist. We saw each other at a college reunion and later I'd heard that he had become a history professor at UNLV, a fact I confirmed on his Facebook. My first week in town, we met over coffee at the MGM Grand, and since then spent hours swapping memories of college and commiserating about our lousy love lives and Vegas. Even in the din of rush-hour traffic I could tell by his tone that something was wrong.

"I got some bad news."

"I'm so sorry, Jonathan," I said, though in his world bad news could mean anything from the death of a relative to the cancellation of his favorite TV show. "I'm in the middle of traffic–"

"You answered the phone."

Shamed by his logic, I swallowed. "That's true."

"I'm calling from Austin."

"All right, just a sec." A woman in a dented Hyundai behind me was honking her horn. A few seconds later, she pressed on the gas and sped past, yelling, "bitch." I turned and slammed on my brakes to avoid a homeless man tying himself to his cart with Christmas ribbon, and pulled into the crowded parking lot of a Mexican restaurant.

"Mina's tour was postponed. She's coming home early."

Mina was Jonathan's Bombay-born roommate and landlord, owner of the luxurious four-bedroom house in a gated community where they both lived. A belly dancer on the Strip, she let Jonathan stay in the house while she went on tour in exchange for modest rent and light housekeeping. She'd asked him to move the last time she returned from Dubai to find the bathroom untidy and wood ants infesting the kitchen, but somehow they'd worked it all out. "Do you still need me to water the plants?"

"Of course, but that's not why I'm calling. Remember I told you that twice when I was sitting at my desk in the living room I saw a mouse run by the dining room table?"

"Yes."

"When I left I set a trap in the kitchen–"

"Good thinking."

"I need you to go over there and empty the trap."

I watched the homeless man now wrapping the ribbon around his chest and pulling his cart like an ox. "Please tell me you're joking."

"Amy," his tone became sharp, "if Mina comes home and sees a dead mouse in her kitchen I will be gone. Do you understand? I will be kicked out. Evicted. I can't afford a move right now in the middle of the semester. I'm behind on all my seventeenth-century stuff as it is."

"Jonathan," I said, my throat constricting, "I really don't know if I . . . isn't there somebody else you can call?"

His tone became gentler. "I wish there was, but you're my best friend in Las Vegas and the only person with keys to the house. I'm so sorry, Amy, but I need you. I need you to do this."

I looked out over Maryland Parkway, the traffic lurching through lights at the end of each strip mall. Cars tailed each other, fighting to get into Target and In-n-Out Burger. A woman made a run across the street as an SUV swerved to avoid her.

"Amy?"

My nose twitched. "All right."

"Thank you so much. You're really a lifesaver. We'll go out for Thai food when I get back."

IT TOOK ME more than an hour to get to Jonathan's house. Popular with Mormons and doctors, Henderson's gated communities offered Vegas's wage-earners at least the mirage of safety and middle-class values–which, after a few months at the Desert Rose, I was coveting too. Just four exits outside of the city, beneath carved sandy hills rose endless cul-de-sacs of boxy identical homes, a frightening triumph of architectural cloning.

Jonathan's house, even with his hand-drawn map, wasn't easy to find. With no landmarks and nothing to distinguish one street from the next, I drove in circles until luck and the process of elimination led me to the galvanic gate that accepted his four-digit code.

Once inside, I scanned the rows of white houses with manicured lawns and plastic yard toys until I found 3257. I opened the series of locks and entered the house. Faux East Asian crafts—an elephant card table, tiger-head mirror, a Buddha plant holder and eight-armed Shiva coat rack decorated the white walls and rug-covered floors. I stepped into the kitchen and saw in dimness the trap, empty, half-sideways on the tile floor.

It was a relief not to see the dead mouse, but Jonathan's recent text—pnt bter or chez thx—meant that he expected me to bait the trap and come back. I opened the jet-black refrigerator, surprisingly well-stocked for people who spent so much time out of town, and scanned shelves lined with Whole Earth and Trader Joe's sauces, spreads, olives, salad dressings, and cheese. I chose a half-empty package of Swiss, took a quick nibble to test it, turned on the kitchen light and knelt down near the trap.

Driving Boulder Highway back to the city in the crushing afternoon sun, I got a phone call.

"Amy, it's me, Olivia. Good news! It was severe dehydration. They hooked him up to an IV and they're releasing him."

"That's great."

"Poor little guy. I'm carrying him right now—he's attached to this huge bag of fluids. They're trying to get his electrolytes up. I'd take the bus, but it's really difficult to manage the cage and his IV."

"Olivia, I'm at my friend Jonathan's way out in Henderson. He's sort of having a crisis."

"I'd stay at this homeless shelter around the corner, but they don't take pets. I'd take a cab but I'm having this problem with my ATM card . . ."

I met Olivia on the corner of Maryland Parkway. She was holding the cage in one hand, and a clear plastic sack filled with pale yellow fluid in the other. Everett, half burrowed into his bed of loose straw, stared at me with one eye.

"You really are my angel." She foisted herself into the car, struggling not to let the tube from Everett's IV get caught in the door. I dropped them off at the Palm 3 Apartments just as rush hour started.

When I pulled into the Desert Rose it was just after six and the autumn sun was already setting. Tucked into my door was a folded note with a hand-drawn heart and the message, "Come by, I MISSS you. Ms. Millicent Misses you too (yum yum, burp!)"

I crumpled it up, burrowed under my sheets, and cranked up the AC.

THE NEXT MORNING, my jaw aching from grinding all night, I snuck out of the Desert Rose early, hoping to avoid Jerry, who returned from his shift the same time that I was leaving for school. At work, I steered clear of the teachers' lounge and the mailroom so as not to run into Olivia, sneaking lunch in my car at the In-N-Out burger. As soon as sixth period ended I made a beeline for the parking lot and hightailed it for Henderson, pulling up to Jonathan's house just after four.

I opened the door, felt the cool of the AC, and turned to the kitchen, bracing myself for an unpleasant sight. I stared at the floor. The Swiss cheese was gone; the trap, a few inches left of where I had placed it, was set and licked clean.

From the refrigerator I took a jar of organic chunky peanut butter. I stirred the hard paste seeped in thick oil, took a quick bite, and carefully scraped the rest beneath the trap's metal spring. I reset the trap, washed the spoon, watered the plants, and locked the door behind me on my way out.

Returning to the Desert Rose late that afternoon, I looked forward to nothing more than a shower, a cold Diet Coke, and two hours of grading so that I could watch my favorite show on TV. Instead, I arrived at my door just as Jerry, hair slicked back, in black sunglasses and his shapeless red uniform, was walking toward my apartment.

"Look who the cat dragged in."

"I'm just getting home. There's no cat. I'm not getting dragged."

He laughed, pulling his left hand from behind his back. "Not you, him." He presented me with a stuffed animal that bore, at first look, a passing resemblance to Mickey Mouse, though closer inspection revealed it to be the mascot of his casino, Hideous Al.

"Oh. Thanks." I opened my door.

"Can I come in?"

"I have grading to do."

"How about later?"

"I don't think so."

"You're acting like I'm a pariah," he said, pronouncing it like "piranha."

"I don't . . ."

"We slept together. Twice! We made love."

I turned my head quickly, fearing that anyone, even a crackhead, might hear him. "Please be quiet."

"Come over tonight."

"Jerry . . ."

"Come over tonight," he took my hand and bent down on his right knee, which made a horrible cracking sound. "Ouch, I need a chiropractor." He laughed. The layers nearest his part were lacquered with grease. "Just this last time. You won't regret it."

I did end up at Jerry's that evening, but only because my favorite show was on HBO and I didn't have cable. We both sat on his bed (he had no room for a couch) and when the show finished his hands slid over to fondle my legs. I stood up.

"Oh, stay. I've got peppermint lotion."

"I can't."

"Call me," I heard him say, as I shut his door.

When I got back to my apartment, the light on my answering machine was blinking wildly. I pressed the button to hear the first message.

"Oh, hi, Amy. This is Olivia Jones. I didn't see you at school today. Good news about Everett. He's doing much better, he's looking a lot like his old self. Tomorrow he gets his IV out. I don't know what you're doing tomorrow after school. Please call me. This is Olivia Jones. Bye."

I pressed the Delete button. I'd have to avoid the teacher's room yet again. The machine beeped and the next message played.

"Amy, it's Jonathan. How are you? Did you get the mouse? Is he dead?

Was it awful? I just want to tell you I am so glad that I had you there to take care of it. I really don't know what I would have done without you. I hope it wasn't too bad for you. Call me. Hope you're doing well. Bye."

Jonathan's tone was loose, as if he'd had a few beers. I took a bite of peanut butter straight from the jar and crawled into bed without taking off my shirt or socks.

THE NEXT DAY at school was the worst I'd had in Las Vegas. I sent a third of the class out with slips to the principal and put another third in detention. The remaining students text-messaged all through my lecture. My fellow teachers blamed discipline issues on the dearth of state taxes, but I believed the problem lay with the students themselves. In a city of poker tournaments, get-rich-quick machines, and millionaire bartenders, there seemed to be zero financial incentive to slogging through *Of Mice and Men*.

When I arrived at Jonathan's house, I took a deep breath before turning my eyes to the floor. The trap was upside down, a few inches away from where I had placed it, and again it was licked clean. I sank to a squat in despair, my elbows jamming my knees.

In dread, I fingered my cell phone. I'd have to let Jonathan know I had failed to do what he'd asked. I thought about asking Jerry for help but knew that I'd pay for the favor. I started dialing Olivia Jones but figured her only input would be search and rescue. Meanwhile, Mina was due back the following day.

Within twenty minutes I found myself cruising identical side streets in search of a grocery store. Despite its efforts, Henderson wasn't quite Middle America. Next to a Church of Latter-day Saints, a Liberace impersonator was walking his poodle. Outside the Midas Auto Repair, two scruffy, barely clad hobos were dueling with car antennae. A cop was writing a ticket to a young woman whose lime-green VW bug had crashed into a palm tree outside of Denny's.

I pulled into the parking lot of a large mini-mart and hurried in past a row of smoking men playing video poker. Near the canned cat food in the back of the store I picked up a bag full of mousetraps. At the checkout counter, a longhaired teen in a Trent Reznor teeshirt was ladling bright orange cheese. I ordered a small tub of nachos, which I nibbled from as it slid back and forth on the passenger seat.

At Jonathan's place, after baiting six traps with a combination of nachos, tabouli, peanut butter, and hummus, I went out to the patio, a bumpy parquet of cut rock, cement, and dry grass. The mountains beyond were rocky and cast in a dull sheen of sunset and haze. Beige, identical one-story homes flanked the yard. In its sparseness the desert night was like winter in Philly; my feeling of imminent failure was just as familiar.

It was on such a night that I had watched my last dinner with Charles unfurl and collapse like an imploding casino. If I were honest, it had been several months I'd been sensing that something between us was off, but the feeling settled like a lump in my throat, strangling the words I might have used to express it. Like a criminal resigned to my sentence, I tiptoed around, dreading the day the jig would be up. I know if I'd spoken up sooner we might not have lasted, but at least I wouldn't have felt like the only one who'd been left.

The sky outside Mina's was speckled and gray now, the strobe of the Luxor refracting the lights of the Strip. The pedestrians who'd survived dodging traffic in the glare of the sun at six would be sprinting at every green light in the hopes of making it home before dark. I despaired of my next day of work, of Olivia Jones, of telling Jonathan I had not caught the mouse, and most of all of avoiding Jerry on my way home. I went to the couch and nestled into its faux-fur cushions, burrowing under a pillow.

THE SNAPPING SOUND was so distinct it called me out from the depths of sleep. I slammed my feet to the floor, switched on the overhead lamp, and rushed to the kitchen. The trap near the sink was flipped upside down and totally still, a tail leaking out from behind.

Stunned, I ran to my car and dug out an oil-stained towel from my trunk. From the edge of the kitchen, I tossed the towel like a horseshoe over the trap. Using a plastic grocery bag as a glove and averting my eyes, I forced myself to pick up the trap. Gagging and holding the bag away from my body, I ran with it out to my car.

Before driving off, I vacuumed and mopped, removing all trace of the hunt from the floors. After locking the doors, I got in my car and drove south on the Boulder Highway in search of a trashcan, taking the first exit into the parking lot of a local casino. I stuffed the bag with the mouse into my purse and entered through a revolving glass door to red carpet, stale smoke, ringing slots, and the scent of fake lilac mingled with beer.

I had only been in casinos twice since arriving in Las Vegas—once to have lunch with Jonathan and once to see an overpriced show about men who wore paint. The local Henderson casino did not have the same panache as the monolithic money drops on the Strip, but it did have something that might be called heart if such a thing could exist in a place where people who couldn't afford to lose money regularly did. At a wicker rotunda, men with white hair slumped together on hard stools playing blackjack. A friendly craps group cheered a short woman crooking her arm to throw dice. A lady with a plastic cup full of quarters cheered on a slot player's every drunken pull. Just beyond the high-limit poker, a hallway with Rembrandt-style portraits led to the restroom where I would certainly find a trash bin.

I entered the spacious pink restroom where a trio of big-breasted women applied lipstick and rouge in front of a mother-of-pearl inlaid mirror. Beneath a knockoff Manet, an attendant smoked while she guarded a heady assortment of perfumes, hairsprays, and gels. I walked towards the chrome trashcan in the corner unzipping my purse.

Just as I brought the bag with the mouse toward the bin, the attendant met my gaze in the mirror, the weight of her reproach lodged in one penciled-on eyebrow. Her knowing look suggested she'd spent many a night watching women like me dispose of unseemly detritus. She took an impossibly long drag of her cigarette, her desert-lined skin growing taut beneath permed silver hair. I washed my hands at the sink, styled my bangs with my fingers, and left with the mouse in my purse.

In the parking lot, I was approached by a woman dressed in a ball gown begging for change.

"Here's five," I said, removing a bill from my wallet. "And do me a favor. Could you take this and throw it away?"

"What is it?" she asked.

"A dead mouse," I said, the words caught in my throat.

"Aw, hell no," she said, dropping the bag to the ground.

I bent to pick up the mouse, clutched it to my chest, and walked to my car.

"Ain't you got ten bucks?" she yelled. "Five's kind of cheap!"

Still seeing no trash can, I got back on the highway and found myself heading away from the city. Mountains crowded with identical homes rose toward the harsh looming sky. When I'd reached the real desert, far enough out to no longer see the lights of the Strip, I pulled into the first gas station next to a neon sign of a cowboy boot kicking a teepee.

Bolstering myself with a breath of night air, I walked to the dumpster at the edge of the parking lot. With a glance at the sliver of waning moon I hoisted the bag, feeling it drop from my hands like a weight.

Instead of relief, I felt an odd twinge of sadness. By morning the mouse would be smashed in a landfill, mingling with paper plates, tin cans, milk cartons, and tires under the glare of the hot desert sun. Ruby had told me live squirrels in Vegas were known to explode from the heat, and I pictured the mouse stiff and baking, crucified on its Victor patibulum. I had not checked the trap to see what its last meal had been.

Heading back on the highway, I swerved down curvy roads on my way past Lake Mead, stuffing my face with the mini-mart nachos and cheese. Las Vegas stretched out below, the lights of the Strip spilling all the way out to the desert at Red Rock. The beam from the Luxor shot over the mountains, bathing Henderson's one-story clones in a crystalline glow. From a distance, the tableau of mountains and light shone with a beauty that faded the closer I got to the city.

Back on my street I cruised past the crackheads in front of Vick's Laundry and jumped when a homeless man stuck his hat out for change. A hooker strolled by with a cane, one foot on high heel, the other encased in a cast. I parked my car in a lit corner, securing The Club to my wheel.

Inside my apartment, I turned on the light, unplugged my answering machine, and got under the covers, my jaw sore from grinding, though I wasn't tired at all. A few minutes later I heard familiar steps at the door.

"Hey, hon?"

Twice Jerry did his shave-and-a-haircut knock, but I burrowed deeper into my sheets.

"I know you're in there 'cause your light's on."

I lay almost still, blinking one boggled eye.

"My aunt Beth's in the hospital. Just thought you should know. I got tickets to the NBA All-Star game. We can just go as friends."

He waited a minute, tried the knock again, and then left.

The air-conditioning from downstairs sounded through my floor with a low rumble that made my dishes and silverware jump. A cockroach ambled across the ceiling with the confidence of an athlete. An alarm on a car was wailing nearby, pulsing repeatedly the same three shrill notes. I turned out my light, and a few minutes later I heard Jerry's footsteps outside my door.

"Hey, hon? I know you're in there. I just saw your light."

I gnawed on my blanket for comfort, folding into my bed.

"You can't keep hiding," he said in his sing-song. "I'll always know where to find you."

My limbs felt like wood and my nose started twitching. I curled my back forward, and tucked in my head, squeezing myself very small. Hugging my feet to my legs I rolled to the ground, landing softly on all fours. Tail flat and nose to the floor, I scurried off toward the AC.

The Fifth Season

Nona Caspers

"Do you remember when all the neighborhood kids had ringworm?" he asked me from his hospital bed, inviting me to imagine, I suppose, that the lesions corrupting his brain were a similar phenomenon. I said yes, but really only one kid in the neighborhood had had ringworm, and it wasn't even ringworm–it was impetigo. Or so I remember.

"Come lie in the bed with me," he said. He said it every time I went to visit him. There was a large window near his bed. Out the window I see gray–perhaps the roof of another building or it could be that the sky was gray every time I went there. The room was on the fourth floor. It was winter. In the beginning it was winter, and then at the end it was spring. But all I see is gray, very continuous, something to count on. I think there was another man in the room, near the door. There was another man, and then later there was not another man. He is gray as well, but shadowy, off to the side.

Marc pulled back the sheet and blanket and patted the space beside him. The bed was narrow, like all hospital beds, but I climbed into that space and lay on my back with my legs straight ahead of me, my arms pressed to my sides–it was what I could do. We would pretend we were still children; or we would slip into that late-eighties, early-nineties script that had enamored Hollywood and the American public: *Philadelphia, Early Frost, Longtime Companion*: gay man dying, loyal friends hold his hand to the dirty end. I felt under the sheets for his hand. There. Warm and muscular, surprisingly life driven. He was dying from the neck up, the rest of his body uncorrupted, muscled, blood-fed. I looked ahead of me at the wall–there was something on the wall, a card or a painting, blue–and I held his hand.

His left eyelid was collapsing. An inelegant drooping into the corner as if gravity were exerting unfair pressure. At first the drooping had given him a lazy, sexy look, but now the skin cloaked more and more of his eye each time I went. His eyes were brown. I didn't go often enough. The small bones inside both his ears were closing in tightly to his eardrums. Nerves shut off, the auditory system smothered. By the time he was admitted into San Francisco General he was stone deaf, but he could read lips and we had a clipboard we passed back and forth. Yellow paper with blue lines.

"Do you want some hot chocolate?" he whispered to me. We had often on winter days as kids, after destroying the snow in our backyards, sipped hot chocolate on stools in his mother's kitchen: dark green cupboards, a photograph of a Oaxacan market on the wall. But the whispering annoyed me–and I was embarrassed that it annoyed me. It was desperate, not child-like but childish–though I don't remember him talking like that as a child.

"Take some money from my bag and go downstairs and get yourself hot chocolate."

"I don't want any hot chocolate," I said.

"You don't want any?" he asked, turning further on his side to see my lips and watch my face.

"No."

"Is something wrong?"

"No, I just don't need any hot chocolate." I had taken money from his bag the week earlier and had returned with two cardboard cups of hot chocolate from a machine in the basement cafeteria. Instant, watery, sweet. A distraction.

A nurse came in with a blood-pressure hose over his neck. He had red hair, diluted by sun or bleach. "Don't get up," he said, gently. "I'll come back." I'd watched him take Marc's pulse the week before: how did he keep his fingernails so clean?

"No, it's all right, I've got to go," I said. I'd been there for over an hour; he slept and then woke; we talked with the yellow pad about the lesions and the possibility of cutting them out with laser technology. But the lesions would just grow back, like thistles.

"What?" Marc asked. He put his hand on my arm and looked up into my face.

"I've got to go," I repeated, slowly, more slowly than necessary. "T h e n u r s e i s h e r e."

The nurse stepped to the foot of the bed and turned his head politely—or to spare himself the awkward deceit.

Marc moved his hand up my arm and sat forward, bringing his eyes to me, pulling me down toward him until our foreheads were an inch apart. I couldn't recall being this physically close since first grade, yet something seemed familiar. A violence. I could see the clear mucus gathering in the corner of the drooping eyelid and the completely unmasked plea in the other. Dark brown. Lighter now than when he was a kid. I could have been there only thirty minutes. Fear and fearlessness. Nothing to lose. Emptiness and grasping. A golden ring around the pupil.

"Hot chocolate?" he asked, his lips not closing around the words as they came from the back of his throat and rode out on his breath. They sounded like "ha chohtlate." He pointed down, toward the cafeteria. I covered my mouth to suppress a nervous laugh and looked away.

A blue print on the wall, blue and yellow and some milky white and I want to say the image was a horse, a print of that famous yellow horse, and that his mother, who had flown in from Minnesota the week before and was staying with his sister Lynn in Richmond, taped the poster there, but I don't think that's true. I don't know how that print got on that wall, though it is true that Marc loved paintings and prints and when he lived in London and New York visited the galleries regularly and when he came back talked about the art incessantly. But Marc had nothing for horses; I am the one who in shorts and teeshirt rode a Shetland around our backyard and into the cornfield behind our houses one summer, until the horse bucked me off and my forearm snapped in two places, and then for the rest of the summer into the school year Marc carried things around for me. A biology book. My coronet on band days. An empty black plastic purse.

The nurse was wearing a white teeshirt and white pants—of course he was. I smiled. Marc could see my lips—I wore lipstick all the time then. "Yes," I said. "Hot chocolate in the cafeteria."

And then I'd be gone, walking quickly past the other man in the bed by the door and turning into the brightness and anonymity of the hallway.

MARC RANDOLF NESSERICH, later known as Marc Wendell Britain. I think I was the only person in San Francisco who knew he wasn't upper-class Protestant: his grandmother was Mexican, his mother and Aunt Zola vacationed with Mexican cardinals and priests. His father, German-American Catholic like the rest of the town, had been a low-level manager at the Melrose Electrical Cooperative. He would have earned little more than the other men in the neighborhood, who labored at the Kraft and Jenny-O Turkey Plants, if he hadn't over twenty years embezzled more than a hundred grand of community profit.

The day the embezzlement news broke in the *Melrose Daily*, Marc wasn't on the bus or in school. He wasn't on the bus the next day, or the next, or the next. I spied him one late afternoon through the evergreens in our backyard; he was wandering around shirtless in a light snowfall, his ill-defined, hairless golden chest flecked with snow. He might have been my first conscious experience of human beauty. Another day I heard him singing Spanish songs and knocking around a golf ball, though he hated golf. And then one day the Nesseriches' house was empty, driveway and backyard barren. Marc visited the neighborhood only once during my high school years, and I was at swim practice.

"What an odd boy," women in the neighborhood often said.

"He's even weirder than you," said my brothers.

But that was later, wasn't it? Wasn't he first just a really sweet kid with dark gold skin, a large head and narrow shoulders?

I can see him out our bathroom window sitting on the swing set in our back yard. He was five, or maybe six. He sat there and waited for me to come out and play with him: barefoot, one toe pushing the swing off from the ground just enough to make motion. He wasn't swinging as much as swaying. The swing swayed and wobbled and he looped one arm around the chain and with his free hand picked at his mosquito bites or the hem of his shorts. He could wait a long time, sometimes until his mother hollered out their back door, and then she'd holler again and he'd look up at the bathroom window as if he knew I was there or had been there. He'd push himself off the swing and slowly make his way across our yard, careful to step around my father's carrot and onion garden, and through the shadows of the evergreens, where he'd disappear.

"Marc!" I called out to him through the window screen. It was June and I could feel the heat from outside move through the tiny screen holes onto my face. He looked up from his swing and waved—his eyes were rounder than other people's eyes.

"Are you coming outside?"

"Maybe. I ate lunch."

"Come out and play."

"Maybe. It's hot."

"The hose," he said and pointed.

My father's garden hose snaked around behind the house and we had on occasion pelted ourselves with water. The water came directly from a ground well that my father dug in our backyard; it was cold, a wild cold, the kind that moves through the skin to the veins immediately and confuses the blood. Spanking cold, my father would say. I stepped down from my stool by the window and a minute later appeared at our back garage door and then ran at him on the swing as if I were going to tackle him. But he didn't scare; he grinned and lifted his shoulders and stuck his chin out in delight. I captured him and pulled him to his feet. I dragged him a yard or two, marveling at his limpness and lightness, how he could allow his body to be taken over, how he would give it to me.

"Stand up," I said, and then he did that too. He was a few inches shorter than I was, though later half a foot taller, and he was scrawnier, less muscled, less self-possessed. I loved him. Once I squeezed his forearm so fiercely that a bright indigo bruise rose up the length of it like a miracle—and I told him to run home and tell his mother he fell from the swing. Another time, in the middle of a ground blizzard, I made him walk behind me through the town and around the S-curve to home. No talking, no touching my shadow on the snow.

Some things he wouldn't do: he refused to eat our dog's poop. Another time I dug a hole in the garden–before my father had planted–and put Marc in the hole. But he wouldn't let me bury him. I got as far as covering his legs, arms and torso to his upper chest–not even to his neck–and he popped up suddenly, shaking the half-frozen black loamy dirt off his shirt and pants, and wiping off his knees and elbows.

At the beginning of that summer, Marc had knocked at our side door: "Do you want to come to my birthday party?" he asked. I said sure and then he took me by the hand and walked me through the neighbor's backyard and to the back of his house. His backyard was browning, needed water, a large expanse of browning grass that led up to the two concrete steps that led into his garage that led into his one-story house. Charcoal gray, the darkest house in the eight-house neighborhood. And dark inside as well. A palpable thickness shrouded his house, as though his father's embezzling had been spinning an aura, a murky tension the color of river water. Marc's mother and father stood ahead of us in the dark hallway, two faceless unformed blobs. No one else was home.

"Who is this sweet little girl?" his father bent at the knees, his belly hanging down between them like a full sac. I was supposed to move forward. I stood still. Marc took my hand–so small. Slightly sweaty but clean feeling. There we are in the dark hallway, the top of his large head at my cheekbone, my fine white hair chopped off under my ears, or above my ears.

"Is this your girlfriend?" his father asked. His mother laughed. "She's his wife," she said. "Lorrie, you're going to marry Marc, aren't you? You're going to be Marc's wife, huh?"

On the table, red party hats and a blazing eight-inch double-layered chocolate cake–yet I was the only guest at the party. Was I the only one invited? Would no one else come? I strapped a hat on Marc's large head, and then one on mine, but the emptiness kept coming and made me pull him closer–his wrist bones settling next to mine. A delicate sharpness. The hat string cut into the baby fat on my neck.

Husband. Wife. One dark, one light. One graduating from Melrose

High School and then flailing around the country in slips and hiking boots until landing in the Western Addition in San Francisco. One fag, one dyke. Post cards. Telephone calls. Two visits. One disappearing for five years, traveling to Mexico, London, New York, answering phones in Soho and memorizing museum plaques. And then suddenly reappearing, on a Sunday afternoon on his old friend's Page Street painted-black doorstep, a nickel-sized Kaposi's lesion passing as a nothing, a birthmark on the tender side of his elbow inside his sleeve.

Toxoplasma gondii. Marc taught me this word. A common parasite in cats, crescent-shaped, ghostly. This was just months before protease inhibitors. On a post-mortem photograph, the parasites looked like fingernail clippings with an eye. Or like sperm without a tail. Floaty, harmless-looking debris that infiltrates the immunologically hijacked blood, travels to the brain, destroys the neuron insulation and instigates the over-production of mysterious white matter. A cross section of Marc's left hemisphere showed a dense network of delicate, wavy branches webbed with snow.

He wrote Help Me on the blue-lined pad.

"What do you mean, help me?" I asked.

He wrote the words bigger.

H E L P M E.

I changed the subject. "Do you remember when everyone went down to the river on Christmas Eve and took off their clothes?" I wrote. Actually, I had turned back from the river out of fear, and when I got home I had told my parents what the kids were doing and they had told Marc's parents. There he is, a ten-year-old boy being hauled up over the bank toward the snowy field by his arm, his mother screaming at him in Spanish and swatting his bare backside and legs.

Marc took hold of my wrist and brought his eyes to mine—a tinge, a memory but not quite.

"Do you need to say something to me?" he whispered.

And just then, for the first time in at least ten years, I remembered.

And he knew I remembered. Not the river scene, but three years later. The beginning of eighth grade, months before his father was busted and he and his family disappeared. I was supposed to be at lunch in the cafeteria, but I was breaking rules, wandering on my own schedule. I decided to go into the art supply room to get something. A certain type of paper. The art room was dark. Everything was lumps, the long wooden tables, the dismal clay sculptures of the previous class. I stepped through the classroom into the back supply room. Past an abandoned stack of something, maybe chairs, half covered with a black tarp. I saw boxes further back. I dropped to my knees and started feeling around with my hands. The smell of boxes and paper and glue.

I didn't know he was in the room, or at least I didn't know it all the way. And then he was flying off the black tarp and landing on my back, collapsing me into a box as his hand ripped at the front of my shirt. He had grown so much bigger than me. His mouth was in my hair and he was tearing strands out with his teeth–that's how it felt. Like he was finding individual strands and yanking them out. His hands were tearing at the buttons of my shirt, one hand pushing down the shirt into my bra.

I didn't yell–was I even afraid? Maybe I didn't want him punished, or I was preserving something, my own reputation–not for sex but for truancy and general misbehavior–already shot. I didn't speak his name. A button jettisoned onto the concrete and pinged, another fell into my mouth. I spit out the button and then I reached up behind me with one arm and drilled my fingernail, the one I kept long for prying open tabs on pop cans, into his fleshy midriff. But the fingernail wasn't what stopped him–was it? A noise, someone came into the art room, the teacher. And then Marc was gone.

I lay for a moment, cheek on the concrete. The cold feels good even now. It could have been a dare. Or payback. Or maybe he just couldn't stand to be alone in his own body anymore. I didn't speak to him for the rest of the school year–what would we say? I still don't know where to put it.

From his hospital bed, Marc continued to look at me. That eye. Immaculate, manipulative, fading into gold now, the pupils shot through with fear and a low, continuous dose of morphine in his saline. His white hospital gown tangled at his waist, exposing a bare hip. Marc's energy, his eyes, his skin, his gestures were returning to the beauty and barbarism of nature. A wilderness radiated from him. Sometimes I felt as if a freshly killed deer were splayed in the middle of the room, its spirit loosened, bragging, obscene, its neck thrown back in morbid ecstasy.

"No," I said, staring blankly back at him. How dare he, I thought. He was blown-open, but I had to keep on going, didn't I? Death waiting around, posing as a fifth season.

"Please, stop looking," I said, and he obediently turned his gaze to the wall.

The yellow horse was galloping across the blue. Not galloping, flying, its muscles shot through with flight. The possibility–that's what the painter was after. The exuberance of the yellow, the defiance of a flying horse, the imagination hurling past reason. On that same wall was something else–a crucifix? Yes, there must have been a crucifix in that room, but not on that wall. Above the bed: a black crucifix with a white figure nailed to the wood; his mother would have put that there as well. I can see the folds of Jesus's skirt, his sorrowful European neck, the resigned, released posture. I can see the long slim fingers hanging over the edge of the wood, beautifully carved, translucent.

I looked down at the pad. H E L P M E. He could never stay in the lines.

"But I want you to help *me*," I wrote, and handed it to him.

He looked excited with one eye. "How?" he said. "How can I help you?"

"I need advice," I said. "This woman has been following me around in her truck. Last week on my walk home from the hospital she rolled down the window and asked me for a date. It would just be sex," I said. Was already sex, every night in the front seat of her truck, parked outside my apartment building, her tattooed carpenter's hand teasing my underwear, pulling the lip down and playfully slapping my bottom.

Marc took the pad from me. "Don't see her," he wrote.

"Why?" I asked. "You've had plenty of sex dates."

He took the pad again. "Look where I am," he wrote. And then he wrote, "You don't know the difference between sex and love."

I read the note and laughed, but he was wrong. I did know the difference, but for now it didn't matter.

"You promised me you wouldn't die for another year," I had written the week before.

"You think I'm dying? I'm not dying," he said, suddenly straight and indignant. He made an extraordinary face, considering the drooping eyelid: he pressed his nose into the air toward the yellow horse, as if he were pressing into a new reality, and then he lay back down, curled on his side, and fell asleep.

"Don't see her," he whispered again now. I promised him I wouldn't, but was already sprawled across her big lap, sex a kind of temporary transcendence. His drooping eyelid collapsed completely, dragging the other lid down with it. He lay on his back and held up his hand. I was supposed to take it; he hated falling asleep alone. He had always hated being alone–instead of sitting in his basement room listening to KWOL like the rest of us seventh graders, Marc traipsed around behind a posse of older neighborhood boys, who predictably taunted him and cuffed him on the shoulder or back of his head.

I set the pad on the hospital table at the head of the bed and stood looking at him for a while. He still wore one ring on his middle finger–it reminded me of a bishop's ring, though I've never seen one. I took his hand. A shadow behind me. His sister. Usually when I was there, she would go to the cafeteria, or hang in the hallway just outside the door. Death duty.

She looked sad. Did I look sad? He was supposed to die weeks ago. Her eyes were round and brown like his. Long eyelashes, thick wavy black hair trailing down to chubby hips. She was a nurse, an RN somewhere in Richmond.

"I wish he would just let go." Lines delivered to me two weeks earlier–and only now do I forgive her.

I pictured Marc on a rope in mid-air. He had swung on a gymnastics rope through the gymnasium in the middle of a school lecture. About a month before his father was indicted. Mr. Ricklick pulled him down, dragged him up the aisles by his thick dark hair.

He's a twenty-nine-year-old man, I thought. Why should he let go?

"Except for the eye, he looks good, doesn't he," she said now. "He would like to look good when he dies."

"Yes," I said. "He looks like a healthy young man."

WHAT IS THERE to say, what can sisters, mothers, lovers, friends say? He was alive and then he was dead, like so many others. Narration only makes him more dead—as we march up and down Market Street in our orange lace bustiers and leather chaps. As we swallow our cocktails and eat tuna sandwiches on the steps of City Hall in tuxedos and wedding gowns. But I have photographs. Age four on his clean-cut front lawn, shrouded in the black and white dress of a Franciscan nun, his sweet round eyes and pudgy face in the habit, devout, beseeching. Age ten on the school bus, thick wavy brown hair eclipsing his ears, his wool poncho—a prize from Mexico City—swinging around his knees. In his mid-twenties, cross-legged on my black-painted steps, imitating (for me?) the bored look of Elvis Presley, whom he didn't respect, paging through an Encyclopedia Britannica, a text he did respect.

There. On the telephone. Three months before the hospital, the late-autumn sun falling onto my bare feet through the bay windows of my small living room, a finger over my free ear so I can hear him.

"Marc? Marc, is this you?"

He was weeping.

"I don't know where I am," he said.

He was in Minneapolis for Thanksgiving, visiting his mother and sisters. He'd had an ear infection for six weeks before he left.

"What do you mean, you don't know where you are? Where is your mother?"

I can hear him breathing into the phone, and I can hear the static sound of a public space.

"I don't know. We're in a mall. I'm dizzy, I lose my balance."

"You're in a mall," I repeated. "They took you to a mall and now where are they?"

"I think they're trying on dresses."

"They're trying on dresses. And they left you alone?"

He got suddenly very quiet. "Yes," he whispered dramatically. This was when the whispering began. "Lorrie, I'm alone."

"No, you're not alone," I said. "Forget that. We'll just stay on the phone until you see them again. Now, get a bench and sit down."

I heard him moving and the shifting of the telephone cord.

"I'm sitting," he said. "A lady wants to use the phone."

"She can't. Now tell me about your trip, are they being nice to you?"

He and Bernie, his mother, had visited the old neighborhood, he told me. It was snowing; the kind of light November snow that floats down like pieces of white ash. The snow was three inches deep on the backyard, undestroyed. "Where are the children?" he kept asking me. "We are the children," I told him. Bernie had taken him for a walk through the yards, but he became frightened of the ice under the snow and he kept falling and she yelled at him.

"I can't hear out of my right ear," he said to me.

"You can't hear anything in one ear?"

Static again and then a new silence. When I was nineteen, I had lived alone for six months in a hollow outside Pyatt, Arkansas. I slept in a mud-floor shack some hippies had left behind; the shack was a mile into the hollow, three miles from the nearest gravel road and ten miles from the nearest house. At night, I lay under sleeping bags and furs and stared into the dense darkness, the grandest darkness I've ever seen, darkness that doesn't end at your skin, but infiltrates your cells, and thickens, and begins to make sounds.

"Bernie doesn't understand," he said. "I'm dying."

And I knew he needed to hear me say what I really thought. "Yes," I said. "You are starting to die."

A long breath, as though he were breathing the words in. And then another long silence that wasn't really silence. I can barely hear the words when he says them.

"I haven't done anything important yet, and now I'm going to degrade myself," he says. "Oh, god, it makes me feel sick–Lorrie, you're not going to write about it, are you?"

And the phone went dead.

THIS DAY ISN'T gray. This day cracks open with some pale blue. Marc's eyelids are closed, in each corner a crusted pool of blood. His face is like a placid lake. I reach under the covers and find his hand: amazingly cold. Spanking cold. Heavy the way a dead cat is heavy. I try to bend his fingers but they pop back up into straight position.

I wait for him to lift his hand. I wait for him to open his one eye and pat the windowless side of the bed. I hold up a photograph I brought with me that morning: he and I lying head to head on the gray carpet in my Dolores Street apartment, staring up directly into the camera. He is confident. Smiling. Legs crossed at the ankles.

An hour earlier, before his mother and sister had gone home for the afternoon to return in the evening, his sister had given me a small brown bottle of liquid opium. "Just a drop or two on his tongue, just if he gets in too much pain," she had said, her brown eyes wet, rims swollen. I sat in the plastic chair and stared at him. The other man in the room was already gone. The bed empty.

I turned the bottle over in my palm.

The day before, I had walked into the room with a cup of hot chocolate and Marc was urinating in the corner by the windows. The IV and oxygen tubing splayed across the floor, white sheets speckled beautifully with red. "Marc, go back to bed," I ordered, but he flung his arms against the wall; he started pounding, howling, no sign of morphine in his eye. The red-haired nurse and two orderlies rushed in and pinned his arms to his sides, pushed him toward the floor, or maybe it was the bed. "Don't do that to him," I yelled, and began to cry, and then for the first time I couldn't stop crying.

The red-haired nurse turned to face me, and he said what he had to say: "Visitors must leave the room."

THE NIGHT BEFORE Marc died, I lay on the floor of my small apartment and cranked up the volume on the stereo—but I could still hear the pounding of my angry sobs against my throat. I had turned the carpenter away. The sun went down and the room went black, and then suddenly I raised my feet and kicked the wall beneath the window; I kicked and kicked until the plaster gave way and a fine white dust powdered the floor. It was an exquisite feeling; I imagine even now the thudding in my feet and ankles like buffalo stampeding, and I wanted to break everything, to bellow, fuck you, you don't understand, you stupid stupid people. Finally, the neighbors knocked on my door, and I stopped, and my breath calmed, and I heard through the open window the wild renegade parrots of San Francisco, escaped from their cages and living in the palm trees on Dolores Street, screeching at the tops of their lungs.

HUSBAND. WIFE. ONE dark, one light. One sitting in a sunny window on Steiner Street twelve years later, and one scattered into the Northern Hemisphere, dissipated molecules, the final diaspora.

And in the backyard, one turning on the hose and chasing the other with water. One screaming and throwing his chest forward, his ribs ecstatic and arching toward the sun and the skin of his round golden belly gleaming as his shorts and underwear slide down and catch on his hips. She swings the hose wildly around her head, like a lasso, and he gallops in a narrow circle, until the end of the hose predictably smacks the back of his head. The water turns pink there—a sudden pink froth—and his screaming shifts tone as he runs to get away from whatever is hurting the back of his head: a darker C-minor chord, a frightened painful bawling.

"Stop!" I shout. He stops.

"Sit down." He sits on the grass in front of me. I can see the back of his head where I part his dark hair. A crooked pink gash. A slit in the back of his head, oozing red onto my fingertips. If I could open the gash and look inside

I would see the human brain, a wormy timeless mass undulating thoughts, feelings, memories–and the infestation, our greed, our fear.

I would see a mass of gray. A rooftop. Wavy branches webbed with snow.

"There there," I said, "it's nothing." I must have heard the phrase on television, or it was something my mother said. He calmed, and I patted the slightly sticky, wet hair into place, and leaned forward and kissed the back of his head.

"Am I going to be all right?" he asked.

"Yes," I answered confidently. "You're going to be just fine."

The Goat's Eye

Kirk Wilson

We're screwing like squirrels in the laundry room, Chloe and I, knocking up against the front panel of Aunt Bug's new Maytag dryer so hard it complains like it's drying a bowling ball. I'm two years older, but I'm her uncle, more or less, and she's my niece, and we've both been hornier than toads for each other since puberty, which is forever to us but to the grand dance of time is nothing. Nothing at all.

It was fate that gave us our opportunity. The same bolt of fate that struck down old Great Aunt Bug left us unchaperoned on the musty lumps of her sofa in her parlour, the only room on the planet still called a parlour by any living human. First we sat close and then we sat closer and our arms touched and the short hairs of them tickled our skins into a bad case of goose pimples and our cheeks burned and we kissed and tongued and then we felt and then we stroked and then we started looking for a room where no one could bust in without a warning racket first and found the laundry. Which is in the cellar of Bug's wheezing, falling-down Victorian castle up on a mesa at the crown of her ranch. And which features a deadbolt on the door and two flights of intervening stairs between us and any of our relatives.

If you climb up in this house and look out from its turrets, you'll see emptiness every way you turn. It's a wilderness, but what isn't? You could run into Geronimo or John the Baptist or just about anybody out there. Terrain-wise, you're looking at high desert and mountains with giant eroded, human-featured figures, ghost stories made of rock, staring back at you on top. In those mountains there are caves and rock shelters with smoked ceilings and walls covered with red handprints and pictures of bears, where you can pick up flint hide-scrapers and arrow points and metates and all kinds of tools that go back ten thousand years. You have to be careful where you reach, especially in wintertime, because rattlers like to hibernate in those caves, but you can hold those tools in your hand and tell how they were used, and put the same hand up against that stone wall inside the handprint that is already there, that has been there waiting for you all that time. Those people had small hands, more like Aunt Bug's. When I was a kid I could pretty much fit my hand in theirs. Now my fingers spill out over the ones up on the wall. If you pay attention on your perch you can watch a couple of roads made of packed dirt run off to nowhere and catch some movement from dust devils and tumbleweeds jumping like they're scared of getting shot. A ragged line of boulders big as dinosaurs stands out there for sentinels, and usually you'll spot a stack of buzzards in the air spiraling down on the latest thing that's died.

Nobody comes looking for us. Nobody hears the pounding on the Maytag, nobody is scandalized or outraged or titillated or even given the option of giving a good goddamn because every soul who might care is two floors away in the creepy, bric-a-brac festooned bedroom where Bug lies dying.

Chloe and I know for a simple fact that not one of the deathwatchers will leave that room prematurely for anything less than an Act of God Almighty, and then it better be a good one, because they all live in mortal, quaking awe of the little woman at the center of their diorama. At the present moment what they fear most is that if they dare to take their eyes off her unconscious form, she will rise up and call her lawyer to write them out of her will.

There's no telling how old Bug is, but it's not much either, in that grand dance I'm talking about. There are stones up in our mountains, I hear, that are 500 million years old. Compared to those stones, people aren't much a part of it. We've been here no time at all. It's only been 1,957 years since Jesus split a hymen from the inside out. Seems an odd way to measure time, but there it is. *How many years do you have?* is what the Mexicans say, like we own our time in this world. I've got nineteen, almost twenty. Chloe's got seventeen plus. I like the way she is alive. The way her mouth stays a little open. The high points of her cheeks are always a little pink, and her eyes always ready to laugh in some way that she keeps private. Right now her whole face has gone so red you can barely see the freckles. We've done all we can do to each other and we're both leaning on the dryer, buttoning up and breathing like horses in a derby. She puts her finger right on my breast bone, touching it through my shirt, and draws a little box and says, *This is where we'll keep our secrets*. And now she does start laughing right out loud. She takes off up the cellar stairs and I go chasing after her, all rubber-legged, and we fall back on the sofa. We stare up at a sky of dark carved wood, way above our heads.

Who do you think she'll give it to? Chloe says.

I don't know and I don't care.

That might be a lie. *That* is *a lie*, Chloe tells me with a look.

I grew up on the ranch. I've worked it since I was old enough to ride. It's the only place I've ever known, so I can't tell you with a straight face that I don't care what happens to it. It's not right to say the ranch is part of me because it's too big to fit in me or anybody, but I'm sure part of it, as much as any creature out there dead or alive.

I don't remember when the two of us have been this still. We're just sitting with our heads thrown back, smelling thousand-year-old dust. We hear a door open and close on the floor above us, up on the gallery where a room full of living people, and probably a bunch of ghosts, are watching another person die. Then we hear a voice from up there, diffusing in all the space around us.

Rascal, come up here a minute.

My sister Rosetta. Half-sister, more or less, except I'm adopted and she's not. Chloe's mama. She's got forty and then some.

I guess they started calling me Rascal because the name they gave me when they took me in is Rasco, after my more-or-less Uncle Rasco who fought the Japs in World War II. That Rasco used to run the projector at the VA hospital, showing movies to the other vets that got their legs blown off or lost their minds somewhere in the war. Some of those hombres, when you would watch them watch those movies, are so far back in that God-forsaken landscape in their heads you couldn't find them with a pack of hounds. I heard Uncle Rasco fought on some islands in the Pacific Ocean. He wouldn't ever talk about the war, and last July 4th he ran his two-tone Ford Sunliner into a whole carload of tourists and got himself and all of them dead. I remember that day especially because it started with Aunt Bug telling me something bad was going to happen because a coyote had killed a black kid, which according to her a self-respecting coyote would rather avoid. I told her coyotes must have a pretty educated palate because I had never noticed a difference between the taste of a black goat and a white one. She said it was no surprise to her that coyotes knew things I didn't. I asked what the bad thing was and she said she wished she knew. Then that night the law came and the dogs went nuts and woke us up, a trooper from the DPS, and told us about the wreck.

Anyway, you could see how there could be confusion with two Rascos around, so the one who was late to the party gets to be called Rascal. My old amigo Pepper Hinojosa told me in sixth grade it sounded like a dog's name. *And what does your name sound like?* I asked him, and before either of us could think of an answer I bloodied his nose on principle, but I didn't really care. Most dogs I know beat most people, role-model-wise.

I make the stairs complain going up to the landing outside Bug's bedroom and Chloe stays on the sofa. The wood in Bug's house remembers when it was alive in trees, I think, because it vocalizes sometimes, not just when you step on it but in the night when nothing's moving.

Did she die?

No, she did not die.

Rosetta's still a pretty woman, Neiman Marcus up and down, black-haired and blue-eyed like Daddy, but she's gotten a little heavy and about half-mean. It's like some kind of ancient female rage has started seeping through her pores. Sad to contemplate, but that's Chloe twenty-some years on, right there. She opens the door and there they all are. Rosetta's dumb-ass husband Randal, who runs a Feed and Seed and John Deere dealership with Aunt Bug's money, giving me his best I-know-so-much-you-don't grin from a wingback chair. Old Aunt Dolly in a corner by the window 'cross the room, staring at the closed curtain like she can see right through it. Dolly always reminds me of a wren, those frail little birds that build nests in any shelter they can find around your house. Our Daddy Stafford, still a handsome old cowboy but looking at the downslope and not as tall as he used to be, sits right on the edge of the death bed with one boot on his knee, the pant leg pulled up so you can see the eagle worked into the stitching on the shaft. And the centerpiece of everything is Great Aunt Bug, her visage rising from the pillow like a pale clay model of a hill that hasn't been rained on in a thousand years. Sixty inches down, her feet make two little peaks in the white chenille bedspread. The room is gray as an eclipse. The day is all sealed out.

Did ya'll find somethin' to amuse yourselves? Daddy wants to know.

Not really.

Good.

Her hands are movin', Randal says.

They are. All packed in blotched and peppered rice paper skin, bulged out with swollen bones and rusty tendon wires attached to gnarly claws, Bug's hands are picking in the most tentative way any moving thing has ever picked at the crocheted fringe along the folded portion of the sheet.

Rosetta says, *Aunt Bug, honey, can you hear us at all?*

We can't know, Daddy says.

I just want her to know we're here is all.

We can't know what she knows or what she hears.

Well goddamnit Daddy I know we can't, but I can want it can't I?

You can want what you damn well please.

She hears, Randal says. *She can be up here on this mountain and you can't whisper howdy-do in church, all the way in town, without her knowin' it.*

Aunt Bug did lay claim to certain powers. She knew when people were about to die, though she missed on Uncle Rasco. She said that was because he didn't go as a result of a sickness. She knew the big things and the little, and all of it seemed to come to her at random. She knew North Korea would invade South Korea on June 24, 1950. She looked up from breakfast that day and said, *Of all the senseless things. Another war just started*. When she was a girl her little brother, our Daddy's Daddy, broke his leg falling down a mine shaft out in the mountains and she dreamed where he was. Without that dream, I suppose, some of us wouldn't be here.

Randal, there are times to talk and times to keep your mouth shut, Rosetta tells him.

We can't know, Daddy says. *She has gone behind the veil.*

Our old Daddy has turned a little mystical on us in his later years. He hasn't started claiming to know things the rest of us didn't, not yet. How Aunt Bug knows is a mystery. I guess the knowing just creeps into her, right through her clothes and skin, or she picks it off the wind or hears it when her house starts talking in the night. Bug claims she inherited this gift of knowing directly from all the Holliday women who came before her. Rosetta says the gift has not been offered to her and that can be the case for all time because she has no use for it. If it's ever cropped up in Chloe she hasn't told me. Maybe Aunt Bug is the end of the line, knowing-wise.

Right then bright light splashes into the room. All of us but Aunt Bug swing and blink. Turns out Aunt Dolly has pulled back the curtain at her window and is tying up the sash. Our heads turn back to Bug to gauge what she will do about all this sunshine pouring through her bedchamber drunk and disorderly without her permission and she does nothing at all. Old Dolly smiles the tiniest baby of a smile and watches a fly worry up against the sun-bright window as though it is the most fascinating spectacle since Creation. She must have heard it buzzing there, and felt a need to see it. She's humming a cheery little tune under the currents of her breath. If she's worried about Bug you sure couldn't tell it. Maybe she figures this whole death thing is just a bump in the road. Or more likely I guess she's tuned in to Dolly radio, as Aunt Bug used to say, on a frequency all her own.

Aunt Dolly don't you think you should close the curtains, sweetheart? Rosetta says. When Rosetta uses that tone of voice it sounds like she wants to pour honey on you, right before she breaks your neck. A beat or two goes by. Then she looks at me and says, *We need to think about what we're gonna serve when people come to the house.*

I *told you already,* Daddy says, we won't need to serve anything. You know people always bring food.

And I told you already you know Aunt Bug would want to provide. That's why

I called Rascal up here, so he could start cookin' some goat. And I can make my potato salad. Aunt Bug always loved my potato salad.

Randal wiggles his finger so that I will lean down closer.

I didn't know Aunt Bug loved anything but Bombay Gin, he says as quiet as he can manage, but not quiet enough.

Randal, you are truly an idiot, Rosetta says. *Aunt Dolly. Sweetheart. That hummin' is about to drive me batshit crazy.*

Rosetta smoothes down her skirt. She crosses to the window, unties the sash, and pulls the curtains to. Aunt Dolly stops humming. Rosetta walks back across the room and gives Randal a look that could shave him.

Light as a mayfly, Dolly opens the curtains, ties up the sash, and picks her tune up where she left it.

I guess y'all want me to cook some goat, I say, and before they can say anything I'm down the stairs. Chloe watches me go past, then gets up and follows me out. The sky is wide open and the wind is picking up. It'll be cold by tonight. I can't tell you why but something sad can happen to a living thing when you put walls around it and a roof between it and the sky. I know I turn more alive when I step outside. In town, they've started building houses that look just alike, in straight rows on a grid of streets that look just alike too. You would get lost in there and never get out except for the street names, which are all the names of birds we never see around here, like Oriole and Scarlet Tanager. I wouldn't know a Scarlet Tanager if it built a nest in my hair. When I started to drive–I was around twelve I guess–Aunt Bug asked me to carry her over there so she could see it with her own eyes. That little old woman looked out the window of my Daddy's truck at those rows of new houses like she was on a grand tour of the moon. She pulled her head back in and shook it, and *Rascal, I believe we have discovered Birdland* was all she had to say.

If I had to live in one of those houses, I know I'd lift up one fine night crazy as a screech owl and take off down the highway. And if I did, if you or anybody did, you'd fly right past the new country club where they waste water keeping the grass green so Randal and his friends can chase golf balls around. That place has a big paved parking lot and a club house made to look like some jet-set villa, with a bar and a restaurant with white linen tablecloths and candles floating in bowls on little boats where the better people of the town can sit and know for damn certain they are the better people, just as good as the better people in Dallas, with Cadillacs and Lincolns just as big and shiny. I went to my high school graduation party there and got drunk and threw up in the swimming pool. I suppose the idea of all those things, Birdland and the town cut up into squares and the candles in the little boats, is to give everybody the feeling they're all tame and secure and tomorrow will be pretty much a replay of today. If you don't need that feeling you can do fine out here.

What's goin' on, Rascal? Chloe says.

We're cookin' goat.

Chloe steps over and gives me a little kiss on the lips which is strange right out here in the daylight, and we move on and come to the pen where I keep some young kids with their mothers. Taking care of them is part of how I earn my keep. That and working cattle, breaking and training horses, and bringing home a little meat I shoot out on the range. I don't remember a time I wasn't fooling with the animals some way on this ranch. They feed us and carry us and pay for everything we need, and they all take some looking after. Even the goats. You might think goats are tough. They look it, and in a lot of ways they are. But when they get the bloat you have to tube them and give them oil and baking soda to keep them alive, and if you keep Angoras and they get caught out in heavy rain too soon after they're sheared, they get paralyzed and die real quick. You can lose your whole herd.

When we eat goat on the ranch it's mostly cabrito. The best meat comes from a Boer kid that weighs maybe ten pounds and has never had anything in its belly but goat milk. Yeah, you're eating a baby, and it might be better in a perfect world to let the goat live out its days, but people like to put that meat in their mouths when it's still tender and sweet. We separate out one about the right size and Chloe picks it up. If you plan to kill a living creature the least you can do is look it in the eye. You need to understand what you're doing, and so does that creature you're about to kill. In this pen we've got plenty of goats' eyes to look into, and they're looking right back at us.

The first thing you notice, of course, about a goat's eye is that the pupil is not round like yours, but is a slit that lays out like the horizon. I read in a book that slit gives a goat a field of vision 340 degrees wide, almost all the way around a circle. I don't know how you'd know that for sure without being a goat, but so the book said. You can believe it if you want to, like the Virgin Birth. Or you can try sneaking up on a goat. It's hard to sneak up on anything that is awake and can see in almost all directions without turning its head.

There's no getting around the fact that that eye is spooky, and maybe it's one of the reasons people associate goats with the devil. The devil looks a lot like a goat, in most of the pictures I've seen. There's a bastard of a sticker burr out here people call a goat's head sometimes and a devil's head other times, and it looks like both those things. But a goat is not a devil. Everything mean enough to live in the universe of rock and sand and cactus that falls off in every direction below Aunt Bug's house is designed to make you bleed. Ocotillo, agave, sotol, scorpions, rattlers, big cats, bears, not to mention weather that will fry your ass all day and freeze it all night. Excepting the occasional human, though, none of it is evil. It just doesn't give a damn about you one way or the other.

I know who you are, where you come from, what you want most, the goat's eye says. *And I couldn't care less.*

We take the kid into a barn where I've got a rack for slaughtering. Chloe's petting it, cuddling. I like the way she nuzzles into the fur, smells what's there. It's no compliment if somebody says you smell like a goat, but a goat smells rich in a way no rich man can. I'm of the school that you comfort the animal a while before you kill it. Some say if you don't the adrenaline will toughen up the meat. I don't know if that's true, but it's not why I do it. It just feels right.

I have a long sharp blade I only use for this. You could shave with it if you don't mind risking your neck. I show Chloe how I pin the kid between my legs and pull its head back from behind.

You don't want to hesitate, I say. *Some people shoot 'em or hit 'em in the head first, but a goat's skull is hard and believe it or not that doesn't always work. The cut is the quickest way, and that's what you want.*

I make one clean stroke across the throat just below the jawbone, all the way to the spine.

We tie on some butcher's aprons and wait a minute until we know for sure the kid is dead, then we hang it up head down and drain most of the blood.

I make slits along the underside and around the legs to loosen the skin, cut around the ass and work out a length of intestine, tie it off with twine and cut above the knot.

That's important so you don't contaminate the meat.

Skinning a kid this small is pretty easy.

I cut off the head, gut the goat, and whack it up just like you do a rabbit, break the back in two places, separate it, and take off the legs. A big goat is a different proposition.

Chloe and I repeat the process with three more kids. I do the slaughtering because she doesn't want to try that yet, but she butchers two of them. You can see the concentration in her face, her lips set, her jaw muscle working and her neck tight.

Do I chop the back here?

A little bit lower. I point. *You want to be right below the front legs and right above the back ones.*

She makes a clean cut through with one swing and the carcass jumps from the blow.

Rascal, did Aunt Bug ever say she loved you?

Hell of a question when you're chopping up a goat.

Did she say it to you?

She shakes her head without looking up. Her black hair is shiny, bouncy. Done up with curlers at night I guess.

Old Bug is hard as they come. But she taught me how to do this, just like I'm showing you. Teaching somebody how to live is better than just words.

Could be that's all we're here for, I think, but I don't say it. Chloe's studying the chunks of baby goat she's just laid out with a cleaver and a knife.

We're here to eat each other, the goat's eye says. *That's the best that I can tell.*

A goat will eat anything, and maybe that's why you can't pin down the taste of goat meat to any certain flavor. Cabrito tastes like the open country would if you could roll it all together and roast a piece of it and put it in your mouth, like sex with a little salt and sugar, like knowing where you come from. You have to gnaw to win the last tasty bits from the sharp points of the bone.

Chloe turns around and gives me that little open-mouthed smile. Rosetta invested heavily with the orthodontist, so her teeth are really pretty. We're both all bloody. We wash up in the yellow well water at the basin behind the slaughter rack, then we start working on the pit. There are a lot of ways to cook goat, but on the ranch we like a welded rebar cage buried in a hole in the ground. The meat is falling off the bones when you're done, but it takes all day.

We're stacking wood in the pit when somebody starts yelling up by the house. *Oh my God, oh my God.* We run up there and it's Rosetta, standing out by her Cadillac, Daddy's pickup, and my hunt-rigged Jeep. She's got a hand over her mouth and she's gone white. There's a dust devil dancing like a baby tornado behind her, off at the edge of the mesa.

What's wrong?

Pappy Holliday, she says in this little voice I've never heard her use.

What about him?

Goddamn Pappy Holliday.

Pappy was a one-eyed Indian fighter and Texas Ranger and Aunt Bug's, and Daddy's, and all these people's most distinguished ancestor. He lost the eye in a skirmish when a Comanche warrior shot his horse out from under him and it threw him eyeball-down onto a long mesquite thorn. He used to live in a lean-to not far from where we are now, all decorated with a bunch of skulls and scalps of Comanches, Apaches, and Mexicans he'd killed. The county is named for him. So is the ranch. He died of lockjaw eighty-some years ago.

Rosetta, what about him?

Goddamn.

Chloe stays with her and I run on up the stairs. The door to Aunt Bug's room is open. Face down right on the rug in front of me is the dusty bronze bust of Pappy Holliday that sat on top of Bug's armoire as long as anyone remembers. It shows him with the patch that covered up his missing eye. Daddy and Randal are standing there staring at the back of Pappy's head. Aunt Dolly is sitting by her window giggling up a storm. She's trying to stop the giggling by humming at the same time, which appears to be a hard thing. Sounds like she might be doing *Turkey in the Straw*. Aunt Bug's mouth and eyes are open wide. She's looking right through the ceiling. The ruined hill of her face has gone yellow like the water from her pipes.

God Almighty, Randal says, *how can that thing be jumping 'round the room? It must weigh two hundred pounds.*

It was not jumping in this world, Daddy says.

Well, Randal says, *it sure as hell landed in this world. Two inches more that way and it would have broke every bone in my foot.*

Turns out Aunt Bug let loose a death rattle and before anybody could properly notice, Pappy Holliday did a swan dive from the top of his armoire. These things can happen in this part of the world and I guess anywhere. On Uncle Rasco's birthday, a month after the car wreck, all the lights in his house came on in the night, and his girlfriend Esperanza said his old border collie was up whining and wouldn't get quiet.

No use looking because it won't be there in front of you, no matter how wide your field of vision is, but there's something going on that we can't reach out and grab.

One thing we do know is that Aunt Bug has left the ranch. That's hard to imagine because there's never been a time for any of us when she was anyplace else. For Randal and Rosetta, this development probably looks like a color picture of the Promised Land. Ninety-six thousand acres and change without Aunt Bug in the foreground. I guarantee you Randal's been sitting up nights in his plaid Bermuda shorts, wearing pencils to the nub so he can try to multiply the current price per acre of Holliday County land by ninety-six thousand. Or drawing little diagrams of five-acre plots he'll sell to Yankees and Californians for twenty times that price. Or dreaming how he'll make water out of dust, irrigate and build a subdivision, a golf club, and an airport for private jets. Of course that means the answer to the secret of the century has to go his and Rosetta's way, and right now Aunt Bug's lawyer Buddy Coleman is the only living human who knows how that tale turns out.

Randal has to figure he's the front-runner in the Aunt Bug rodeo. He and Rosetta have pretty much invested their lives making it that way. Every Sunday in the front pew at First Baptist, where he's a deacon and she sings solos in the choir. Three legitimate, baptized kids. She's School Board. He's Chamber of Commerce. They watch Ed Sullivan on the biggest television you ever saw. They send out Christmas cards with their pictures on them, where you can count every one of their teeth.

Meanwhile Daddy, the only serious contender left in the field after Uncle Rasco's demise and the only one likely to keep the ranch in one piece, has to figure as a genuine dark horse. Three ex-wives who swear he's Satan, never saw a skirt or a highball or a game of five-card stud he didn't like. And then to top it off there's me. I was adopted as a squalling babe after one of Daddy's intimate acquaintances at the time, a lady named Lucinda I never properly met, pushed me through her birth canal and took off with a drummer in a country band. Some claim I am my Daddy's son after all. But nobody really knows, not me or Daddy or anybody else. Whatever you might say about him, and there's a lot you could say, he stood up and took me in, and when he told Aunt Bug about it all she said was, *A spotted dog has spotted pups*.

They can put that on my tombstone for all I care.

Aunt Dolly has quit humming. She's working her hands one around the other in her lap. The curtains at her window are closed. Daddy tries to shut Aunt Bug's mouth and eyes, but they keep popping open. He gives her a kiss on the forehead. Rosetta strides in and starts to tidy up. If she's still worried about Pappy Holliday putting his nose through the rug, you can't see it. She pulls the sheet up over Aunt Bug's face. She tells Randal to go out and call the undertaker. Undertaker, now there's a word for all time. Before Randal can make it down the stairs, she yells after him to bring some vaqueros in from the bunkhouse and figure out how to get Pappy back on his perch. *Aunt Dolly*, she says then, all sweet and chirpy, *why don't you go down and make us a nice pot of tea?*

Know what a fulcrum is? Well, Aunt Bug was the fulcrum in this old world, and now she's gone everything will tilt a whole new way. I guess I want to look at things the way I know them one last time. Before Rosetta can think of anything for me to do, I go down the stairs and out to my Jeep. Chloe has wandered over toward the edge of the mesa. She's standing there staring off at the mountains. I pull out my spotting scope and set it up to see if any pronghorns are moving, and find a good bunch off at the base of a peak, maybe two miles out, maybe further. There's a pretty stout mess of wind, dust moving every direction. I tie down the windshield so I can feel it when I drive. I take the .30-06 off the gun mount and throw the bolt back to open the chamber. I know it's clean and well-oiled because I'm the one that cleans it, but I look anyway because that's the right thing to do. The bore is so shiny it would work like a fun-house mirror if you could crawl down in it. I've got the scope sighted in at 300 yards, so I won't be looking that prong buck in the eye. He'll never see the bullet coming. He won't have time to think much of anything besides *what the hell*. That's just how it is, because I can't exactly walk up to him and ask his permission. I put the rifle back in the mount. Chloe has come over and wants to go but I tell her she belongs here with her mama, and besides somebody needs to finish the pit.

Who do you belong with? she says. I fire up the Jeep.

I look into her face before I pull away and know it's one of those pictures I will see forever, as long as I have eyes to close and memories.

There used to be an ocean out here, volcanoes and flying dinosaurs and mountains of ice and people decked out in paint and feathers dancing up in the caves. I'm not sure all of that is gone, completely, though it is invisible, at least for me. Maybe old billy goat can see it. I know there is something that will chill your blood down in the evening, when it moves just outside the little circus ring of things you can perceive. Soon enough this old world will be there too. You can already see its bones. It's finished, and there will be a new world walking on its grave. You can feel that world's impatience. It can't wait. It'll be air-conditioned, and paved, and all quiz shows and deodorant. That much you can tell already.

I've got up a pretty good head of steam now, bouncing like a wildcat down the old ranch road and eating sand when I open my mouth to give out a grito. Maybe I'll bring back a buck and maybe I won't. Maybe I'll just keep going.

Graham Greene

Percival Everett

I had done some work on the reservation nearly ten years earlier, helping to engineer an irrigation ditch that brought water from a dammed high creek down to the pastures of Arapaho Ranch. I slept on a half dozen different sofas during the seven months of the project. The tribe paid me well and I left, thought that was the end of it. Then just a few weeks ago I received a letter from a woman named Roberta Cloud. I was not so much surprised by the call as I was by the fact that she was still alive. She'd actually had a friend write for her as she was blind now, the letter stated. The friend said that Roberta needed my help. It was a short letter, to the point, without many details. The letter ended with an overly formal "Until I see you I am sincerely, Roberta Cloud."

I made the drive up from Fort Collins on a Thursday. I left in the morning and stopped at Dick's Dogs in Laramie for an ill-advised early lunch. I loved the dogs, but they never loved me back. I drove into a stiff early-winter wind that caused my Jeep to burn more gas than usual. The high-profile, flat-faced vehicle felt like it was on its heels as I pressed into the breeze. I hit Lander midafternoon and drove straight through to Ethete. Ethete was just a gas station with a convenience store. There was a yellow light at the intersection that flashed yellow in all four directions. I stopped and grabbed myself a cup of coffee.

A heavyset woman rang up my drink and the packaged cake I'd put on the counter.

"Think it will snow?" I asked.

"Eventually," she said.

I nodded. "Can you tell me how to get to Roberta Cloud's house?"

"She's on Seventeen Mile Road."

"Where on the road? Closer to here or Riverton?"

"Did you know it ain't seventeen miles, that road?"

"How long is it?"

"Changes," she said. "I've never measured it myself Some people say it's only thirteen miles. Dewey St. Clair said it's nineteen, but I think he just said that because he was always late for work."

"How will I know Roberta's house?"

"She's at the first bend. There's a purple propane tank in the yard. Big one."

"Thanks."

I drove back to Seventeen Mile Road and turned east. After a couple of miles I saw the bend and there was the big purple tank. Someone had scrawled Indian Country across it in white paint, but the last letter of the first word and the last two of the second were worn off, so it read India Count. I rolled into the yard and waited behind the wheel for a few minutes. A black dog came trotting from the house next door. I got out and opened the back of my Jeep. I placed a carton of cigarettes on a stack of three new dish-towels and a twenty-dollar bill on top of that. The dog walked me to the door.

I knocked lightly. I didn't remember Roberta all that well. I recalled only that she was the oldest person I had ever talked to. She looked to be ninety back then. The gift was customary. I didn't know if she smoked, but the tobacco was important. I knocked harder and a woman called for me to enter. I did.

Roberta Cloud sat in a rocker across the room, backlit by the sun through a window. She didn't rock.

"Ms. Cloud?"

"Yes?"

"It's Jack Keene. "

"Mr. Keene, you came."

"Yes ma'am. You call, I come. That's the way it works."

"I could get used to that," she said.

"I have a few things for you," I told her.

"Thank you, Mr. Keene." She pointed to the table.

I put down the towels, cigarettes, and money. "Please, call me Jack."

"Sit down, Jack."

I sat on the sofa under the window. The sun came through the glass and hit my neck.

"I was wondering if you got my letter," she said.

"You didn't give a phone number and I knew I could get here faster than the mail."

"And here you are."

"Here I am. What can I do to help you?"

"I want you to find my son."

"Ma'am?"

"My son. I'm one hundred and two years old. I'm going to die and I want to see my son one last time. I haven't seen him in a bunch of years, maybe thirty."

"Ms. Cloud, I'm not a detective."

"He's a good boy. I was twenty when I had him and he never gave me any trouble."

I did the math. "Ms. Cloud, that would make your son eighty-two years old."

"I reckon that's right."

In my head I did more math. I was told once that the average Native American man lives to be forty-four. I wasn't sure I believed the statistic, it being so shocking and sad, but I was certain it wasn't a gross exaggeration. Ms. Cloud's son would be defying the odds if he were still alive.

"So, you're telling me you haven't seen your son since he was fifty-two years old."

"His name is Davy."

"Do you know where I should look for David?"

"Davy. His name is Davy. That's what's on his birth paper. His name is Davy."

"Davy." I looked at Roberta Cloud's wrinkled face, her cloudy eyes. I wondered if she could see at all.

"When I met you years ago I knew you were a good man," she said. "And here you are."

"I'm glad you think that," I said.

"That's why I wrote to you."

I didn't know whether to feel flattered or like a sucker. "Ma'am, I have to say that I don't think I'm the person to try to find Davy."

She nodded. "You'll find him. I believe with all my heart that you will find him."

"Why do you believe that, ma'am?"

"Let's just say I have a good feeling about you." And then she let out a high little laugh that seemed incongruous.

"I see."

"The last I heard he was working in the restaurant in Lander. The restaurant would be a good place to start."

"There are many restaurants in Lander, Ms. Cloud. Do you know the name of the restaurant?"

"No, I don't." She reached over to the table beside her rocker and picked up a photograph. She pretended to look at it and then pushed it toward me.

"Ms. Cloud, eighty-two is kind of old to be working in a restaurant. Working anywhere."

"Here's a picture of Davy."

I took the photo and looked at it. I looked at the olive-skinned man with a long braid. He looked familiar. The man in the picture looked to be in his midforties. "It's an old picture, Ms. Cloud. Do you think I'll be able to recognize him?"

"You'll know him when you see him," she said.

I wanted to ask her if she was sure he was still alive, but thought better of it.

"What's his birthdate?" I asked.

"The second of December," she said quickly.

"The year?"

She directed her useless eyes at the ceiling. "I don't know," she said. Maybe she was crying.

"Ms. Cloud," I started.

"Mr. Keene," she said, her voice softer than before. "I'm going to die in one week. I can't stop it, that's the way it is. I know you will find my Davy."

There was nothing for me to say. Actually, there were many things I could have said, but none of them to Roberta Cloud. But I said the one thing that I could say to her and that was "Yes ma'am."

"Well, you had better hurry, Mr. Keene. The clock's ticking." She laughed.

Needless to say, I did not. Hurry, that is. What was I supposed to hurry up and do? I rose, bid her good-bye, and walked out into the cold March air. I looked at the propane tank and was sorry it had been so easy to spot. I stood just outside the door and heard no movement from inside. I wondered briefly what had prompted me to respond to the old woman's letter. Briefly, because I answered the question in short order. I was there because I was a stupid do-gooder, a typical idiot with a slight messianic complex. I thought I'd come up here and the old woman would ask for something simple, like a repair on the aforementioned propane tank, and I would do it, feel good about myself, and help out an old woman. I got what I deserved for being a nice guy.

I climbed into my car and drove to the reservation office. Maybe this would be simple. Perhaps Davy Cloud, if he was still alive, which I doubted, was living only miles away on the reservation. As I parked and got out I peered up to see that the sun was giving in to a sky that looked like snow. Inside, I found a lone woman sitting at a desk behind a long, high counter.

"What can I do you for?" she asked.

"A man could hear that a couple of ways," I said.

"A man could," she said. "But a man won't."

"Fair enough." I put the photograph on the counter. "I'm looking for this man."

"I'd be looking for him, too," the woman said. "He's a looker."

I nodded. "But he's about eighty now."

"Oh."

"His name is Davy Cloud."

"No Davy Cloud," she said. "There's a Roberta Cloud. No Davy Cloud."

"He's Roberta's son."

The woman looked at me with a sidelong glance for a second. Then she might have shaken her head. I wasn't sure.

"Could you check?"

"Check what?"

"Don't you have a register or a roll or something?"

"Yes, we have a list of everyone in the tribe. Is he Arapaho?"

"He's Roberta Cloud's son."

"Okay, I'll look up Roberta." She walked to a desk and sat at it, facing a computer screen. "We just digitized what we have. Here's Roberta. No mention of a son. But that wouldn't be that strange. Eighty years ago some people just had their kids and that was it. No paperwork, no nothing."

"A reservation phonebook?"

She came back to the counter, reached under it, and pushed the thin volume that was the phonebook toward me. "Look for yourself. One Cloud. Roberta Cloud."

"I believe you," I said. "Do you have any old phonebooks?"

"No."

"Is there a library on the reservation?"

She shook her head. "There's a library in Lander."

"Thank you. Sorry to come in with such strange questions."

"Every week some wasichu comes in here looking for an Indian nobody knows."

She was joking, but she had used Lakota slang for a white person and it kind of rankled me. "I'm not white," I said.

"You're not Indian," she said.

"True enough. Have a good day, ma'am."

I DROVE TO the library in town. It was late in a steel-gray afternoon. I asked the cliche of a librarian at the reference desk if they had old phonebooks. They had some for Lander and a few for the reservation. Apparently the reservation hadn't started keeping a phonebook until seven years earlier. Still, I looked through all of them. I had nothing better to do with my time.

I found a computer, got online, and found a couple of David Clouds. Not one was Native. All were young and none were in Wyoming. And as usual I felt a little sullied by having been online.

I drove to a diner and tried to find some food. It should have been easy, given that I was in a restaurant, but it was not. The chicken soup tasted like soap and the club sandwich's only memorable attribute was that it was enormous. The waitress was an older woman who seemed well aware that the food was substandard.

"I would ask you if everything's okay," she said and left it at that, just filled my mug with coffee and walked away.

When she came back, I asked her how long she'd worked there.

"Twenty years," she said.

"That's a long time," I said.

"You bet your sweet ass that's a long time. Now every week feels like twenty years."

"Sorry," I said. "You ever have any Arapaho men work in the kitchen?"

"A couple. A Sioux guy worked the kitchen last year."

I showed her the photograph. "You ever see him?"

She studied the image. She gave it a good, very long look. "Nope, never seen him."

"That picture was taken about thirty years ago," I said.

She turned her head to the side like a dog and said, "There is something familiar about him."

"So, maybe he worked here?" I asked.

"What's his name?"

"Davy Cloud."

She shook her head, but said, "He does look familiar. But all Indians look alike to me."

"Well, okay then."

"No, he hasn't worked here since I've been here. I know that much."

"Thank you."

"Sure thing."

"Can I ask you something?"

"Shoot," she said.

"Is this chicken soup?"

She glanced quickly back at the window. "That's what I'm told. It's bad, right?"

"Tastes like soap."

"It tastes exactly like Palmolive dish soap. Exactly like it." She smiled at me as if we were sharing some important knowledge.

"Why didn't you mention this when I ordered it?"

She shrugged.

I put the photo back in my breast pocket.

I WALKED INTO two other restaurants, for no reason except that I had time to kill and didn't know what else to do, showed the photo, and got strange looks. When it was getting late I wandered into a rundown tavern with pool tables and a jukebox and ordered a beer. I said hello to the woman who was working the bar. A couple of bikers shot a game behind me. I thought, what the hell, and pulled out the photograph.

"Excuse me, miss, but have you ever seen this man?" I asked the bartender.

"What are you?" she asked.

"What do you mean?"

"Are you a cop?" At the word *cop* I heard the pool game stop briefly. "You some kind of private eye?"

"No, I'm an engineer."

That didn't help clear things up at all, so I decided to change my story. I told the next person that Davy Cloud had come into an inheritance. The heavyset blond young man with two sleeves of tattoos showed great interest.

"Is there a finder's fee?"

"No, I'm afraid not."

"Then why are you looking?" he asked.

"Friend of the family."

"Fuck that." He went back to playing pool.

"Let me see that picture," a woman said.

I did.

"I know that guy."

"You do?" She was about twenty and wouldn't even have been born when the picture was taken.

"Yeah, that's that Indian actor. What his name?" She bumped her forehead with her fist a couple of times. "Damn it. Sherry, come over here."

Sherry did, along with three leathery bikers. They all looked at the picture together.

The first woman said, "What's that guy's name? He was in that movie with Hal Kilmer."

"Val Kilmer," Sherry corrected her. She thought, gently pounding her own forehead with her palm. "Graham Greene. He was in that *Dances with Wolves.*"

"Val Kilmer wasn't in that," a biker said.

"The movie was *Thunderheart,*" Sherry said. "I know my movies. Yeah, that's Graham Greene."

I looked at the picture. I'd seen both of the movies and he did look a little like Graham Greene. In fact, he looked a lot like Graham Greene. Then I felt like an asshole for thinking that maybe the two men looked alike, as if it was because they were both Indians.

One of the bikers stared at me. He had a cliché red bandanna tied over his hair. "You know this guy?" he said, more an accusation than a question.

"Trying to find him for a friend."

"Why?"

"Some inheritance thing," the first guy I'd talked to said as he was taking his shot at the table.

"How much?" the biker asked.

"I don't know. The guy in the picture is about eighty years old now."

"Eighty? What the fuck does an eighty-year-old need with an inheritance?" The biker let loose a high-pitched laugh and his friends laughed with him.

I shrugged and took the photo back from Sherry.

"Thanks," I said.

"You're welcome," the biker said, not sincerely.

"That's Graham Greene," Sherry called to me when I was at the door. "I'm telling you that's Graham Greene."

AFTER A NIGHT in a motel I returned to the library the next morning and looked at images of Graham Greene. The man in my photograph did look a lot like Graham Greene, but also different. Regardless, I didn't know where to look next. I decided to try the sheriff's office.

The inside of the office was as nondescript as the outside and in fact so was the sheriff. He was a new sheriff, though he was over fifty. I could tell because his clothes were so neat and crisp. His dispatcher was out sick and so he was manning the desk, he told me. I showed him the photograph.

"Looks like that actor," he said.

"I know."

"What's his name?"

"Graham Greene."

"No, that's not it. He was on that Chuck Norris television show." He scratched his head as he looked out the window. "Floyd something. Westerman. Floyd Westerman."

"This man's name is Davy Cloud. He's Arapaho and he's about eighty now."

"Why do you want him?

"I promised his hundred-year-old mother I'd find him."

"You're shittin' me."

"I wish I were." I tapped the picture. "I can't find out anything about him. I was thinking maybe he has a driver's license."

"And you thought you could just wander into the police station and have somebody look that up on a computer, right?"

I blew out a breath, feeling pretty stupid.

"Well, let's take a look," he said. He laughed.

"Really?"

"Why not?" The sheriff used the computer on the counter. "What's the name?"

"Davy Cloud."

"David Cloud," he said.

"Davy," I repeated. "It was made clear to me that the name is Davy, not David."

"Doesn't matter," he said. "No Clouds at all."

"Okay, thanks, Sheriff."

"What are you going to do?" he asked.

"Beats me." I looked at him for a second. "What would you do?"

"You got a birthdate for Davy Cloud?"

"Day, month, but no year."

The sheriff snorted out a laugh. "Then I'd give up."

"You would?"

"I would."

"Thanks, Sheriff."

I LIKED THE sheriff's advice. It made complete sense to me and I would probably follow it because there was nothing more I knew to do. I could not drag my carcass all over Wyoming looking for someone who was probably really a carcass. But before admitting defeat I decided to go ask around on the reservation one more time. I felt guilty because my search was really half-assed. That was due to my complete incompetence and also a sheer lack of any fundamentally important information. All I had was an old photograph, and for all I knew the man in it was an actor.

I PARKED IN front of the little store at the flashing light. It was just starting to snow. I walked inside and grabbed a cup of coffee and walked up to the register. The same heavyset woman stood behind the counter.

"Remember me?" I asked.

"You were in here asking about Roberta Cloud."

"That's right. I found her. Thanks to you. Tell me, do you know Ms. Cloud?" I sipped my coffee.

"She used to come in more, but I haven't seen her in a long time. Why were you looking for her?"

"Wants me to find her son."

"Her son?"

"He's eighty-two years old."

The woman laughed.

"So, you don't know him."

"I didn't even know she had a son."

"Here's his picture. It was taken forty years ago, I think." I handed her the photograph.

"Never seen him."

"He doesn't look familiar to you?"

She shook her head.

"Like an actor?"

She studied the picture again. "Nope."

It pleased me that she didn't think he looked like anyone else. I put Davy Cloud back in my pocket. "My name's Jack."

"Delores."

"Delores, after Roberta, tell me who is the oldest person on the reservation?"

Delores looked at her feet and then out at the snow that was falling now in earnest. "It's going to be a mess," she said. "I'd guess that it would be Regina Shakespeare. I don't know how old she is, but she's almost as old as Roberta."

"Where is her house?"

"Last I heard she was living over on Yellow Calf Road."

"Where's that?"

"Off Seventeen Mile before Plunkett. Plunkett is where the tribal office is."

"Okay. How will I know her house?" I asked.

"Never been there."

"Thanks, Delores."

"Can I ask you a question?" Delores looked at my eyes. "Why are you doing all this?"

"I don't know. An old lady asked me to do something for her and I said I'd try."

"You could have said no," she said.

"I suppose I could have. But I didn't and here I am."

"You must have hurt somebody along the way, I guess."

"Excuse me?"

"You must be guilty about something."

I stared at her for a long few seconds. "Who isn't?"

I FOUND MY way to Yellow Calf Road. There were two houses on the dirt lane and they faced each other. On the porch of one lay a big black dog, a Doberman mix perhaps. The dog raised his head as I got out of my car and so I made the reasonable choice of trying the other house first. I walked through the deep yard and onto the narrow stoop. I knocked. I heard grunts first and immediately came barking as five or six dogs ranging from medium to huge came tearing around the corner of the house. They lunged while I tried to remain calm and slowly walk away. They did not chase me all the way to my car, but rather disappeared much as they had appeared. I looked across the road at the Doberman mix. His head was down again. I noticed smoke coming from the chimney pipe.

I walked to the other house and stepped onto the porch. The dog looked up at me and then closed his eyes. I knocked. A young man came to the door. He might have been in his midtwenties. He had two long braids that fell over his shoulders.

"I'm looking for Regina Shakespeare," I said.

"What do you want with her?"

"It's a long story, but I just want to ask her about Davy Cloud."

"Who's Davy Cloud?" he asked.

"Roberta Cloud's son."

"I didn't know she had a son. And who are you?"

"My name is Jack Keene. I'm a friend of Roberta."

"You can come in, but it won't do any good to speak to my great-grandmother. She's got Alzheimer's."

"I'm sorry," I said.

"She's in and out."

I stepped into the house. An old-fashioned wide-stance wood-stove kept the place very warm.

"Gammy," the man called her.

The woman sat in an old wheelchair. She didn't look up.

"Gammy, this man wants to ask you a question." He looked at me. "Go ahead."

"Ma'am, sorry to bother you, but do you recall someone named Davy Cloud? He's Roberta Cloud's son."

"Roberta Cloud," Regina Shakespeare said, surprising her great-grandson. "Why, she's even older than me." She let out a strong, throaty laugh.

"Do you know anything about her son?" I asked. "He'd be about your age."

"Alder wood pops too much, don't you think?" she said. She held up her index finger and smiled at the man. "What's this?"

"It's your finger, Gammy."

"Alder wood pops," she said.

The young man looked at me.

"Thanks for your time," I said.

"Sorry."

THE HIGHWAY WAS nasty as I drove back to Lander. The temperature had dropped suddenly and every curve looked like black ice to me. The snow was falling heavily now. I made it to a motel and lay in bed and did nothing. It was only Friday night and I had exhausted every avenue I could think of. I wondered what I was supposed to do for a week and then I remembered that if I waited a week Roberta Cloud would be dead. At least, she had told me she would be. I would have to go to her house the next morning and tell her that I had failed, that there was no way I could track down Davy.

I fell asleep wanting to dream about finding Davy Cloud, but I didn't. I dreamed about an old girlfriend that I'd never loved. And so I woke up in a bad mood.

THE WORLD WAS buried in snow on Saturday morning. My car along with it. I raked the windshield clear and then chipped and scraped off the ice. My fingers were numb when I started my engine. I returned to my room and let the car run for a while. I wanted the heat in the car and I wasn't sure if I could even shift and steer with my hands as frozen as they were. I snapped on the television for a weather report and there was Graham Greene talking to Val Kilmer in *Thunderheart*. Greene's character was complaining about Kilmer's character having a vision.

I FELL IN behind a snowplow on the highway and though it was slow going I felt more confident about the safety of the road. But that was short-lived as the plow turned around at the reservation border and I was left to push through six inches of snow with my Subaru.

There were a couple of cars and a pickup parked at Roberta Cloud's house. I tramped through the snow to her door and knocked. A young woman answered.

"Are you Mr. Keene?" she asked before I could say anything.

"I am."

"Come in." There were two other women inside the house and a tall man who drank from a large travel mug.

"What's going on?" I asked.

"She's dying," the man said.

"She's been asking for you," the woman who met me at the door said. "Who are you?"

"A friend," I said.

"Let's go then," she said. She led me into the room where Roberta Cloud lay on the bed under quilts.

"He's here, Roberta," the woman said and left.

"Mr. Keene, you're back." Her voice was so weak, so soft I could barely hear her from five feet away.

"Yes ma'am."

"I knew you would find my Davy. Davy, my Davy." Roberta Cloud reached out her hand. She was so weak that I thought I could feel her life slipping away.

I stepped close and took the old woman's hand. It felt like a baby bird. Her bones felt like nothing. I said nothing.

"Davy, my Davy," she whispered. "I've missed you so much. I love you."

I didn't make a sound. I rubbed the back of her little hand with my thumb.

"It's been too long," Roberta Cloud said. She said that several times until her voice just trailed off.

I watched her face. I felt her leave. I didn't even hear her last breath. She was just gone.

One of the women came in and I looked up at her. She left and I heard her tell the others that Roberta Cloud was no more. There was no crying. I let go of her hand and stood up. She looked peaceful. I toyed with the idea that I was partly responsible for that. I also felt terrible that I had lied to her. I told myself it was not exactly a lie. I had simply let her assume something. But of course I had lied.

I left the room and joined the others in the kitchen.

"So, who are you?" one of the women asked.

"Ms. Cloud asked me to come here and then asked me to find her son, her eighty-two-year-old son. I couldn't find him."

"That's because he died when he was a boy," the man said.

"Excuse me?"

"He would have been my great-uncle, I think," one of the women said. "Granduncle?"

I looked back at the bedroom.

"What did she say to you?" the woman from the door asked.

"She thought I was Davy," I said.

"And so you were," the man said. "So you were."

Harte Lake

Vanessa Hua

The last step was to unload the unnecessary weight. Anna Murata looked at the brilliant blue, not a cloud in the fall sky. She set down her backpack, removed the heavy rain pants, waterproof jacket, and wool socks, and tossed them into the backseat of her car. She strapped herself into the lightened load and set out on the trailhead at nine o'clock in the morning. Her destination was Harte Lake, elevation 9,500 feet, latitude 36 North, longitude 118 West. The date: October 10, the first anniversary of her husband Ken's death.

A year ago, as they pored over a map for their upcoming trip, Ken stopped talking midsentence and tumbled to the floor. She shook him, screamed his name, and crawled to the phone to call 911. While waiting for the paramedics, she put his head in her lap and straightened his glasses. She could not save him. She did not remember driving to the hospital, following the ambulance, parking their car, or filling out forms—only the moment when they were unable to revive him. An artery in his brain had burst. He was dead by the time the ambulance arrived, maybe by the time he hit the floor, and she was left alone after thirty years.

On this trip, Anna wanted to remember Ken as he was, on the last trek they were meant to take together. Out backpacking, they had depended on each other the most. She would spend three days on the twenty-four-mile loop, Friday through Sunday, following the itinerary and packing list he'd laid out. She'd grown more sluggish in the last year, but she vowed to push through the hike.

She put on his sweat-stained Cal baseball cap. They met at the university in 1969, squares among the hippies. Both their Japanese-American families had been forced into the internment camps during World War II. She and Ken met in one of the first classes in Asian-American Studies, and they were married the following year. They had stayed together for decades, despite—

or because of–the losses and betrayals they had inflicted upon each other, and that their country had once inflicted upon them.

She was more attractive at fifty-four than when she had been in her twenties–sturdy while others her age sagged. If she had once been beautiful, she might have mourned the loss of her youth, but her plainness had sustained her. She kept a garden behind her lemon-yellow Berkeley bungalow and ate cruciferous vegetables and whole grains, redeeming herself with these small virtues.

The first half-mile of the trail was flat, alternating between meadows and groves of trees before climbing steeply. Where the trail petered out, Anna checked the route against the topo map, trying to make sense of the rippling lines of elevation. Navigation was new to her; peering at maps with feigned interest, she'd always left it up to Ken.

Laughter and conversation came up fast behind her. She stepped to the side and a family passed by: a mother, a father, a teenage girl, and a young boy. They weren't going far, judging by their thin sandals, fanny-packs, and single bottle of water shared between them. The sandy-haired boy, maybe eight, with a narrow fox's face, trailed behind. He halted and picked up a stick, which he banged against the trees. After a few more steps, he used it to dig into the ground, flinging stones and clods.

His parents called for him–"Wyatt! Wyyy-at!"–and he dropped the stick and ran to catch up.

Anna waited until she could no longer see or hear them before she started walking. She picked up the stick and hurled it into the trees. She and Ken had no children. She'd mentioned the trip to a few friends but couldn't imagine them or her siblings coming with her. She had to take this hike alone. She pushed forward with two spring-loaded walking sticks. Although she used to disdain extra equipment as unnecessary coddling, her knees and back ached without them. The pack bit into her shoulders and pulled at her chest. Winded, she rested, took a long drink of water, and looked at the steep switchbacks up the mountain. Was this a mistake? She and Ken had trekked farther before, but she'd hit the trail later than she'd intended. She would have to hike faster or risk arriving at the campsite in the dark.

THE WINTER AFTER Ken died had been unusually rainy, and many sites were snowed in until late in the summer. Some had been closed for the entire season. She imagined the frozen campsites, never receiving the airy touch of spring nor the deep, still heat of summer nor the fading warmth of autumn. Come winter, fresh snow would fall on packed drifts untouched by the present. If she burrowed into the snow banks, what remained of the past would be hers.

Several times, Anna climbed over fallen trees, grabbing their branches and hoisting herself, then jumping or sliding down. Each time she landed, she wobbled for a moment. With each jolt, she could see a flash of Ken in motion–the way he knelt to weed a tomato plant, reached for a platter high up or pulled her head to his chest. She scraped the back of her knee on a tree. Wincing, she stopped to check the damage–two long scrapes, and a trickle of blood–when a ranger loped up from behind her and asked to see her wilderness permit. She turned around, showing where it was tied to her pack. He wore green shorts and a button-up shirt, with a hat clapped over a short brown ponytail. No wedding ring, and looked to be in his early twenties, with a scraggly goatee, which might have been an attempt to add a few years to his smooth baby face. Billy was embroidered on his shirt pocket. He needed nothing more than what fit into his small pack. Was endurance a test of how little you could survive on? Proof of how much you carried inside yourself?

"This is the best time of year to go," he said. "After the crowds are gone."

He said he was going into the backcountry for a few days, first to Pear Lake and then to Bodie Lake, to check the conditions. She realized that he might be the last person she would talk to for days, and she had to resist calling after him as he disappeared from view. That was the unspoken rule of backpacking: you kept to yourself. Each hiker strapped on forty pounds to escape the crowds, and the only permissible topic was trail conditions, asked in the most concise manner.

If the first day's hike wasn't too difficult, she might recommend it to the group that organized outdoor trips for girls, the latest in a series of non-profits where she had worked. From her messy cubicle, she did the books, cut the checks, and clamped down on expenses. Ken had been a partner at a big law firm in San Francisco. He always said that she did enough good for the both of them, though each recognized they could live well on his salary alone. In the year before he died, Anna had come to believe that her noble calling was nothing more than a hobby. She resented his compliments about her good deeds, but how could she ask him to stop? She poured water onto a handkerchief and wiped at the slashes on her leg. The thin scar would join the others from a lifetime of walking through brush.

Going uphill on the last stretch, she slipped in the dirt, her right ankle rolling to the side. Shit. She yelped, using her trekking poles to catch herself. She dropped her pack and sat down on a boulder. She massaged the tender ankle, flexing and moving it from side to side. Anna hobbled her way over the crest, stopping every few yards until her ankle felt steady again. She descended toward Harte Lake. This was her favorite part of every hike, when she caught the first glimpse of her destination. Here, Ken would move ahead, scouting for a campsite while she trailed behind. She had felt serene in the knowledge that he would find a safe, comfortable place for them. Even now, she could see his back, broad and muscled, exposed after he dropped his pack. The way his exquisite muscles rolled and pitched beneath his thin shirt. For a moment, she could not breathe, electrified by her desire.

She set up camp on a sloping patch of ground backed by pine trees. On the other side of the lake, a field of specked granite boulders led up the ridge. A flash of green–a tent? A bush. The solitude made her uneasy, and she had to admit that she had counted on there being neighbors who could help if anything went wrong. She assembled their battered two-person tent. The walls sagged, no matter how tight she staked the pegs, but it would have to do. Their routine had been for Ken to raise the tent and put on the rain fly, and for her to inflate the air mattresses and unfurl their sleeping bags. She eased her boot off her swollen ankle and slipped on a pair of Tevas.

Without the backpack, she felt lighter. She walked into the chilly lake, up to her knees, and washed off the grime. She trailed her hand in the water, watching the ripples spread to the other side of the lake. The luxury and dread of freedom opened before her.

Anna retreated into tasks. She grabbed the water filter from her backpack, and threw one end of the tube into the lake. She visualized the grit, giardia, and other foul microbes bunching against the filter, unable to reach her. Nothing tasted better than water that was out of reach of most people. She could pump all day, draining the lake.

To escape the thickening mosquitoes, she climbed into the tent. She probed her ankle, puffy and sore, and tightened the bandanna. She was drifting off when she heard a creature, a marmot maybe, knocking about her gear. It wasn't loud enough to be a bear. Hey, she shouted, hey, hey, and it shuffled off. Anna slept for an hour and awoke as the sun was starting to set. Alpenglow lit the granite above the lake gold-orange as she tried to start a fire, but the kindling flared and the logs never caught. She pictured Ken lighting the fire, and all the little tricks he did to get it going. Anna snapped a stick in half and threw the pieces in the pit. She was able to light the fire when he coached her. Why hadn't Ken been a better teacher? No. She had been a poor student, following without understanding or memorizing. She hated him for undermining her. For acting like he would always be there.

Anna gave up. She sat in the dark, waiting for her self-heating package of beef stew to warm. She took a few bites. Ken used to plan elaborate campfire meals—couscous and steak at dinner, burritos at breakfast—but she'd thought prepared ones would be easier. The noodles were slimy and the beef chunks smelled like dog food. She dug a hole, buried the rest, and went inside the tent.

She curled into a ball, holding herself in the sleeping bag, when she heard a plaintive animal cry in the distance. Like a baby's wail. Now, and on other nights since he died, she longed for the child that she never had with Ken. She regretted not having some part of him that would live on. Not the genetics of it, his re-born puckish dark eyes or dimples, which she could revisit in photographs and memories. She did not want a companion or a substitute, but someone else who had experienced him, in private, without the world intruding.

Two decades ago, she had miscarried. During the ultrasound, the doctor said he could no longer detect the baby's heartbeat, and soon sharp cramps turned her inside out. Gray clumps and bloody clots. Broken helpless incomplete unfit.

They were already picking names. Michiko. Emi. Hitomi. Keiko. Ken was sure the baby was a girl. Within months, Ken wanted to try again, to help them to start over. She miscarried again and yet again, four times in all, her body unable to hold onto a child. Did the babies know she feared their all-consuming need? She grew up in a family of seven and saw how her parents had lived for their sons and daughters, and no longer for each other. She did not want to share her husband's love. Ken, the only son in his generation of cousins, wanted a child of his own blood. Anna had tried, for him, but never longed for a baby.

They stopped having sex.

She recoiled when Ken stroked her cheek, his touch a reminder of her perceived failure as a woman, a wife, a mother. He began spending late nights at the office and going on weekend business trips. He took showers at night instead of in the morning. He confessed, after Anna found a crumpled receipt from a San Francisco bistro that she wanted to try out with him. She had liked the looks of its black awning and cheerful red and yellow storefront.

That was what wounded her: he had experienced what she wanted, with someone else. He was giving up on the life they were meant to have together.

WHEN SHE AWOKE the next morning, her ankle still throbbed. She decided against moving on and went for a walk around the lake. She saw no other hikers. She wondered what the solo ranger was doing. Meditating at sunrise, smoking pot at twilight, and bounding cross-country, his life ahead expanding, not narrowing.

With each step, she expected to see Ken round the bend to greet her. She grabbed a handful of trail mix, his favorite—coconut, dates, chocolate, and peanuts. She could hear his low, delighted *mmm-mmms*. She reached her hand out to the rough brown bark of the lodge-pole pine behind her. The solid bulk comforted her at first, and then she trembled and dropped her hand—sickened by its solitary life. The trees lived for hundreds of years, alone, dropping cones that needed a forest fire to explode them and release their seeds. Their survival depended on forces beyond their control.

At sunset, the wind stirred and Anna could see fast, faint clouds overhead. A storm was supposed to blow in on Tuesday, but she planned to be back home by Sunday evening. She would get an early start, gulp down a couple packets of oatmeal, power down the mountain, and take a late lunch at their favorite hamburger stand. She buried the rest of her dehydrated spaghetti dinner and climbed into the tent.

She nestled into her sleeping bag. She delighted in her aches, even the twinge in her ankle, proof that she had pushed herself to the limit. She was too excited to fall asleep, anticipating her return. What she had looked forward to the most—before she set foot on the trail, before she left her house in Berkeley—was to get through the trip. She only had to last until the next morning to prove that she could survive without him. In the year since Ken had died, she marked off special dates this way. His birthday, their wedding anniversary, Thanksgiving, and Christmas. She focused on the end rather than on experiencing the event itself. The day was speeded up, disregarded, and afterward she savored the accomplishment of getting through it.

IN THE MONTHS after she learned of his affair, they had pledged twice to make the marriage work. It fell apart each time. He could not forgive her for not wanting children, she knew. She could not forgive him for wanting more.

The other woman did not want a family, not until she made partner, and maybe not after, he told Anna. The knowledge burned her, to think that he might be with his lover if she had been willing to have children.

On the eve of their third and final reconciliation, they had camped in Desolation Wilderness. It was the first time they went backpacking in more than a year, after they began sleeping in separate bedrooms. They passed the first day with exceeding politeness, commenting on what they saw on the trail. They could agree on the beauty of a dead tree, struck by lightning, or discuss the geologic forces that shaped a granite peak, but could not talk about their past or their future.

At sunset, he said he was going for a walk around the lake. The low, slanting light turned him gold, his skin glowing and his black hair shining. He was hers to lose, she knew. He was almost gone.

"Back in awhile," he said.

"Wait."

He stopped and turned.

"Can you go by the store?"

"What do you want?" He had a half-smile on his face. An old joke of theirs, to ask for impossible foods in the middle of nowhere.

"Ice cream. Mocha fudge. With hot sauce."

"I'll do my best." He disappeared into the trees.

She put on her jacket and pulled out bags of couscous and dried mushrooms, and then packed and repacked their food in the bear canister, in the order of when they would eat it. She spent another fifteen minutes gathering twigs and fallen branches for the fire. Her busy work done, she walked to the edge of the lake. She could see Ken already on the other side, popping in and out of the bushes. She wished he would hurry. He returned a half hour later, his hands behind his back. He took out a capful of snow from a slow-melting patch under the trees.

"Will this do?"

She had scooped a loose handful, marveling at snow in June. "Thank you."

She put a careful measure on her tongue. He clapped his hands around hers, the heat melting the snow into rivulets between her fingers. Out in the wild, they would know nothing of a nuclear war, a terrorist attack, or an alien landing that ended civilization. They alone would hold onto the perfection of the world that existed before calamity. That night, inside the tent, they zipped the sleeping bags tight, past their heads and pulled the drawstring on the hood. The mummy bag bound their arms and legs. Although she could not see him in the darkness, she sensed him looking at her.

"This is all I have to give," she said.

He sighed. "This is all I need."

They kissed and rested their foreheads against each other.

IT WAS SILENT on the morning of her planned departure. Anna fumbled for her watch—8:30 a.m.! Usually, while camping she was up by 6:30 or 7 a.m., awakened by the discomfort of sleeping on the ground and her excitement to start the day. The light coming in seemed strange, though. Something on the roof made a spatter pattern, filtering kaleidoscope shadows—clumps of pine needles? And when she touched the side of the tent, it pushed back. She unzipped the tent door and poked out her head. She looked up. Was that volcanic ash falling through the sky? Or pollen? She reached her hand out to feel the cold wet flakes. Snow, drifting overnight to two feet or more around her. She had gone to sleep in a world of greens, blues, and browns, but now everything was white flurries. The sky was confusing, the color of dull, wet concrete. A light layer of snow covered her backpack, which sat under the tent vestibule. Her food was tucked in the bear canister, a hundred feet away.

She sat back, zipped the door shut, and sank into her sleeping bag to salvage the residual heat. Her stomach rumbled, and she scrounged in her pockets, where she found a half-eaten energy bar. They—she, now—had been lucky too long. She and Ken had gone over what to do in case of emergency. If a bear attacked? Stay on your feet for as long as possible, and then lie in a fetal position, using your backpack to protect vulnerable areas. Create a diversion by banging pots and pans. In a forest fire? Run into the lake or river. Take turns bobbing up to check when the fire has passed. Broken leg? Get the victim back to the tent, keep them warm and elevate the leg. Run like hell for help. And even, what to do in a snowstorm? Stay put, stay dry. Zip the sleeping bags together for warmth.

In each of the scenarios, Anna now realized, the plan involved both of them.

By early afternoon, the snowfall had lightened and cracks of blue broke through the clouds. The snow was now about three and a half feet deep, judging by the height next to the tent. Worried that conditions could worsen, she decided to hike out the eight miles. She'd leave behind her gear. Snow hid the trail, but she figured she would keep walking downhill. She struggled to break through the heavy, wet, snow, and within minutes she was exhausted and soaked. Her foot plunged into the powder and pain shot through her weak ankle. She pin-wheeled and fell. Panting, she willed herself to rise before her clothes were soaked. After a half hour and progressing only three hundred yards, she turned back.

She changed into dry clothes and huddled in her sleeping bag, trying to warm up, before she spent an hour digging for the bear canister, using the lid of a pot to dig through the snow. She thought of the stew that she had buried in disgust. Hunger dug at her. She made many false starts before she heard the dull thump of metal on plastic. Yes. She cradled the black canister in relief, her hands wet and stiff, scratched and bloody from the ice. Her ankles and feet were numb but she could still wiggle her toes.

Back in the tent, she upended the canister and poured out a packet of oatmeal, a few crumbs of trail mix, a couple of granola bars, scrapes of peanut butter, and one freeze-dried meal. She inhaled the musty, earthy smells of the trail mix and took a small handful.

She told herself that help was on the way, that it was an early winter storm that would soon pass and melt away. Besides, she had registered at the ranger station, indicating that she had set out from the trailhead three days ago. But—they did not know when she was returning. What if the rangers thought she was already gone? There was no one to expect her at home. A home that was starting to fall apart, without Ken's repairs; a home, in truth, that she did not know how much longer she could manage on her own.

NO ONE HAD been expecting her at home, the night she started her affair.

A decade after his betrayal and their reconciliation, Ken introduced her to the man who became her lover. He and Jack Olson, both playing singles at the Tilden Park golf course, had been paired up. The two lawyers had a beer at the clubhouse after their round, and Ken offered to take out Jack and his wife, Becky, who were both new to town. Ken and Anna were always looking for other childless couples who did not have to cut their evenings short because of the babysitter, who did not spend hours conversing about potty-training and summer camps.

Ken, Jack, and Anna were all in their forties. At twenty-eight, Becky seemed younger, favoring overalls and brightly colored clothes and ponytails. She was adopted from South Korea and raised in Minnesota, where she said there was one lake for every adoptee. Jack, the son of a Korean War veteran and his war bride, looked almost fully Asian, with a strong jaw and a faint tilt to his eyes. His Swedish origins were manifest in his height and his hair the color of dark honey.

The Olsons were always game for whatever Anna proposed, though she caught them giving each other quick looks, raised eyebrows and set mouths, resigned to the evening's adventures: Ethiopian food. Pilobolus dance. Kronos Quartet. It irked her that they tolerated, rather than enjoyed, her suggestions.

"Why don't you ask them what they'd like to do?" Ken asked.

"I do! But then they ask what we're up to," Anna said.

"Maybe that's all they want," he said. "For you to decide."

His refusal to take sides or judge others had maddened her more each year. It made her feel low, unkind for having an opinion. Long after his affair, Anna held a part of herself back. She would never give herself completely to him again, and this knowledge had protected her.

The old fears of Ken cheating returned in the presence of a younger woman. Anna studied them together: did their hands linger when passing the wine? Did they lean close when talking? But when Becky didn't understand a reference, it was Jack who smiled at Anna, their own little joke.

Becky had yet to find a teaching job because they were thinking of starting a family. "It wouldn't be right, to get hired, and then have a baby so quick." She could resume her career later, in a few years, after the kids were in school.

Jack called when his wife was visiting her parents and Ken was in New York on a business trip. "Why should we both eat frozen dinners?" he asked.

They went to an Italian trattoria, his pick, where the food was bland as she supposed he preferred.

She flushed in the candlelight, aware of his steady gaze. Afterward, he leaned down to kiss her by his car, hidden in the shadow of eucalyptus trees. In bed, she ran her fingers along his downy back, where the skin was young and smooth, in contrast to his weathered neck and his arms. For two decades, she had been with no one else besides Ken, and she reveled in discovering a new body. She stroked the hairless patch on his thigh, rubbed bare by blue jeans. This was also where she caressed Ken. Disorienting, to see the same purring effect on another man.

The thought of having children panicked Jack, she suspected, just as it had stricken her. He married a young wife to put off fatherhood and never suspected that Becky would be so eager to start trying. Anna had long tried to understand her husband's infidelity, and was learning through this deception. The first encounters were excitement and pleasure and discovery. Without commitment or expectations, you had none of the problems in your marriage. You despised the spouse you were cheating on and then blamed them for driving you away. She wanted Ken to see Jack look at her with longing. To remind him of what he had and of what he stood to lose. Ken was as powerless as she once was. As lacking.

EVERY FEW HOURS, she left the tent to dig the snow away from the sides and to pack it to shield the walls from the cutting wind. Snow slid into her boots, melting and soaking her feet. The wind knifed through her, each gust pushed her further past the limit of what she thought she could endure. Each slap was proof that her numb face could feel still more pain. Snow fell faster than she could keep it away. She feared the tent would break, collapsing into a blue shroud onto her face.

Stupid, stupid. Why did she leave behind her foul-weather gear?

She ran her tongue behind her teeth, across the roof of her mouth, but could summon no saliva. She tilted her water bottle back, desperate for a few drops. Unable to wait for the snow to melt in her bottle, she stumbled to the edge of the lake, where she broke through the crust of ice with a kick. She drank deeply, shuddering from the chill. For dinner, she ate a bit of dry oatmeal and a lick of peanut butter. Her stomach knotted in hunger, and she turned her head away from the dwindling food, resisting the temptation to eat it all. Now she regretted what she had wasted on this trip, the spilled trail mix and the two dinners she did not finish. She craved a vanilla milkshake, cheeseburger, and curly fries from Ikeda's, the roadside stand along I-80. And to share the meal with Ken, who let her eat his fries. Indulging her. At this, she wept, the tears stinging her marble cheek.

WEDNESDAY AFTERNOON, AFTER the storm let up, snow drifted higher next to the tent. As night fell, the temperatures dropped, and ice, her condensed breath, built up inside and outside of the tent. She tried to be still. When she touched the wall, ice fell and melted, making everything wetter. She'd never been so cold. She thought of her parents' bonfires, the heat billowing against her face and the flames blinding. They had died three years ago, within months of each other, her mother of stomach cancer, her father of a heart attack. They died without ever speaking of what happened at the government camps, with their barbed-wire fences and tarpaper barracks in the high desert. Searing summer heat. Bitter winter wind. Snow swirling on frozen mud. Pain swallowed. She had learned her silences from them, the silences that lengthened like shadows between her and Ken.

She rubbed her hands along her cheeks, her neck, her ribs, her thighs, and her feet, to check the wholeness of her body. Each breath, a second. Sixty breaths, a minute. It was impossible to judge how much time had passed. How much longer she would remain clenched. How close she was to dawn. She watched individual drops of water track down from the roof and along the side of the tent, wiggling snakes.

An airplane whined above. She ran out of the tent, waving her orange sleeping pad in the air, and shouting. She unscrewed her flashlight and held the mirror to the sky, trying to catch its attention. The airplane flew past. Too high. She staggered back. She was going to die. Snow would drift over the tent, and she would succumb to sleep. Hikers would find her body in the spring. Rotten, bloated, black—or the bones picked clean.

She tried to conjure specific memories of Ken. To bear witness. The first time they met in college, when he asked to borrow her notes. His shy smile. His concentration when he made gnocchi, the fat larvae falling off the spoon into boiling water. How defeated he looked after his father died.

SOME DETAILS, SHE will never forget.

Just before she began her affair, Anna had thought she was entering menopause. At forty-four, she suffered hot flashes and night sweats, and sometimes her period skipped a month or two. She was relieved that she would no longer have to deal with the monthly mess, awkward condoms or diaphragms.

When she went in for a check-up, her doctor told her that she was pregnant. Almost two and a half months along. A change-of-life baby, and she and her husband should consider genetic testing. Her husband. Judging from when the baby was conceived, it was not his. They had not slept together in October; they were down to having sex once a month or every other, and on special occasions.

She did not want to mislead Ken, to play father to a bastard, nor did she want to escape into a life with her lover that seemed much like the one she already had.

"You seem distracted," Ken said. They were in bed, spooning for a few minutes before sleep.

Her appointment for the procedure was the next day. She felt the baby roll and spin within, even though she knew it was impossible at this stage. Less than two inches long, but with a miniature brain, fingers and feet and lips and eyes—eyes!—beginning to develop. Her last chance to be a mother, to reverse the failure of her miscarriages a decade ago. Maybe Ken knew about the affair and was waiting for her to tell him. She imagined the bolt of anger ripping across his face. Her tears. She would have said she wanted to hurt him. To make things even. She was sorry and now knew that they belonged together.

"It's nothing," she said. Although she kept this secret to protect him, she hadn't realized it would distance them. How she would flee from him, over the years, into other rooms, for a walk, into the car for long drives. At times, she despised him for not guessing and leaving her heavy with this burden.

In the last year, she had come to wonder if Ken's early death was retribution. Why was he taken from her? A life for a life. It seemed the only reasonable explanation.

What if she had kept the baby and never told Ken who the father was? Her boy would have been nine this year. She had decided it would have been a boy. He may have even looked like Ken. He and her lover had the same broad shoulders and broad noses. She and her son would huddle to outlast the storm. Or her son, back with friends in the Bay Area, would alert authorities that she was lost in the snowstorm. Or the three of them would still be together. Ken, with a son, would be more cautious, would have gone in for more check-ups to catch the condition that killed him. But no. She had made different decisions that led to today.

Her attempts at an explanation were misguided, Anna had come to see. Foolish. Her miscarriage—divine will, or nature's? His affair—whose fault? Her affair? Her abortion? Impossible, to judge if her good intentions hit their mark, or the worth of her sin. She could not imagine who was keeping track, and why she would matter. Only this she knew: she would die alone.

FRIDAY AFTERNOON, A week after she set off on the trip, a helicopter whump-whump-whumps in the thin mountain air. Though it hasn't snowed again in the last day, the drifts remain too high for her to hike out. Weak as she is, she climbs out on wobbly legs. "Help, help!" She beats the pans together. The helicopter passes again overhead. It circles twice, and she knows she will be okay. She sinks to her knees. The reflected sunshine is blinding and beautiful. Snow glistens on tree branches and boulders, soft, fluffy, pristine, and harmless as cake frosting. The granite peaks in the distance are tipped in snow, in sharp relief against the sky, as if outlined with a black pen. A ladder falls down from the sky and a man helps her get in a basket. He wears mirrored sunglasses in which she can see a tiny haggard reflection of herself.

He extends a hand covered in a puffy blue glove and as she reaches up, she stumbles and falls against him. She feels the moist heat of his breath against her ear. "Easy now," he says. "We got you." Up, up they go, up the beanstalk, up the charmed rope into the sky.

Strapped into her seat, she gulps down an energy bar and a sports drink. The rescuer covers her with a blanket and slips headphones over her ears, so she can hear them above the shaking roar. Her fingers tingle painfully and her belly aches from the first food she's eaten in days. She wiggles her toes, rolls back her shoulders, and inhales deeply as her body returns. The men are talking about the lost ranger, who set off from the same trailhead. He is missing.

"Where to?" the pilot asks.

"Not sure. The ranger told the station that he was going to check out some lakes, and there's several in the area."

"I saw him," she says. "On the trail."

The rescuer turns to look at her. "What did you say?"

"I saw him. Billy."

"Where?"

"To Pear Lake. Then Bodie Lake."

He nods and points out to the right. The helicopter wheels back around, and she closes her eyes. Flagging them down took almost everything left in her, and the rumbling whirling is rocking her to sleep. She is slipping away when she hears him cry out—"There, there!"

A life saved. Surely, it must mean something.

Impressions of a Family

Cathy Warner

My father is dying. He's been dying all week. I knew it when I saw him today, opalescent and shrunken, bony in the white bed.

His wife, Janice, had called on Christmas Day to say he'd had another stroke after Thanksgiving. She hadn't wanted to bother me during the holidays, but one of his lungs collapsed and he contracted pneumonia. It wasn't urgent, she said.

"I can come down in a few days," I'd said.

"The boys are coming, too, on the twenty-eighth." She paused, and I could tell she was calculating how to squeeze all of us into the condo.

"Don't worry, I'll stay in a hotel. I was going to visit Jared soon anyway."

I'd hung up the phone, returned to the living room where my mother and grandmother arranged presents around my Christmas tree while Grandpa dozed. There was a box set aside for my son, Jared, and a small cluster of gifts for my sister, Hope, and her twins, just in case she called with an address.

"My father's had another stroke. I'm going to fly down," I'd said.

"That's too bad," my mother answered as she handed me a gift, looking not at all sorry. "All that drinking was bound to catch up with him."

I wished Janice had called sooner, but I've always been peripheral in my father's life. He left when I was eight, and I didn't hear from him again until he showed up at my high school graduation with Janice, his third wife. They've been married twenty-five years, and in their world I'm a comet, rarely in range.

People cluster near my father's bed, the center bed in the triple room at Golden Age Acres. Janice introduces Jared and me to two men, their wives, and a clump of kids perched on the end of the bed watching *The Price Is Right.* Luke and Mark, my half-brothers, are real estate agents from Great Falls, Montana, and products of my father's mystery decade. I've seen their photos displayed in the condo, but we haven't met before. Janice's youngest daughter, Lisa—my stepsister, I suppose—sits in the chair beside my father's bed. She is massively pregnant, and her four-year-old stands on her shrinking lap, with a spoonful of applesauce aimed toward my father's mouth.

"Open up, Grandpa," she says.

His lips part under the pressure of the spoon, but his eyes are vacant. He swallows like a gasping fish.

Janice leaves her place at my father's arm, and I shuffle in, nudging Jared in front of me. It's the first time Jared and I have been together since August when he moved in with his father, my ex-husband, to attend an arts high school.

I lean alongside Jared's shoulder, which tops mine now, and squeeze my father's flaccid hand. I remember it firm and huge, tugging me across Victory Boulevard into his appliance store, and capable of a killer slap.

"Hi, Dad." His eyes flick in my direction. "I brought Jared to see you."

"Hi, Grandpa." Jared inches closer and peers at his grandfather. The last time they met was almost a year and a half ago, after my father's first stroke, and Jared was pissed that he missed his first day of high school to visit some stupid stranger, as he put it.

My father lets go of my hand and reaches for Jared's. "Straight on 'til morning," he says, quoting Peter Pan, his voice hoarse.

I see their interlocked palms—pale and fading, strong and tan. The last time they held hands was also in a hospital. Jared's newborn fingers, tiny pearls, curled around my father's index finger, firm and golden. My father had driven the length of the state to meet his first-born grandchild, only to kiss us both, buy Jared a stuffed giraffe from the gift shop, then turn around and leave within twenty minutes.

I can tell Jared thinks I'm the only link between them, the one who holds them together. But I feel the inverse, the force with which their lives have forged me. First, my father's distance, cool as ice in a whiskey glass, even before he left, then Jared's infant need that demanded all my time, all my attention, all my wonder, and then evaporated before I was ready. I rest my hand on theirs for just a moment before Jared wriggles from our grip.

"I'm glad you came." I kiss Jared on the cheek as he backs away from the bed.

"I'll wait in the car," he says and leaves the room.

"Where's Tink?" my father asks.

"He's Peter Pan today," says Janice, patting my father's hand, explaining his lapses, as if I didn't know the story. She's been Pope-like, orchestrating today's reconciliation. "It's good you're here." She surveys the room. "Any word from Hope?"

"No."

Hope stopped talking to our father and Janice—mostly Janice, she's the verbalizer—when she was pregnant with the twins, and Janice was livid that Hope didn't marry the father. With our family history, it was probably just as well. She gradually dropped contact with the rest of us, most recently me, once I stopped sending her money. She's an alcoholic and gets evicted so often I can't find her anymore.

"You're sure?"

"Positive."

"That's just like your sister." Her mouth settles in disapproval.

After my audience, Janice's oldest daughter, Linda, ushers me to the activity room. She sits on a couch and I join her, next to an old woman trying to crochet and shaking uncontrollably. The scent of mock oranges through an open window help mask the odors of urine and pine cleaner.

"We need to talk about Dad's memorial," Linda says. "I want to serve salmon salad at the reception; he loves it. What do you think?"

"Fine with me."

I didn't know that my father likes fish or that before the stroke he and Janice ate a fish dinner at Linda's house every Friday, surrounded by grandkids. My father golfed with her husband every other Thursday. Linda knows his best friends from work and the homeowners' association, his favorite hymns, and that he wants to donate his body to UCLA Medical School. She's the daughter with the father I always wanted.

LUKE AND I stand in line at Taco Bell, assigned by Janice to bring dinner back to the condo.

"Dad was thinking about buying a summer place out our way. I showed him a little ranch he liked last spring." Luke wears boots with mud embedded in the lariat stitching. He drags his heel across the dirty tile.

"Were you born in Great Falls?" I ask.

"Mark was, but I was born in good old Burbank. We didn't move until 1965, after Dad sold the appliance store. I was four."

"Then you were born the same year as Hope," I say. "But Dad didn't leave us until '65."

Luke thrusts his fists in his pockets and looks at the floor. "My mother never said, but I always thought it was something like that."

"I'm sorry," I say, and I am. Sorry that we grew up with lies and unspoken fears and that my father never told all of the truth or apologized. Sorry that he used my mother, Hope and me, and Luke, Mark, and their mother as tester families until he got it right with Janice and her daughters.

"Water under the bridge." He smiles too brightly. "Anyway, things turned out okay for us."

We unload tacos and burritos in the kitchen. Janice looks satisfied and hums a tune that might be "Amazing Grace." I contemplate phoning my mother to reveal that my father's secret life began while they were still married. I imagine she is long past caring; that I am too.

I walk into the living room and sit on the arm of the couch next to Jared, who has his portfolio open on the coffee table.

"That's a lovely landscape," one of the Montana wives says. "Did you paint it from a photo?"

"No, it's home. I painted it from memory."

"You don't live in L.A.?"

"I do now, with my dad. But I used to live in Napa with my mom."

"Oh. Well, it's very impressionistic."

"Thanks. I was trying to capture reality in terms of the transient effects of light and color."

I can tell he's been waiting all semester to use that mouthful.

"I'd say it was a success. Who's your favorite painter?"

"Monet, Manet, Pissarro, any of the Impressionists, really. But for technical skill, I'd have to say Renoir."

"He's my favorite too."

"I read that Renoir always wore a hat when he painted. Do you know why?"

She pauses. "So he wouldn't get sunburned, I guess."

Jared laughs. "No. He thought the sun would damage his brain, and he wouldn't be able to distinguish between all the shades of gray."

I put a hand on his shoulder, my smart funny boy, and give him a quick squeeze.

JARED IS OFF for a day of skiing with friends in Big Bear when Janice calls my hotel room early the next morning. "The boys took their families to Disneyland, and I don't feel like being alone. Will you come over for coffee?"

"Of course." I don't feel like being alone either, but I was so glad to hear Jared had made friends that I didn't want to interrupt his ski plans.

Driving to the condo, I think back to when Don and I took Jared to Disneyland for his tenth birthday. We had a silent three-hour fight in the car on the way down after I insisted that Don accompany Jared into the men's bathroom at the rest stop on I-5. Don refused and waited at the door instead.

"You have to let him breathe. He's not going to disappear," he'd said.

I spent our day at "The Happiest Place on Earth" standing in line to buy popcorn and Cokes and holding Mickey Mouse sweatshirts and souvenir cups while Don and Jared went on rides that made me motion sick. When the three of us were finally closed into a car in the Haunted House, I had a fierce desire to clutch Don's hand, but kept it on the metal bar instead.

I think of Luke and Mark, arms wrapped tight around their wives' waists and clasping their children's hands as they herd them through Mr. Toad's Wild Ride, Snow White's Scary Adventures, and the Matterhorn. They will wave while the kids steer cars on the Tomorrowland Autopia, and pretend they can see around corners.

I ARRIVE AT the condo, drink coffee and read the *Times* while Janice returns calls from well-wishers. Her voice, sharp as her diamond cocktail ring, reports my father's temperature, food intake, and consciousness ratio, which she pegs at 15 percent. She talks about her grandchildren; how the nine-year-old wears eyeshadow, throws her hair back, and sings, "Hit me baby, one more time." The little kids insist on Lucky Charms and eat breakfast by the TV watching aliens with TV sets built into their stomachs.

"What is the world coming to?" She laughs, a pleasant sound, unlike my father's stern voice.

He called last Christmas just as Grandpa, Grandma, Mom, Jared, and I were sitting down to a turkey dinner.

"Well, how's the weather up there in Napa?" he'd said.

"We had a big storm blow through a few days ago. Six inches of rain."

"Uh, huh. It's been dry here, only a quarter inch this month. And the damn smog gets worse all the time."

"What are you and Janice up to?"

"Nothing much. We spent the weekend in Huntington Harbor with Lisa's in-laws. They've got a boat and took us around the canals looking at Christmas lights."

"That sounds like fun. How are– "

"Say, we're headed over to Linda's now. How's Jared?"

"He's doing great. In fact, his– "

"Good, good. Well, I just wanted to say Merry Christmas."

"Merry Christmas."

Of course my dinner was still hot. Conversations were always like that. Don used to tease me after I hung up frustrated. "Just the facts, ma'am," he'd say, like the detective on *Dragnet*.

Janice continues her calls. I write thank-you notes for flowers and lasagnas, prowl the hallway, and study the jumble of photos that give the impression that my father and Janice raised six of us. There's a sixteen-by-twenty-inch Olan Mills portrait taken several Easters ago of Luke, his wife, and two boys, Mark, his pregnant wife, and their toddler, all clad in pastels. Janice and my father smile in front of a Silver Anniversary banner. Don, Jared, and I hug Goofy outside Cinderella's castle at Disneyland on that tenth-birthday visit. Hope's date's hair is longer than hers at her senior prom. There's a framed color photocopy of a picture I took of Hope's gap-toothed twins posed at the door of their kindergarten. Linda, her husband, and their three kids relax on the beach alongside a giant sandcastle. Lisa and her husband kneel against a tree and balance their daughter on a red tricycle. A grainy sonogram of their imminent baby is tacked to the wall. I marvel at this fantasy family. What if we were real?

JANICE AND I join my father at the convalescent home shortly after ten. While my father sleeps in front of us, Janice rubs his bony feet through the thin blankets. We make small talk and greet visitors from work and the neighborhood.

"Oh, you're the teacher from Napa," they say. "Isn't your son the one who's attending the high school for the arts? He wants to be a painter, right?" I'm invariably surprised that they've heard of us.

An attendant brings in lunch. The curtains between beds are open, solids are returned to the kitchen in exchange for purees, and "Just one more bite" becomes a prayer, a family's tangible sign of hope. Janice feeds my father, though he seems barely conscious and there's nowhere for me to go. I feel trapped while he's helpless as a newborn bird, and with each meal less able to prove his love for her.

"He ate well, didn't he?" she asks.

"Yes," I lie.

Janice and I head to Mimi's Grill for our lunch, where she complains how appalling it is that Max's wife—Max is in one of the beds next to my father—has hired someone to sit with him at the hospital.

"Where is her loyalty?" Janice shakes her gray-streaked head. "I know it sounds trite, but money can't buy love."

"No, it can't," I say as I remember the birthday and Christmas checks my father sent after he reentered my life—always, it seemed, inside the least emotional greeting cards he could find. I pucker my lips around the straw in my iced tea.

"You know," Janice says as she slips her Mastercard underneath our ticket, "your father does love you and Jared. He's so proud of you both. He knows he hurt you, and he's sorry, truly." She dabs her napkin on her lips and reaches into her purse for her lipstick.

"Thank you for saying so," I answer, wondering if the sentiments are my father's or hers, or if the distinction even matters.

WE RETURN TO Golden Age just after five. I flip through a magazine and try not to watch while Janice feeds my semi-conscious father dinner and the paid sitter feeds Max; it seems an invasion of privacy. Bob, in the far corner, surrounded by his small family, eats nothing.

We stay, and I rest a tentative hand on my father's foot through the blankets while we pretend to watch a little television with him, though he hasn't opened his eyes since dinner. At seven-thirty, Janice decides it's time for us to leave.

"Sweet dreams, Dad," I say, shouldering my purse.

She kisses him goodnight and slips an ice chip down his throat.

AFTER HIS SKI trip, I lure Jared to the Best Western with the promise of all-you-can-eat pizza and R-rated in-room movies. When I pick him up, Don's new wife, Rhonda, answers the door, wearing designer sweats. She fills the doorframe with her big hair, big teeth, and big breasts. "You're early, Jared's in the shower." She pauses. "Won't you come in?"

"Thanks."

We'd both prefer that I wait outside, but it's dark and sprinkling and that wouldn't be civil, and we try to be the poster family for modern divorce.

A naked Christmas tree and three full Hefty bags sit in the entry.

"Excuse the mess. I don't have everything back in order yet."

"What's the rush?"

"The new millennium." She pauses for me to add a mental duh. "We're having a huge New Year's Eve party. Stop by if you get a chance," she says, knowing I will decline.

Jared takes the stairs two at a time, stepping around boxes of ornaments. He's carrying his portfolio on one shoulder. His wet curls glisten.

"Hi, Honey."

"Hey, Mom."

After he's eaten seven slices of pizza, and about eighty-seven people are killed in Jean-Claude Van Damme's latest movie, I ask Jared how he likes living in L.A. Instead of answering directly, he spreads his portfolio over one of the beds. He's done dozens of sketches and almost as many paintings this semester. He holds each piece, framing it with his delicate fingers.

"There are five principles of organization," he explains as if he's giving a school report. "Balance, movement, contrast, emphasis, and harmony."

He has me compare a series of charcoal sketches, and we determine that I favor irregular rhythm, and asymmetrical over radial or formal balance.

"You're catching on, Mom. Now, there are five basic elements of design: line, shape, color, texture, and space."

I study watercolor, oil, and pastel renditions of the same still life until I can correctly identify realistic from abstract shape, dark from light values, actual from simulated texture, and positive versus negative space.

He shows me an experiment in Pointillism. "Everything is made up of tiny dots using only primary and secondary colors. What do you think?"

"It feels static." I do my best to sound like an art critic and not a mother who wants to snatch her son back for purely selfish reasons.

"Exactly. The precision of color sucks all the life out of it. That's why I like Impressionism. This is my favorite." He holds up the painting of our yard in Napa.

From across the room I see everything clearly, the dilapidated barn, the almonds and magnolia in flower, chickens pecking near the pond. When I come close, the images blur and become indistinct. They could be anything.

Jared falls asleep while I floss my teeth. He's sprawled across the bed-spread, face down, elbows angled under a pillow, legs arranged like the number four. I pull a corner of the bedspread over him, sit on the bed's edge and rest a hand on his back, feeling the shallow rise and fall.

When he was a baby, Jared couldn't fall asleep without my hand on the round of his back. Until he was three, I eased him into his crib after our ritual rocking and countless verses of "Bye Bye Baby Bunting." I stood for long minutes with my hand across his spine waiting for the breath of sleep. Gradually, I retracted my hand into the space above him, feeling the connection between us diminish. Finally, I'd turn to tiptoe away, but often he sensed me move, and I'd repeat the process again. I was everything he wanted, and everything I could give him was enough.

But I wonder now if that was ever completely true. Because Don was there, too, often taking my place on the second and third rounds of hand-on-the-back sneak-away. My marriage is over, but Don did not evaporate from Jared's life the way my father evaporated from mine. My son has a father whose love is visible and present.

I lift my hand and crawl into my bed. Jared doesn't move.

JARED LIKES ME this morning and asks me to take him to the Rose Parade tomorrow. "It's an awesome study in color and line."

"It depends." I park on the street.

"I mean, if Grandpa doesn't kick off tonight."

"That's rude." I open my door.

"Sorry." Jared shrugs.

"But it's also true."

Don is a landscape architect who specializes in ripping out lawns and flowerbeds and replacing them with gravel. He calls it xeriscape. This morning he is washing his truck with some eco product from a spray bottle, no hose in sight. He pretends not to see me while I walk to the front door with Jared's portfolio while they talk.

"Dad said okay."

"Great. I'll call you."

"I love you, Mom." He hugs me.

I hug too hard. He bounces into the house.

I walk toward Don who looks up, rag and spray bottle in his hands. "I'll probably be over really early tomorrow," I say. "I hope it won't interfere with your New Year's plans."

"It's fine. It'll be good for the two of you. Jared won't say it, but he misses you."

I nod. "He seems happy here. I'm glad."

"I'm sorry about your dad."

"Thanks."

"I never liked him." He smiles, quick and sad, a lapse in the usual reserve.

"I know. Thank you for that." I return the smile and remember the afternoon I told Don about my father.

"What kind of scumbag runs out on his family?" he'd asked while we were twined in bed. "I will never leave my family. When I get married, it will last forever." It was a proposal, a confession, and an opportunity for someone to hate my father for me.

AFTER TAKING SHIFTS at the Golden Age with my fading father, we gather for New Year's Eve at the condo. Linda supervises cookie-making with the kids in the kitchen. Lisa, feet up in a recliner, discusses pregnancy aches with the Montana wives. Luke and Mark make a grocery run to Von's, and Janice and I borrow folding chairs from the clubhouse. The adults have a chatty dinner, packed in the dining room, while the kids take over the living room. We eat green salad from bags, pre-made garlic bread, and the sympathy lasagnas. It's a reunion-like atmosphere, punctuated with awkward silence when we remember why we're gathered. We talk about everything, except my father.

Later, the kids want to play charades or Pictionary, but Janice decides games are too festive, and we watch a colorized version of *It's a Wonderful Life* instead. There's sniffling at the end when the townsfolk pay homage to Jimmy Stewart's principled and self-sacrificing George Bailey, and Linda passes around Kleenex. I step onto the balcony and stay outside until I'm chilled. I can't help but think of my father. Would I have been better off without him? What about his second family? If he could choose to live over, would he head straight to Janice?

The kids clamor to stay up until midnight, but the rest of us lack celebratory spirit. At eleven—it's midnight in Montana the grownups say—we open three bottles of sparkling cider and one of champagne, which is left untouched either in deference to my father's twenty-six years of white-knuckled sobriety (no Twelve Steps for him), or fear that if alcoholism is genetic it will kick in tonight. We toast and sing "Auld Lang Syne" while the kids bang pots and pans on the balcony.

JARED IS A kid who sticks to his New Year's Resolutions. "What did you resolve, Mommy?" he used to ask, showing me his crayoned list.

"Nothing." I'd reply. No resolution, no failure.

This year it's different. Alone in my hotel room, I can't sleep. There's a party in the hotel lobby, firecrackers in the street, and a new century ready to impact me. I take a sheet of stationery from the bedside table, place it on the Gideon's Bible, and write resolutions for the first time in ages:

I will learn how to mother from five hundred miles away.

I will stop punishing Jared for leaving me. Becoming independent is his job.

I will keep in touch with Janice after my father dies.

I will think of one good thing to say about my father at his memorial service.

I will try to appreciate Rhonda and her love for Jared.

I will forgive Don for being human enough to leave after I kept pushing him away.

I want to write something about coming to understand in a deep way the difference between being alone and being abandoned, but I can't figure out how to phrase it. I fall asleep with pen in hand and wake at four to my alarm.

JARED AND I are crowded and freezing on Colorado Boulevard waiting for the Rose Parade in the pre-dawn, huddled in sleeping bags on lawn chairs culled from Don's garage and clutching my father's promotional thermoses, filled with cocoa. Jared sings Christmas carols to keep his teeth from chattering. I pull the sleeping bag over my ears and watch his breath steam the air.

"Close your eyes," he says.

I obey and hear him open the ice chest and clunk around. I burrow further into the flannel. It smells faintly of Don's aftershave. I drift into the scent and scenes I don't often let myself recall. My unspoken *don't leave me* breathed into his neck, his chest, when we'd save our disagreements for the cover of night and the shelter of bodies.

"Okay. You can look."

I open my eyes to dawn and Jared holding a black plastic plate arrayed with crab puffs, sushi, and ruffle-cut radishes, and a plastic champagne flute filled with orange juice and a strawberry. "Compliments of Rhonda."

"Hold on." I fish a bag of Winchell's donuts from my purse and add them to the spread. "Happy New Year!" I raise my flute. We toast with a plastic *click*.

"Art school's pretty great, isn't it?" I say to my pink-cheeked grinning son.

"Yeah." Jared snaps a radish and chases it with jelly donut.

"I'm glad you're here." I sip the juice. "Not glad, exactly, but happy for you. I'm sorry I blew up when you wanted to come." I'd been nasty, saying he was just like his dad and my father sliding from one family to another when it was convenient. "I never meant a word of it. I want you to be happy."

Jared chews and nods.

"Leaving is what growing up is all about. This is where you should be now. Forgive me?"

"It's okay, Mom." He wipes his nose on his sweatshirt sleeve.

"I have this idea," I say. "How about the two of us drive to Chicago this summer? We can check out the Art Institute."

"Really? That would be so awesome."

"Really." We clink again.

THE NEXT MORNING, there's an empty bed, freshly made in my father's room. All that remains of Bob is a stack of photos on the tray-table at the foot of his bed.

Our leave-taking begins. My father lingers in his netherworld, and his assorted children must return to their lives. "Call us for the memorial," we tell Janice and Linda. Janice says she'll copy our addresses, so we can keep in touch. "Great," we say between hugs and handshakes, and we mean it, for another few weeks, until the reason our lives collided no longer exists.

My plane departs in a few hours and Janice leaves for a few minutes after she feeds my father lunch, so I can be alone with him. I'd blurted "I love you" instantly upon my arrival last year after the first stroke, scared by the tubes in his nose. He was startled, but answered, "I know, and I love you too." That settled, there wasn't much left to say.

Today his eyes are closed and I imagine his mind is far away. He breathes roughly and floats in his Neverland. I kiss his cheek, hollow and too soft, not the sandpaper I remember, and pull the chair close to the bed. I reach for his bruised veiny hand and scrape my mind for other memories.

There are fragments: sitting in his lap while he read the *Herald Examiner* and drank scotch and soda until he passed out. Being spanked for finding the *Playboys* he hid in the bathroom. The time my sister and I sat at the dining-room table in our party dresses and Mary Janes until midnight waiting to shout, "Surprise" on his birthday, while Mom rotated dinner from oven to table and back and dabbed her eyes with her apron. All memories his absence would eclipse, except one, my eighth birthday. He bought me a Bobby Vinton album and plastic record player and told me how I almost died at birth and how he, giddy with relief after hours of praying to a God he wasn't sure existed, took me in his arms and named me.

He left two days later.

I take a long look at this man, my illusive father who won't speak my name again, and decide I'll ignore much of his life. What will I remember? That he phoned on my birthday and Christmas, that I called on his birthday, Easter, and Thanksgiving, sent vacation photos and Jared's school pictures, and still remained outside his orbit? I tell myself he was scared of his past, afraid to risk forgiveness, so he withdrew, the way I did with Don and almost repeated with Jared.

His hand is cool and still as I close my eyes. There will be no deathbed apology, no confession, no declaration of love from him. I will never hear his voice again. A tear slides down my cheek. Mine will be the last words between us.

"I've missed you, Dad, but I love you, and I know you love me," I remind us as I snuffle. My shoulders quiver and my pulse quickens. I think about telling him that I know he did the best he could when I was young, but those words don't feel quite right. "You couldn't do any better back then," I say. "And later, neither of us could bridge the gap. But we each tried, in our own way." I squeeze his hand. "Let's forgive each other, Dad. Okay?" I feel the slightest flutter of his fingers and then he is still.

When Janice returns, I kiss her and my motionless father one last time, retrieve my purse, blot my eyes with Kleenex, and fumble through the curtain separating the beds. Heading for the door, I see Max staring in the vicinity of the television. A soap opera airs, on screen people recover from brain tumors today only to be shot next week. Max's lunch tray is untouched. His sitter is nowhere to be seen, and the nurses, too busy to feed patients, eventually return uneaten meals to the kitchen. My temples throb as I step toward his bed.

"Hi, Max. I'm Faith. Are you hungry?"

He looks at me.

"I thought I could feed you lunch, if you're hungry. Is that okay?" I hold a spoonful of pureed peas in the air.

Max looks at me vaguely and opens his mouth.

The Intricacies of Post-Shooting Etiquette

Brian Evenson

I

One winter morning, watching Bein read his breakfast paper, Kohke decided to kill him. He stood behind Bein, aligned a pistol barrel with Bein's skull and worked the trigger. He had reasons for wanting Bein dead, but watching his lover shake about the floor, smearing blood on the linoleum, he could not bring those reasons to mind.

The pistol must have wavered when he pulled the trigger, for Bein did not seem to be dying properly. After a writhing agony he fell still, attempting to catch his breath. And then, calmly, he asked Kohke to call an ambulance.

Unable to bear the thought of shooting Bein again, Kohke carried the pistol from room to room, finally submerging it in a pitcher of orange juice. He telephoned for help. Paramedics arrived, the police alongside. The first extracted Bein. The second discovered the pistol, remanded Kohke to custody.

In an interiorly-mirrored room, Kohke began to lie. He had not known the gun was loaded. He had pointed it at Bein only as a prank. He had thought it a novelty cigarette lighter, not a real gun. He lied even about matters of no consequence. Slowly the lies accumulated, crowding each other awkwardly. Yet, when the police received word that Bein, rolling into surgery, had absolved Kohke of blame, they grudgingly released him.

IN THIS FASHION a measure of uncertainty slipped into Kohke and Bein's relationship. Never having shot anyone close to him before, Kohke had difficulty unraveling post-shooting etiquette. Was the relation terminated?

Kohke wondered, as he waited for Bein's release. Could they be said, now, properly, to have a relationship? Had the shooting freed him of sexual and emotional obligation to Bein? Or had any potential release been countermanded by Bein's refusal to blame him?

What, wondered Kohke, did Bein actually know? Officially the shooting was classified as an accident. Perhaps even Bein himself believed it to be an accident: after all, he had not seen Kohke pull the trigger. *Or perhaps,* thought Kohke, *Bein has only classified it such so as to be able, later, to avenge himself against me.*

ALONE IN THE large bed, beset with uncertainty, Kohke had trouble sleeping. He would awaken, the stench of gunpowder strong in his nostrils, feeling he had been shot. The day after the accident he contemplated visiting Bein in the hospital, but he could not bear to see Bein so soon, partly from shame, partly from fear of violating post-shooting etiquette. How does one apologize for shooting someone? *Sorry to have shot you, Bein* didn't ring properly, but neither did *My apologies for the accident, Bein*. On the second day, he stayed away because he could develop no convincing lie to justify his first-day's absence. By the third day, the pattern was fixed. Visiting Bein now would seem unusual.

He kept himself apprised, bribing an intern named Chur to provide him daily reports. It was from Chur he learned of Bein's transfer from critical to stable condition. From Chur, he learned that bullet fragments had lodged in Bein's brain, causing blindness. He was told that the second bullet–

"The second what?" asked Kohke.

"Bullet," said Chur.

"Bullet?"

"Yes, of course," said Chur. "Mr. Kohke, you fired twice."

Second bullet? He had no memory of firing a second bullet. Indeed, just the opposite: he remembered shooting once and not again. How had he managed to blot out this second bullet which, according to Chur, had rendered Bein immobile, paralyzed from the neck down?

Presenting himself at the police station, he asked to examine his arrest report. The sergeant assigned to the case chatted at him idly while Kohke thumbed through the file. Yes, he saw, there had been two bullet wounds, one in Bein's skull, the second in his back. Two cartridges were absent from the orange juice-drenched pistol. He had fired twice. His body had pulled the trigger while his mind remained at a safe remove.

RESEARCH LED HIM to understand where he had gone wrong. The caliber of the pistol he had found in Bein's top drawer had been woefully inadequate. It was, he learned during an awkward park bench conversation with a war veteran, more appropriate for the slaughter of dogs, small children.

The police had the gun now. Despite his awkward success soliciting the veteran in the park, Kohke could not imagine entering a munitions shop to purchase a more powerful weapon. It went contrary to his character. Nor would the police so easily excuse a second incident.

Perhaps, he thought, *the relationship has successfully terminated and I will never see Bein again*. Or perhaps when Bein did come home, crippled, he would prove a different man. A so-called *new man*. Then, the circumstances that had culminated in the shooting would not accumulate again. Yet even in the best of circumstances, Kohke was not certain he could bear living with a man he himself had crippled.

IN THE MIDST of such reflections, the hospital telephoned. Bein would be released in four days. He had requested that Mr. Kohke take him home. Was Mr. Kohke willing to accept responsibility for Mr. Bein?

No, he said, *all apologies*, and recradled the headpiece.

He sat beside the telephone, scrutinizing the pale lampshade. Apparently the relationship was not terminated after all, but continued to limp on.

It would look suspicious both to Bein and to the police if he refused to take Bein in. He could ill afford suspicion. He had been hasty, foolish.

Holding his hand out to the lampshade, he greeted it enthusiastically.

Getting up, he went to look at himself in the mirror. In the glass he could still perceive the old, pre-shooting Kohke, largely intact. *Hail, fellow*, he thought.

"Bein," he said to the mirror. "What a pleasure to see you again."

Watching his face as he said it, he saw no revelation of anything, let alone guilt. Surely Bein, blinded, would notice less than he. He closed his eyes.

"How was your stay?" he heard his voice smoothly say. "I must apologize for not visiting. I had been informed that healing takes place more rapidly in solitude."

I will keep him off balance, he told himself. *I will give nothing away. I will maintain the upper hand.*

II

HE COULD NOT imagine rolling Bein's wheelchair over and over the spot where Bein had been shot. Yet he was concerned that moving would excite his suspicions, allowing Bein to gain the upper hand. Compromising, he rented a new apartment in the same building—one floor lower than the original apartment but identical in every other respect: three dusty rooms, doors sufficiently wide to admit Bein's wheelchair, the final room with a window opening on an airshaft.

At the appointed day's appointed hour, he walked to the hospital. Bein was slumped in the circular drive in his wheelchair, a nurse posted beside him. *You're Mr. Kohke?* she asked as he approached. He nodded. *Kohke?* said Bein.

Kohke nodded again. "Hello, Bein."

"What's wrong?" asked Bein, face squinching.

"Not a thing," said Kohke.

"I don't want to go home with him," Bein said to the circular drive.

"Nonsense," said the nurse.

"I didn't think you'd come," said Bein. "Why did you?"

"I'll leave you two alone now," said the nurse, smiling grimly, then slipping away.

"Well, shall we set off?" asked Kohke, briskly jabbing the wheelchair apartmentward.

They traveled several rugged blocks without speaking. As they passed other people, Bein would turn his head, directing one ear or the other toward their voices. *His ear is his eye*, thought Kohke, listening to the faint clack of the wheels.

"What's wrong?" Bein asked again.

"Nothing," said Kohke.

"Why do you do this?"

"Do what?"

"Refuse to share your feelings with me."

"Bein," said Kohke. "I beg you."

When Bein wouldn't stop speaking, Kohke set the brakes on the wheelchair and abandoned him. He crossed the street and looked at Bein from the other side, watching the foot traffic flow around his lover. He could hear the sound of Bein's voice, see his lips move, but could make out none of what the voice was saying. He stayed, waiting for the moment when Bein would realize he was no longer present.

Was there a way to end the relationship immediately? Could he abandon Bein on the corner?

He stood watching Bein's mouth move until he could not bear it, then watched instead Bein's wheelchair, and finally turned to watch the traffic light as it turned, then turned, then turned again.

WHEN HE LOOKED away from the traffic light, it was growing dark. Bein was just as Kohke had left him, still slumped in his chair.

"You came back," said Bein, as Kohke affixed his hands to the grips. Kohke employed a bright voice to respond, the same voice he employed with dogs and small children: "Of course I came back." Reaching down, he levered the brakes off, began to rotate the chair about.

"We're going back?" asked Bein, pale eyes staring not at Kohke but above him, at Kohke's nonexistent hat.

"Back?"

"To the hospital."

"You've been released, Bein. You can't go back."

"Where am I to go?"

Kohke did not answer. He began to push his lover down the sidewalk, clicking over cracks until they reached the apartment building. Holding tight to the chair's vulcanized grips, he took Bein up the steps backwards, drawing the chair up a tread at a time, shaking him, regressing a few treads, turning the wheelchair about until he was convinced Bein would be unsure of how many flights they had mounted. Then he was at the door and had opened the door and they were both in.

"Welcome home," he said. He lifted his ex-lover out of his chair and into the bed.

"This is my bed?" Bein asked. "It doesn't feel like my bed."

"Nothing feels the same after you've been shot, Bein."

"How would you know?"

"That's just what they say."

"We're not going back to the hospital?"

He could not bear Bein's face up close. Kohke kept casting his gaze about, finally letting it rest upon the buttons of Bein's shirt, a string of tiny, bland faces.

"No," said Kohke to the buttons. "You're done with the hospital. You're home now."

Bein turned his head slightly, dimpling the pillow's case. "Take me back."

Kohke left the room, went to the kitchen. He was thirsty. The refrigerator was unplugged. When he opened it he found that the air inside had turned. He plugged the refrigerator in, closed it.

He listened to the hum of the refrigerator. He could hear Bein's voice abuzz in the bedroom, still speaking. He could not hear what he was saying. He went back, stood with crossed arms in Bein's doorway.

Bein fell silent, whorling one of his ears toward Kohke. He stayed like that, motionless, regarding him with his ear, as Kohke grew uncomfortable.

"What is it?"

"It doesn't feel right," said Bein.

"Don't be crazy," Kohke said.

"What's changed?"

"Nothing. It's all the same."

"It doesn't feel the same."

Kohke went back into the kitchen. He wandered all around the kitchen and then left the apartment. There was the hall, the floorboards brightly polished and throwing light up against his shoes. There was the light switch, apparently innocuous, the paint worn thin upon it. He went back into the kitchen, looked at the refrigerator until he couldn't stand to look any longer. Thirsty, he opened it, found it empty.

He went back to Bein's room. Standing in the doorway, he watched him. Slowly, Bein smiled.

"The sea," said Bein. "I no longer hear the sea."

THE SEA, THOUGHT Kohke later, sitting in the hall just outside the apartment. *What sea?* There was no sea. They were hundreds of miles from the ocean, there was no river or other water within sight or hearing of the apartment. The bullets had damaged Bein's thinking as well as his vision.

"The sea?" he had repeated, standing before Bein.

"Yes," said Bein. "I don't hear it . "

"I don't recall having heard a sea," Kohke carefully stated.

"You wouldn't," said Bein.

"What is that supposed to mean?"

"Is the window open?" asked Bein. "Open the window and you'll hear it."

Kohke looked back at the window leading into the airshaft. "I have to go to work," said Kohke. "I can't bother with that now."

"Work?" asked Bein. "You, work?"

"I've changed, Bein," lied Kohke, "I really have. I'm a new Kohke."

Bein contorted his face in a fashion the meaning of which Kohke found difficult to determine. Backing his way to the front door, he left.

ON A PARK bench, ogled by a veteran whose hands fumbled deep within his pockets, Kohke considered life with Bein. Bein had come home with him, which Kohke reluctantly classified as *promising*. Bein had mentioned nothing about the murder attempt, had not blamed him. Also *promising*—unless Bein's silence was seen as biding his time so as to exact his revenge. Yet how, he asked himself, could a paralyzed man take revenge? *Disappointing*, though not yet *cause for alarm*, Bein sensed the wrongness of the apartment, felt despite the identical floorplan that he was not at home. Such wrongness, Kohke suspected, could lead to recognition of other wrongnesses, and must be corrected.

Yet the sea? What was this talk of the sea? How could it be classified?

Deserting the bench he returned to the apartment building, borrowed the key for his former apartment from the manager. He went from room to room, listening, first with windows closed, then with windows open, then some opened, some closed. He turned on the water, listened to the pipes tick. He was unable to identify any sound that even remotely recalled the sea. He stood on his toes, squatted down. There was, he saw when crouched, a faint rust of Bein's blood still marring the pebbling of the linoleum. Hurriedly, he left.

Bein's brain must have fused two memories, dredging a past sea into his present life, or simply evoking water from empty air. *The sea*, he told himself, returning the key between thumb and forefinger to the manager. *He wants the sea. The sea is what he'll have.*

III

HE PURCHASED A tape recorder and a cassette series entitled *The Soothing Power of Nature*. In the back room, he opened the window, plugged the recorder in, set it on the sill. The cellophane crackled stiffly coming off *The Soothing Power of Nature*. He dropped the cassettes into the airshaft, except for one, marked *Aqua Vitae*, which he inserted into the machine.

When he pressed play, he heard a short feed of blank tape, then the sound of waves. He listened for a time, set the recorder to play continuously.

BEIN WAS LYING on the bed, his head sunk deep into the pillow, his blind eyes wandering the upper rim of his orbits.

"Good morning," said Kohke. "How are we today?"

"Give me to someone else," said Bein.

"We don't know what we're saying this morning," said Kohke, his voice cheery. "Do we?"

"One of us doesn't," said Bein.

Kohke positioned the wheelchair next to the bed, tugged Bein over until he was beside it. He forced Bein's feet onto the floor. Slipping his arms around Bein's chest, he locked them behind his back. He heaved Bein up, dropped him into the chair.

"No need getting dressed today," Kohke said. "We won't go out."

Wheeling Bein to the table, he began to feed him. Bein chewed, then sat awaiting the next bite, mouth ajar. Kohke poured him a glass of orange juice, expecting to see the pistol's snub as the juice in the pitcher drained away. He clacked the glass's rim against Bein's teeth.

" I hear it now," said Kohke as Bein swallowed.

"Hear what?"

"The sea," he said. "I hear the sea."

"Sea?" said Bein. "What do you mean?" And, once Kohke wheeled him back, pushed him back into the bed: "You're hearing things, Kohke. Imagine that."

THE CASSETTE RAN nearly constantly. Despite Kohke's efforts at preservation, it acquired a dull hiss, degenerated into a sound hardly recognizable as water. It had been a mistake to buy the tape, to try to simulate something that hadn't existed in the first place. Yet, now that it was done, Kohke felt he had committed himself.

Oddly, as the tape deteriorated Bein perked up, claimed to recognize what he heard as waves. Kohke could not tell if Bein was toying with him or if, somehow, he heard it now. Perhaps it was simply whatever dementia that had first caused Bein to believe the sea existed had now returned. It had all gone wrong, Kohke felt, and there was no putting things right. Better to let the tape run down to its own extinction.

This was how Kohke came to identify the waning of his relationship with Bein. When the tape snapped, the relation would end and he would be free of Bein. He wasn't certain how this end would occur, but he was certain it would.

Bein began begging Kohke to take him down to the sea. He wanted to touch the water's edge.

"You wouldn't feel it," said Kohke. "No point."

No, insisted Bein, his face would feel it. He wanted Kohke to carry him down to feel the breeze, then out into the water in his arms. They would walk out until Bein's face was floating, licked by the waves.

"Like a lily," Bein said.

I can't stand it, thought Kohke.

He was tied to Bein, obligated to him until the tape broke. Still, there were distractions. There was the veteran in the park with his fluid and somewhat inarticulate consolations. It was better than nothing, though all the while he thought of Bein alone in the apartment, the tape winding slowly down. There was shopping, his imaginary job, other excuses. Yet each time he went back he found the situation less bearable.

He considered simply leaving, abandoning Bein, letting him starve to death, though he worried the neighbors would hear Bein's cries and rescue him. When he had nearly worked up sufficient nerve to desert Bein, the hospital called, inquired after Bein's condition. How was Mr. Bein recovering? Was there anything they could do? They would call again, the intern said. It made Kohke feel he was under observation. *A courtesy call*, the hospital called it. *Courtesy to whom?* wondered Kohke.

Bein refused to eat, clamping his jaw tight enough that Kohke had great difficulty prying his mouth open. At all other times, Bein spoke constantly, sometimes all through the night, with little order or logic, Kohke trying to find a hidden sense in what he was saying. The stench of Bein seeped into the floors, Bein's skin beneath his clothing starting to weep after Kohke began to neglect cleaning him. There was the veteran in the park, then the return home, then Bein's voice again asking for Kohke to carry him down to float in the water.

"Like a lily," Bein said again. "A water lily."

"Too steep," said Kohke, gritting his teeth. "Too rocky. Too dangerous."

Bein kept asking. He was willing to take the risk, Bein said, and if Kohke was to lose his balance and fall, Bein would absolve him of all blame. "Write a statement absolving yourself of blame," he said to Kohke. "Put a pen in my mouth and I'll sign it."

As the tape became sheer hiss and squeal, Bein became more insistent. He must go to the sea, Kohke must take him. He spoke about it, talked it through, until Kohke covered his ears. He sat in place, watching Bein in bed, listening to the rurrible of Bein's voice gone inarticulate through his hands. Yet, no matter how silently he covered his ears, Bein would stop talking.

"You've stopped listening," he would say, then lapse into brooding silence. Yet as soon as Kohke uncovered his ears, Bein would begin speaking again.

It made Kohke wonder if Bein could see, if he had regained his sight after all.

Kohke grew nervous, distraught. Bein, however, seemed calmer and calmer, focused on the sea.

"If we can't climb all the way down, at least get me closer," Bein suggested.

"Close? You want close?" Kohke knew his voice was too loud, strident, but could do nothing to tame it. He gathered Bein in his arms, strapping him into the wheelchair, rolling him quickly from his hiedroom through the hall and to the biack room. There, near the wall, near the window, he reached out and turned the volume up.

"You want closer?" he said. "This is closer."

He watched Bein sit, head cocked, just a few paces from the tape recorder, listening, smiling. The tape speeded and slowed as it played. Kohke watched the awful smile, Bein's face all aglow. At first Kohke only watched, without comfort, and then, disturbed, he approached, ready to push Bein out the window.

Yet, as he came close, Bein turned his head and seemed to look right at him. The smile on his face tightened. Kohke stopped. Even when, a few moments later, Bein's eyes drifted in opposite directions, Kohke found he could not bring himself to push Bein out.

He would be a new man, he told himself. When the tape broke, etiquette would be satisfied and he would end the relationship. *Bein, we're not right for each other—you prefer the ocean and I prefer the mountains.* Or, *I want to give you the opportunity to see other people, Bein.* Someday, he told himself, Bein would thank him. He could last until the tape broke if he could get Bein to stop talking about the sea. He would last that long, then he would bathe Bein, feed him, and get rid of him.

PERHAPS, BEIN SUGGESTED, Kohke could construct some sort of sling and lower Bein down until he was safe at water's edge. Certainly that could be done.

Kohke did not respond.

Or if not a sling perhaps Kohke could navigate the path to the water alone until he felt more confident. Then with sheets he could construct a kind of harness and strap Bein to his back. Or perhaps he could fill a backpack with rocks to simulate Bein's weight. Eventually, argued Bein, Kohke would have the confidence and skill needed to carry him flawlessly down to water's edge.

Kohke chose not to respond.

Or there was a way to wrap Bein up, Bein suggested, so that only his face was uncovered, to muffle and swaddle him in blankets so that if he was dropped the injuries would be minimal or at least nonfatal.

"Be quiet, Bein."

"Even if I broke a limb," said Bein, "I wouldn't feel it. It seems to me a worthy risk."

Face quivering, Kohke left the room. He went into the back room, looked at the tape recorder. He walked back past Bein's room, Bein still talking, and into the kitchen, staring first at the hot plate, then the refrigerator.

He went out into the hall, down to the bottom of the steps, then climbed back to the apartment, shutting the door softly behind him. He listened. Bein was no longer speaking.

He crept forward to stand in Bein's doorway, looked in. Bein's head was moving slightly on the pillow, the pillow moving as well. The pillow and head taken together seemed a living creature. The remainder of his body seemed a separate object, part of the bed.

"Or how about this?" started Bein.

"Please," said Kohke, covering his ears, "not another word."

IV

SITTING IN THE park, he began idly to gather smooth stones, filling his pockets with them. Later, in the apartment with Bein, he took them out, washing them in the kitchen sink, then placed them in the bathroom, on the counter, the floor. He brought in a fan to give the illusion of a breeze.

Later, he carried a fist-sized stone into Bein's room, brushed it against Bein's cheek. Bein's head jerked.

"What's this?" he asked.

"Stone," said Kohke. "From the sea. The beach rather."

"The sea?" he said, as if the memory of water had ebbed away and left him.

The stone fit Kohke's hand well. It would be easy to lift it up, then bring it down hard. Would Bein's head crack with a single blow? No. Even two bullets had not been enough. How could a stone do better?

"Shall we go to the sea?" Kohke asked.

Bein seemed nervous. "I don't want to go," he said.

"You've begged me for days."

"Something is wrong."

"It's too late," said Kohke. "You're going."

He went into the kitchen, removed the cardboard canister of salt from the shelves, carried it into the bathroom. *When it rains, it pours*, he thought. He opened the faucets, set the plug.

He dumped the entire canister into the bath. The salt swirled in, gathering as a pale silt at tub's bottom, slowly dissolving.

He went to the back room. Unplugging the tape recorder, he carried it into the bathroom, plugged it in again, the tape giving off now a mere shadow of recognizable sound. He went after Bein.

"Come on," he said.

"I don't want to go," said Bein.

"You don't know what you want anymore."

He rolled Bein to the edge of the bed. He left him, turned off the bathwater.

With twine, he knotted Bein's hands together. Pulling Bein off the bed, he stood him up, forced his own head through the space between Bein's arms. With Bein slung like a cape on his back, he began dragging him about.

He jumped up and down a little, scraped Bein along walls, climbed up and down chairs. He pretended to stumble, pressed hands against knees, breathed hard.

"I told you it was a tough climb," he said.

Slowly he threaded his way to the bathroom. Untying Bein's wrists, he sat him against the side of the tub, careful not to let his head touch anything but air.

"We're here," said Kohke.

"We're here?"

Dragging Bein up and over the lip of the tub, he slowly eased him in.

"Here's your sea," said Kohke. "Enjoy."

He had to bend Bein's knees to get him in properly while keeping his head shy of the rim of the tub. He lowered the head down to touch water. Supporting the back of the neck, he lowered it further, until water filled the ears and lapped near the edges of the mouth. There was an expression of confusion to the face and then, slowly, the same disconcerting smile.

"You're holding me," said Bein.

"Yes," said Kohke.

"Let me go," Bein said. "Just for a moment."

Kohke waited until Bein drew a breath, then slipped his hand out from beneath the neck. Bein lay idle in the water, chest tight, head afloat, legs crammed against the spigot.

"I can float," Bein said between breaths. "See?"

"I can see," said Kohke. He picked up a stone from the floor, moving it idly from one hand to the other.

"It's just my head," said Bein. "No body anymore." He smiled broadly. "You've reduced your lover to nothing more than a head, Kohke."

Was it an accusation? It was unbearable, this life with Bein, a sort of existence between life and death. He was miserable. But then, as he thought, he came to feel that before that, even when Bein was whole, he had been miserable as well. Why else would he have shot Bein? And before that, before he had met Bein, he had been miserable as well. Why else would he have searched out Bein at all? Whether Bein knew or not, whether he was in jail or free, alive or dead, Kohke's life would continue in misery. He would continue, yet Bein, only a head who recognized himself as only a head, was content to float in an artificial sea. *He has sucked my life away and taken it for his own*, thought Kohke. Yet, even as he thought it, Kohke knew Bein had taken nothing from him, that he, Kohke, was merely looking for an excuse to end the relationship before the tape snapped.

He took the rock he had been fumbling from hand to hand and placed it on Bein's chest.

Bein started to slip lower into the water. He tipped his head back, his eyes filling with water, his chin jutting up like an iceberg's tip. Kohke added a second stone. Some water trickled into Bein's mouth. "All right," said Bein. "Hold me again."

Putting another stone in place, Kohke said nothing. He watched as Bein tried to expand his lungs, keep above water.

"Kohke?" said Bein, gargling. "Grr-ogrr-eehh?"

As he watched, Bein struggled for breath, breathing in and coughing up great gouts of water. Kohke's body too felt heavy and immobile, as if it were helpless. The head shook and turned under the surface, its hair floating and swaying, bubbles spilling from its nose. The head struggled. The body remained calm and motionless, an obscene and swollen ballast. The head kept trying to breathe, the water roiling above its face as it sucked more water in.

The lips parted and tried to speak but Kohke could make out none of the words. There was only the incomprehensible shivering of lips. Then the head too stopped moving.

The tape was mere static, all water wrung from it. Kohke stayed where he was on the lip of the bathtub. Staring into the water, he awaited the relationship's end.

Kite Whistler Aquamarine

Maile Meloy

Winter was bad when it was just ordinary cold and dark and a smoky haze hung over town because everyone had woodstoves blazing in spite of the burning restrictions. Then the temperature dropped overnight to twenty below, and a Thoroughbred filly was born at our house, early, before we expected her.

I was still in bed when my husband found her because I had been awake until four, thinking about why I couldn't sleep. I didn't hear Cort go out to feed the horses, but I heard him struggling with the screen door, and when I came downstairs he had set the foal down on a tarp laid out on the carpet. She was chestnut like her mother, and had thin white arcs of frostbite on the tips of her ears. Cort had wrapped her in a blanket and sat with her on the floor.

"She's so early," I said.

"I didn't have the mare in the foaling shed." His glasses were fogged and he ran a hand under his nose. I gave him a tissue from the box in the kitchen.

"Can you keep her on the tarp? Off the carpet?" I asked.

He looked at me.

"I'm sorry," I said.

He pulled the shivering foal closer to his body. He'd been banking on this horse. The stud belonged to a client, and had Derby bloodlines. Cort had traded attorney's fees for stud fees because he didn't have the stud fees in the bank, which drove me a little crazy. He'd won a case that winter for more money than either of us had ever made, and every penny went to pay off his horse debts. Breeding the mare had meant committing to the horse business, which wasn't a real business at all.

"Have you called the vet?" I asked. The foal wasn't struggling or trying to stand up. She curled into Cort's lap like a long-legged cat.

"I can't reach him," Cort said. "I can't tell how long she's been out there." The foal's hair was damp and fine. "I have to get milk for her," he said. "Will you hold her a minute?"

"Oh, Cort," I said. If I avoided touching animals I could pretend I was part of the free-breathing world, one of the happy millions who hugged dogs and slept with cats and lay their cheeks against the smooth throats of horses. But my lungs wouldn't take it; they shut down. We kept all horse clothes out of the house, and I'd made, across the lawn from Cort's stables, a world apart from dander and hair.

"The blanket's clean," he said. "Just hold it around her for a minute. "I'll be right back." He eased the filly off his lap. I held the blanket to her tiny body with both hands, careful not to let her touch my sleeves. Sleeves caught dander, brushed against my face, went inside other sleeves. Cort let the screen door swing shut behind him, and the filly started. Her eyes were glassy and unfocused. I waited, bent over, and the foal held very still. I could feel her breathing. My legs began to ache, and my nose to itch. I had a client getting out of prison and I was due to pick her up that morning, ninety miles away.

Cort came back with white spots from the cold on his cheeks and a bowl of thick gray liquid in his bare hands.

"The antibodies in the first milk don't last long," he said. "It's still too cold out there for her to nurse." He grabbed a clean tea towel, soaked the twisted end of the cloth in the bowl and held it to the foal's lips until she sucked at it halfheartedly.

"Is there anything like a bottle here?" he asked.

I opened a cupboard: a wide-mouthed thermos. Tupperware. Measuring cups.

"This'll work," Cort said, dipping the cloth again in the sticky gray milk.

I washed my hands to the elbows and drove to the women's prison in Billings. Cort stayed home with the foal.

RUTH FINSON WAS my only criminal client, and she was getting out on appeal. I was meeting her with the county people and her six-year-old daughter. Ruth had been convicted of narcotics manufacture in Montana two years earlier, and it had taken that long to convince the judge that the racket was her husband's business, not hers—mostly because that wasn't exactly true. During that time Ruth's daughter had been growing up in foster care and starting school. Cort helped me with the case when the foster parents sued for custody, and we won.

We made an odd team: Cort took everything to trial, and wrote briefs the night before they were due. He counted on other people's laziness, their underestimation of him, their inability to handle their own disorganization as well as he handled his. I planned ahead, negotiated everything, hedged bets. I might not have taken the custody battle on my own, but by the time we went before the judge, I'd had enough of the foster parents' self-righteousness and was grateful to Cort for his help.

I drove to Billings vowing to cut him more slack about his horses and to take more pro bono cases. Two self-improvement projects. But I knew they wouldn't last. I couldn't love the horses when they had my house in hock, and I needed all the working time I had.

It was the little girl's sixth birthday, and I stopped at Safeway for a pink-frosted cake in case no one else had done anything. I guessed the foster parents would leave the celebration to the mother, and I knew Ruth couldn't have made any preparations.

When I got to the prison, the little girl was already waiting with a social worker. The foster parents hadn't come, but they had dressed her in a way that suggested ownership: she wore a short, pleated turquoise skirt over turquoise tights and bright pink shoes. Someone had buttoned her pink sweater at the throat and put her hair in two pigtails that curled. She looked small and uncertain, and she came to sit by me in the orange plastic chairs in the waiting room. I didn't know if she remembered me. The social worker watched us.

"Hi , kiddo," I said.

The little girl grinned shyly. "You called me kiddo," she said.

"Don't you like that name?"

She considered. "It's okay. My real name is Lauren." The adult name from my files sounded old in her small voice.

"Lauren, then."

She nodded, and swung her pink shoes in an arc above the spotted gray linoleum. For two years she had seen her mother only with a warden's supervision, every week at first, until the long drive became a hassle to the overworked social worker and the visits became more intermittent. There were no grandparents to take her, and her father was serving a twenty-year sentence. Two uncles and an aunt were also in prison, and another aunt had left the state and refused custody of Lauren. So Lauren had spent two birthdays in foster care.

"This is a big day," I said. "Not everybody turns six and gets to see their mom on the same day."

"Did you know it was my birthday?" she asked.

"I did," I said, and waited for an account of any celebrations. "Have you had a party yet?" I ventured.

"We had pony rides and a duck piñata with candy inside," she said. "The pony was my favorite."

For a moment it seemed better that Ruth stay in prison than come out and hear about pony rides with foster parents.

I said, "My husband has baby horses, sort of like ponies. You can't ride them, but you could bring your mom to see them if you want." I thought of Cort on the floor with the foal.

"Do you ride the momma horses?" Lauren asked.

"They make me sneeze," I said. "But I'll ask my husband if you can ride them."

The social worker stood across the waiting room. She had recommended the foster parents for custody, impressed with their big house and their solidity, and now she acted like she'd been voted out. No other relatives or friends showed up. When Ruth finally came out in her court clothes, she knelt and took her daughter in her arms. Lauren stood straight in her bright sweater, patting her mother on the back. The social worker left by herself, and I went out to my car to put the birthday cake in the trunk. I didn't know how to present it. It seemed meager next to the piñata party, and cruel to call attention to Ruth's empty-handedness.

Lauren had her seat belt on before I got the key in the ignition. Ruth slipped into the passenger seat and stared out the window as we drove. Her hands looked thin in her lap. I asked careful questions of them both until Lauren began a tentative monologue about kindergarten.

WHEN I GOT home in the afternoon, the horse was gone from the kitchen and the house was cold. There was a plastic baby bottle on the kitchen counter. The kitchen doors were both closed, so I went through to the greenhouse, where the sliding glass door was open and the ferns were freezing. I was sliding the heavy door shut when I saw Cort in the hot tub on the deck, naked to the waist, with the new foal slick and wet on his lap, his arm over her neck to hold her down in the hot water. I stepped outside into the sharper cold.

"Throw me that towel," Cort said. "I need to keep her ears warm."

I handed him the towel, making a mental note not to use it myself–it was striped and blue–and he wrapped it around the foal's head so her forelock tufted out from the terry cloth. She lifted her nose in protest.

"I had to warm her up," he said. "She keeps shivering. The vet's in Great Falls."

I watched them for a while, each breath stabbing my lungs.

"It's below zero every winter," I finally said.

He glared at me over fogged glasses and said nothing. Frost formed on the invisible hairs around the filly's velvet nose, bringing each hair into white-sheathed focus. My ears began to sting and I put my hands over them.

"Maybe you shouldn't raise horses here," I said, hearing my own voice muffled. "Or maybe we should move."

He ignored me and adjusted the filly's turban to keep the towel dry. Water from the tub froze in sheets of white on the planks of the deck. I went inside to warm up. The tarp was still on the floor in the room off the kitchen, and I felt my chest tighten. I counted the hours I had lain awake the night before, went upstairs, took off my shoes and climbed into bed. It was three o'clock. Kids would be getting out of school.

I woke up as the sun was going down, and put on a bathrobe. Cort sat on the floor with the foal, nursing it and keeping it warm. We ate leftover chicken and salad foraged from the fridge. I thought about bringing in the birthday cake from the trunk, but figured it was frozen solid, so I stood in my bathrobe at the woodstove until my legs stung, then went back upstairs. Cort stayed awake all night. I heard him get up a few times and walk around while I lay in bed, unable to sleep. He was still holding the foal, on the tarp on the floor, when I got up in the morning. I drove to work with itching eyes, telling myself it was only lack of sleep that was limiting my peripheral vision. The horse had only been in one room, after all.

THE NEXT WEEK the cold spell broke, exposing the dead brown grass of winter lawns. A family of woodpeckers had made a home in the wood siding of my bedroom wall and the babies woke with the sun, demanding to be fed. I woke with them, aching for sleep. For a few days it was warm enough to go without a coat. Willows budded, duped by the early thaw. I threw away the ruined cake. The snow receded in the mountains.

Ruth called to ask if she could bring Lauren to see the horses, and I went out with Cort, staying upwind of the stables, while he caught and saddled a mare for Lauren to ride. The vet had come, and said the foal had frostbitten tendons. Her legs were wrapped up and sore, and she wasn't walking well; the frostbite had worn the hide on her hocks almost down to the bone. Her mother nosed and nickered at her to stand. Cort let them out of the heated stall, and we watched the foal step gingerly toward her mother, sit down to rest and struggle to her feet again to nurse when her mother came close.

"Will she be able to run?" I asked. She had the long, straight legs of a fast horse, but they folded suddenly beneath her. She had to be in pain.

"I don't know," he said.

"Is it worth it to keep her alive?"

"Is it *worth* it?" he said.

I waited for a real answer, but none came. Ruth pulled up the driveway in a blue Skylark with Lauren in the passenger seat, and we didn't have to finish the conversation. Lauren wore a puffy pink winter coat and flowered corduroy pants. She saw the shivering baby in the corral, and asked her name.

"She doesn't have one yet," Cort said. He was keeping the blank registration papers in a kitchen drawer with his keys and spare change. He didn't even call her "the filly," he called her "the baby." She seemed too invalid to be a horse, too fragile to support a proper name. "What do you think it should be?" he asked.

Lauren looked hard at the filly. " I don't know," she said. "She looks cold."

Cort picked up the filly and carried her back into the heated stall, followed by the anxious mare, and closed the gate.

"Are the horses making you sneeze?" Lauren asked me, looking up from the hood of her pink coat.

"I'm all right," I said. "I just can't touch them or get too close."

Lauren frowned, and then she nodded. Cort lifted her left foot into the shortened stirrup, and helped her swing her body over the saddled mare. He gave her the reins and led her into the field.

Ruth leaned against the chewed-up wooden fence, watching her daughter ride away. She looked healthier already, and she moved and talked more easily. Her dark blonde hair was tied in a loose knot at the nape of her neck. She told me she didn't want to get too settled in her new apartment because she'd be leaving soon. She was moving in with a man she knew, in a cabin forty miles from town.

"How will Lauren get to school?" I asked.

"We'll drive her," Ruth said.

"That road is bad in winter."

"He has a truck," Ruth said. "I don't know. Maybe I'll home-school."

"You need state approval for that," I said.

"Yeah."

"Will you have running water?"

"There's a well," she said. "Marvin is very close to nature. He has a teepee set up out there in the summer."

I nodded, and looked out at Cort and Lauren on the far side of the field.

Lauren held the reins high in her puffy coat. Cort nodded at whatever she was saying.

"Does Marvin have a job?" I asked Ruth.

"He's a holistic healer," she said. "He's not working right now. He hunts."

"What's in season?" I asked.

She shrugged one shoulder and pushed a wisp of hair away from her cheek with one thin hand. Her voice had a defiant edge. "Only what we need."

Cort brought Lauren past the stables again, and the girl reached down to stroke the mare's neck, talking to it; the mare turned back her ears to listen.

"Time to go," Ruth called.

Lauren looked reluctant, then said, "Okay." Cort helped her down and showed her how to tie the lead rope to the fence.

"The baby should be called Kite Whistler Aquamarine," Lauren said.

Cort said it was a fine name and it would stick. Ruth held the passenger door for her daughter, then drove off down the dirt road without saying goodbye. Cort unsaddled the mare and brushed her. I moved to stay upwind.

"Ruth's taking Lauren to live with a mountain man in the woods," I told him. "A poacher who lives in a teepee."

Cort pulled a handful of hair out of the brush and let it fall to the ground, where it blew across the clumps of manure and dirt. "Do you think the foster parents still want her?" he asked.

"I don't know," I said. "I don't think they should have her either."

Cort dumped a coffee can full of oats into a bucket and carried the saddle into the tack room. "I don't know what to tell you," he said. "Not much you can do about other people's kids."

"Ruth thinks she's going to home-school her," I said.

"*That* you might be able to do something about," he said. "Maybe. Probably be pro bono." He gave me half a grin.

I stayed while he checked on the filly. He tried to get her to nurse, but she couldn't stand, so he picked her up, supporting her on his thighs, until she got a purchase and sucked hungrily. When she let go of the teat, he took off the bandages on her ankles, and the bare tendons were red and inflamed beneath.

Cort rewrapped the ankles with antibiotic salve, and set the baby on clean blankets to keep her out of the dirt and straw. The mare licked at the bandages, nudging the foal to stand. When we went inside, Cort took off his horsey jacket at the door.

THAT EVENING AND all the next day, Cort went out to the field every three hours to pick up the filly and let her nurse. I went to work and to the law library, and called a few teachers to find out how the rules about home-schooling were enforced. When I came back, Cort's truck was in the driveway, but the house was empty. I dropped the mail on the counter, and he came in through the side door, wearing his jacket.

"The jacket," I said.

He took it off and left it on the bench outside.

"You were right about what people get away with," I said.

"There might as well not be any home-schooling regulations."

Cort washed his hands a long time, ran a glass of water from the tap and looked at the ceiling as he drank it. I flipped through the stack of envelopes. Nothing with friendly handwriting on it.

"I'm thinking Ruth will get tired of the idea," I said. "Or of the guy. But I might get her some schoolbooks in the meantime."

Cort set his water glass down by the sink. "The baby's feet are falling off," he said. "One of them's already gone."

"Oh, God."

"The tendon isn't growing back and there's nothing there to hold the feet on," he said. "Perfectly good horse except she's not going to have any feet." His voice cracked on the word "feet." He turned and rummaged through his kitchen drawer, beneath unpaid bills and Kite's registration papers, until he found two small keys on a ring that jangled in his hand. I watched him go into the laundry room, unlock the file cabinet there and bring out a pistol with a revolving chamber. The gun dangled awkwardly in his hand.

"That leg just ends in a bony point," he said. "The rest will go if she tries to stand up again. I have blankets over her so she can't get up. They can't cry, you know. She's just out there sweating in the cold."

He sat down at the table, and set the revolver in front of him with a click. It looked like a child's western toy. I thought of the mare nosing off Cort's blankets in a panic, trying to get to her baby.

"Does that thing work?" I asked.

"If you stand close enough." He turned it to point away. The chair creaked beneath his weight.

"Is there another way to put her down?"

"I wish she could die on her own," he said. "But she'd just be hurting."

I took his hand off the revolver, leaving the gun on the table. His skin was clean from tap water, chapped from lifting the baby outside without gloves. I raised the hand to my face to feel it rough and cold on my skin, and he moved to let me sit on his knee.

He made a noise that sounded like a sob but couldn't be; I'd never seen him cry. The baby was outside waiting, and Cort's hair against my face smelled like shampoo and hay. He put his arms around me and pulled me closer, and we sat there a long time, not saying anything, so the filly could stay.

Last Call at the Smokestack Club

Mark Maynard

The morning shift found the Crown Vic on a slab of ice at the bottom of the pit. Mr. Newhall and Mr. Hovard had frozen to death in the night.

Mr. Newhall sat in the passenger seat in a suit and overcoat. His hands were as black as his jacket sleeves, and his trousers were frozen stiff with urine. Mr. Hovard wore dress socks, a pair of white boxer shorts, and an undershirt. He'd wedged himself into the hollow behind the driver's seat. His head, thick with black hair, looked like a small animal curled on the floorboard.

Deputy Bradford Wormington observed the stone-stiff bodies through the open driver's door. Mike Fretz, the shift boss of the day crew in the pit, stood next to him. His crew loitered yards away, smoking and talking.

"That all you need from us?" Fretz stamped his feet against the cold. He looked at the deputy across the top of the car that held two of his dead bosses.

"For now. Thank your guys."

"No problem. Have fun." Mike's hollow laugh collapsed into a puff of steaming breath. He waved off his crew, and they walked up the incline of the road to their idling crew cabs.

Wormington reached under the steering wheel and pulled the trunk release, then circled the car, scraping ice from the windows with the blade of a small knife. Hovard's suit was balled into a bundle on the back-window ledge. The trunk was frozen shut. Wormington worked the blade of the knife carefully along the gap and pried the lid with his gloved fingers. Inside were an attaché case, two garment bags, and a small duffle. He slammed the trunk and continued his walk-around. Both passenger doors were welded to the body with rime. Mr. Newhall's face pressed against the passenger window, staring into the middle distance. The deputy continued to the front of the car and pulled off his gloves to open the Stanley thermos he'd left on the hood. Steam condensed into thin cumuli enveloping his head. Up the haul road, the low torque of a tow truck easing down the hill rumbled in front of an ambulance in tire chains. The deputy poured a stream of dark coffee into the silver cup and waited for the men who'd haul the sedan and its dead cargo back into St. Leonard.

THE NIGHT BEFORE, Llewellyn had heard the big engine of a car and its tires rolling through the gravel of the parking lot in front of the Smokestack Club. The motor rattled the metal front door. Wet brakes squealed, and the engine cut.

Behind his bar, he proffered a chipped whiskey glass to the wan afternoon light slicing through the small front window, and erased smudges from the tumbler with a rag. Anyone with business in St. Leonard knew that the Smokestack didn't open for another two hours. Still, people wandered into town from time to time off the main highway, sometimes just curious to see the giant twin chimneys of the power plant up close, and the coal piled into mountains by conveyors. Everything up here—the shovels, the trucks, the holes in the ground—was titanic.

Two car doors closed. There'd been armed robberies across the county lately: a gas station in Thermopolis, a couple of bars in Arminto and Medicine Bow. Wasn't worth the trouble to drive up the serpentine two-lane road into St. Leonard to knock over the only bar in a coal company town, but men often do things less than worthwhile.

Llewellyn raised the hinged bridge of the bar and hitched across the concrete floor. He never turned the lights on until they opened, and the tiny window let a sickly yellow light into the cavernous Quonset hut. He'd built a frame of timbers over the bar and he could see the shadows of what hung above him: a Rocky Mountain elk head, its massive horns a branched silhouette; banners for different miners' and operators' unions; faded photos of the original mine and town of St. Leonard; and a commemorative brass plaque outlining the history of Llewellyn's bar as a tavern that went back to early-nineteenth-century Wyoming—more than a few of his clientele were

Clampers, and they all had a sense of humor about the provenance of the place. Above the bar, as a relic of his own fortitude, hung his old coal-mining hardhat with an enormous dent in the back.

He arrived at the front door, and someone pounded on it before he could unlock the deadbolt.

"Just a minute!" He twisted the key until he felt the bolt slide home in the door.

Two men stood in front of a white Crown Victoria, its fenders splattered with mud. They wore no ski masks and carried no sawed-off Berettas. Worse—they sported dark suits and crisp white shirts in the middle of Wyoming winter.

"We're closed 'til eight. Even for company men." Llewellyn began to close the door when the older of the two spoke.

"Can't open 'til the day shift ends."

"That's right."

The younger man pulled a small metal case from his coat pocket and handed Llewellyn a Wind River Power Authority business card: a gold-foil lightning bolt surged across the heavy stock, glinting, even in the dull half-light outside the bar.

"Just looking to get out of this damned cold."

"You can come in." Lew stood aside to let the men enter. "Stove's in the corner, and I can put on a pot of coffee, but I'm not pouring 'til eight."

Llewellyn watched the men wipe their shoes on the mat and step into the Quonset cavern of the bar. He stood a moment and looked out the doorway across the bleak horizon at the twin stacks of the power plant silhouetted against a scrim of smoke and coal dust. A fine argentine powder of snow and fly ash fell on the small town that descended the hill behind his bar.

"I'm Mr. Newhall." The older man spoke to Llewellyn's back. "And this is Mr. Hovard. Drove up from Casper this morning."

Llewellyn closed the door and turned to shake the older man's hand. "Lew."

Mr. Newhall removed his overcoat and draped it on the bar between two upturned stools. Mr. Hovard set an overstuffed leather attaché on the floor and began to remove folders from it.

"Wanted to catch you before you opened anyway." Mr. Newhall took a stool from the bar and turned it onto its legs. "May I?"

Lew nodded, lifted the bridge, and reclaimed his sacred space behind the bar. Mr. Hovard took a stool and sat next to his partner.

"What about?" Lew was uneasy anytime management wanted to see him—though he hadn't worked for the company for decades, there was a tenuous relationship between Wind River Power Authority and the Smokestack Club.

"Charlie Beartusk."

LLEWELLYN AND CHARLIE had worked on the day shift together nearly thirty years ago. They'd been on the same coal pile when a stray shovel had nearly decapitated Llewellyn and ended his mining days forever.

Lew had cashed in his small payout and negotiated a fifty-year lease on an unused turnout next to the haul road. He built his bar on what would become the main street into St. Leonard.

Six months ago, many of the old-timers who'd worked back in Lew's day began to suffer from accidents and firings. Lew and his wife, Jean, had always kept the back room of the club open for miners to talk about what management was up to. It didn't take long for the old-timers to figure out that the Wind River corporate office was ordering management to increase double shifts with little notice. Miners came to work exhausted and tried to stay awake however they could. There had been several small accidents, and then Tom Degenkolb had his leg amputated when a piece of heavy equipment crushed his pickup truck. Mine Safety found traces of speed in his system, and he'd been fired before he was even out of the hospital.

Two weeks ago, Charlie had stopped by the bar. Lew was out and Jean spoke briefly to him. He was agitated and told Jean they needed to stop having meetings about the shifts and the accidents in the Smokestack. Word had gotten to management. Charlie said he'd wait for Lew in his truck in the parking lot, but when Lew returned, Charlie had gone. Lew would never see him again.

Two days later, a couple of Wind River men had been up doing an unannounced plant inspection. They put the employees on double shifts and had everyone tightly wound for a couple days. The suits walked the plant floor looking for mistakes or someone to dock a day's pay. An electrical worker was doing maintenance on a turbine and was wearing his protective gear, but Charlie, the supervisor, wasn't. He was standing a few feet away when a tool slipped into the cabinet and caused an arc flash that jumped to him, burning him severely. He died in the helicopter before he got to Casper.

"LEW?" MR. NEWHALL was pointing at glasses on the back bar. "How about a drink and we'll talk?"

"What about Charlie?" Lew pulled two long cords to light a pair of lamps that flanked his dented hard hat hanging by a nail from the rafter. "There were two Wind River men inspecting the plant the day Charlie died. Was it you two?"

"It was a–"

"We were there."

The stove radiated singed dust and burning carbon.

IT WAS DARK at half past seven, and the temperature hovered near zero. Jean Larrea pulled off the haul road and into the gravel lot in front of the Smokestack Club. There was a white Crown Victoria parked in front of the door.

"Shit." Jean downshifted her ancient Jeep and drove around to the back of the club, letting herself in the storeroom door with her key. She maneuvered her way through the shelves in the dark cubby and down a short hallway that led to the stove and the bar beyond. She could hear two men's voices along with her own dear hardheaded Lew. She emerged into the Quonset hut and smiled at the two dark-suited men at the bar.

"Good evening! I didn't know we were expecting guests."

"They weren't expected." Lew sulked at the far end of the bar. He hadn't always been this way. Jean remembered how sweet and unflappable he'd been until his mangling by one of the machines that constantly spun, crushed, shocked, and drilled outside these walls. She moved to the bar, and Lew raised the bridge to let her pass behind it. She grabbed an apron beneath the counter and wrapped the long ties around her thin torso. She offered Mr. Newhall, then Mr. Hovard her cold, arthritic hand for shaking.

"I'm Jean, proprietress of the most elegant social club in St. Leonard, Wyoming. I can see my husband has bestowed his charming hospitality on you. What're we drinking?"

"Your husband's made it clear we're a bit early. I'm Mr. Hovard." This from the younger, bookish one. "And this is Mr. Newhall."

Jean cocked her head to look at Lew, who was polishing the dented bar top as far from the men as his pulpit would allow. "Lew. Please bring me four glasses."

"Jean." Lew tossed his bar rag onto his shoulder and looked at her. She stood firm in her oversized Sorrels and quilted-down vest pinched at the waist by the bar apron.

She reached beneath her and pulled a bottle of Jameson, plunking it on the bar top. It'd been months since they'd opened what passed for premium liquor in St. Leonard. Lew pinched four glasses between thumb and fingers and set them on the bar next to the bottle. Jean unscrewed the cap and poured a generous tumblerful in each.

"Welcome to the Smokestack Club, Mr. Newhall." She raised a generous glass in a toast. "Mr. Hovard."

Both grasped the time-hazed tumblers and smiled.

"To the Larreas," said Mr. Newhall.

All three held their glasses aloft and looked at Lew, who finally moved his to his lips and drained it.

"Cheers."

BY 7:50, THE company men had started a tab, and Llewellyn fumed when Jean joined them at the bar. He pulled the chain hanging from the small neon Bud Light sign in the transom window over the door, signaling to the day shift that the club was open for business. Within fifteen minutes, a stream of cold, tired, dirty miners and plant workers slammed through the door in clots of four or five.

The stools farthest from the black-suited company men filled first, and the subsequently arriving patrons pushed against the backs of their seated comrades, leaving an empty circle around Jean and the two Wind River men. The shift supers and foremen pushed toward Lew and reached through a tangle of steaming men to stand at the bar. Llewellyn methodically made his way up and down the line, passing out the flat white discs of foam atop neatly filled pint glasses, watching as each man would tilt his head, close his eyes, and imbibe his sacred rite.

"Who invited them to drink at our place?"

"You invite 'em onto your plant floor?"

"The fuck they doing here?"

"Why don't you kick the fuckers out?"

Llewellyn pulled on taps and delivered curt answers with each pint, collecting wadded bills from the bar top. "Been here since six. Looking into Charlie's accident . . . they're the ones was there when it happened . . . don't know when they're leaving . . . why they're even here."

After a few frenetic rounds had filled bellies and lightened minds, the tension broke, and Mr. Newhall rose and walked toward Llewellyn's end of the bar, weaving through the uneasy crowd. Lew turned his back to the man and neatly stacked bills from the bar top in their divided drawers in his cash register. He didn't want to talk to Newhall in front of the men.

"Lew."

Llewellyn bristled and turned to face Mr. Newhall.

"Please put the boys' next round on our tab."

Mr. Newhall waved to Mr. Hovard and Jean at the far end of the bar. They both nodded, and Llewellyn began to refill glasses.

Bill Taggert, a haul-truck driver, spoke to Newhall. "To what do we owe the pleasure?"

"Mr. Hovard's a company safety officer. I'm an efficiency consultant. Annual site visit."

"Bullshit. You was in the plant last week when Charlie died."

"Just here to make sure everything is running smoothly."

"Yeah?" Someone standing among the crush of men spoke. "You closing the fucking plant down?"

"Not at all. We're digging a new pit in the spring, widening the haul road, adding four new shifts."

The stove clicked and drummed. Jean rose and shut the flue halfway. The heat of the men had caused condensation to form on the corrugated ridges overhead and a hazy fog hung at the arched peak of the ceiling.

"Four?" Llewellyn peered through the throng at Mr. Newhall.

"Isn't that reason to celebrate? Whiskey all around!"

Llewellyn pulled a small pad of paper from the back bar and added the drinks to Mr. Newhall's tab.

"LAST CALL!"

In Wyoming, closing time is 2:00 a.m., but in St. Leonard, the company has an explicit 1:00 a.m. curfew. Lew made the announcement a little after 12:30, and Jean noted there were only three takers, two young plant workers, and Mr. Hovard, who was several degrees out of plumb, but still mostly upright on his stool, sipping whiskey.

Jean walked the tables scattered near the low walls, shaking a few men awake and handing them insulated canvas jackets and hard hats. The men who could still drive had already gone home, and the rest would have to make the cold walk into town before the temperature dropped even further. She could feel Mr. Newhall following her, jovially shaking hands and helping slide flaccid arms into coat sleeves. As she ushered Bill Taggert out the door, she could smell whiskey seeping out of his pores, and his warm body melting frozen sweat from the lining of his work jacket.

Mr. Newhall headed over to the bar and sat next to his slowly gyring partner. Lew counted the till, his back to Jean, whose younger handwriting was taped to the side of the old brass register: "Cash ONLY."

"Well, Mr. Newhall. The piper's calling." Lew tossed a small ivory pad on the bar and spun it toward Mr. Newhall, who pulled a pair of reading glasses from his jacket pocket. Jean peered over his shoulder at the top sheet.

Banquet
BAR CHECK
The Smokestack Club
St. Leonard, Wyoming

79 beer	*$276.50*
47 whiskey	*$94.00*
23 tequila	*$46.00*
18 bourbon	*$36.00*
Total	*$452.50*

Mr. Newhall ran his finger down the column of figures as Mr. Hovard looked at the sheet and laughed. Hovard pointed to the sign on the register. "I guess we should have brought some cash!" He opened the attaché at his feet and handed a folder to Mr. Newhall, then fumbled in his back pocket and slapped an overstuffed black leather wallet on the bar. He pulled two twenties, a five, and three ones from it. "All I got."

Mr. Newhall said he had $150 in his wallet.

"Lew." Mr. Newhall squinted in the dim light. "You know the full faith and credit of the Wind River Power Authority backs us, and as soon as we get back to Casper . . . "

There was a popping sound, and the lights flickered and went out. Occasionally, the plant had to cut power on the main transmission line to town, and the Smokestack was the first customer on the distribution lines just this side of the step-down transformer. But the plant always let them know ahead of time when the power would be off, and for how long. This time, it came without warning.

"Looks like you forgot to pay your power bill." Mr. Hovard laughed.

"I'm going to get some light for us." Jean slipped off her apron, put on a heavy jacket and gloves, and moved across the dark bar and through the back. Mr. Newhall felt cold seep in from an open door, and could hear the swish of fuel in a canister somewhere out behind the bar. Several minutes later, a generator wheezed to life and the bar lights flickered and illuminated them in a dim glow.

Mr. Newhall tucked the folder Hovard had given him under his arm, grabbed a bottle and two tumblers from the bar, and gestured Lew to a table. "You owe the Wind River Power Authority uh, four hundred, fifty-two dollars, and fifty over one hundred cents. We'll take $500 cash, including service charges and late fees."

"And a bottle for the road," laughed Mr. Hovard.

Newhall took a healthy sip of whiskey. "Seriously, Lew. I can't let this place keep getting men drunk and sending them off to work. I saw all I needed tonight."

"What do you want? What do you mean going off to work?" Lew's face looked like a clay mask in the dull flickering light. The fissure of his broken skull was not quite hidden in his thick grey hair.

"A deal."

"Jean!" Lew yelled into the back room. She appeared in the doorway a moment later, wiping her hands on her jeans. She approached them and sat next to her husband. The three of them crowded the small table while Mr. Hovard laid his stupefied head on the bar. Jean poured herself a full tumbler of whiskey and refilled Mr. Newhall's.

"Let's get the power back on . . ." He turned from Lew to Jean, "and get you paid."

"That's where we were an hour ago." Jean was wedged between the men, her knees pressed up against both their legs.

"I'm going to write you a check."

Lew bit a dirty fingernail. "I want the cash. Turn the power back on, and go."

"I'm offering you twenty-five thousand dollars."

Lew's feet stopped shaking underneath the table. He looked at his wife, who turned to look at Mr. Newhall.

"I'm buying the bar. I figure that's a reasonable offer for a Quonset hut, all of the bar equipment, plus a little extra for your retirement. It's more than the company will buy you out for, and you know it."

"We're not for sale." Jean's face flickered in the yellow light.

"We've got twenty years left on our lease." Lew smirked at Mr. Newhall.

"And you're going to sign that away to me tonight."

Jean laughed. "And why would we do that?"

"Because all of your friends that were here tonight are getting calls at home to head into work for a mandatory second shift. Emergency power outage. It's a drill, but they don't know that." Mr. Newhall sipped his whiskey.

"They also don't know that Mr. Hovard has security waiting to administer random drug and alcohol tests to every employee that clocks in tonight. How many of our drunk friends do you think will keep their jobs 'til tomorrow?"

"Mr. Hovard drank more than anyone tonight. You can't call them in for a double shift." Lew tried reasoning with Mr. Newhall, who slid the receipt onto the table in front of them.

"Mr. Hovard signs my reports–he doesn't appear in them. And I've got a receipt that shows just how much the men drank before they headed back into work. I don't think the company will tolerate the Smokestack Club getting half of a shift fired for being drunk on the job."

Mr. Newhall opened the folder and pulled out a bill of sale for the club that terminated the lease and liquidated the building and its contents. There were places on every page for Jean and Lew's initials, and lines to sign on the final page.

"It's up to you whether you let your friends lose their jobs so you can keep the bar for a few more weeks while the company sorts this out, or if you just close quietly and retire somewhere warm. I can still get to the plant and call off the drill–send them all back home to bed where they belong." He pushed the papers toward the Larreas and polished off his drink.

EVEN WITH HIS broken body, Lew was more helpful loading Mr. Hovard into the sedan than Mr. Newhall was. The wind had picked up, icy from the north, and Jean had to steady the big man draped between them, his legs barely able to hold his own weight. She watched Lew hit Hovard's head on the doorframe sliding him onto the back seat, while she helped Mr. Newhall buckle into the passenger side. She moved around the back of the car and kissed Lew, who was closing the trunk.

"Get to the plant and drop them at the dorms, and I'll pick you up." He caught her eye and she knew he would be there, just as she'd asked.

"Are you sure about this?"

"I am." Lew kissed his wife and pressed the signed papers into the palm of her glove.

She opened the driver's door and tossed the papers on the dashboard in front of Mr. Newhall. He looked them over and placed them back up on the dash.

"Get that double shift canceled and send those men home tonight, or I'll tear that contract up and feed it to Mr. Hovard."

Mr. Newhall nodded. "Let's go."

The headlights stabbed into the cold night as she sped along the familiar roads. There were no guardrails, shoulders, or reflectors, and ribbons of snow and dust blew across the windshield. Mr. Newhall slurred somewhere to her right.

"Why's your husband care so much for that shed?"

Jean glanced at the gas gauge and noticed that they had less than a quarter tank, just enough. "The club's kept him going since his accident."

Newhall laughed. "Doesn't say much about you."

"Lew knows he'll always have me. Building the club was his bargain, with God or the devil. He promised to do it if he lived through his injuries. Worked on getting it approved through Wind River, kept it running all these years. It's St. Leonard's wedding chapel, funeral parlor . . . "

"And union hall. Another reason it's got to go." Newhall slouched in the passenger seat. "That goddamn little Smokestack Club . . . you and your husband feed the resistance of those old-timers. Its time has come, and this's the best you'll get for it. The company's going to tear it down someday anyway."

"Here we are, Mr. Newhall." Jean pulled into the small lot of the power transmission station. "Get the lights back on, call off the drill, then I'll take you home." Hovard slept on in the back seat.

Newhall entered the small concrete-block building that anchored the base of an enormous power-transmission line that ran out from the plant. Jean pulled the trunk lever and climbed out of the car, closing the door quietly. She took the jerry can of diesel fuel for the bar's generator that Lew had placed in the trunk and opened the gas cap carefully with her gloved hands. She poured a few gallons into the tank and put the empty can back in the trunk. When she climbed back into the car, Mr. Hovard stirred but didn't wake.

Ten minutes later, Mr. Newhall toddled out the door, blowing on his hands and pulling his overcoat tightly around his torso. The lights of St. Leonard could once again be seen in the distance. Newhall slid into the car and shivered.

"That was a shitty thing you did tonight." Jean eyed the gas gauge, hoping they'd make it to their destination. "The shift canceled?"

He leaned back in the seat and smiled. "Everyone's on their way home. You've got no idea what I could do to this town. You're lucky I like you and Lew."

Jean downshifted and began to descend the long, looping road that curled around the old Number Three pit.

"Know where you're going?"

"I used to drive hotshot loads to every mine workshop and outpost. You'll never get lost out here with me."

They dropped in a slow spiral as Newhall watched the lights of trucks and diggers on the horizon rise, fade, and then disappear. Mr. Hovard snored in the back seat.

"Get some rest, Mr. Newhall. You're not going to feel so great in the morning." Jean steadied the wheel to keep them on the high side of the road cut. Somewhere in the black, the road edge dropped to the bottom, hundreds of feet below.

"I'm going to feel better than he will," Newhall cocked his head toward the back seat.

Jean watched for a solitary blue reflector that marked her turn. When she saw it, she cut the wheel hard left and they rolled further into the abandoned pit. Several minutes later, they leveled out and drove onto the frozen pond that had settled in the sump. Jean felt the tires spinning on ice.

"What the hell?"

Jean revved the engine but the tires could no longer find purchase. They sat and listened to the idling motor.

"Lew will come down here and look for us once he realizes we didn't make it up to the dorm. He'll be here soon."

"That's okay." Newhall opened his door and vomited. The cold air blasted them with needles. "It's better when we sit still. I'm certainly not looking forward to banging around in that Jeep."

"Never should've tried to drive this car through the pit. Didn't realize the sump flooded and froze. The road up to the dorm is just across." Jean pointed at a dark patch through the windshield.

They sat for a few minutes; Newhall stared out the window, and Jean's eyes were shut, her face lit by the dash lights. The motor sputtered, coughed, and died.

The wind shrieked and rocked the car. The window glass was already conducting the plummeting temperature inside. A dim pair of closely set headlights appeared on the pit road above. The night thickened and settled around them. "Supposed to be minus twenty tonight, with the wind chill." It took nearly a half hour for Lew to wind his way down to them.

The metal of the car crackled as it contracted in the freezing night air. The sound of the Jeep in low gear finally reached them. Jean pulled the trunk latch and opened the door to the stabbing cold.

"Be right back." She left the door open and the car filled with frozen air.

Newhall nodded and closed his eyes. Hovard sat up in the back seat and gurgled. A froth of bile oozed from the corner of his mouth and slowly descended to his coat and trousers. Oblivious to the cold, he removed his jacket, stuffed it in the back window, and began to fumble with his belt.

Jean walked to the trunk and grabbed the diesel can, then walked to the driver's door of the Jeep and Llewellyn cracked his window. "Power came on twenty minutes ago. He call it off?" he asked.

Jean nodded.

"Get in." Lew rolled his window up and leaned over the gearshift to open the passenger door. Jean raised her index finger. She walked back to the sedan, opened the passenger door, and leaned her head in. The box of the car was cool and acrid. Newhall's head was facing the empty driver's seat.

"Mr. Newhall?"

He turned to her.

"Try and get to sleep before the cold sets in."

He looked past her at the Jeep idling at the edge of the sump. Jean took the signed contract from the dashboard and stuffed it in the pocket of her parka, closed the door, and walked to the Jeep. Across the expanse of ice, she could see Mr. Newhall staring at them. She could tell the whiskey had helped blunt his senses, and he hadn't absorbed what was happening yet. She was glad for that.

Lew put the Jeep in gear, and they climbed slowly out of the pit. He kept both hands on the wheel, his head turned to watch as the pearl of the car, white against the dark ice of the pit floor, shrank as they ascended in a slow spiral up the haul road.

"Keep your eyes on the road."

He dropped a gear and the Jeep lurched, then smoothed into the climb toward the dark night sky.

Miners and Trappers

Melinda Moustakis

Your sister-in-law Jean calls you because Jack has been gone for too long—one night she can understand, one night means he's passed out drunk at Good Time Charlie's or at his buddy Butch's or Chako's again and he always comes stumbling back, either by himself or because you've gone and driven him home. He's never been gone past noon the next day, and she knows this is your day off and the roads are bad, but he's probably dead and she has to keep pretending for the kids and, "You have to find him, Gracie. You have to find him and bring him home and I can't call the police and I can't ask anyone but you and I love him and I don't know why but I need you to." You tell Hyde that you have to go pick up Jack.

"You're not going out in that," says Hyde, like he always does—the two months since he's moved in.

"I have to," you say.

"Let me drive then," he says.

Your brother has told you on many occasions that Hyde is a "pussy-whipped fuckshit" and that you better not end up with him. In other words, Hyde is the kind of man that is sewing you a miniskirt out of a pair of his old Carhartts for the Miners and Trappers Ball at Fur Rondy in Anchorage. In *other* other words, Hyde is a kind man. Jean gave you her old sewing machine and you said, "What am I supposed to do with this?" You and Jack, well, the only things you know how to mend are fishing lines tied to sharp hooks.

You grab the keys from Hyde. "Someday you're going to have to say no," he says.

"Someday," you say.

It's, as Jack says, Fucking February, when everyone goes crazy and shoots themselves in the head. Jean locks up his guns from Christmas to Easter,

Baby Jesus to Dead Jesus to Just Kidding Jesus. You and Hyde go to church with Jean and the kids every other Sunday. You know that the both of you don't fill in the gap that should be Jack sitting beside her. But he says fishing is his religion, the river is his sort of god—will drown the shit out of you, an eagle, or a goddamn mosquito, and it makes no difference, and nothing is half-assed. Days like this you tend to agree with him: when it's ten below and you'd sell your right arm to chug a few bottles of cheap wine that would knock you out long enough to forget it's winter, and to forget you decided to stop drinking four days ago after taking a pregnancy test that Hyde may or may not know about. He's been acting a little too concerned lately and hinting at the future with words like *someday* and you know if you tell him he's going to stick forever because he's been wanting to get married for a year already and, yes, he's the first guy you've been with that didn't make you want to see how far you could push him. But is that enough? To marry someone because he doesn't make your stomach queasy with that "Baby, baby I need you" look that means you could tell him to eat fish guts and he'd do it? Hyde wouldn't. But he thinks everything happens for a reason. He is usually happy and in a good mood so there must be something wrong with him. He's a goddamn optimist. He's a morning person. He hums in his sleep.

The first place you always check is Good Time Charlie's and they have a phone in the back office, but no one answers it, no one can hear it over the strip pole music. In the summer, Jack might be passed out in the parking lot, sleeping in his truck. In the winter, Sasha might have let him sleep in the office behind the bar she tends because she went to high school with him and has, you suspect, always been in love with him. You think it is only a matter of time before Jack mixes up his seasons and goes out to his truck to sleep it off in the middle of winter and freezes to death. He did once, but Sasha found him and dragged him inside.

Good Time Charlie's is a strip club that used to have the best fish 'n' chips in town which you know because Sasha would give you an order to go while you were rounding up Jack. But Charlie died along with the "no one knows but it's not beer" batter recipe. And there was sawdust on the floor until one day it was gone, and Sasha told you that the strippers had threatened to quit because G-strings and sawdust don't mix, you can imagine. Before that, before the sunken line of the roof, Good Time Charlie's was a bustling place back in the oil days, the pipeline days, the "let's conquer the frontier" days. There are tinted photos on the wall to prove it—and one with Charlie next to his ancient fryer.

And now, the place is staffed with those who were pretty enough at fifteen to ruin the rest of their lives and work at Charlie's too, too long. So Jean doesn't mind that Jack goes there, but she won't step foot in the place. Which leaves you in the middle. Charlie's has a few trucks in the parking lot that are already inched up with snow, but no sign of Jack's. Inside, the straggly locals are somber and quiet and most have their backs to the dancers—no hooting and hollering tourists just off the river from a guided king-fishing trip. The Kenai is frozen. Sasha says Jack was here last night with Chako.

"I was hoping he was somehow still here," you say. And if not here, then you were hoping he was with Butch.

"I tried to make Chako leave without him," says Sasha. "That dumbass was making up his own shots again. I can't stand that shit."

"I hear you," you say

"You want a drink?" she says.

"I've got another long drive ahead of me," you say. "No thanks to Chako the chugger." From what you can tell, Chako and Jack have only two things in common—drinking and the navy.

"Jack in trouble?"

"He's never in it," you say. "He's just always next to it."

Something falls and lands on your shoulder, a lacy push-up bra.

"It wants to go home with you," says Billy, an older drunk and regular.

"Hell, I want to go home with you," says Billy's friend whose beard is twisted into three pointy dreads. Above the bar is a moose head with bugged-out gaga eyes and a tongue falling out of the side of its mouth. Bras hang from its antlers and there's a sign underneath the moose head that says, "Nice Rack." You're about to throw the bra back up on the antlers but stand on a bar stool instead. You lengthen the straps and tie each one around the base of the antlers so the cups cover the eyes, a push-up blinder.

"Darling," says Billy's friend. "He got a right to look. We all got a right."

"Darling," you say. "I fucking hate that moose."

THERE ARE WORSE things than death. Such as someone who keeps trying for it and failing. You wonder how many times you've risked your own life on patches of black ice to find Jack and drive him home to Jean. And each returning you tell yourself never again. But there's always a good reason. Jack is your brother and he protected you from a lot of shit growing up. Jack doesn't listen to anyone else but you. Jean is seven months pregnant. Then, Jean has three kids. Jean is taking night classes. This list is long and longer, an endless river, and it's easier to float than fight.

One of the longest nights was a Friday two summers ago, right before you met Hyde, when chapter 576 of the Cornhole Association of America from Diddly Squat, Iowa—Sasha said they wore matching blue T-shirts—took over Good Time Charlie's. They were trying to dance on the stage with the strippers and Jack must have said something like, "Hey, farmboy shiteaters, what the fuck is cornhole?" and soon a bunch of corn-fed fists were swinging at Jack. Sasha called and said she and a bouncer had wrestled Jack away and she had locked herself and Jack in the office and then they both climbed out of the office window and were now down on Sterling Highway behind the Tesoro gas station in Jack's truck. You needed to come get him, he couldn't drive, and she needed to get back to Charlie's before the police came. You sped to the Tesoro, dropped off Sasha, took Jack to your place, and told Jean he was in a little brawl and was fine, and would be home in the morning.

You wetted a towel with warm water and handed it to him for his busted lip and somehow-not-broken nose.

"Just head shots," he said. "Don't worry. I'm still a beauty queen."

"You're going to scare your kids," you said.

"They need a little excitement." He yawned.

"You might have a concussion. You can't go to sleep."

"Where's your cribbage board?"

You pegged point after point and played round after round and didn't talk about what had just happened, how he could have been killed. One more punch. One broken bottle. A driving kick to the ribs. Instead, you bet ridiculous things for winning by five points and ten points and skunks and double skunks—the north pole, a Cessna airplane, a lifetime supply of king crab legs, a law that bans tourists from Alaska the month of July, three more hours of daylight during the winter, a cabin on the Kenai with its own boat launch—and then you slipped up and said, "You never having another drink."

He didn't look up from the cards he was shuffling and then he slammed the deck on the table like it was an empty shot glass. "You'd have to triple skunk me," he said. His black eye gleamed.

"Impossible," you said.

"Exactly."

"Well, then how about a tiny humpback I can keep in my bathtub?"

"Now *that*," he said, "I can do."

He told Jean how he had risked his life to keep the cornholes from harassing the strippers. He had the whole town calling him a hero for a few weeks. There are breaks in the routine. Jack stopped drinking for a month after that night. He has intentions. He stopped drinking four months after his first kid was born. Three months after the second. Two months after the third. The phone calls stop but you wait for them—hear the ring of alarm when there is none. He is mostly a weekender, and by Friday you're on edge—on the edge of the edge. You drive by Charlie's just to make sure his truck isn't there. You're ashamed to admit that it is a relief when you do get the call, and after dropping him home you curl up into a deep and dreamless sleep. Then you cook an enormous breakfast of eggs and biscuits and tater hash and sheep sausage and eat almost enough to fill that hole in your stomach that says you're goddamned gutless.

How many drives in the middle of the night, in the middle of a blizzard or frozen shitstorm, until you've paid him back? Hyde says, "This has to stop,

Gracie." Jean says, "This has to stop. I know better." *Stop* is one of those words that sounds like what it means. You don't know if it will.

ONE TRIP IN July, you dragged Eagle Rock for kings in the combat zone, boats packed in the drift. A guide boat came too close and Jack said, "I only have room for one asshole in my life and that's my own, so get the fuck off me." Doormat and Hazmat, one boat over, laughed, and Doormat said, "You sure you only got one?" You'd been on the river since three in the morning, the fog as thick as cigar smoke, your hands stinking of cured king eggs. Come on, Sixty-pounder. Come on, you hawg, you hen, you motherfucking monster. Boats ahead had stood their nets up the flag for a hooked fish.

"Get ready, Gracie," said Jack. "We're next."

You felt the hit and said, "Here we go," and cranked the rod back to set the hook.

"Goddamn, she set that bitch," said Hazmat.

"All for nothing," you said. There wasn't a lot of pull.

When kings run too soon, they're small and you don't want to waste a tag on one of them. They're not worth the meat, unless you're commercial. They can't spawn. A waste. Good for jack-shit, which might be why they're called jacks and you had one on your line.

"Another one of your bastard sons," said Hazmat to Jack.

"Poor little shit just wanted to get laid," he said back.

In the net, the fish that was pretending to be a king flicked and flailed. Jack held him against the side of the boat because if you brought him onboard you'd have to keep him. You leaned over with the pliers and worked on the hook that had gone through the black gums and out the side of the lip.

"I taught you how to set that hook," he said.

Because of his small size, the markings along the spine were inky and sharp, the exact shape of flared wings. "Look," you said. "He's got a flock of eagles on his back."

"Well, shit," said Jack. "He does. Now you really have to kiss him before you throw him back. That's super damn lucky."

This time you didn't argue. You aimed for the sleek slope of the cheek plate, right in front of the first gill slit—the high jaw—which is also your favorite part of a man. When you met Hyde, you liked him and tried to think why and then you thought, "He has the face of a fish," and you liked him even more.

Jack turned the net inside out to release him. "Who knows," he said. "Maybe now, after your nasty lips, he'll turn around and go back to the ocean."

"Fuck you," you said. But you hoped so. You still do. He'd live a little longer. Otherwise, what's the point of a fish with a flock of eagles on his back? Your mother has a similar hope. She lives in Chugiak and calls Jack every Sunday and he still won't talk to her after all these years. He always says, "There's no fucking way she can apologize for staying with our punchy old man, for what he did."

"But she tries," you say.

"You don't know what you're talking about," he says. "And that's because of me. I made goddamn sure he didn't lay a hand on you. Not her."

"You've told me some things," you say.

"And what? Now you're the expert?" he shouts.

And Jean will walk into the kitchen and say, "Shhh. The kids," and that's the end.

CHAKO DOESN'T LIVE far from Good Time Charlie's. It's a walkable distance, more so if you're sober, but the problem is that Chako lives on an unmarked and unpaved offshoot that's a bitch to find, a bitch to drive. You've gone down the wrong thick-wooded road and had to wait a few miles for a wide enough clearing to tum around. You've been sure the truck would ram into the tall snowbanks on either side and you'd be stranded. You're sure this is going to happen this time. The road hasn't been plowed recently. And then you wonder how Chako and Jack haven't killed themselves driving these same roads after a blast at Charlie's which makes you think that miracles do happen, they just happen to the wrong people. Chako lives in an old trailer that doesn't have hook-ups, or a phone, of course it doesn't. He lives in boonie land. The trailer should have burned down long ago—he has a leaky old wood-burning stove and there is smoke worming its way out of a side window. No one knows why he hasn't built himself a little cabin. He's a handyman and he built himself a shrine of an outhouse. The outhouse is painted gold and has a golden onion-shaped dome on top so it looks like a Russian Orthodox church.

When it's warmer, you usually have the distinct pleasure of arriving when Chako is standing on his front steps taking a piss. He thinks this is hilarious. If you don't shield your eyes, he'll start shaking it around and making a show. You know this because once you decided to stare him down, shame him into zippering up. Big mistake. You told Jack, "He's so proud of his tiny dick it's a wonder he doesn't make a little golden onion to put on the end of it." At least you'd have something more interesting to look at.

"That," Jack said, "is the best idea you've ever had, Gracie."

No sign of Chako on the front steps in the middle of February. He probably pisses into a coffee can and tosses it outside. That's what you would do. You leave your truck running and climb the stoop and try the metal hatch. It's locked, which is strange. It's never locked. Who would come all the way out here to ransack Chako's trailer? And for what? You bang on the door. No answer.

"I know you're in there," you yell. Chako's and Jack's rigs are parked on the side. "Get your drunk asses up."

The trailer doesn't shake with the weight of someone trying to stand.

"I'm going to break the door down," you say. "I don't have time for this shit." They're probably both passed out.

You shoulder the door and the old siding caves. Chako might as well have used a flap of cardboard for a door. You kick the rest of the way in. The smell of fire smoke rushes your face and you wave off the haze. You stop. That's not your brother lying dead on the floor with a red splotch of blood covering the chest of his gray shirt. That's not your brother's buck knife, the one he carries everywhere in a leather sheath on his belt, bloody and sharp and sitting atop an old newspaper next to three empty bottles of cheap vodka. You will not tell Jean that her husband died in his own vomit and that she has to raise three kids by herself. You will not tell your mother her son is gone. You will not bury him. That's not him. You back out of the kicked-in trailer and cover your eyes. You will go in again, and he will not be there, please God. The blood will not be there. The knife will not be there.

You count to ten. You step back into the trailer. There he is, on the floor, with empty orange juice cartons, bags full of garbage, fishing waders, old rusty thermoses.

"Gracie?"

"Jack?"

He moves his head. "Help me up," he says.

"Don't move. I'll go find someone. I'll call an ambulance."

"I'm fine." He props up on his elbow.

"You're not fine. Chako stabs you and you think you're fine?" You kneel next to him.

"He didn't stab me," says Jack. "Someone came and picked him up for a job."

"I thought you were dead." You look around for something clean to press to his wound.

"Well, I'm not," says Jack. "Not even close."

"Here." You grab the newspaper.

"Newspaper isn't going to do shit," he says. "The bleeding's stopped. Just hand me my jacket." He sits up and groans. You place his jacket on his shoulders.

"What do you mean the bleeding's stopped?" You can't believe the blade didn't cut a vein or artery or slice through his heart. Maybe it did. Maybe he's going to slump forward and bleed out any second.

"Vodka," says Jack. He uses you as a prop to stand. Then he looks around. There's a fourth bottle, half empty, and he grabs the neck. "For the drive to the hospital."

"Fine," you say. "And we should take this." You pick up the red-streaked knife and drop it into an empty cereal box. When you lose a piece of yourself, say a finger or a leg, you're supposed to bring it with you to the hospital. And for a while, the knife was a part of Jack.

You crutch him down the icy steps to the truck. Once the heat's blasting, the fumes of vodka, vomit, and fire smoke are sickening. You breathe out of your mouth. "You going to tell me what happened?"

"Wasn't planning on it," he says.

"Jesus, Jack."

"I believe his name was Jesus *Christ*."

"You tell me or you're walking," you say.

"You wouldn't make me walk." He looks out at the frozen trees. "But I'll tell you anyways." He takes a swig. Then swirls the bottle and takes another long drink.

"I'm listening."

"Gracie, Gracie. Always listening." He laughs.

"Goddamnit, Jack."

"You won't tell? Not even Jean? Not even that pussy boyfriend of yours? What's his name, Hicky, or some shit?"

You grit your teeth. "No one."

"All right. I did it."

"You did what?"

"I stabbed myself in the chest," he says. "I don't remember doing it, but I must have."

"That's it? That's all you have to say?"

"I remember pulling the knife out," he says. "And thinking that would do me in. But then I woke up, figured I wasn't going anywhere–poured vodka on it all and drank some more."

"What about Jean and the kids?" you say. "What about me? You go apeshit on us all and you think it's a goddamn joke. I mean, I'm pretty sure I'm pregnant for god's sake. You're my brother. I can't do this without you"

"I hate to point out what's obvious," he says. "But you already did."

"You know what I fucking mean." You pound on the steering wheel.

He isn't fazed. "Does Hicky know?"

"His name is Hyde." You collect yourself, if there's anything to collect. "And maybe."

"Oh god," says Jack. "He's the kind of guy who knows when you're on the rag, isn't he? When will Gracie be bitchy? When won't she put out?"

"Sounds like you know a lot about it," you say.

"I'm right, aren't I?" he says.

"You're drunk." Which you somehow always forget when you're talking to him.

"I'm a lot more than that, Miss Slut."

"Watch it."

"Don't worry," he says. "You're going to be a terrible mother. The goddamn worst."

"I am," you say. "I really, really am." Because you can't even take care of your own brother, much less some helpless blob of a baby and when did you make the promise, "I will go down into the darkness with you," and when did you decide to keep it and your laughing sounds like you're crying, and your crying sounds like you're laughing. This is how you drive the snowy twelve miles to the hospital in Soldotna.

THEY ADMIT JACK and you hand over the cereal box with the knife. You tell them how you found him and you have no idea what happened. They shrug and say, "It's February." You call Jean and tell her only that you're going to sober him up before you bring him home, which might be a while. You almost don't call Hyde, but when you hear his voice, you ask him to come to the hospital in Soldotna, that it's about Jack. The receptionist hands you a mug of coffee. In the lobby is a mannequin covered in fish hooks, articulating flesh flies, bright spinners and lures. You've heard the stories. Fishermen come in snagged and the doctor takes out the hooks and puts them on the same place on the mannequin. There's a line of papers taped on the wall next to her and the top one is titled, "Name the Manikin." You go down the list. Fish Hook Franny but then someone crossed out the *r*. The next two have definitions. Tina, my ex-wife. Marla, the fatass bitch sleeping with my husband. Then there's Fish Hook Hussy. Fish Hook

Hawg. Fish Hook Fuck-Up. The Fish Hook Totem. The Lures of Eagle Rock. Dolly Varden Voodoo. Which is immediately followed with Vagina Voodoo. The Hook Keeper. The Fisherman's Curse. Fish Hook Whiskey. You try not to want the vodka Jack left in your truck. Fish Hook Hallelujah. Your favorite: WHAT I FUCKING FEEL LIKE RIGHT NOW scrawled in caps. Because they always find the most vulnerable parts—a treble hook at the base of the throat, ears and hands covered with tied flies. But the one that makes you cringe is the hook straight through the eye.

Jack probably won't remember this night, the hospital, your conversation on the way. You will. And if he does remember, he'll make a story out of it. "Some crazyasses broke in, looked like they rolled in mooseturds, and tried to steal Chako's stove, Can you believe it? That stove was Chako's great-great-grandfather's. He hauled it on a snow sled across the tundra in 1875. I said, 'You're not taking this stove, you fucks. Have anything else. Have a bottle of vodka.' But they didn't want that. So one of the two starts acting real cagey like he thinks he can take me. And I pull out my buck knife and say, 'You better think about what you're doing,' and I would have made a mess of him, if not for the slimy newspaper I slipped on in Chako's trash-stash of a trailer and before I know it the guy is standing over me and I've been stabbed and then he spooks and runs off with the other guy and without thinking I pull that shit out." You'll be the nag of a sister who bitches him out on the way to the hospital. Chako will hear the story so many times he'll believe the stove is worth something, start telling his own stories about his wild great-great grandfather.

The doctor comes out. You think, "He's dead. I shouldn't have moved him."

The doctor says, "Well, looks like he's out of the woods."

"Yes," you say. "Those damn woods."

They've determined the wound is self-inflicted by the angle of entry. The knife barely missed a vein, but all he needed was stitches. They're going to keep him overnight, do a psych evaluation when he's sober. You call Jean and tell her he's going to stay the night on your couch, a record bender this time. Chako was making up his own shots again and she says, "That goddamn Chako. I could kill him." Jack was supposed to do inventory at the auto-part store he co-owns with Doormat.

Hyde arrives with smoked salmon that was in your fridge and some crackers.

"There was an accident," you say. "He's OK. I can't tell you about it."

"But you will?"

"I will." You squeeze his hand. "Soon."

"Jean's not here?"

"Jean's not supposed to know."

"I think you should call her," he says.

"I think he should have to tell her."

"Is there anything you need to tell me?"

"Not now." You lean your head on his shoulder.

"You know what I do, while I wait for you?" he says. "I sew like my grandma."

You could go home, but you wouldn't sleep anyway. In the morning, they release Jack. Even they fell for his line of bull. Jack probably promised the guy a deal on a used transmission. The first thing he says when they wheel him out is, "Hicky, what are you doing here?"

Neither of you answer him.

"Chickenshits," Jack says. "You both thought I was gone, didn't you? And I bet *he* thinks you tell him everything, right, Gracie?"

You freeze.

Jack raises his eyebrows at you. "What, now you don't have anything to say?"

TWO WEEKS LATER and you're at Fur Rondy. You still haven't had a phone call, not even from Jean just to talk. They're probably staying with your cousins in Anchorage. You and Hyde are staying with your mother in Chugiak since it's not too far away You watch the blanket toss and go ice bowling and see the snow sculptures on Ship Creek. One of the first-place winners is called *Qasida*—Aleut for *go fish*—and shows an open-mouthed fisherman in a kayak struggling to catch a giant halibut that is right underneath him, fighting for its life, pulled up from the depths of the ocean. The fisherman has speared the halibut in the head and rides the wake. One more flip, one more thrash, and the kayak will capsize. Either one could win. You don't know if "go fish" is a command to the fisherman or a raised fist in support of the fisherman's demise.

For the Miners and Trappers Ball, you and Hyde dress up as lumberjack and lumberjill in matching red flannel shirts and work boots. You in the Carhartt miniskirt that Hyde made. You spot Jack and Jean on the dance floor, swaying to the slow music, their arms wrapped, their legs tangled. Her face is smashed into his shoulder. He has his chin tucked into her hair. If they could swallow each other under the streamers and glowing lights of blue, they would. But there's something about the way Hyde touches the arc of your back and keeps time with his fingertips–and you make up a stupid little song–*timber, timber, timber, you hold me just tight enough.*

Old Car

Michelle Willms

Hannah walked beside her vanishing father. His body, once strong, had reduced like soup boiling for far too long. Her father adjusted his straw hat with its former black ribbon, now salted gray with dried sweat. Hannah couldn't bear to look at him any longer and stole a glance through the rough-hewn fence rails separating their farm from the Millers' next door.

She saw the dilapidated old car that Mr. and Mrs. Miller's seventeen-year-old son, Isaac, kept parked in deep ruts behind their barn. Driving automobiles was strictly prohibited in their community, but allowances were made for teenagers like Isaac, who was taking part in *rumspringa*.

It was Saturday, and Hannah wondered at the car being home at all. It was common knowledge among the families that on Friday nights Isaac and his friends drove the old car out of West Kootenai for the weekend and picked up Amish girls along the way—girls who placed lighted lanterns in their bedroom windows to signal to the boys that they too were ready to go to a hoedown, to camp in the Purcell Mountains west of their community, or to drive east and go swimming in Lake Koocanusa. And for reasons Hannah never spoke of to anyone, she also knew that sometimes the youth traveled into a city, likely Libby or Kalispell, to attend parties with the English, those people who were not Amish.

"Help me with this," her father said.

It had rained the night before, so Hannah and her father set to the task of cleaning the simple wire-mesh filter atop the rain barrel. He held the frame while Hannah used a twig to scrape out a potpourri of fallen things: leaves, maple keys, lifeless insects.

As she and her father worked, Hannah wondered if her mother had spoken with him about the improper question she had asked. Hannah knew better than to ask such questions of anyone, even her mother, who from the time

Hannah was a little girl had always encouraged her to turn away when one farm animal mounted another. Yet at sundown the day before, as Hannah and her mother sat up in a tree together picking peaches for jam, Hannah felt desperate to understand the mystery. "Mother," she said, knowing that to finish her sentence would quite surprise her mother, like a pin-pricked finger.

"Yes, Hannah?" her mother said, reaching for a piece of fruit.

"Can you please explain the mystery to me?"

Her mother's hand quivered before plucking a peach and placing it gently into a basket balanced within the branches.

"What do you mean?" she said.

Hannah spoke quickly. "What I mean is that I'd like to know about the mystery that happens between a man and a woman when married, and how a woman comes to bear a child."

Her mother sat unmoving. Hannah gripped a branch to steady herself, wondering if she might be punished once home for asking such a question.

When her mother finally spoke, she averted her eyes and said, "That is between a bride and her bridegroom, and God, Hannah. Some knowledge, when known too soon, becomes a burden. Be patient. You'll know soon enough, when it's your time to be married."

Her mother continued picking as though nothing had happened, but Hannah's eyes filled. Having recently found a thin book with glossy pages fraught with images of uncovered men and women physically engaged in a way that both confused her and made her cheeks burn, Hannah wondered if what she saw was the mystery. If she could only understand it, then perhaps her shame would lift. She wanted to confess to her mother that while the images appalled her, she continued turning the pages in awe. But to confess to her mother would take away the one last joy Hannah felt she had left in life–sitting in Isaac's car and helping herself to his belongings.

Hannah looked away from her father's bony fingers and tried to lift up the remnants of a firefly from the corner of the filter with her twig. Hannah, only thirteen, was too young to place a lantern, yet that didn't stop her window from brightening with a special kind of light each Sunday night when Isaac's car rolled safely back into the ruts, the two headlights illuminating her white eyelet curtains for a moment, only to quickly extinguish and leave her in a shroud of darkness. A wellspring of joy would bubble up inside her when she heard his car door slam at a distance, for as she imagined Isaac walking away, she believed the car to be hers again. Then from Monday to Friday, Hannah watched each morning as Isaac and his father emerged from their house wearing their simple black shirts and trousers. Isaac harnessed their family's horse while his father secured their small black buggy to travel to work where they made wooden furniture together; the moment their horse and buggy turned the corner, Hannah would emerge from her house, bend low, and dash to Isaac's car.

Her father set the filter down, and together they peered inside the barrel. Their reflections rippled dark on the water with the bright blue sky mirrored behind them. When her father smiled, Hannah turned her face away and stood up. Her eyes darted back to the Millers' property. Sitting alone inside the old car made her feel happy, something she no longer felt at home. Hannah missed her friends, and though her parents had taken her out of school early to help on the farm, with great reason, Hannah felt like an altogether different person—jarred-up and pickled in sadness and farm sweat.

As Hannah's father slowly bent upright, she looked to him again.

"That's enough water for a wash," he said, and nodded toward the hem of her plain black dress caked with dung from mucking out the barn. The brown under her fingernails and between her toes didn't bother her today because it was Saturday, bath day.

"You will help your mother when I'm gone," he said. The hot summer wind could not winnow away the sadness from his heavy words. Hannah wondered if another letter had come for him. He stroked his long beard, as he often did when he seemed deep in thought. They both looked down at his fist, clutching a large tuft of his dislodged black and silver hair—hair he had not shorn since the day he'd married Hannah's mother. Surely another sign that the cancer in his blood would push him toward heaven sooner than she or her mother thought. It had already been arranged by Hannah's parents and the Millers next door that the Millers' eldest daughter and her husband would purchase Hannah's family's farm after Hannah's father passed away. Mr. Harrow and Mrs. Harrow, Hannah's parents' close friends since childhood, had offered to section off three acres of their farm and sell it to Hannah's mother, and when the time came to claim it, the men in their community would work together to build Hannah and her mother a house.

AT LEAST THAT had been the Harrows' plan. Last spring, after the news of her father's illness the winter before, Hannah's mother had gone to assist Mrs. Harrow's labor, but when her mother returned, she collapsed into Hannah's father's arms. Instead of announcing the sex and name of the newborn, she said between sobs, "Abigail's gone. They're both gone. There was so much blood." Mrs. Harrow would not be the first woman to perish during childbirth along with her baby, nor would Hannah's father be the first man to get cancer and die. In spite of his failing state that spring, Hannah's father had helped Mr. Harrow make a coffin for Abigail and the baby. Their Amish community gathered in the back field of the Schmidt property, which served as the community's graveyard. As Hannah watched her father struggle to help dig the burial hole for Abigail and the child, her throat ached and her mouth dried. When she couldn't bear to watch him any longer, she fixed her gaze beyond the group, out toward the expanse of the meadow, where patches of white bittercress flowers and blue forget-me-nots ran toward the western mountain range's skirt like a large bolt of patterned whole cloth rolled across a table for pattern-cutting.

The congregation had formed a large circle around the burial site, and Hannah looked to Mrs. Schmidt, who stood next to Mr. Harrow by the head of the grave. Mrs. Schmidt reached over and gripped Mr. Harrow's, her brother's, hand. Mr. Harrow's gaze was fixed on the coffin resting on the ground close by. His skin had turned the ashen color of old wash water, and Mrs. Schmidt looked no better. Her eyes like wet stones, the dark circles beneath them, the shadowy hollows in a creek bed.

Hannah thought Mrs. Schmidt an amiable woman, and her walnut streusel cake was the best Hannah had ever tasted, but Mrs. Schmidt had recently said something that had caused Hannah to lose much-needed sleep. When Mrs. Schmidt had dropped off a pitcher of her apple-cider vinegar mixture for Hannah's father, she said to Hannah, "Should it be God's will, this family remedy will help cure your father's cancer, but should it not be, we can trust God, Whose ways are higher than our ways." Hannah had taken the pitcher from Mrs. Schmidt, having never before considered that her father's dying might be a part of their loving God's will. Mrs. Schmidt had never regained her rosy hue after her daughter, Sarah, had left their community the year before. Was this also God's will? Hannah knew Mrs. Schmidt must have believed it so, and yet Mrs. Schmidt stayed firm in her faith. It was difficult for Hannah to understand Mrs. Schmidt's patience and surety.

Hannah had looked again to her father holding a spade next to the deepening grave, his forehead smeared with dirt. Isaac touched her father's shoulder and handed him a handkerchief before he leaned in to whisper into her father's ear. Breathless, her father wiped his forehead and walked toward Hannah and her mother. He stood beside Hannah, and though none of the other men wept, her father held the grey kerchief over his eyes, the fabric's color darkening.

Soon thereafter, six men used ropes to lower the coffin into the ground before the bishop spoke upon God's love for His people, and prayed. Mr. Harrow, Hannah and her parents, and Mr. and Mrs. Schmidt, along with the five Schmidt boys and some of their wives and children, each took up a handful of earth to sprinkle on the coffin. Next, Isaac, with his older brothers, his father, and Mr. Schmidt worked quickly to restore the mound of earth back into the burial plot.

Mr. Harrow knelt down and touched the burial mound, his hand trembling. When he rose, Hannah's father wrapped his arm around Mr. Harrow's shoulders, and slowly turned him. Together they walked at length through the graveyard to the edge of the property to face the mountains. It was then that Mr. Harrow bent forward, his body shaking, and released a grievous howl that echoed off the mountains and returned as the startling sound of a baby crying. Hannah reached for her mother, who pulled her into a tight embrace.

When Hannah's father and Mr. Harrow returned, Mrs. Schmidt touched her brother's shoulder gently and said, "There is a great deal of suffering at present, Noah, and yet surely we can trust God's perfect will. He has good plans for you yet. May His peace be upon you."

Mr. Schmidt, who stood next to his wife, nodded. He gripped Mr. Harrow's other shoulder, giving it a gentle squeeze.

Hannah watched as Mr. Harrow's dark brow furrowed and his clear blue eyes filled with storms. Mr. and Mrs. Schmidt removed their hands from his shoulders and looked confused by his expression.

"Is this God's perfect will, Anna?" asked Mr. Harrow. "For surely such pain, on such a day as today, is no more the will of God than the fall of man, nor all of the pain and suffering that followed thereafter."

Hannah looked to her mother, who shook her head slightly, which could mean anything: don't speak, don't stare, don't fret, but Hannah didn't know which.

"I fear you have mistaken what I mean, Noah," said Mrs. Schmidt, stretching her hand out toward him.

"I do not believe I have, for you said, 'Surely we can trust God's perfect will.' Dare I say, as of late you serve your thoughts to people like a helping of food they never asked for, Anna."

"I only seek to bring you comfort, Noah," said Mrs. Schmidt, imploringly.

"There is no comfort to be had this day, Anna, for my home is empty."

Hannah's father said gently, "Your anger is misdirected, Noah. Shall we take a walk again?"

Before Mr. Harrow could answer, Mrs. Schmidt said, "You have lost greatly indeed, brother, but I feel this loss too. Abigail was dear to me also. Was I not also beside her, only three days past, on that woeful night? And beside you?" Mrs. Schmidt raised the back of her hand to her lips and stifled a cry. Mr. Schmidt stepped closer to her.

Hannah recognized this behavior well enough; when she had attended school, close siblings might be babbling quietly together outside in the schoolyard one moment, like water in the slow turn of a river, only to quickly change course the next, their volume rising, their words rushing swiftly and crashing upon each other in rapid bursts. During harvest time, when the sun reckoned a family's work hours longer, this happened all the more, and if the teacher took notice of the quarrel before the siblings resolved it on their own, she would say to them, "As two voices sing unto the Lord, they will eventually find the harmony." Then she would have them sing a hymn together until the peace between them was restored. And if that didn't work, the paddle.

"I believe there to be no falsehood in Anna's words," said Mr. Schmidt, his voice deep, "and if you have reached your conclusions by studying Scripture independently, Noah, then—"

"You have never known me to be a rebellious man, Daniel. If you wonder at my studying Scripture independently, I have not. I have come to this knowledge only by saying the Lord's Prayer, in which I have always found great comfort. When hope filled our home, I prayed 'Thy will be done,' as a declaration, as though it were already so, but now in my darkest hours, I find that I pray 'Thy will be done' as a petition, for surely such pain and loss cannot be the will of God."

Wearily, Mrs. Schmidt lowered her hand. "How can you speak to me so, Noah? For how am I to think upon God's will otherwise? How can I bear to think otherwise? My home, once filled with hope and cheer, feels empty, yet I find peace and new hope within my understanding of God's will, so what is it you charge me with, brother? Trusting God's plans? Trusting His goodness?"

Hannah, who had found it difficult to breathe through the siblings' exchange, exhaled deeply when the storm in Mr. Harrow's eyes appeared to be passing, and his river turning, for his voice had softened.

"No," said Mr. Harrow. "I seek to offer you rectification, for I have heard you express your understanding of God's will quite freely with others as of late, and though you seek to bring comfort, you may injure."

"As I think upon it now, Noah and Anna," said Hannah's father, "I believe you will agree with me when I say we have yet to hear the bishop or ministers teach upon God's will as absolute or supple, and being so, perhaps it is wise that the subject depart from everyone's lips, henceforth."

Mr. Harrow and Mrs. Schmidt stood in silence for a time, looking at Hannah's father.

"You are right to say so," said Mr. Harrow.

"Indeed," said Mrs. Schmidt.

"And if I may say so," said Mr. Schmidt, "and I feel that I must, such strong words, dare I say even accusations—even on a day such as today when surely any man in your position should be given forbearance, Noah—may burden you with regret later, and injure those who love you. But rest assured, dear brother, we understand that grief is a heavy burden to carry, and we are here so that you might not carry it alone. Anna has prepared a bed for you, and you may stay with us as long as you like so that you will not return to an empty home, nor will you be far from your family."

Mr. Harrow bowed his head. "I am humbled. Forgive me," he said, stifling his own cry now. "I am not the man I was three days ago, who awaited the joyous birth of my child with Abigail. It was not my intent to injure you, Anna."

"Nor was it mine to injure you, Noah," said Mrs. Schmidt. "Forgive me." She reached her hand out toward Mr. Harrow, who stood hunched. Mr. Harrow took it at once.

NOW, MONTHS LATER, having cleaned the water barrel filter with her father, Hannah set out two plates with boiled eggs, a slice of cheese, and a cut of bread. She pulled her chair up tightly to the table. Shortly after receiving news of her father's cancer, what Hannah considered The Letter Plague began. Letter after letter had come for her father, always from a distant relative, and always in need of his help, and this day, Hannah's heart sank when her father placed an envelope on the wooden table before her.

"I must leave this afternoon," he said.

Her mother, who was working in town, would stare at the letter when she was home, and nod and say, "It's for the best."

Hannah said nothing.

Whenever Hannah's father arrived home from his journeys, he retched for days on end while Hannah held the pail, cleaned his face, and covered his shaking body on the floor with a warm blanket while he whispered to God, "Thy will be done." Hannah wondered at times if her father's prayer was a declaration, or a petition. She wished her mother were home to comfort her and her father, but her mother worked at a quilt shop from open to close every day, where she sewed intricate puzzles of fabric together by hand under electric lights while tourists looked on. The money she earned ensured that they would not lose their family farm before Hannah's father died, as they had come close to doing when Hannah's father fell ill.

Hannah could not tell her father what he ought or ought not do—she risked getting the paddle if she did so—but his sickness had already rendered him unable to manage the work on the farm. Anger rose up and she feared she could hold her tongue no longer. She pushed her plate forward.

"May I please be excused to do my barn chores?" she said, staring at the wood grain of the table.

"Hannah—" he said, but the loud scrape of her chair being pushed back overpowered his failing voice.

She ran to the back door before he could say any more and quickly pulled her work tunic from the hook, tied the strings tightly around her waist, and slipped her shoes on. She ran toward the barn to yell at the bull, or whatever creature came across her path first.

"Do these distant relatives, who call upon him in times of sickness, also yoke a lame ox to plough their fields?" she yelled. The chickens grew silent and stared at her with cocked heads.

She stomped into the barn. "Why won't you heal him?" she screamed to God. Carrot, their friendly barn cat, cowered and then ran away. Dust motes caught in a beam of light captured Hannah's attention, and in three steps, she pressed her face against the barn board to peer through the hole where a wood knot had popped out. She took stock of the Millers' farm, looking for family movement, but only the corn stalks swayed.

Hannah dashed across the yard, pulled the car door open, and slipped in. She sank down into the burning bucket seat, and soft-clicked the door closed. It was sweltering inside. Sweat beaded on her hairline and the crest of her upper lip as she sat quiet and still, allowing herself to feel fully abandoned by her father. She removed her white *kapp,* knowing this would displease him, and pin by pin she unfurled her bun and let her long hair roll down her back. Unable to bear the heat any longer, she slowly rolled down the window, her eyes scanning the yard before she began her ritual.

Unlatching the glovebox, she pulled Isaac's bag of Twizzlers out. She peered inside, sad to see the bag was almost empty, save three licorice sticks. Her stomach cramped with hunger pangs. She pulled out all three pieces and rested them on the dusty dashboard while she carefully plumped the bag and repositioned it back in the glovebox. Her father was most likely preparing the horse and buggy to leave, and Hannah sank down even further so as not to be seen. She braided the soft and pliable Twizzlers and took a bite.

Next, like a stealthy cat, Hannah crawled into the back seat where burgundy upholstery thinned to pink in the well-worn places. Tufts of stuffing poured out of a large tear along the top of the middle seat, like a cattail gone to seed. Hannah pulled the loop handle where the seat folded down, the contents of Isaac's trunk at her full disposal. She reached in and held up ripped blue jeans and a teeshirt with cut-off sleeves, pushing the fabric of Isaac's garments against her face and inhaling deeply. His clothing smelled sweet and musky, like rain and fire smoke. She threaded her head and arms through the shirt holes and wore it over her dress.

Hannah considered her time in the old car to be her *rumspringa*—or at least her *sitsitspringa*—because *rumspringa* was no longer an option for her; by the time she was old enough to place a lantern her father would be years gone, and her mother would need her at home to continue working each weekend, lest they lose their small new farm on Mr. Harrow's property.

Yet she longed to go camping next to Lake Koocanusa and tried to find contentment by imagining herself there with Isaac and his friends, her face aglow by the firelight at dusk as she grilled fresh fish and roasted potatoes over a cooking fire for them. When she served the food, everyone would say, "Thank you, Hannah," which she didn't hear very often anymore from her tired parents. Next, someone would ask God to bless the food and the hands that prepared it, being her hands. When the meal was over, she and the other girls would leave the boys to walk into the shallows of Lake Koocanusa, where they would wash the plates. And during that time, she would freely ask the girls about the mystery, and the girls would tell her everything, unlike her mother.

Hannah reached into each of Isaac's pants pockets to find his cell phone, and then turned it on. The phone buzzed with a new word-message. Hannah touched the name Sylvia and read: "FYEO I no u said ur not looking for sumthin srs, IMU. can't wait 2 touch u again and 4 u 2 touch me." Beside the message were small pictures of a purple eggplant and a peach. Rather quickly, Hannah imagined Isaac and a girl touching each other uncovered. She shook her head in an effort to rid herself of the thought and lifted the floor mat where she'd found the glossy-paged book before, both relieved and disappointed to see it gone lest she feel tempted to look again.

Word messages were not what she wanted to see most, so she touched a little square box on the screen that she'd learned through trial-and-error would lead her to pictures. There was a very old photo from half a year back of Isaac standing beside an English girl with his arm over her shoulder and a cigarette dangling from the corner of his mouth. His pupils were large black saucers, and the whites of his eyes looked overlaid with the pilling of fine red yarn. In the background, some other teenagers she recognized from her community wore teeshirts and pants, and they held cans up to their mouths.

She touched an arrow, and another old picture appeared on the screen—one of Sarah Schmidt holding her baby, born out of wedlock. Though Sarah grinned, there were dark circles beneath her eyes. From the pictures on Isaac's phone, Hannah guessed that Isaac went to visit Sarah about once every two weeks, beginning a few months back. Hannah touched the screen again and saw a new picture of Sarah and her child, now sitting on a blanket together and stacking wooden blocks. Hannah smiled and took another bite off the strawberry-flavored braid, her mouth filling with saliva, and paused mid-chew. She looked closer at the photo. The details in the background were grainy, but clear enough to cause her to inhale deeply through her nose.

A man lay sideways on Sarah's couch, his arms knotted over his chest, his hat resting over his face. Hannah recognized the thinning legs pulled up tight into his stomach, and a big toe poking through a wool sock tip that she'd darned several times. Why was her father at Sarah Schmidt's house? Before she could try to piece together what this meant, a head poked through the old car's rolled-down window.

"Caught you!" Isaac said.

Hannah threw the phone, as though it burned her hands.

"What are you doing in my car?" he said. "And why are you wearing my clothes?"

"I'm sorry," she said, refusing to meet his eyes as she hurriedly took off his teeshirt. She grabbed her bonnet and opened the door. Outside, her hair fell over her shoulders. She turned to leave.

"Wait," he said, "you can't just go. I need to take inventory."

"I'm sorry," she said again, turning back to him. "Please don't tell my parents."

Hannah looked down as they stood in silence for a moment.

"Get in the car," he said, "while I look over my stuff. I thought maybe a squirrel or raccoon was getting in through the rust spot under the mat, eating my food and messing up my stuff, but wouldn't you know, it was just you."

Hannah found it difficult to breathe, as though she'd fallen backwards off a rearing horse. It was hard to move.

"Can you please just get in the car?" Isaac said. "I don't have all day. I'm picking up a friend."

Hannah met Isaac's eyes, expecting a leer of consternation, but instead, he gazed softly. She moved back toward the car. Hannah purposefully left the door open and faced forward in the passenger seat, as Isaac stared at her from the driver's seat.

One of Hannah's cousins, whom Hannah had recognized in Isaac's party pictures from the city, spoke ill of Isaac one evening during a family dinner by saying, "Isaac's gone hog-wild in *rumspringa*, crossing lines he ought not cross. He stopped picking us up on the weekends. Says he's exploring Montana's badlands alone. I'll say. Hopefully he'll still be able to find his way Home."

"No good comes from unkind words," Hannah's father had corrected, "especially where young people are concerned. Isaac works hard with his father, but the weekends are his alone during *rumspringa*—as they should be—to do as he pleases before making a baptismal commitment to the Lord. I'm sure he'll find his way Home yet."

"Isaac shows generosity," Hannah's mother said. "His mother tells me that he gives most of his wages to his father. Though the Millers' farm does well enough, there are already nine children to feed, and Mrs. Miller is pregnant again."

Her cousin's cheeks flushed and he bowed his head. Everyone ate in silence, with only the occasional sound of utensils scraping stoneware. Hannah watched sidelong as her father lowered his hand beneath the table, no doubt to grip her mother's fingers for a moment, as Hannah was the only child her mother had ever been able to carry to term.

Isaac gripped the steering wheel. "How long have you been breaking into my car?"

That's not how Hannah saw it. The accusation weighed like a millstone.

"Well, if you won't answer that one, then answer this one: How's your father doing?"

His question caught her by surprise—nobody asked anymore. She turned to him, unsure of what a teenage boy would know of her beloved father, whose body disintegrated more and more daily, like a farm tool strewn carelessly into a field to rust and crumble under the hot sun and driving rain.

"He has cancer," she said.

"I know," Isaac said. He reached for the glovebox and opened it. He smacked the Twizzlers bag repeatedly while looking at her. "Empty."

Hannah glanced at the phone she'd thrown on the floor when Isaac had caught her by surprise. He followed her gaze and leaned his face down toward her thigh to reach for it by her feet.

"You smell like cow manure," he said. "You put my clean clothes over your crap-caked dress." Hannah's cheeks burned. "How far did you get through the pictures?"

"Not far," she said. "I saw the pictures of Sarah and her child."

"Yes, Schmidty and little Schmidts," he said.

Hannah remained silent.

"Oh," he said, and turned to Hannah, who sat perfectly still, staring out the windshield. "Did you see him?"

Hannah nodded, fighting hard not to cry. She thought about her grieving mother and how her father would suffer through a shunning when the bishop learned he had engaged in the mystery with Sarah Schmidt, which somehow created a child. Did that make the child her half-sibling? And who would care for her father if he was forced to leave the community, for surely, she'd stay with her mother?

"Your mother knows," Isaac said. "And she supports the decision. I reckon they didn't tell you because you're only eleven or twelve."

Hannah turned to him and said, "I'm thirteen, and my mother would never agree to my father being with another woman."

"What?" Isaac said, tilting his head. "Schmidty and your father? No, she lets him sleep on his couch after his chemotherapy treatments at the hospital."

"What are chemotherapy treatments?" she said.

"It's medicine that the English created to heal cancer," he said, "and sometimes it works."

"Does this mean that my father's not going to die?"

"The doctor said the treatment seems to be working for your father."

Hannah slapped her hand over her mouth to stop a cry from escaping. After a few deep breaths, she pressed her eyes with her soles of palms, as though the pressure might hold back her tears. She imagined her father as an old man, the wrinkly skin on his hands and arms as soft as worn leather, enveloping her in a hug as warm as morning ash in the woodstove.

Isaac handed her his gray handkerchief, and she pressed it to her eyes. The hopelessness that had circled and cawed above her dying father like an ever-present carrion bird, flew away. She looked at Isaac with reddened eyes, unable to suppress a smile.

"Does the church leadership know?" she said.

"No," Isaac said. "Just me, your ma, and Schmidty. Though I reckon when your father's well again, a secret like this will eventually burden him to the point of seeking out the bishop to tell him he's broken the rules of the *Ordnung.*" Hannah nodded, knowing this of her father too.

"But your father tells me there are other Amish communities where the *Ordnung* may allow chemotherapy," Isaac said. "Perhaps you'll resettle there."

"Perhaps," Hannah said quietly.

Her smile faded. She quickly pressed the kerchief to her eyes again to conceal her face, thankful that Isaac didn't seem to notice her chin dimple, or new tears springing. Their community in West Kootenai was the only home Hannah had ever known, and she didn't want to leave.

"I respect him for wanting to live honestly," Isaac said, "and I've decided to live honestly too. That's why I'm not getting baptized into the church."

Hannah lowered the kerchief and turned to him. "Really?" she said, her hand moving involuntarily along the upholstery of the bucket seat as though it were the soft skin of a friend's hand. She felt saddened for Isaac's family, and saddened that his car would eventually leave with him.

"Really," he said. "I was ready to get baptized, and I started looking at the Amish girls around here for one to court and eventually marry, but then I ran into Schmidty and little Schmidts when I was bringing your father to the medical center in Libby. Sarah looked rough, and her little guy didn't look any better. I offered to drive her home, and when I carried her bags into the apartment it was . . ." Isaac shook his head. "It was a bad scene: mostly empty, no toys, and it would have sent my mother into one of her cleaning fits. I left everything I had in my wallet on Sarah's table when she put little Schmidts to bed, and I told her I'd be back. If I get baptized, I'll have to stop helping her, and I won't do that to a friend." Isaac looked toward his house.

"My mother will suffer at my leaving. And I'll be sad to leave her too." Isaac turned to Hannah. "You still see your friends, what with working the farm now, and all?"

Hannah shook her head, glad to speak of something other than departure.

"Surely you still see them at the weekly hymn sing," he said.

"I'm too tired after a long day's work to go," she said.

"But look at you now," he said. "You're a good farmer, and that's half as much as the other girls can say."

Hannah held back a smile. "Don't encourage pride," she said.

"I'm not. See, sometimes when I'm working on my car, I can see you through the fence over there." He pointed to the small vegetable garden that Hannah kept. "I watched when you found the dead rat over there, that your orange cat reduced to the likes of a pile of red ribbons. You didn't flinch–just picked it up on the tip of your spade and threw it into our cornfield."

Hannah look down at her calloused hands and smiled at his words.

"You were strong," he said, nodding at her, "and then you threw it into our cornfield," he repeated. "And then you threw it into our–"

"I'm sorry," Hannah said.

"Not a problem," Isaac said. He nodded and smiled. "Just wanted to hear that you knew you did wrong."

A breeze blew through the car and Hannah turned toward her and her parents' farm. She watched the sea of wheat ripple beyond the fence. Her expression changed. Isaac followed her gaze.

"You ready to hold a scythe?" he asked. "What do you have over there, thirty acres?"

"Forty," she said. "I wish the field was in its seventh year, so we could let it lie fallow."

"Well, no need to worry about harvest. It's already been settled that come harvest time, my father, my brothers, and I will help you."

"You won't be gone by then?"

"No," he said. "I'm to help you and my father harvest before leaving."

Hannah laced her fingers together and looked down at them in her lap.

"Would you like to come to the hospital with us today?" Isaac asked.

"I'd like that very much so."

"Good. I'm picking him up at our meeting place in half an hour."

Hannah swung her legs over the side of the car.

"Where're you going?" he said.

"I can't go to the hospital smelling like cow cake. I need to wash first."

"Nobody will care how you smell," he said. "It's a hospital. Come back in."

She turned her body back into the seat slowly. Isaac looked away when Hannah coiled her hair back into a bun, pinning it carefully, before securing her white *kapp* in place.

He opened his car door and picked up a backpack that Hannah hadn't seen him set beside the car. He unzipped it, and then carefully drew up a large camera and handed it to Hannah.

"Be careful. It's new," he said. He leaned over and pushed a button that made a small square screen light up. "Now press this arrow button to the side," he said, "to look through my pictures from last weekend. Schmidty, little Schmidts, and me went camping at Glacier Park. I've got some good photos of them standing by some of the lakes, and I even got a picture of a few mountain goats."

Hannah smiled as she looked through all the pictures. She noticed plumes of smoke in some of the pictures.

"Wildfires?" she said.

"Yeah. They've started on the western side of the park. They were far enough away."

Hannah handed the camera back to Isaac. He gently lowered it into his backpack. Next, he pulled out a new bag of Twizzlers and opened it with his key-chain pocketknife. He tilted the bag toward Hannah, the smell of sweet strawberry candy filling the air between them. She smiled and pulled out two pieces. Beside Isaac, Hannah watched the fields, her thoughts on the strength it would take to swing a scythe. Hannah imagined working in the wheat field alongside her father for many years to come, but in their West Kootenai community for the last time. Would everyone feel cheerless, or would they still sing hymns unto the Lord together as was customary, to quicken the work of the harvest and to draw their thoughts away from the dull ache in their bones and the new blisters forming on their soles of palms? It would be difficult for Hannah and her family to leave their community, surely, but something her mother had said to her through the years came to mind: God did not give us His light so that we might dwell on the shadows and darkness. And so, Hannah looked to the dusty dashboard, to the mottled steering wheel, then through the windshield as she ran her fingers over the soft, timeworn upholstery once again, wondering if within the new community where she and her family might settle, if a girl might be allowed to have an old car of her own.

Sasquatch Seeks a Mate

Aharon Levy

Tonight he'll call himself Steve. He bounced around when he was young, long stretches with no name at all and others when they called him whatever came to mind. Steve's one of the few that stuck, as good as any.

He's here because he's heard that if you can't get laid at Stanley's, you need to check your pulse. That's what the kid at the gas station said anyway, handing him the fake ID and a few bills as he pocketed the mushrooms Sasquatch had brought down from the mountain. The kid, who never seemed to listen to Sasquatch with more than one ear unplugged from his iPod, always had a hell of a time understanding his accent.

"You from Atlanta or something, man?" the kid asked him tonight, then nodded without waiting for a reply. "Nice and warm there, I bet." They looked together at the misted peaks, past the bright buzz of Stanley's Patio in the middle distance.

Sasquatch is not sure of his own age. He can count—of course he can count—but there's been no reason to. Somewhere between ten and fifteen, he thinks, but his bones have been telling him that his life is more than half over, it's time, it's time to find a mate. He's tall, he's fully haired, and the ID is just a precaution. He's managed this long without one.

The bouncer didn't even glance at it. It's one of the advantages of being what he is. Which is what? The question has not bedeviled him—Sasquatch doesn't spend much time in contemplation, it's not in his nature—but still he wonders, staring at the evidence of his thick fingers, feeling the pinch on his shoe-trapped feet (big, but no bigger than the rest of him). Sasquatch hasn't had schooling, but he knows about evolution. He's overheard plenty of talk radio on the subject, and gathers that the split with humans, among whom he has spent his whole life, must not be so ancient. He remembers the joke the kid repeated again and again until Sasquatch understood: "You got any Polish in you? Well, you want some?" Sasquatch laughed when he finally got it, in a voice so loud and deep that the kid was scared. He'll have to watch that tonight.

Stanley's isn't as crazed as it seemed from the gas station, but it's early, the peaks still calling to him with a little bit of light. Sasquatch feels for his stash of money, built up through visits down the mountain. He finds it implausible that these greasy bits of paper have any value, as implausible as someone having thrown out the shirt he now wears, found in the gas station Dumpster after one of his exchanges with the kid.

And here are the first few females, teetering on pointed shoes and collapsing onto moldy bar stools, most of them far too short but the two at the end broad-shouldered, exposing flesh to pull attention away from their size.

He walks to the bar and nods at the women.

"You're a big one, aren't you," says the taller, giving off a pungency of fruit, whether from her own flesh or the bright slushy drink she's sipping through a straw, he can't tell.

He grunts, mutters, "Drink?"

She blinks, takes a moment to realize what he's asked, indicates her almost-full glass. "Not ready to double-fist yet." She sticks out her chin. "But what'll you have?"

Sasquatch feels excitement at the odor of alcohol—like wild apples fallen from the tree, only sharper and stronger—but shakes his head. "Nothing."

"Come to the right place, huh?" She laughs with her mouth open, head thrown back. Out of the corner of his eye, Sasquatch sees her redheaded friend stare at him unhappily.

"I can . . . I can . . ." His voice, ordinarily so deep, has taken on the whiny flutter that he uses to imitate birds. When he is alone, he can entertain himself for hours producing the urgent chirp of grosbeaks, the questioning twitter of soras, but wonders now: where had he learned this skill? Why does it feel as much a part of him as his knowledge of mushrooms? He is caught by such questions, pointing back at the cave-darkness of his own origin. "I'm not from here," he says, and feels a betrayal to the mountain behind him.

"Foreign, huh?"

"Foreign?"

"That accent. Are you, like, an exchange student?"

"Clara, they're here," says her friend, and Clara—he should have asked for her name immediately, given his too—is distracted.

"My friends," she says to him, then looks back at the redhead. "We're talking."

The redhead rolls her eyes. Sasquatch can see the interest in Clara's posture, but now that there is competition he knows he cannot win.

"So where are you from?" Clara asks, and takes a long drink through her straw.

He thinks of the trailer where he spent the winter, years earlier, the door opened to him during a storm. The old man and woman hadn't asked any questions, just made a space for him on the floor, taught him how to open cans of beans, found him clothing that more or less fit. He'd been wandering for years by then, and with their silence they'd almost convinced him he was no different from them. When spring came they'd begged him to stay but he hadn't.

"Bozeman," he says.

Again she laughs. "You're funny."

He feels his stomach tense, then realizes it's a compliment.

"Strong and silent, huh?"

"Come on," says the redhead, more urgently. Clara gets up, keeps her eyes on Sasquatch, but when he doesn't say anything she turns and disappears into what has become a crowd.

He insinuates himself into a group of arm-pumping, laughing women, moving in rough time to a song that even Sasquatch, isolated as he is, has heard dozens of times over the summer just past. For a few minutes, the dancing works, and denimed buttocks grind against him indiscriminately. But then there is a slow song, and as quickly as he entered the group he has been disgorged to sit at the bar, drinkless.

It is a strange place, Stanley's, neither inside nor out, the bar's bright light dying in the patio's far corners, the overhang drawing a line against the sky above him, the wood floor echoing the emptiness beneath it. And it seems more crowded each second, the trees hanging over its perimeter less and less reachable. The air, though, is still comforting, pine rising above everything else. He breathes deeply and smiles.

"Morgan!" There is a slap on his back and every muscle tenses, ready. He turns to see a wide-bodied, red-faced man in a sweatshirt, peering at him inquisitively. The man shakes his head, holds up open-palmed hands. "Sorry, bro. My bad. You look just like a buddy of mine."

The man walks over to an identically dressed group, points at Sasquatch, and laughs. "Morgan!" someone in the group yells, and when he acknowledges them with a wary nod, they send him a beer.

After that, Sasquatch surrenders. He buys himself another drink, pointing wildly at the bottles behind the bar until the bartender brings him something. Her mouth is a red smear, and her eyes shift too rapidly for him to see their color. He shoves three bills at her and she says, "Too much, too much," but doesn't hand any back. "Next one's on me," she insists, and the next one comes immediately. Sasquatch has already drained the first and presses more bills into her hand, her eyebrows going up as she tucks the money into her pocket. She winks at him, puts a finger to her lips, and before Sasquatch can ask what this means she has gone to the other end of the bar.

Talking has become easier now. A group has sprung up, mushroom-like, around him, and Sasquatch tells a story—he can't remember whether he's ever told one before—about the kid at the gas station. Halfway through, he loses the point of what he's saying, why he's talking about peeing onto the highway, but the group at the bar keeps nodding. He pushes himself up and runs into someone, a man who shoves him, then steps back and barks a laugh when he gets a look at Sasquatch. "No way am I going to fight you," the man says, shaking his head. "No way."

Sasquatch catches sight of Clara but when he stumbles toward her she is gone, replaced by a laughing girl who surely isn't old enough to be in here. His bones tell him not to give up, he can find Clara, but then his bladder speaks and he can barely remember what to do. He shuts his eyes as he guides himself into the panicky cave of the men's room.

When he emerges, tall women are everywhere, striking confident poses, laughing.

"I'm foreign," he yells to one over the music, and she leans in to hear him before whirling away.

"I'm from far away!" he says to another, who nods and gives him a thumbs-up.

A third shakes her head when he speaks, miming that the music is too loud. She takes him by the wrist, flips back her hair with her free hand, and guides him to a table. Their seats are muffled in pine needles from the tree above, and it is dark. Sasquatch can't tell whether this is Clara until the fruit scent reaches him. He closes his eyes, smells the damp dirt under the patio. "I'm a stranger here," he says.

"I know just how you feel," Clara says. "I'm from Kentucky." She lays a hand on his arm. "So what's your name, again?"

Sasquatch finds that he can't summon what he's been calling himself. The alcohol is a woodpecker in his head. "I don't remember."

She laughs at this, hands held far out in front of her face, head thrown back, and after a moment he joins her. The sound of his voice drives her to more laughter, and he releases himself, laughing as he would if he were alone, howling up now at the few visible stars.

"So how long have you been out here?" she asks when they stop laughing. Her palm rests on top of his fingers, cool, smooth as a grebe's egg.

He shakes his head and she goes on talking. "It's strange. I've been here four years, you know, for school, and it still doesn't feel like home."

He nods. He's noticed this gesture comes with equal ease to him and to humans. "How old are you?"

She tsks. "You're not meant to ask that." She purses her lips, cocks her head, giggles. "Twenty-three."

Sasquatch looks down at his hands, vaguely outlined on the table. The kid from the gas station hasn't aged in all the time Sasquatch has known him, and Sasquatch has concluded that humans are like stones, unchanging, unlike himself. "You seem younger," he says quietly.

She leans in to listen and doesn't giggle. "I guess that's a compliment." She smiles—a flash of white teeth in the dark—and says, "So what do you do?"

He draws in his breath at the sudden volume to her voice. "I spend time outside."

"Yeah." She leans back. "It's great, isn't it."

He follows her eyes, sees that she is looking up the mountain, feels something tremendous surge within him, overtaking even the alcohol. "Good water up there."

"What?"

"Leaf piles too. Keep you warm." There are river flints to shave with. Twigs to clean teeth. Foliage thick and springy enough to cover up the evidence of passage. He could tell her all of this. He leans forward at the same moment she does, and when his mouth meets hers it is flooded with the taste of fruit.

After a moment she draws back. "Your breath's a little . . ." She sees the look on his face. "No, no, it's fine." She kisses him again.

This is something Sasquatch has never imagined, and he doesn't want to surrender it. But eventually Clara draws back again and smiles at him, hand at her face.

"Come," he says, and reaches for her arm. He tugs on her, pulls her up slightly. The walk is easy, he thinks. He can carry her if he has to.

Her eyes widen and she pulls back. "Whoah," she says, massaging her wrist. "Don't know your own strength, huh?"

"Come with me," he says, but even to his own ears the words are slurred.

She stands, arms crossed over her chest, looking down at Sasquatch. Her jaw is set, her right foot is pointed back toward the bar, but she doesn't move. As he opens his mouth to speak, as clearly as he can, about the birds, the roots, everything that waits on the mountain, the lights come on behind her.

The bartender—not the woman but a man as hairy as Sasquatch himself—

calls out indifferently, "Finish up." He taps a wobbly stack of glasses with a knife. "Party's over, come on."

"I should go," Clara says, shifting her feet, looking down at them. "My friends are waiting." She looks at Sasquatch and chews her lower lip a moment. "But this was fun." She turns, takes a step, turns back. "Here." She pulls out a piece of paper from her purse, rummages for a pen, writes something, hands him the folded sheet.

The bartender turns on the rest of the lights and the isolated table is part of the patio again, each pine needle and table splinter suddenly clear and shadowed. Sasquatch's gut throbs and his eyes water at the illumination. Clara's nose wrinkles as she looks at him. "Wow, your shirt's really messed up." She glances a moment at the paper in his hands, then shrugs, smiles—another flash of teeth—and walks off.

Sasquatch blinks, rises, opens the sheet. On its surface are semi-familiar markings. What can they mean? He looks up toward the now-invisible mountain, tries to imagine its comforting bulk and finds that he cannot. But it's there, he tells himself, it's waiting. "Go home, go home," the bartender yells to the remaining many. "Get out, get out, try again tomorrow."

Sk8r

Siân Griffiths

June, 1985.

IF IT HAD been night, the neighbors wouldn't have stared at Ilsa in the back of the squad car. In darkness, the blue and red lights overhead might strobe her mother and Harold into sight, but Ilsa would have remained invisible. The fight was between those two anyway; it had nothing to do with her, but California's fierce late-afternoon sun exposed them all.

"Sit tight," the officer had said as he shut her in. Ilsa imagined he wanted not so much to protect her as to contain her until the on-call social worker arrived.

On the lawn, her mother looked, as usual, like everything was under control. Even though it was Saturday, she was wearing one of her office skirts, always a little too tight. Ilsa's mother believed that, if she squeezed in, her clothing would remind her hips and waist that they were supposed to be smaller. Her thighs would snap to once they saw that she wouldn't give in to laxity. That's why she was so valued at Clemmons, Stein, and Barco. In battles of will, she always won.

On the opposite side of the lawn, in the middle of a ring of officers, Harold bent over with loud, shoulder-racking sobs. His grey ponytail hung limply down the back of his Hawaiian shirt. Hate filled Ilsa's belly like soup, hot and substantial, a food she could live on. Weeks ago, she'd found the gun while looking for scissors. From the back of the squad car, Ilsa now wondered if the moment she first touched her finger to the cool metal had set all this in motion.

ON THE MORNING of the last day of school, she'd been digging through the forbidden drawers of her mother's armoire when her fingers hit the heavy barrel—so much to know, too quickly. No matter how many times she turned the gun over in her hands and in her mind, it wouldn't make sense.

She got on the bus, went to class, and after school ended and yearbooks were signed, she rode the bus home again and walked through the development to the hill because it was the one place she could think of where the world was large enough to hold what she now knew. She always loved the moment when she passed the last hedge at the end of the neighborhood, the moment when the lush green lawns abruptly stopped. The lemon trees and lime trees and orange trees and grapefruit trees, the ivy and the olives, the power-washed pavement and crisp blue swimming pools and chlorine-tinged air, the manicured palm trees and the oleander—everything that made her neighborhood her neighborhood suddenly ended, and the place revealed what it really was: dry brown hills and sage, rattlesnakes and coyotes.

Though she looked and saw her hands were empty, Ilsa could not make them light again.

THE BOYS WERE there that afternoon. They weren't always. Sometimes, Ilsa walked through the construction and all the way to the top of the hill only to watch the lines of cars waiting at the light where Central teed into Chicago Avenue, but that day, they were there, starting their summer the way they would continue it. Four of them. Three sitting at the edge of the drainage ditch watching the fourth ride his skateboard up and down the curve of the concrete, the closest thing to a half-pipe the suburb had to offer. The skater touched the lip of his deck to the lip of the ditch, clipping it or kissing it, depending on how you looked. The move would have been cool if he had pulled it off, but the board caught, sending him running down to the dry bottom of the ditch while the other three laughed. The sun shone in their hair as they flipped it from their eyes. The helmets that their mothers insisted on sat in a tumbled heap.

Ilsa wanted all of it: a skateboard, a group of friends to laugh when she fucked up, a mother who gave enough of a damn to ask her to be careful.

She hadn't expected anyone to sign her yearbook. She hadn't asked.

Becky Mills, too popular to even know Ilsa's name, had seen it on her desk and assumed, scrawling her standard "2 cute + 2 be = 4gotten" before handing it to Vince, who added "L8r sk8r."

The boys' laughter was soft as it floated up to where Ilsa knelt at the top of the hill, the grit biting into her knees. When she first started watching them, she was afraid they would catch her. The dry desert grass and tumbleweed were hardly enough cover. But she had watched them for a year now, from when they first got their boards and tried to ride, and not once had one of them ever thought to glance up the hill. The worry that they would see her had grown into a wish that they would. She wanted nothing more than for them to look up and spot her spying on them. They would know her as the girl they went to middle school with, another Gage Gator, the quiet girl blending in at the middle of the class. But in this light, they would also see her as something more. They would recognize her as one of their own and would invite her down into the ditch. They would lend her a board and teach her to skate. Vince's note would be true, whether he meant it or not. Sk8r: what she was. Sk8r: the word not filled with a stupid, meaningless number but with an upturned infinite loop, with wheels that spun forever, rocketing away.

If wishes were horses, beggars would ride, her grandmother used to say. Maybe it was enough to be invisible. The scissors were there, in the forbidden drawer, thrown in among the tumbles of condoms, a half-used coke vial, lace and satin lingerie, and, Ilsa now knew, her mother's gun. The hot day hummed with wheels rolling over concrete. Then more. Footsteps.

Ilsa recognized the steps running up behind without having to turn. They belonged to Angie, the foster kid who'd come to live with Susan next door; Angie, forever wearing heavy brown orthopedics with a yellow and white Humpty Dumpty on the side, shoes any right-minded six-year-old would have been embarrassed to wear; Angie who was ten, two years younger than Ilsa and stunted small as a first-grader; Angie, who every other kid in the neighborhood avoided. Their parents forbade them to hang with her. She had too much history, too much experience. They moved to this neighborhood in the first place to keep their kids safe from her kind. Bree, the little snot who ran the fifth grade, spread rumors of all the things she was supposedly too innocent to know: Angie fingered herself under her skirts during Social Studies; Angie gave some Mexican kid a hand job in the bathroom; Angie pressed her flat chest against the principal and said she'd suck him off if he let her sit on his lap and call him Daddy.

"Guess what?" Angie said.

Ilsa started back through the development, kicking up dust as she went. She couldn't remember the last time it rained. Angie followed her. Clomp, clomp, clomp. "Mom says we're going camping this weekend and you can come."

Ilsa stopped and gazed at the wide holes that would be pools or crawlspaces and the narrow holes that would just be the spots where something buried went, a box for electrical lines or water mains. Someday this would be all groomed and finished and neat, another expensive neighborhood adjoining their own. Stucco and Spanish tile. The honest brown of the dirt would be made green with grass and flowering shrubs and automatic sprinkler systems. Someday, these places would be off-limits, but they weren't yet. The closest hole was deep and narrow as a grave. Ilsa jumped in. The earth was cool around her, and she thought maybe it wouldn't be so bad to be buried alive.

Angie stood, illuminated by sun, at the top of the hole. "So, do you want to? Go camping?"

"No." Ilsa lay down and closed her eyes a moment. She imagined the roll of wheels, and the pull of gravity carrying her up and down the sides of a ditch. She felt the freedom of the air as she left the concrete, letting her board kiss its rough lip, then leaving it quickly, stomping back down and traveling away. Skating would be a love affair. The concrete might betray you, but it was always there. Dependable. If you skated long enough, maybe you could master it. Maybe that's how love worked. Love could be bright and shining as the California sun in the sky over her hole.

"Mom rented *Dark Crystal*. Want to come over and watch?"

"She's not your mom." Ilsa squinted up at Angie, who looked away. In profile, she wasn't so weird.

Angie said, "She's mom enough."

Ilsa closed her eyes again and let the cool of the hole seep in deep. "She could give you up any time. She could take you back." If someone looked across the land, they would not see her. She'd vanished. She could disappear altogether.

When Ilsa opened her eyes again, Angie was still there looking down at her. If only Angie would go away, Ilsa wouldn't have to be like this. If only Angie would realize that Ilsa was no more her friend than Susan was her mom.

Angie sat down on the side of the hole and dangled her legs, swinging them in and out of the shadows. Susan said Angie had been through two rounds of parents before she was fostered out. Her own father raped her before she was two, so the state gave her to an adoptive uncle who did the same. "He saw rape as the ante and raised the bet," Susan had told them the day Angie was due to arrive, laughing as if poker jokes could make the whole thing a funny anecdote from the past. "Broke her femur and cracked her skull." Angie had been in ten homes before Susan's. Ilsa couldn't see how anyone who'd lived through all that could still be so fucking clueless.

"Is your mom going out with Mr. Gillespie tonight?" Angie didn't wait for Ilsa's answer. "Seems like he's over every night. Mom said she saw him crying by the lobelia yesterday. Grown man and everything, she said. I thought he was in a band or something. Can you cry if you're in a band?"

Ilsa scrunched her eyes tighter and wished Angie a million miles away. She wished Harold had even one bit of the self-control that her mom did. The guy was all enthusiasm. Smiles, and energy one moment, horse tears and self-pity another. He had no in-between, no normal. Her mother said he had an artist's temperament, but Ilsa knew better. His guitar was a front, a way to fake coolness when you weren't actually in any way cool. Harold had the liquid eyes of a spaniel. They might work on her mother, make her think she was loved, but Ilsa knew he'd turn those same eyes on anyone. He was too stupid to love for real. He loved like a dog loved: everywhere.

At school, he was "Mr. Gillespie." Leave it to her mother to date a substitute teacher. And not just any substitute teacher, but one with a greying ponytail. He'd filled in for their art teacher in their last week of school and was all uptight about scissors, showing the kids over and over how to hold the blades and pass handle first, as if seventh-graders weren't old enough to know, as if scissors even ranked a spot on the scale of threats at Gage Middle. The kids carried the scissors open, blades out, breaking into short jogs just to cheese him off. "Isn't this right, Mr. Gill's Pie?" they would say. Kids could smell weakness, and Harold was too dumb to realize that he made things worse by being kind. He bought in every time, hurrying over saying "heavens, no" and turning the scissors gently in their hands, tears already trembling in his eyes. Heavens, no. Good heavens. He was always bringing heaven into it—but that didn't stop him from taking Ilsa's mother to one dive bar after another to watch him and his stupid surfer throwback band.

Angie's voice pulled Ilsa back into her hole. "Mom and I never see a babysitter when they go out. You've got one though, right? Does your mom pick her up or something?"

They were spying on her. Spying as if any of this were their business, as if Ilsa weren't old enough to take care of herself, or to babysit other kids for that matter. Ilsa was damned if she was going to give Angie or Susan one bit of gossip.

Ilsa's silence didn't matter. Angie ran on and on. "You hear the Night Stalker struck again? Shot a man and raped his wife. Mom says it's only a matter of time before he hits Riverside. She says no one is safe anymore, not even here. It doesn't matter where you live."

Ilsa opened her eyes and pulled herself out of the hole. What would Susan think if she knew her mother had a gun? Would that shut her up? What if she stuck the gun right in Susan's face and fired? A blank maybe. Just enough to give her a scare.

"I'm going home," Ilsa said, wishing that were enough to make Angie leave her alone.

HER MOTHER'S BLACK BMW was parked in front of the house, shining hot in the late afternoon sun where people could see it and remember that, single mother or not, she had made her way. Angie was saying something about the elementary school talent show, about Bree and her friends dancing to the new Madonna, chattering on as if Ilsa cared. Ilsa shut the door in her face while Angie was mid-sentence, the only way to make the talking stop.

"You can fix yourself dinner tonight?" her mother called. "Heat a burrito or something? I have to go out."

"Harold? Again?"

"It's our anniversary. Two months."

"Anniversary means a year, not a month."

"Can you just be happy once in a while?"

Her mother rounded the corner and froze. Her thick eyebrows, red from where she'd plucked them back, met in a crease. Her nails were painted purple. Her lipstick, an even-darker shade. "Ilsa, those had better not be your new jeans."

"No," Ilsa lied.

But her mother already had her, nails scratching the belly skin as she pulled the waistband searching for the tag. "Fuck, Ilsa. Those were Gloria Vanderbilt." Like cutting the legs off changed what they were. It had been hot that morning, and Ilsa didn't have clean shorts. She could point out that her mother hadn't done the laundry in a week. She could say that the girls who mattered wore Guess now anyway. She could say that, looking for scissors, she found a gun.

"Tell me you at least have a bra on." Her mother snagged the collar of Ilsa's teeshirt to expose a bare shoulder.

Ilsa squirmed away. "God, mom. Get a grip." Heat rushed over her. She didn't want breasts, let alone a bra. She didn't want clean clothes or to be the kind of girl men leered at. Who needed jeans in the summer in the desert? She liked them better now that she'd cut them off below the knees. Maybe if the boys in the drainage ditch saw her in them, they would see her as a girl with potential, a girl they could hang out with. Better yet, maybe they would not see her as a girl at all. Maybe she could be just another skater without all that sex crap messing things up.

"I don't know why I buy you anything nice." Her mother pulled off her work blouse and threw it across the sofa. Standing in front of the window in her emerald green bra, she dug through the pile of plastic-wrapped dry-cleaning and selected a beaded sweater two sizes too tight. The neckline dipped low, offering her cleavage. Ilsa supposed that's why her mother had chosen it, as if Harold needed incentive.

Her mother pulled the sweater down over her hips, trying to cover the roll at her waist, lowering the neck further. Pursing her lips in the window's reflection, she puffed her hair and pressed in the fat at her sides. "We're going to get dinner before his show."

"The Night Stalker struck again," Ilsa said. "Killed a man and raped his wife."

"Ilsa, don't start."

"Could be Harold for all you know."

"Christ."

"Okay, but if you come back and find my stomach guts all over the living room, just remember I'm not the one who decided you should go out with Harold."

"I don't fucking need this."

"We don't need Harold either." Ilsa was named after a movie she had never seen. Her mother had once told her that the movie contained all you needed to know about love: a lot of bustle and drama leading to heartbreak. The goal was to look classy throughout the whole disaster, to be stronger at the end.

"Damn it, Ilsa, can't you think about what I might need once in a while? You think I can spend all my time working and shut up like a nun with a twelve-year-old who thinks she knows it all? Think again."

"You only like him because he does what you say."

"I'm not having this conversation with a child." Her mother rummaged through her purse. She pulled out her kit and chopped coke on the mirror, moving the powder into a line that Ilsa knew better than to cross. She hacked at the coke as her teeth clipped her words: "I work damned hard. I get you everything you need. Nice clothes that you cut to shreds. Pretty little bras you won't wear. A good house in a good school district. Don't you dare deny me my little bit of happiness." She snorted quickly, leaning her head back so that nothing was lost.

For a moment, everything was still. Then, a smile began to pull at the side of her lips. She wiped her nose quickly and glanced at her watch, all poise and power, once more in control of herself and the situation, just as she liked. The last five minutes might never have happened. She scooped everything back into her bag. "I need to go. Don't stay up past ten."

Her mother rarely snorted at home. Coke was her work friend, the one she could call on when things got intense, when the hard deal had to be made and she needed an extra edge. Even so, the coke didn't bother Ilsa like the gun did. She couldn't say why. Maybe because she knew the coke was off-limits. She thought about it from time to time, how it turned any moment happy. There was something to that. If Ilsa took the smallest amount, though, her mother would notice it missing. But the gun? Ilsa had taken the gun from the drawer and held it in her palm and felt every piece of her changed by its weight, and no one knew any different. She could do it again. She could take the gun whenever she wanted.

Ilsa put a frozen burrito in the microwave, then locked the front door, leaving the chain unfastened. Even with the Night Stalker out there somewhere, Ilsa knew that her mother and Harold would stagger in sometime in the early morning. If she left the chain off, if she was lucky and they didn't laugh too hard as they crashed into the walls and fumbled for the light switch and for each other in the dark, Ilsa might sleep through the whole thing.

WAS IT A week later that she found the puppy head? She'd gone again to watch the boys, and there it was: nestled amongst the dried weeds and dirt, the head of a yellow Lab that had been no more than a couple months old, sitting at the base of a telephone pole at the top of the hill. The golden fur shone softly in the sun. From the front, it looked like it was sleeping. From the back, it was cleaved. She wondered if they used an axe, or maybe a knife.

It must have happened recently. The round bone of its skull was still pink with blood, and only a few flies buzzed around the red meat of its neck.

Below, the boys were skating. They didn't know about the dog's head. They didn't know about Ilsa. They didn't know that Harold had been over every night that week. They didn't know about guns. They knew about gravity and wheels and nothing else.

Ilsa couldn't understand what the head meant or what it was doing there. Why would anyone kill a puppy? Why would someone leave its head at the edge of a housing development at the edge of a neighborhood? She supposed she should be frightened, but she wasn't. She wanted to pick it up. She wanted to stroke its little head and make it come back to life, grow a new body, something, but if she touched it, she would only make the head that much more dead. Even sitting there, absorbing the sun, it wouldn't have a living puppy's warmth. If she touched it, she'd know all the breath it didn't hold. It would be too light or too heavy for its size. She wouldn't be able to look at the eyes anymore and imagine it to be sleeping, or to forget that the back of its skull was open as a head should never be.

Thank god Angie wasn't there. Angie would jump straight to the nightly news her foster mom never missed. Susan would say it was Satan worshippers or the KKK or kids who listened to AC/DC and Ozzy Osbourne. She'd say again as she always did that no one was safe. She delighted in how unsafe they were, how much less safe they were every day.

Laughter floated up from the boys. One of them had fallen again and lay on the bottom of the ditch, hugging his skinned knees to his stomach and calling his friends a bunch of fuckers before he rolled to his feet and laughed with them.

She could go to them. She could tell them about the puppy head and bring them up the hill. They'd be bound to her then. They would have all seen something amazing, something incomprehensible, and they would not ever be able to disown that knowledge. In the fall, at school, when they saw her, they would nod hello—and in that nod would be the knowledge of the puppy head and a world that was beyond what anyone could fathom or explain.

Even as she had the thought, she rejected it. Telling would be a form of buying them, and she wouldn't buy the boys, not even with the horrible currency of that head. She wanted and didn't want to share this knowledge. She folded her arms tight over her braless chest. No, she thought, the dead puppy wasn't a way to buy friends, but a kind of poison. Spreading it might bind them, but in a way that would only fester and corrupt.

She should bury it. She should kick it down the hill a little ways into the sage where no one would ever know about it except for her. Instead, she kneeled and watched the boys try their tricks for one another, always ultimately failing but trying again. She let the sun and the boys' laughter soak into her.

THE FIGHT THAT ended with police cars started over Saturday lunch. School had been out three weeks. Ilsa was bored with summer but more bored with Harold. She'd have taken any excuse to get away from the table that day, but her summer was empty, so they ate their sandwiches together, like a family, her mom had said. She smiled across the table to him and went back to spreading her mayonnaise.

Ilsa had slid the gun into her back pocket that morning, an oversized teeshirt hiding it from sight. She didn't know why she had taken it and didn't want to think about what her mother would say if she found out that Ilsa had been through her stuff.

Or maybe she did want her mother to find it. Maybe it would remind her mother that she existed, that she wasn't just a moving doll to dress up in designer clothes. Maybe Ilsa needed her mother to see that the world did not revolve around Harold. The gun in her back pocket was a kind of truth or dare, asking how much her mother loved her and what she would risk to prove it.

Harold dabbed a glob of mustard from his mouth with a paper napkin. "Goodness, I've been here so often lately, I might as well move in."

Even as Harold said it, they all knew the failed joke for what it was. A hint. A request. He'd smiled that stupid, sheepish smile, like he was apologizing for even having an opinion. Ilsa was terrified that her mother would agree. He'd come home with her the night before and seemed to settle in for the weekend. He brought a bag.

But when her mother's head shot up and she stared at him with her I'm-going-to-make-partner confidence, a joy rose in Ilsa like she hadn't felt in as long as she could remember. This was the moment. It came sooner for some than for others, but her mother was about to crush Harold as she had crushed other men who tried to infringe on her power to define the terms of their relationship. The smile had already spread over Ilsa's lips as her mother said, "I really don't think you're the one to make that call."

Later, Ilsa would realize that she had misjudged just how tenacious a weed Harold was. The man dug in his roots. He might snap, but he wouldn't pull. The curtains were drawn against the afternoon sun, and in dim light of the stained-glass lamp hanging over their kitchen table, his Hawaiian shirt looked all the more tragic: the optimism of it, the false insistence on youth, the gentle flowers in the face of her mother's glare. He said, "I just meant that I care about you. I want to spend my time with you. I thought you felt the same."

"Don't you think you're moving awfully fast?"

No, Ilsa thought. No. Her mother could not soften.

"If we're moving fast," he said, reaching out to take her mother's hand in his own, "it's because I love you." Ilsa felt herself folding inside, a kind of perverse origami, her stomach becoming a crane or a cup. Harold smiled across the table, looking all gentle and kind, and her mother smiled back. She was going to give. The toughest deal-broker in the firm was yielding to a pony-tailed man with flowers and parrots on his shirt.

Then hopeful Harold went a step too far. "My lease is up on Friday. My landlord says if I want to renew, I need to tell him tomorrow."

"That's what this is about," her voice was dead level. She dropped his hand.

"No, sweetheart, no."

"Don't fucking sweetheart me."

"I'm just saying that the timing is good. It's like a sign."

"Sign my ass. I notice you're not offering to cover any of the mortgage payment."

"Well, I figured if you were paying that anyway. I mean, it's your house."

"I see." Her mother got up and started pacing.

Ilsa quietly gathered her plate and put it in the sink, the gun's grip grazing the skin of her back as she moved. Neither Harold nor her mother noticed. "I think I'll go out for a little while," Ilsa said to no one. They could be at this all day. If blades could shoot out of a face, they shot from her mother's. Harold tried the teary eyes defense, a poor choice. Ilsa slipped out.

"You're taking this all wrong," Harold said behind her. "I'd like us to move to the next step in our relationship."

"The step where I pay for all our shit?" her mother said. Ilsa heard a crash. "Whoops. There's one new plate I'll need to buy." A second crash. "There's another."

Ilsa shut the door before she had to hear more. She turned to find Angie in her face. "What's going on in there?" Angie asked, straining her neck to look around Ilsa as if she could see anything through the closed door.

"None of your business."

"Sounds like they're having a fight."

Thank you, Captain Obvious. Ilsa started walking toward the development. Angie stood rooted, unable to decide between the drama of the fight she'd clearly been spying on and the lure of Ilsa herself.

Ilsa walked. An old man aimed a rifle, shooting the pigeons from his palm tree, as Ilsa had seen him do on many afternoons. She supposed it was one way to spend retirement, though what was so precious about his palm tree was anyone's guess.

For the first ten years of her life, she thought her father died at sea. In hindsight, she didn't know where she got this idea. They were watching TV one day and a commercial came on for aftershave and somehow that bottle with the ship sailing across it, or maybe the actor himself splashing his face and hugging his daughter, or maybe something else altogether made Ilsa say, "I wish I'd gotten to know him before he died."

"Know who?" her mother said.

"My dad."

"Who said your dad was dead?" And that's when the whole story came out. He wasn't the rugged sea captain Ilsa imagined. He hadn't fought wind and sea trying to get back to them. He hadn't even fought traffic. Her father was just another loser in the long line of losers her mom would date, a man who left when his knocked-up girlfriend was eight months along, saying that he was moving to Alaska to be closer to the fishing grounds and to get the hell away from her–one of the last men to say when the relationship was over. He told her she could send his stuff along or donate it to Goodwill or burn it for all he cared because he wasn't coming back.

Had he stayed, Ilsa might have been just another Jennifer, just another Heather. Instead, he left her mother to binge on black-and-white movies all night for the last month of her pregnancy. Ilsa could picture her mother staring coldly at the failed romances, absorbing them all as she rebuilt her strength. Her mother would pick herself up, take control, transform her life, but not before Ilsa became Ilsa.

Angie's feet slapped against the pavement as she ran to catch up. No one that small should run so loudly. The girl had no idea how to move in her own body. Every motion was awkward. The Humpty Dumpty shoes didn't help, but Ilsa doubted Angie would be any quieter in sneakers. "Leave me alone," Ilsa said, "I want to think."

"I'll think with you."

Anger churned in Ilsa's throat, setting in her jawbone with every slap of Angie's shoes. Ilsa stared ahead and walked faster, hoping Angie would give up and go home. Ilsa wondered if the skaters were out. She wondered if the puppy head still lay where she'd found it, hidden under the weeds she'd piled on, or if the crows had pulled it out to peck its eyes.

Angie was going on about the Night Stalker again, delighting in the danger of darkness. "Mom says most people break into houses during the day so they can steal stuff while people are at work. Not him. He looks for places where people are home so he can rape them before he hacks open their throats. You can't protect yourself. You just have to hope he doesn't come to you. Hope he picks some other house. Then one day, they find the prints of his Avias outside your window, and you're done."

Ahead, a group of girls meandered through the holes, their heads bent toward one another as they giggled. Angie hesitated, then hurried on before Ilsa could leave her. Ilsa didn't really know them well, but she knew who they were: Bree, Laura, and some girl whose name began with an M or maybe an N.

Bree, a skinny blonde with a sour smile, turned as they got closer. She put her hand on her hip and narrowed her eyes like some gossipy socialite housewife, a stance undoubtedly learned from her mother. The neighborhood was full of mothers like hers. They'd sip Long Island iced teas after playing a round of tennis at Victoria Country Club, but their favorite sport was judging career women. Sure, Ilsa's mother could buy into the neighborhood. She could buy herself a Beemer and buy her daughter clothes every bit as expensive as their daughters', but at the end of the day, she couldn't belong. As much as Ilsa wanted to be fine with that, as much as she wanted to scorn them right back, at that moment all Ilsa could feel was anger at her mother for what she was: a coked-out trader who serial-dated losers.

"Ho-ly shit," Bree said. "Angie finally found someone desperate enough to hang out with her."

"We're not hanging out," Ilsa said. She should have kept her mouth shut. She should have kept walking. She knew even as she stopped that it was a mistake.

"Could've fooled me."

"She's following me. Won't leave me alone."

In the stark heat of the afternoon sun, Angie's face blanched. "We are hanging out," she said.

The girls laughed. Their carefully brushed hair, home-highlighted with lemon juice, shone white in the sun. Ilsa looked at Angie. She had a chance to do the right thing: to let Angie have that little bit. Why not allow her the one friend she had in the world? Who else would ever value Ilsa as much?

Only, the fact that Angie worshipped her was exactly the problem. Ilsa was no one to admire. "Get away from me," she said. "Leave me alone."

Angie's eyes trembled with tears. "We're friends."

"No, we're not."

"We've always been friends."

Under the glaring sun, the hot stares of the watching girls burned Ilsa, as did Angie's groundless faith. Ilsa felt the day closing up around her, folding like an envelope to seal her in. Saliva swam hot around her tongue. There was nothing to say, and she did the only thing that came to her. She built that saliva into a ball and spit.

Angie stood trembling, the blob of goop and bubbles sliding slowly over her cheek, mixing with her tears. The other girls bent over with laughter, and Ilsa walked away toward the silence of the hill overlooking the ditch.

For an hour or so, she turned the gun in her hands as she watched the boys skate, knowing that she would never walk down that hill to join them and that they wouldn't have her even if she did.

HAROLD'S BLUE VW Beetle was still in the driveway. Fuzzy dice hung from the mirror because he was a cliché, because he was the kind of person who believed that you could substitute-teach and be in a band. Because he was the kind of guy who played Beach Boys songs like they had relevance. Because he was the kind of man who cried over his eggs in the morning for no reason at all. Because he was just another cheese-dick boning her mom.

Inside, her mother was yelling again, or still yelling. Her voice carried through stucco, past the bougainvillea and bottlebrush. Ilsa considered her options. It had to be three o'clock. The afternoon was hot, and she was thirsty. Maybe she would hide out in the backyard, see if she could find any last oranges on the tree and wait for things to blow over.

No. She needed a tall glass of water, heavy on the ice. Then maybe she could sneak in to get her swimsuit and sneak out again to pass the rest of the afternoon in the pool. From the sound of things, her mother and Harold weren't likely to notice her.

She went to the side door of the house and crept into the kitchen. The gun had worn her back raw, so she took it out from under her shirt and laid it on the counter, wondering again why she hadn't had the guts to point it right in Bree's face and imagining what might have happened if she had done just that. In the living room, Harold had resorted to suicidal threats. "You're what I live for." He was crying so thick and hard that his words came out gurgled. "You're all I live for." This over a woman he'd known a few months.

"More like, I'm what you leech off," her mother said. Ilsa rolled her eyes as she crossed the kitchen. They were still stuck in the same part of the argument where they'd been when she left. "Put your fucking pills away and go cry your river somewhere else. I'm done."

"I'm serious. I'm doing it."

"I'll get you the water to wash the bottle down."

Good, Ilsa thought. It was over. The only thing left was for Harold to leave. She stood by the water cooler, calculating how much she could pour before its glug gave her away. The last thing she needed was Harold coming in and trying to enlist her to his cause.

But it was her mother who came into the kitchen. She froze in the entry, her eyes locked on the gun. Ilsa couldn't move, her mind consumed with calculating how much trouble she was in. A lot. More than she'd ever faced. Her mother strode across the kitchen and grabbed the gun.

"I can explain," Ilsa said, but her mother didn't seem to hear her. Ilsa might have been another fruit basket or barstool to her mother, who strode into the living room before Ilsa could figure out what had just happened.

"You think you want to die?" her mother's voice dripped with sarcasm. Ilsa pulled the cooler's tap, her hands shaking almost too much to hold the glass still. Every molecule of her body needed that water, something to steady her. Her mother's voice was hurricane-strong, unswerving and relentless. "You really do? You think you can test me? Let's see how much you mean it."

The gunshot startled the glass from Ilsa's hand. It smashed on the Mexican tile at her feet, a shard grazing her ankle as it flew.

"You still want to die?" her mother said. Ilsa ran to the doorframe to see her mother fire two more rounds over Harold's head. The wall behind him was ruined, three bullet holes surrounded by flaking plaster, but Harold seemed to have pulled himself together as her mother shot.

"You're trying to kill me," he yelled.

"If I wanted to kill you," she said, "I wouldn't have missed."

THAT WAS THE line she told the cops when they arrived. By then, Ilsa had finished a Dr. Pepper, sitting on the front steps and watching Harold drive his Beetle over their yard and Angie's and on to the Winchesters' and the house beyond them, going up the block and back, tearing everyone's grass to shit. The policeman talked kindly to Ilsa before closing her off in his car to wait, but he was less forgiving of her mother.

"My daughter wasn't home," she told him. "I would never have fired the gun with Ilsa in the house." When she saw the disbelief in his face, she changed tack. "That bastard was threatening us," she said.

"As I understand it, ma'am, he was threatening harm only to himself."

"Exactly," she said, thrusting her chin at the cop as if he'd just proven her point.

IN THE BACK of the car, Ilsa closed her eyes. It all would have been okay if it weren't for everyone watching. Then she might have been able to figure out the degree of her guilt. She liked the contained world of the cruiser, its cocoon. Maybe if she could stay in here long enough, she could grow into something beautiful, but that did not seem likely. Didn't girls grow up to be like their mothers, whether they wanted to or not? She had practically put that gun in her mother's hand. She would have been happy to pull the trigger.

Only a little sound leaked in over the hum of the air conditioner. She liked the way it made everything outside unreal, a movie with the volume muted. She liked the distance it created. The only problem was the light, how it let the neighbors line up and witness. She couldn't turn off their eyes. She couldn't mute their memories or their mouths.

Next door, on their front steps, Angie held Susan's hand. Maybe this disaster made Ilsa and Angie even again, but Ilsa doubted it. She could no more understand why she had spit at the one friend who wanted her than she could understand why a person would behead a puppy or why her mother would fire a gun at a man she loved or why a stranger would break into someone's home only to slit his throat or why a father would leave his daughter before she was even born. Ilsa watched Susan and Angie's delight. Maybe the only thing threading people together was a deep, unfathomable ugliness.

This would all be over soon. Harold would go back to his sad apartment, wherever it was, and renew his lease. Ilsa almost allowed herself to feel sorry for him. If this went to court, her mother would hire a good lawyer and Harold would not. In the end, nothing was actually harmed except for the wall.

She closed her eyes and again imagined the pavement rolling below her feet, letting it carry her over its ups and its downs, feeling it moving in her hips and shoulders. The pavement and wheels spoke to each other in that voice she loved, hushing only as the board reached toward the sky, speaking again when it stomped back to the ground.

Except she knew neither the ditch nor the board was her place. Her place was on the hill, not quite above it all. She was the girl who sat where the dead dog's head looked over the lanes of traffic, watching one wide intersection of lives.

That Room

Tobias Wolff

The summer after my first year of high school, I got a case of independence and started hitchhiking to farms up and down the valley for daywork picking berries and mucking out stalls. Then I found a place where the farmer paid me ten cents an hour over minimum wage, and his plump, childless wife fed me lunch and fussed over me while I ate, so I stayed on there until school started.

While shoveling shit or hacking weeds out of a drainage ditch, I'd sometimes stop to gaze out toward the far fields, where the hands, as the farmer called them, were bucking bales of hay into a wagon, stacking them to teetering heights. Now and then a bark of laughter reached me, a tag end of conversation. The farmer hadn't let me work in the hay because I was too small, but I beefed up over the winter, and the following summer he let me join the crew.

So I was a hand. A hand! I went a little crazy with that word, with the pleasure of applying it to myself. Having a job like this changed everything. It delivered you from the reach of your parents, from the caustic scrutiny of your friends. It set you free among strangers in the eventful world, where you could practice being someone else until you were someone else. It put money in your pocket and allowed you to believe that your other life—your inessential, parenthetical life at home and school—was just a sop to those deluded enough to imagine you still needed them.

There were three others working the fields with me: the farmer's shy, muscle-bound nephew, Clemson, who was in my class at school but to whom I condescended because he was just an inexperienced kid, and two Mexican brothers, Miguel and Eduardo. Miguel, short and stolid and solitary, spoke very little English, but rakish Eduardo did the talking for both of them. While the rest of us did the heavy work, Eduardo provided advice about girls and told stories in which he featured as a trickster and deft, indefatigable swordsman. He played it for laughs, but in the very materials of his storytelling—the dance halls and bars, the bumbling border guards, the clod-brained farmers and their insatiable wives, the larcenous cops, the whores who loved him—I felt the actuality of a life I knew nothing about yet somehow contrived to want for myself: a real life in a real world.

While Eduardo talked, Miguel labored silently beside us, now and then grunting with the weight of a bale, his acne-scarred face flushed with heat, narrow eyes narrowed even tighter against the sun. Clemson and I sprinted and flagged, sprinted and flagged, laughing at Eduardo's stories, goading him with questions. Miguel never flagged, and never laughed. He sometimes watched his brother with what appeared to be mild curiosity; that was all.

The farmer, who owned a big spread with a lot of hay to bring in, should have hired more hands. He had only the four of us, and there was always the danger of rain. He was a relaxed, amiable man, but as the season wore on he grew anxious and began to push us harder and keep us longer. During the last week or so I spent the nights with Clemson's family, just down the road, so I could get to the farm with the others at sunup and work until dusk. The bales were heavy with dew when we started bringing them in. The air in the loft turned steamy from fermentation, and Eduardo warned the farmer that the hay might combust, but he held us to his schedule. Limping, sunburned, covered with scratches, I could hardly get out of bed in the morning. But although I griped with Clemson and Eduardo, I was secretly glad to take my place beside them, to work as if I had no choice.

Eduardo's car broke down toward the end of the week, and Clemson started driving him and Miguel to and from the decrepit motel where they lived with other seasonal workers. Sometimes, pulling up to their door, we'd all just sit there, saying nothing. We were that tired. Then one night Eduardo asked us in for a drink. Clemson, being a good boy, tried to beg off, but I got out with Miguel and Eduardo, knowing he wouldn't leave me. "Come on, Clem," I said, "don't be a homo." He looked at me, then turned the engine off.

That room. Jesus. The brothers had done their best, making their beds, keeping their clothes neatly folded in open suitcases, but you got swamped by the smell of mildew the moment you stepped inside. The floor was mushy underfoot and shedding squares of drab linoleum, the ceiling bowed and stained. The overhead light didn't quite reach the corners. Behind the mildew was another, unsettling smell. Clemson was a fastidious guy and writhed in distress as I made a show of being right at home.

We poured rye into our empty stomachs and listened to Eduardo, and before long we were all drunk. Someone came to the door and spoke to him in Spanish, and Eduardo went outside and didn't come back. Miguel and I kept drinking. Clemson was half asleep, his chin declining slowly toward his chest and snapping up again. Then Miguel looked at me. He slitted his eyes and looked at me hard, without blinking, and began to protest an injustice done him by our boss, or maybe another boss. I could barely understand his English, and he kept breaking into Spanish, which I didn't understand at all. But he was angry—I understood that much.

At some point he went across the room and came back and put a pistol on the table, right in front of him. A revolver, long barrel, most of the bluing worn off. Miguel stared at me over the pistol and resumed his complaint, entirely in Spanish. He was looking at me, but I knew he was seeing someone else. I had rarely heard him speak before. Now the words poured out in an aggrieved singsong, and I saw that his own voice was lashing him on somehow, the very sound of his indignation proving that he had been wronged, feeding his rage, making him hate whoever he thought I was. I was too afraid to speak. All I could do was smile.

THAT ROOM—ONCE you enter it, you never really leave. You can forget you're there, you can go on as if you hold the reins, that the course of your life, yea even its length, will reflect the force of your character and the wisdom of your judgments. And then you hit an icy patch on a turn one sunny March day and the wheel in your hands becomes a joke and you no more than a spectator to your own dreamy slide toward the verge, and then you remember where you are.

Or you board a bus with thirty other young men. It's early, just before dawn. That's when the buses always leave, their lights dimmed, to avoid the attention of the Quakers outside the gate, but it doesn't work and they're waiting, silently holding up their signs, looking at you not with reproach but with sadness and sympathy as the bus drives past them and on toward the airport and the plane that will take you where you would not go—and at this moment you know exactly what your desires count for, and your plans, and all your strength of body and will. Then you know where you are, as you will know where you are when those you love die before their time—the time you had planned for them, for yourself with them—and when your daily allowance of words and dreams is withheld from you, and when your daughter drives the car straight into a tree. And if she walks away without a scratch you still feel that dark ceiling close overhead, and know where you are. And what can you do but what you did back in this awful room, with Miguel hating you for nothing and a pistol ready to hand? Smile and hope for a change of subject.

IT CAME, THIS time. Clemson bolted up from his chair, bent forward, and puked all over the table. Miguel stopped talking. He stared at Clemson as if he'd never seen him before, and when Clemson began retching again Miguel jumped up and grabbed him by the shirt and pushed him toward the door. I took over and helped Clemson outside while Miguel looked on, shrieking his disgust. Disgust! Now he was the fastidious one. Revulsion had trumped rage, had trumped even hatred. Oh, how sweetly I tended Clemson that night! I thought he'd saved my life. And maybe he had.

The farmer's barn burned to the ground that winter. When I heard about it, I said, "Didn't I tell him? I did, I told that stupid sumbitch not to put up wet hay."

Thirst

Ashley Davidson

It's brown out here, nothing but teddy-bear cholla and sagebrush, an hour from downtown Phoenix. Stacy reads the street names aloud—Palm Oasis, Blue Sky Way, Sunshine Beach—as if to suggest that the distant whir is not the highway at all, but the soothing, drowsy ocean. Beside her in the empty passenger seat is a pink gift bag containing a crocheted blanket and two ice-cream-cone rattles that Monica and Dustin's baby might someday grasp in both fists. The rattles, when shaken, sound to Stacy like they are filled with cherry pits.

Last year, Stacy drove out to Monica and Dustin's housewarming in this same unfinished subdivision, way out in the boonies, past Buckeye even, 200-and-somethingth street. The house was a foreclosure, a palatial stucco two-story with a clay-tile roof and a soaring pillared entryway. Inside, the grey marble was slick and cool; even hushed voices skipped across it like rocks. Monica and Dustin's old furniture had looked shabby, dwarfed by the cathedral ceilings—something so gaudy and depressing about all that space. And yet. Stacy had spent most of the visit trying to shake the feeling that she'd lost something—a credit card, an earring, some mislaid item that, by its absence, threw her off balance. Behind the house was a paved street lined with empty lots. There was a sprinkler system, a green lawn, a pool shaped like a kidney bean, the kind of neighborhood that, seen from the air, appears orderly, comforting in its sameness.

At the housewarming, as Monica gave the tour, Stacy had trailed her fingers along the white walls of the hallway and imagined herself living here instead. She imagined the pad of Dustin's bare feet, the huff of his breath in the half-dark.

"What do you think, Stace?" Monica had asked. The other guests had already gone back downstairs. It was just the two of them, looking out the window of the master bath at the far highway, the worn-down trenches of arroyos crisscrossing empty scrubland.

"Big," Stacy said.

"Huge." Monica smiled. Stacy could see she was a little anxious. She needed someone to tell her: Everything will be okay.

"It's nice," Stacy said. "Really nice." In the mirror doors of the bathroom closet, she'd caught sight of a hundred selves turning to face a hundred Monicas.

"Thanks," Monica said, relieved. "It's a lot of house."

Today, a full year later, the subdivision remains unfinished. The builder went under a few months before Monica and Dustin bought their house. Went under is exactly how Monica had phrased it, as though Stacy were to picture the man sinking, one hand reaching for the fading light, here where the air is so dry swimming pools must be refilled every third day, where Stacy has only to tighten her fist to split the parched skin of her knuckles, lick her lips and wait ten minutes to taste blood.

SHE COASTS ALONG the wide, vacant streets of the subdivision, blacktop barely used, smooth and tranquilizing. Part of her wishes she could ride around on it for hours, never arrive at the baby shower. She's wearing the clothes she taught in, the armpits of her red polo shirt and the inner waistband of her chinos sweat-soaked. New teachers complain that the uniform makes them look like Target employees, but Stacy is used to it. There are thirty-plus kids in a class, and the air-conditioning in the portables can't handle that many bodies, even small ones, all of them producing heat. April and already in the hundreds. Heat radiates up from the asphalt. In the afternoons, she wades shin-deep through it to get to her car.

Stacy is thirty, but part of her is still waiting for her real life to start and, of course, that real life would begin with a fresh change of clothes. She's seen Dustin only a few times since the housewarming, when he came to carnival or to the enchilada fundraiser at the school where she and Monica teach. This distance has helped some.

The pinch-pots the first-graders made shift collectively, rattling against each other in a shallow cardboard box in the backseat, waiting to be fired in the kiln at the high school. Stacy leans over the steering wheel to read the address numbers, unnecessary; only one house on the block is occupied.

Dustin's work truck is parked on the street with a half-dozen other cars, Dusty's Lock and Key stenciled on the side panels. Stacy notices the load of bleached gravel he's spread over the front yard to save on water.

Monica has told Stacy how ragtag herds of javelina will occasionally wander through the subdivision, fan out around a swimming pool, and lower their snouts to drink, concentric rings expanding across the chlorinated blue surface. A few months ago, a neighbor of Monica and Dustin's one cul-de-sac over, to whom they'd never actually spoken, shot his wife. The wife, like Monica, was pregnant, although not visibly so; they only found that part out later. The woman might not have known it yet herself. When the police arrived, the man was sitting with his feet in his pool, watching the rings radiate out from around his shins.

There are still only a few dozen residents in the subdivision, designed to house two thousand. Stacy imagines these lone neighbors stumbling out into the streets after the shooting, squinting, dazed, like survivors of some freakish supernatural disaster—a microburst, a blast of irradiating white light.

Monica stopped working last month, earlier than planned. She's petite, her wrists tiny, and even at twenty-four weeks the pregnancy had appeared enormous. She'd waddled, sighing when settling into chairs, her bangs ruffling in the current of air blown up from her bottom lip. She's stayed home since her leave of absence started. It seems creepy to Stacy, to spend all day alone out here, one street away from where the man shot his wife and was led from the house, grim and penitent, old before his time.

Stacy hears women's voices over the church echo of the doorbell, but it's Dustin who opens the door in a faded red ball cap and paint-splattered Levi's. He has grown a thick dark beard out of season, as though to appear more fatherly. Stacy smiles to cover the little stab of tenderness she feels for him scratching his beard now, self-conscious of it.

"Hey, Stace," he says, as if she still lives next door, though she hasn't seen him in almost four months. "Weren't sure you were gonna make it."

Dustin lived in the apartment beside Stacy's for almost three years before he and Monica bought this house. Stacy used to meet him on the stairs; they were outdoor stairs, inlaid with smooth pebbles. If Dustin ascended them quickly, the sound of his work boots striking the concrete slabs would ring out, reverberating against the side of their building. The first month she lived there, he helped Stacy carry up a dining-room table, setting each chair down carefully to avoid scuffing her linoleum and then brushing off the backs, as if dusting the shoulders of a little boy to make him look respectable.

Once, late at night, he'd kissed her in the parking lot, then apologized immediately, said he'd had one too many, dragged the back of his hand across his mouth as though to wipe the incident away. Then for weeks he'd avoided her, until finally Stacy had done the only thing she could think of: locked herself out of her car. It seemed so obvious a gesture and yet, after retrieving her keys, he pocketed her twenty dollars easily, made no show of refusal. If he stood on the landing to have a cigarette, Stacy invented reasons to go out. He is soft-spoken, but back then his voice lingered like smoke in the air. He quit when he moved in with Monica—these were the sort of mundane details Monica relayed to Stacy in the lounge or standing around on recess duty: small, awful weights she fastened to Stacy's wrists and ankles, cinching the knots.

Before all this, before Monica and Dustin ever knew each other, Stacy had known them both separately. Stacy had watched through her peephole as Dustin led other women up the stairs, women who twirled, dipped back over his arm, ending a long and complicated dance.

Today, Monica is in the den at the back of the house, where the sliding glass door would look out on the pool, if the curtains weren't drawn against the heat. There are new sofas, large and white, and Monica's mother, aunts, cousins, old friends of hers from high school—all women closer to Monica than Stacy is, even after eight years in the adjacent portable. Monica's thick auburn hair is swept back in a black exercise headband. Her face is plump.

The slits in the sleeves of her beaded turquoise blouse expose pale, freckled arms. The blouse stretches tightly over her large belly, her skin moist when Stacy bends to hug her, as if she has been teaching in the portables all day too.

Stacy helps Dustin arrange trays of bacon-wrapped dates. He asks about school, humming under his breath as she answers. He's polite, friendly, but Stacy senses his attention is elsewhere, straining to catch Monica's voice in the next room.

THE DAY STACY introduced them in the parking lot of her apartment complex, she'd just loaned Monica a sky-blue peasant dress. It billowed in the rippling heat. They were on their way out, headed for the movies, where it would be cool. Dustin was just coming home. The way he looked at Monica, Stacy wished she'd been wearing the dress instead, wished the crocheted neckline had revealed honeycombs of her own skin. It was Monica who'd teased Stacy about him that day, until they got to the theater, a huge multiplex, bigger than a Walmart.

It took him a few days. When Stacy finally opened the door, she'd felt buoyed by the warm currents of air flooding in to equalize the air-conditioned chill. She'd been wearing slippers and always returned to the fact of them, ratty pink terry-cloth, as if they were partially to blame. Dustin had looked nervous, standing there.

IN THE DEN, Stacy hears Monica retelling the story of the man who shot his pregnant wife as she emerged from the master bath upstairs, in a house identical to this one. Stacy imagines curtains of steam rising behind her, towel turbaned around her hair, her knitted brow, the split second of confusion. Maybe they had debts. Maybe she'd been carrying on with a married man from another cul-de-sac—meeting him at night in one of the abandoned houses, the air inside it stale, only slightly cooler than outside, their breathing amplified by its bareness, the wife's moans echoing through the cavernous rooms.

Dustin goes out to grill on the patio. Stacy brings him the silver platter; a wedding gift, bright coins of sunlight glitter across it. He's been drilling holes around their pool to install a wrought-iron fence. They've drained it—it costs too much to maintain, Dustin explains—but the baby could still fall in. Stacy descends the steps into the empty concrete basin, walking down the slope to the deep end, arms extended, balancing one foot in front of the other as if very high off the ground instead of underneath it.

Dustin tells her about the flash flood a few weeks ago. How the banks of the arroyos turned green with stickyweed and bullheads, until the moisture evaporated and the dirt split and curled. People forget how much is alive out here. Before he drained the pool, he'd skimmed off scorpions, millipedes, drowned kangaroo rats. A lone, mangy coyote once waded in to drink. Stacy imagines the coyote trailing off across the vacant lots: glassy-eyed, haggard, the last of its pack.

Dustin lifts black-striped chicken breasts and turkey burgers off the grill with tongs and transfers them to the platter, Stacy adjusting the placement of her hands. Less than a foot separates them. There's the hiss of grease, the smoky heat rising off the grill only slightly hotter than the air. She looks straight into the grizzle of beard, the place on his throat where it smoothes out into skin. If he lifted his eyes, he would see what has been there from the beginning, from the very first day they passed each other on the stairs outside the apartment complex.

The first time Monica brought Dustin to the school, they folded up cafeteria tables and marked the floor with masking tape. The gym filled with cakewalk music, with the bumbling vibration of the popcorn cart. Stacy tore tickets off a wheel, watched Monica touch Dustin's wrist lightly, his forearm, his elbow. Children thrust forward dollar bills, Stacy struggling to make out their voices, the tearing of the perforated tickets suddenly very loud.

"You don't mind, do you, Stace?" Monica had whispered, as if she were simply borrowing her lip balm, something small and trivial that could be easily replaced.

"Why would I mind?" Stacy had asked. She couldn't admit she'd seen them already, hushed and clumsy on the landing.

"You can take those in," Dustin says, nodding at the burgers on the platter. Stacy blinks up at him, as if years have passed here, out on the patio.

Inside, pink paper plates announce baby, with matching cups and napkins. Stacy holds her burger with both hands, wipes her fingers, raises lemonade to her chapped lips, each movement a blaring, self-congratulatory reminder: baby! baby! baby!

They've closed off some of the extra rooms to save on cooling bills. They like living out here. Quiet, private. Stacy wonders how they can afford it on Dustin's income. They've chosen Ruby as the name.

Stacy thinks about the house where the man shot his wife. It stands empty now, like the others, but eventually, once the hardened splatters have been scraped off the walls, shattered mirrors replaced, grout scrubbed down with bleach, it will appear normal but for the steam of its invisible past.

Dustin stands to gather plates, the sort of routine thoughtfulness Monica no longer notices, no longer even considers worthy of mention. The veins on the backs of his hands are swollen from working outside in the heat. From where she's sitting, sinking into a white chenille blanket thrown over the sofa, Stacy sees him press the plates down inside the kitchen trash, tie up the bag and haul it out.

Monica unwraps diaper bags, teething rings, a pair of string underwear small as a slingshot. The women cackle. Stacy watches Monica's face through the joke gifts: a bottle of Advil the size of a mason jar, earplugs. If the cattiness of the gifts affects her, there's no outward sign of it. The skin at the corners of Monica's eyes pinches, something Stacy has not noticed before—maybe it's the baby weight. Monica shakes the ice-cream-cone maracas and whips her head to one side, a flash of auburn hair. This is what Dustin likes: Monica's flair, the red blotches that bloom on her neck and chest when she's upset. She's the type of woman who would surge forward to meet a deer rifle: Go ahead. Here I am. She'd pull open her robe.

Stacy traces her fingertip along the wall, laughter echoing through the bottom story of the house. The stairs are carpeted, absorbing the clomp of her ergonomic clogs. The stairwell is crowded with wedding photos: Monica's head thrown back in riotous laughter. In the background, Stacy stares out from a table of bridesmaids, her eyes squinty and deep-set, holding a fancy stick of crystallized rock candy for sweetening iced tea. The candy stirrers had caught the light like objects of geological value and Stacy had studied hers through the inevitable locksmithing metaphors: the heart a safe, a vault, blah, blah; it required patience, finesse, a stethoscopic ear. Dustin toasted her for introducing them, and Monica sitting at the banquet table beside him went momentarily out of focus, pins-and-needles prickling up Stacy's spine. The guests all turned to acknowledge her then, as if she'd held the door for them, retrieved a fallen coin.

IT'S WARMER UPSTAIRS. Monica and Dustin's bedroom door is cracked. Stacy reaches out a full arm's length and pushes it the rest of the way open, as if this is the thing she has spent three years working up the courage to do. The bed is loaded with ruffled pillows, like a fake bedroom on display in a JC Penney's. Stacy walks into the master bath, runs the faucet, traces a crack in the cheap generic bar of soap beside the sink, steps up to regard her repeated reflection. She lifts her shirt, examines the mosquito bites across her lower back. She imagines the wife of the man one cul-de-sac over examining herself this way, checking for softness in her stomach or the backs of her thighs, until, satisfied, Stacy lets her shirt drop down again. The upstairs hallway is dim, lines of light leaking out from under the doors, carpet plush and white. There's a softness up here Stacy had forgotten, insulating it from the voices downstairs, which rattle in the air ducts.

The coolness of the first door handle is surprising. It's a small room, white, empty. The second door opens into a wallpaper of pastel-colored balloons. There's a crib, a farm-animal mobile, a small yellow changing table.

STACY HAD RUMMAGED through her purse in the entryway of her apartment, flustered, until she found a pen. *Monica,* she scribbled on the back of a crinkled receipt. The inadvertent brush of his fingertips along her palm, accepting it, was the last time he ever touched her. Dustin had stood there a minute, as if he wanted to say something besides "thanks." "I have to go," she'd said, grabbing her purse.

She went downstairs and got in her car. Her hands were shaking. The residue of his touch tingled on her skin. She would get supplies for the third-grade peacock project. She felt better, making the list in her head: paper plates, glitter, blue and green feathers, but once she got to the store she stood at the head of an aisle, gripping the cart handle.

"Excuse me?" a man asked. She looked down at her school clothes, realizing only then that she had forgotten to change. Unspeaking, she'd led the man to the toothpaste aisle, walking in front of him, scanning the shelves until she located the brand he wanted. Thank you, he said. I never would have found it myself.

EVERY MORNING, STACY passes Monica's portable on the way to her own. At first, hunched over her purse, fumbling for her keys, she'd glance up and see the two of them leaning against the sun-faded siding. She'd have to look up a second time to make them vanish. It happens less now, since the long-term sub started. Sometimes it's only Dustin standing there, smoking the cigarettes he gave up.

"Stace?" Dustin asks.

She turns from the window, confused, vision still imprinted with the brightness of the scene she's been staring absently down on: white gravel, cookie-cutter houses, desert. His face softens, but she doesn't wipe her eyes or duck her head to dab them with her sleeve.

"I'm not finished," he says finally, running his palm along a wallpaper seam. "I still have to do the trim."

Light filters through the angled slats of the blinds, illuminating dust mites stirring in the air between them.

"Which house was it?" she asks. "The guy who shot his wife?"

"That one," he says, coming closer. The house's hedge is completely desiccated: a rattletrap of oily leaves gone papery brown. "Over there."

He smells of barbecue smoke. His forearm grazes her elbow—he doesn't even seem to register it, but the touch, after all this time, makes her draw herself upright.

"It still doesn't seem real," he says, scanning the room.

"Having a kid?" she asks.

He nods and the hairs at the back of her neck prickle with sudden awareness: of the warmth of his body in the stuffy room, of a distant throaty ticking in the shafts of the closed-off air vents, of the friction, his palm running back and forth along the sanded railing of the crib.

"It isn't yet," she says.

"It is though, Stace." His voice is gentle, but there is also a firmness, a finality. "It is."

She wants to ask Dustin what the man was thinking. If he'd felt trapped or if he'd simply imagined his life differently. No doubt, that morning, examining her fleshy abdomen in the mirror, the wife had also imagined things otherwise, the way we sometimes will.

Upstream Vertigo

C.R. Beideman

In bed with the lights out in a house in Montana, John hears in the distance a train's whistle. He feels its drumfire through the floor and through the walls and through his chest. It reminds him as he begins dreaming: the world clacks along.

THE LOCOMOTIVE IS a burnt orange SD70AC operating on Montana Rail Link track with ninety-nine cars, including, front to back: eighteen pipe flatcars strapped with three miles of ExxonMobil pipeline; twenty-four open-top hoppers containing seven million pounds of coal; nine center-beam flatcars stacked squarely with lodgepole timber; thirty-seven boxcars stuffed with bulk ag fertilizer; and twelve chain tie-down flatcars laden with six Boeing 737 fuselages. Of the boxcars and hoppers, thirty-nine are graffitied by different artists with red, yellow, blue, and green Krylon[1].

Walking the thin corridor between trains, John Jones, the engineer, sees magpies on the raised siding. As the sun rises, shafts of pale yellow reach through the industrial thicket and between cars, wrinkling the corners of John's eyes. On the boxcars he reads ballooned graffiti letters and thinks POW!!! or BAFF!!! because each car is like a comic panel and he feels half reader and half superhero, like in dreams, and also he thinks of hobo marks scratched on sidings: [///]–this is not a safe place. [˄\]–a beating awaits you here.

John's son's birthday is today.

---

[1]Balaz is one such artist. He is sixteen, white, lives with his single mother in Spokane, does okay in school. He tags bridges and trains and his favorite color is green. The engineer likes Balaz's art the best; he likes the moss color and the sharp slanting letters.

Gravel crunches under his boots. He wears overalls and instruments hang from his belt. Bending to inspect coupling, his knees separate. He smells oil and cold steel and he touches the worn rail. A brassy harmonica rises above the hiss of brakes and gong of ball-peen hammers. The melody seems hidden in the railyard orchestra. John approaches the musical car, the inside curtained with shadow, and touches his flashlight. The melody halts. He moves his hand from the flashlight to his shaven upper lip. His nose is wet in Laurel's high valley air, and his gloved finger leaves soot. Hesitating, John reads his pocket watch. He flicks the gold clasp open. He feels the weight, imagines the complex movement within, and snaps it closed.

He walks back to his locomotive–northwest bound through Bozeman, Helena, and Missoula before joining BNSF track in Spokane. John prefers this northwest route through Montana because it follows the Missouri and Clark Fork down the Divide, and backward currents give him vertigo.

John's marriage was worn away by his schedule. He missed too many birthdays. Canceled too many fishing trips.

Gripping a vertical handrail, John climbs into the cabin; his long limbs seem to fit the engine's high step. He jaws mechanically on the radio, flips the knife switch, primes the pumps. The air horn pierces the morning; birds caw and scatter and resettle. Diesel burns in his heart. He feels the forged scream of the weighted rails in his veins, and he releases the hand brake.

John bends the iron. He's on live track again. He passes houses with drooping wires beside a trash-filled ditch separating the rail from the city. The houses have bad roofs and are split into A and B apartments where low-income families mow the grass leaving tufts around plastic sandboxes. Then, behind chain link, storage units in long rows repeat until replaced by an enormous freshly plowed valley into which John accelerates.

John pulls a newspaper clipping from his overall's back pocket and reads the *Missoulian* headline:

CITING "TRACK GEOMETRY ISSUE," JOINT INVESTIGATION BY MRL AND THE FRA CONCLUDES NO FAULT IN DERAILMENT PLUNGING THREE BOEING FUSELAGES INTO THE CLARK FORK RIVER

When John looks up from the clipping, he's crossing the Yellowstone River. Looking down, he does not see the surface, but a page with banks for margins, and each emerging insect is a letter. John believes the insects selected by fish spell the name of God.

The tight cabin's bathroom door opens and clicks shut. John turns his head slightly. His conductor smiles. John nods. The heavy engine drones, interrupted by sharp indicator beeps. John's clutching a wet chemical cloth in his overall's front pocket. The conductor turns to read the assistant panel. John pulls out the rag and covers the young man's nose and mouth, who kicks until he's limp.

"DON'T STOP THE train for what won't stop the train, John. Can you do that?" the instructor asked.

"Sure. Simple," John said. Hand black with oil and calloused and heavy, the instructor reached up and held John's shoulder. John's eyes had to focus, to pull back from miles ahead. He gaped. The instructor's eyes were like a frightened child's.

"Ya don't understand what I'm tellin' ya, John."

FARSIGHTED, FACE SUNLIT, he looks ahead for cattle or stalled trucks. Flanked distantly by the Absarokas and the Crazies, their snow looks like low far clouds to John. Semis on I-90 flit in his left periphery;[2] lined by cottonwood, on his right the Yellowstone roils with spring melt, the color of rich chocolate, fish pressed to the rocky banks. Moving upriver, the train

---

[2] Balaz grips the Krylon can loosely and shakes it until the clack sounds like a speeding metronome. His pack lies at his feet. He's alone and in danger—he sees the guard's light sweeping steadily among the parked rail cars, but he doesn't care. This is going to be his masterpiece. He sprays in long strokes. His arm doesn't tire. His mind yields to his muscle memory. Just as he's finishing, the sharp light in his peripheral vision calls him back from reverie. He has no time to enjoy his tag. The guard says nothing, but raises his nightstick. Balaz drops the can, reaches down for his pack, and sprints to his exit hole in the fence topped with razor wire. Breathless and safe on the other side, he looks back and smiles.

looks fast, but John feels like the train is submerged, stuck in slow motion, like in dreams.

John was put on leave during the investigation. He tied a whole suitcase of flies, all the same pattern. He just sat there in his basement apartment in the light from the tilted lamp, gripping hook after hook into the vise, mechanically wrapping thread and copper wire over pheasant tail and peacock herl. But he never fished them. And when he ran out of material, he stopped tying.

He remembers the fisherman who stood far below in aquamarine water, casting a fly as John ran the steep, cedar-pricked ravine above. Waist deep, the fisherman waded slowly to shore as the teal fuselages slid down the mossy bank, tearing hulls on the riprap, titanium shrieking through the ravine. Pressed by whitewater, they lay in the river like dud torpedoes. They were meant to fly. They drowned.[3]

Approaching Bozeman, John sees a large M of painted white rocks halfway up a mountain: [/\/\]–tell a hard-luck story here. The train rolls under an Interstate overpass. Utility vehicles are stacked at the crossing there with mountain bikes and kayaks tethered to specialized frames. John sees a canoe. His heart sinks. Under the next overpass, he counts hobos–some are tucked back up the concrete ramp inside sleeping bags, others stand in a parallelogram of sunlight, watching tags scroll by. One sits and writes on cardboard with a black marker, then hands the marker to another hobo. John's hands are filmy inside his gloves.

His wife moved his son too far for visiting, with John's schedule. He mailed some comics yesterday: Batman and Superman. "Can you do that?"

---

[3] Balaz rides with his mom in her Vibe to his dad's. His pack smells like Krylon and he presses it under the seat with his heels. It's sunny and the windows are down, but Balaz doesn't feel anything but sticky ink fouling his circulatory system.

"I'll get custody–you don't come cheap, kid–then you won't have to."

"But she's a psychotic bimbo," says Balaz. He recognizes tags on the overpass as they go under. He tags because it turns his brain off, it's like meditation. If he's still around it's because he has that.

His mother snorts into her coffee. Balaz bites his fingernails.

his son asked him once, with the colorful page open, pointing to Superman stopping a runaway train.

Leaving Bozeman, the overhead sun commands a sky so big that it bends. John's pulse slows. He notches back the throttle lever and travels back in time: At the Missouri confluence, John nods to Lewis, Clark, and lovely Sacajawea camped on the bank. Men sit sketching and cleaning guns among canoes and horses, and the river flows languorous behind them. John notches back a thousand years. The Blackfeet tribe has raised tipis on a plain under a squat cliff. On the plateau above, barefoot runners push buffalo through cairns, funneling them to the cliff where they spill over, a black waterfall, kablooey. They shake the earth.

John steps back and enters the bathroom. The conductor lies tied and conscious. Between his bite is a roped-up neckerchief. John avoids eye contact. He vomits into the cabin toilet, kablooey. Raising his hat above his crew cut, he washes his long face.

AFTER DINNER,[4] JOHN sat his son on his lap at the vise. He tilted the lamp shade and gripped the hook into the shiny silver pincers. "You have to be patient. Or it won't come out right. Don't get frustrated. Use sparse material. Tomorrow, you're going to catch a fish on a fly you tied yourself."

"What's it like?" his son said, taking the bobbin and pinching the thread tag to the shank and making long, inefficient wraps around it like a swing going over the top bar.

"Not so loose. Keep the bobbin close to the hook."

His son tightened his wraps, winding back toward the hook point.

---

[4] Balaz's tongue slides over his braces. The bimbo cooked lasagna, Balaz's favorite.
"May I be excused?"
"You haven't touched your dinner."
"I don't like it," Balaz says.
"Maryanne worked hard cooking for us."
"Let him go, honey."
Balaz pushes his chair out and scrapes his food into the trash. *Let me go,* he thinks.

"It's like being in control . . . like you spin the world."

His son sped up his wraps, already becoming automatic.

"Slow down near the point."

He got pricked. John held his son's finger and watched the red bead form. The phone rang.

"Go ask your mother for a kiss."

JOHN'S TRAIN CHUGS along the Missouri, so close in places he could dive in. Chalky sagebrush provides cover for swift jackrabbits; glaring white pelicans cluster on a shoal, and sandhill cranes—the last dinosaurs—stalk the reedy side channels. A sandstone canyon wall rises above and shadows the train. The timeless landscape, for miles and miles, exists for John or for no one. Against this expanse, he and his train might be small models, John thinks.

He decelerates. His radio makes noise. "On the advertised," John assures the radio voice. John takes his oil can—antique with a long nozzle—and climbs out the window. The ultraviolet breeze whispers on his face. The air smells empty, like dry snow. Standing atop the locomotive, he realizes that it's too late to turn back. He'd never really meant to go through with it—until he read the *Fortune* article:

"Most rail corporations would like to get rid of as many workers as possible," says General Secretary of Railroad Workers United. "They believe they can operate trains with a single employee . . . These are mile-long trains carrying every kind of hazardous material you can think of through communities."

Holding the oil can in both hands, John scissors his long legs and steps off the engine onto Exxon's pipes. He walks to the next car, jumps and runs to the next, on and on, running and jumping, faster and higher until he reaches the open-top coal cars, where he begins squirting oil like hot fudge. The oil can gurgles oopka, oopka. From John's belt hangs a small butane torch.

THE AIR HORN screamed CALAMITY!!! But the hobo ignored it, so John could only sit and wait and watch and be made spectator to death—which John saw was not a dance, or a bout, but a sure fall of the scythe. The hobo walked on the track in the ravine high above the Clark Fork, facing the train. His hair was dreaded. He wore an auburn beard that may have been fiery red in the past. His bone structure showed. His exposed penis was brown and bent. Understanding that he could not stop the train in time, understanding that the hobo had already punched his ticket, John vented the air pressure for an emergency stop anyway. His humanity was on the line. "What in God's name are you doing!" his conductor yelled. And the fuselages went into the teal river. And the hobo liquefied like red paint. And John embodied the hobo, feeling the pressed air on his skin, releasing hot urine that splashed back. The rails cried. John braced for the smack, trying to hold himself together.

CRANING HIS HEAD out the window, John sees a line of white contrail arcing the sky, and as though from a bygone steam engine, a plume of black coal smoke trails gloom across the horizon. John grabs a harmonica off the dashboard. He looks at the neat row of holes and blows a few notes. The row looks like a station, John thinks, looking for tiny locomotives inside. Instead, he sees a harmonica-playing hobo in a dark boxcar. The conductor kicks the bathroom door. John accelerates to seventy toward Toston Dam and flicks open his pocket watch.[5]

As the sky fades from robin's egg to royal blue, John sees that the red coal fire has ignited the lumber, which burns hard yellow, and he sees a helicopter shadow on the far canyon wall, morphing like cave art in flickering light. A voice bleats on the radio. Something flits in his left peripheral and

---

[5] As the bedroom door opens, Balaz hears the hallway grandfather clock gong the hour. He sits at his new desk, facing the wall.

"Go apologize to Maryanne. You made her cry."

"Did she pick all this out? All the furniture?"

"She's in our bedroom. Knock."

"She doesn't want me here."

"You can decorate. No pins in the walls."

"This is a guest room."

"This will get easier," says Balaz's dad.

draws his gaze. Carp are breaching the river, hundreds of them trying to fly. Shafts of sun through low purple clouds illuminate their gold scales.

JOHN AND HIS son sat in a canoe, casting flies. The river was still except for wind waves against the wood freeboard, echoing like the inside of a guitar. The channel deepened before the dam, more lake than river.

"Why can't we catch one, Dad?"

"They're not feeding."

"So why do they jump like that?"

"Don't know. But they can't be caught."

"They're like . . . like gold coins."

JOHN WEEPS. HIS chest rises in starts, too heavy to lift all at once. He tastes bile in his sinuses. He wipes his eyes, leaving coal smut.[6] Now the fertilizer is burning, John thinks. And the fuselages are melting. Their skinless titanium screams horribly. They writhe like burning baby snakes. John imagines the steam, the searing boil when the train derails into the river, one car after another hammering into the dam, the toxic deluge annihilating Toston and swamping Townsend and dispersing into Canyon Ferry Lake, high-marking the shore with chalky ash, silver trout and gold carp strewn like coins by a hole in a pocket. John knows this will poison the river; the fertilizer and

---

6 Balaz's stepmom says, "Come in."

"I'm sorry," Balaz says.

"It's okay, honey." She's drinking red wine. It's difficult for Balaz to see her after she's been crying.

"I love your father very much."

"Okay."

"I know you hear us arguing."

"Screaming."

"Are you going out tonight?"

"Why?"

"I have your spray paint." She pulls his backpack out from under her bed.

coal and oil will seep through the surface to the silt and linger there like footnotes at the bottom of a page.

John turns his head from the sunset-bronzed track. There in the river before the dam, a man is fishing, completely alone. The fisherman sits in a little boat in the channel, with a fish on! Childlike excitement[7] suddenly consumes John. He believes he can hear the reel's high-pitched whir. The fish jumps, shimmering in peach light. "Drop the tip!" John yells. "Give him slack!" The fish jumps again, this time behind the boat, and again, this time at the front, so the fisherman has to spin all the way around. Then, with a great leap, with airborne head shakes, the fish gets away. The fisherman's rod was bent, alive, divining, enchanted, now limp. Still absorbed in the dance, the fisherman watches the ripples spread before he sees hellfire and rows for the boat ramp. Reaching the far shore, he flies a drone. John removes his gloves and turns his eyes to the dam, to the floating orange buoys. Face dark, beads of sweat in his furrows, eyes twitching with salt at the corners, John pulls the air horn like a bandit pulling reins. His lever

---

[7] Balaz reached up to hold his father's hand as they walked along Latah Creek under a high bridge. "See the arches?" his father said. "It's built to resemble the roman aqueducts."

"Aqua ducks," said Balaz. An empty sleeping bag lay open in the dark against the wall.

"Hobos," his father said. Balaz squeezed his hand. And when the train rumbled above, he tried to run back out from under the bridge; he was sure the whole bridge would fall down upon them. But his father wouldn't let him go.

"Wait," he said. Then Balaz saw the sprawling, colorful tags that stretched up the piers. The distance between their grandeur and his crayons seemed insurmountable. Lost in their unreadable language, he forgot the charging train.

"What do they say?"

"I can't read them either," his father said. "They're like a secret code." When the train was gone, Balaz heard the wind and the pigeons high up in the arches. "Hobos use codes, too," his father continued. "Helpful marks scratched along the line."

"What for?"

"It's not safe to hop trains. They say things like *helpful lady* or *man with gun*." Looking up, Balaz's father stretched his neck tight revealing his stubble follicles. "If I could do it all over again, I'd leave everything behind and ride the rails."

At first, Balaz didn't understand what that meant.

hand tremors over the emergency brake. *NOW!* He closes his eyes. He sees his son. He grips the lever, and he lets it go.

His train passes by the fisherman and the dam. As it rides a narrow shelf, high above the river now on the other side, John notches to a walking pace. He feathers the air horn: whippoorwill, whippoorwill, it calls. John prepares to step off, while he's still between worlds.[8]

8

By lamplight, Balaz carves his tag into the new desk. He recalls the train yard hobo marks, from his forefathers. He takes pills without water and lies on the new bed waiting to feel if he's numb, but it's hard to tell. Then he unwraps a single razor from a whole box of them, and places the cardboard cover in the empty wastebasket. Preparing to cut three slanted lines into his wrist [///], he gets a text from a friend.

"Dood your famous!"

Balaz taps the link. He watches drone footage of a glowing freight train nearing a dam, mirrored in the still water. He raises his phone to his nose to read his tag, BALAZ, stretching the entire car, wheels to rim, with an aurora of green chemical flame soaring against the soot black sky.

Wagli Yelo

E. G. Willy

In the parking lot a car radio was playing a rock-and-roll song by some boys in Reno. It sounded to Walter like it came straight from the prairie. Not all of it but some. Walter liked rock-and-roll. He thought that guy who wrote "Rumble" was a fine musician. Mr. Link Wray. And it was a shame that so many radio stations had refused to play his music. It was wild and light all at once.

A long time ago, Walter had bought the records for his kids at the five and dime. He'd discovered songs like "Ramrod," "Bombora," and "Cannonball." Songs only an Indian could write. Walter had seen some kids from Los Angeles on the television. They were dancing in no particular style, just letting their bodies go. They were young and thought they were discovering something, that this dance was new, but Walter had witnessed this sort of dancing all across the prairie when he was growing up, folks who'd never learned to move properly, soddies, soldiers, and townies, folks jumping and moving to one beat.

When he'd met Eve, his first wife, at the dance in Chamberlain, a white man dancing with a Brulé woman, these were the moves he'd had, arms waving, feet stomping. Being born under a station wagon on the reservation, they were all he had. Nothing formal. Just a simple beat. Folks dancing to it. Not much to look at. A guy trying his best to impress a gal. Eve had accepted his ignorance. Walter thought he should go down to the parking lot and talk to the owner of the car, find out what was playing.

He leaned over the landing, then slowly pulled himself back, his throat tightening. His stomach fluttered. He pulled his hat lower over his head. How had they found him so quickly? He'd left them a day ago in a field outside Elko, tires shot out, right out where they'd chased him. But the Buick was in the parking lot, the windows down, the radio turned up all the way. Walter peeked over the landing again to make sure he hadn't seen wrong. No, it was the Buick. Same car. It looked like they'd put on a new set of tires, but otherwise it was the same car. Could he be wrong on that? He'd seen hundreds of cars in his life that looked the same, right down to the scratches on the bumper. He squinted, made out the ding he'd carved on the hood with the round from the range rifle. How could they have found him here? Was it a fluke? Or did they know something he didn't? Walter swallowed, leaned against the wall. The doors opened and closed. Boots landed on the pavement.

Walter hurried to his room, picked up the bobcat fur, his barn jacket, the range rifle. He had no other articles in the room, but it still felt like too much time had passed, as if moving fast didn't really matter. Walter pocketed the key, went along the landing toward the stairs.

"Come on," he told himself. "Think straight for a damned change."

Walter arrived at the stairs, saw he had misjudged the time. The boys were striding toward the staircase. Walter backtracked. He slid on the balls of his feet toward the ice-maker at the end of the landing, slipped in behind the machine. It was a bulky device, newly installed. It had sharp stainless-steel edges, was painted a gray that forced the eye to miss it. Behind that, a utility closet. If he opened the door to the closet, they would hear him. And the rifle would be no good. They would be armed.

Probably not showing it. But they would have something. He pushed himself flat against the machine, heard the whir of a motor, the sound of Freon pumping.

There were seven rooms on the second floor, all with doors that faced the highway. The young men went to the first two doors. They knocked in unison at each.

"Yes?" came the reply. A businessman. A traveling man on a trip. "You boys need something?"

"Howdy, mister."

"Hello."

"We're looking for our uncle. His name's Walter Wright. Wondered if you'd seen him. Tall old guy. Skinny. A cowboy."

Walter recognized the voice. Alan, the kid behind the wheel, the one that had called the shots.

"I don't know anyone by that name," said the businessman.

"He's an old cowboy gone lost. You might've seen him around," went on Alan. "We're real worried about him. See, we think he can't see so good now, maybe he's even lost his mind a little bit. The whole family's worrying."

"No, no, I haven't. Old cowboys in Nevada. Plenty of them around," said the businessman. "Sorry to hear that about your uncle. But he'll show up soon enough."

"You didn't see anyone walking around the lobby, say?"

"Sorry, I'm not in the business of watching folks. Not my business. Good luck though with your uncle," said the businessman.

"Wait, mister . . . we were hoping . . ."

"Sorry, son, I ain't interested," said the businessman. "On top of that, I can't help you."

The door closing. Alan swearing. Steve knocking on a second door. "Hello, someone in there?" asked Steve.

No answer. Someone called from the first story, "What you making noise for?"

"Nothing," Steve called back. "Just checking on someone."

Two more doors. One would be Walter's. The other would be that young couple he'd met the night before. Young man thinking of making a career in rodeo, his gal not sure she wanted this life for herself. Walter felt a line of sweat already creeping down his back. Old man's sweat, strong in odor, the tang of fear. He pressed himself deeper into the alcove of the ice-maker, his back now against the utility door.

The rodeo man didn't answer. Walter heard the hiss of the shower as its hot water rushed through the pipes in the wall. The rodeo man wouldn't hear them, was still in the shower. There was a clank, the sound of pipes jumping in their settings as he turned off the water.

More swearing, then the next two doors. "Hey, this door's open," said Steve. "Anyone in it?"

"Looks like they cleared out."

"Go on in and see if there's a tip on the nightstand."

"Will do."

Steve went in the room, came out a moment later. "Hot shit."

"What you got?"

"Twenty dollars."

"Damned smart," said Alan.

The next door was a few feet from the ice-machine. Walter saw the back of Steve's denim jacket, the round of his shoulders. The young man was smoking. He took a final drag off his cigarette, tossed the burning butt over the landing.

"You think that old fart should be here?" asked Alan.

"Why shouldn't he be?" said Steve.

"I don't know. Seems like we've come a long way just to teach a dog a new trick."

The door opened. The voice of an elderly man, saying, "Can I help you?"

The young men asking if he'd seen Walter Wright. They'd heard he was staying there. They were his sons, had come early to pick him up but there was no one in reception to give his room number. The sweat on his back. Walter wishing he had the nerve to pull out his weapon and fire, then telling himself to wait, to sit this one out. Shooting them would do nothing but change his course from the reason he was here in the first place. Those two boys showing up at his place, shooting his dogs. Walter coming on them. They were just like their father, Clyde F. Briggs, repeating the man's sins, returning to their own vomit. Though Walter had lived through the death of animals, he accepted that he was the engine that had driven hundreds of thousands of horses on rail cars to Chicago and St. Paul. This shame, of animals so hungry that they ate manes and tails of those packed in the cars with them. Horses screaming. Walter riding sometimes with them, taking his pay at the end if the brokers refused to pay up front. Why couldn't

Briggs do the same, keep quiet about his wolves, find a ragged peace in silence? Briggs seemed to be bragging about his past in that newspaper story they'd run a few weeks before, a "remember when" piece. Talking about killing things as if it were his right. The good old days. Then those kids, inspired by this historical rehash, killing more.

"No, no one here like that," replied the elderly man. Then, "Say, what did you say your name was?"

"Well, thanks for your help," said Alan. "Sorry to bother you."

"Yeah, we won't bother you anymore," added Steve.

"I'm sorry, who are you?"

The door to the room stayed open. The elderly man watching. The sound of boots on the landing. Alan saying, "Goddamn, he's a slippery one." And then the engine from the Buick groaned. The driver gunning the throttle. The car peeling out of the parking lot. The acrid odor of burning tires wafted over the landing. Walter leaned against the wall, took a few breaths.

Annie, the rodeo man's gal, found Walter leaning over the railing, watching. "I found the softest pair," informed Annie as she handed the gloves to Walter. "They won't hurt your hands."

"That's awful nice of you," said Walter. He cleared his throat, coughed, said, "These are perfect."

"I have my moments," said Annie.

Walter stared at the gloves, said, "I'm all breaking apart. That's what happens when you get old. Get folks' pity."

"You okay, Walter?" asked Annie.

"Well, I sure am."

"You went distant there for a second. I saw."

"Yep."

"I do that too," said Annie. "I get to wondering about things, choices I've made."

"I was thinking rough thoughts," admitted Walter. "Kind of worked up." He didn't add he was thinking of killing someone. Not in the present. In the past. He had those thoughts. When you are asked to do something like killing, it becomes complicated. When you first fire on a man, your shot won't go straight. No matter how a man points his weapon, he can't shoot a person. Walter had seen plenty of that, men shooting up a bar. Forty or fifty shots are fired and no one is touched. And now he was wishing he'd shot those two boys. Walter had friends who would have shot, who would have cleared those boys off the landing like trash off a deck.

"I got to ask this, Walter," said Annie. She looked to Walter as if she wanted to hide her concern but was unable. "Does your family know you're out here riding around?"

"Well, no, they don't."

"And your wife?"

"She can't know," said Walter. He felt his voice breaking again, his breath rattling in his lungs. But there was nothing he could do about it. "She can't know," he said again.

"Are you sure, Walter?"

"You got to be careful," replied Walter.

"What?"

"Careful of how you feel," said Walter quickly. "Make the right choices. A man will promise something, but it will take more time than he knows to get to that promise. You'll know when he says that. But after a while he doubts himself. He doubts you. And he wonders if his promise was any good. We men don't read things too well. We can't tell if we're loved or not. So, you got to say what's in there. Not saying does nothing for a man."

"You mean, my boyfriend, John."

Walter said, "I mean anyone you love."

"Is that why you're out here?" asked Annie.

"Something like that. I lost my wife a while back. Sent me on a bad course. Now I regret it. Sorrow. The things I should've said and now I can't. So now I feel I have to talk all the damned time. Let folks know."

Annie thought about this, said, "I'm not sure I love him yet. I'm with him now, though, giving him a chance."

"He's a good guy."

Annie already had another cigarette lit. Her face was flushed. And Walter wondered if he should have given any advice.

Annie referred to the gloves to change the subject. "They're a little worn, Walter. I hope you don't mind."

"No, I don't. You didn't have to do that for me."

"Like I said, I'm a nurse. I see a pair of torn-up hands, I have to do something. It's like second nature to me."

"That's mighty nice of you."

They spoke for a few more minutes. But words were useless now. They were both filled with the awkwardness of Walter's advice. Annie went in to take the next shower. She said something about how men should always take the first shower and leave the bathroom to the women. Walter wished he hadn't spoken out.

Walter went down the landing, crossed the road to the horse barn where he'd stabled Lucky. The man who'd put up Walter's horse also ran the motel, though Walter figured he was the last to ride through this town in some time. Not so many horses nowadays, just cars flying by on the Interstate. He gave the big appaloosa a flake of second-cut alfalfa and a coffee can of oats, then checked on the barn horses. They were going swaybacked, and their teeth were twice as deep front to back as they were wide. At least twenty years old, maybe a little older. But their hooves were good, and it was clear that the motel man cared for them. Walter brought them each a handful of oats, whispered through the stall doors, calling each horse *kola*, scratching their heads.

Outside, a car horn honked. Walter peered through the slats of the barn. No Buick. Just a horn. He looked at his watch. It was nine. Getting late. He brushed and saddled Lucky, talking to himself as he worked, thinking of Eve, why he'd left her. He wished it were otherwise, that folks could go back and change things.

He swung up on Lucky and gave the horse a click. The appaloosa was feeling good and came out throwing his head around, checking his surroundings. They trotted out on the road. The rodeo man's gloves fit well, worn and well-used, a cowboy's gloves. Walter figured he'd bought himself a few more days of riding. If those boys came up on him again while he was out there on the road, he'd make sure to shoot them quick, leave them silent somewhere. That was how it would be. They'd lost their chances.

"Come on, *kola*," he said to Lucky. "Morning smells fresh."

THEY STOPPED AT the Shell station on the Interstate so Walter could buy a map.The kid at the station came out to look at the big appaloosa. His hands were greasy, and his hair was slicked back in the fashion of mechanics. Though the kid was young, it looked like he'd been long at this job, the type that had done a lot in a short life.

"That's a hell of a horse," said the kid. "I had me one just like that when I was ten. Couldn't keep me off of him."

"First horse?"

"Yep."

"What you do with him?" asked Walter.

The kid handed Walter the map, said, "Sold him for five hundred bucks so I could buy me a car. Sometimes I wished I didn't do that. I still remember that horse. He was strong as hell. The car, well, it was no good. Now I feel like a fool. But you can't feed a horse on oil and gasoline. No, sir. And no one wants a horse nowadays. Just can't get around on them."

"You find a good place for him?"

"No, no, I didn't. They kept him for a couple of years, then sent him to the Ken-L Ration processing plant over in California. Sons of bitches. Turned him to glue."

"Sorry to hear that."

"Yep. Life ain't fair."

"What do I owe for the map?"

The kid sniffed. "I'm supposed to charge you a dollar, but you can have it for free. A guy rides up on a horse, asks for a map, well, you don't get that. Old days. Just like the movies. I'll tell the boss someone stole it."

"I appreciate that."

"My pleasure," said the kid. Then, "You going a long distance?"

Walter nodded, said, "I'm getting on somewhere."

"Shit, I'm stuck in this damned station. Got bills. Got an apartment. Wish I were somewhere else."

"Glad you told me about your horse."

"Yep."

The kid pulled his hands along his coveralls, wiped, gave his head a nod. He looked like he had something extra to say. Walter folded the map slowly over his knees, delayed turning the reins over on Lucky.

"I called him Ricochet," offered the kid. "A damned stupid name now, but I thought it was something. You know, like adventurous."

"This one here is Lucky," said Walter.

The kid put out his hand, let the appaloosa smell him. "A real old gentleman."

Walter pulled up by the railroad tracks and checked his map. Somehow, he'd gotten turned around in his thoughts and was facing the railroad yard. He gazed over the tracks, smelled the metallic odor of filings, grease, and urine. He knew this place.

But it was different now, all gone. The boarding house on Main Street, staying far from Madame DuFran's house of Three D's. Moving farther along when trucks came to the roads, hauling six cars a day and clearing far off as he could. The tracks were the same, following the road. He looked at the sky, checked his watch.

"Those boys scared me," he told Lucky. Lucky shook his head, waited.

Why couldn't he tell the kid at the gas station that good horses were always saved? The best never went to the plants. And only those parts of the horses not good enough for meat were turned to glues formed through the hydrolysis of the horses' collagen. It came from the skin, bones, and tendons. He was an expert in every part of this trade, but he never spoke to people about it. Most already knew this anyhow, had seen their parents and cousins go through the same. The whole country knew the story. Telling the kid what he thought would've just been returning to something no one wanted to hear about.

Walter rolled a cigarette, placed the map on his saddle, followed the railroad tracks east. He whistled the tune to a song that once had lyrics but now was just a comfortable tune. Lucky kept one ear back, listening.

"Just one detour, *kola*, then we move along."

Lucky's nostrils flared. He had his head into the wind and took in the odors flowing up the road. Walter clicked the big horse. Lucky hesitated before stepping forward again.

"What you smell?" asked Walter. "You know something?"

Clyde F. Briggs had a home that was built in the Great Depression, a busted-up old house that had once stood at the edge of town but was now surrounded by postwar homes and shoddily constructed strip malls. A home out of place, poorly painted, larger than the others that were around it. Walter noticed the mailbox with the door open, the porch swing with a couple of pillows on it, the sheriff's patrol car parked sideways in the painted asphalt drive. Behind it, the Buick.

Walter pulled on Lucky's reins. "Goddamn."

Someone had spilled the beans. They'd probably come to his farm in a group, bullied his old friends. The sheriff would've gone by the motel after those boys. And they'd be looking for him there again. The information those boys in the Buick were talking about. They knew he was coming.

Walter came over on the reins. He rode angry west, back into town, complaining and cursing.

The kid at the Shell station recognized him, wondered out.

"What's wrong? The map no good?"

"It's fine. Worked like a map should." Walter dismounted, handed the map to the kid. "You can put it back in the rack. I won't need it now."

"Save me explaining the inventory," noted the kid.

"Well, there you go."

"You need anything else?"

Walter nodded to the phone booth by the light pole.

"That phone work?"

"It does."

"You got change for a dollar?"

"Sure do."

The kid went to the cash box, came back with change. Walter tied Lucky to the handle of the phone booth. The kid watched him from the door of the station. Walter turned his back, dropped a quarter in the slot.

He counted the rings, five, six, seven, eight. A woman answered on nine. "Hello?"

"Is this the Briggs' residence?"

"Who's calling, please?"

"This is Walter Wright. I'd like to speak with Clyde F. Briggs, please."

There was a pause. Whispers. Other people in the room. A man said, "Get him to say where he is." A rustling of chairs. Another man was talking loudly.

"Can I ask what this is regarding?" asked the woman.

"I'd rather speak to Mr. Briggs, if you don't mind," replied Walter.

"Can you wait a moment, please?"

"I sure can."

There was more conversation, someone hushing another person, a man swearing.

"Who's this?"

"Is this Clyde F. Briggs?"

"Yes, it is. Who's this?" Clyde F. Briggs had an old voice, the cracked, overused kind. Walter heard the Oklahoma accent still in there, though it was distorted and struggling.

"Mr. Briggs, my name's Walter Wright. You don't know me, but you and I were in the same business."

"Who?"

"Walter Wright."

"Do I know you?"

Clyde F. Briggs asked Walter who he was, again. Walter imagined it must be hard for the old guy to understand him, so he began with the newspaper article. Then he told Clyde F. Briggs his business, about the horses he once ran.

"They scream. And it's like nothing you've ever heard," said Walter.

Clyde F. Briggs replied, "I didn't kill any horses. I didn't kill a single horse ever. Don't know what business you're talking about. Must have the wrong number."

"No, Mr. Briggs, that's not why I'm calling. You did it with wolves. You know, you killed Scarface. I saw your picture in the paper. They did a whole 'remember when' piece on you."

"What about it?"

"Well, I'm not sure you know this, but that wolf you shot was my son's dog, not the wolf you said it was back then. I should've come and told you that when you did it in the first place, got it off my chest. He worshipped that dog. Like most kids his age, that wolf was the greatest thing he could've known. I thought you should know. Lots of kids. Folks too."

"Who's this?" asked Clyde F. Briggs.

"Walter Wright. I used to broker horses. Did some rodeo. But mostly I just had them killed."

"Who's this?" asked Clyde F. Briggs. "Who's calling?"

"We killed some things, Mr. Briggs. I did. Just as you did. Thought I'd ask you about it. See how you made out. You got Old Scarface. I figure you might have some regret too. Just thought I'd call. See if you had regrets like I did."

Walter listened to Clyde F. Briggs breathing. His lungs were rattling, old guy's lungs, like Walter's.

The woman came back on the phone. "I hope you've had your fun, Mr. Wright. You've got my dad all worked up."

"I'm sorry. But I just thought I'd let him know, him killing Old Scarface, how we got something in common. Read about him in the paper. Brought some memories back. Then his grandchildren coming around, doing the same thing. See, my dogs are my dogs. I don't shoot his horses. His grandkids shouldn't be shooting my wolves right there in front of me like they don't care about what a man owns."

"Maybe it wasn't my dad giving the interview. Did you think about that?"

"I did. I got to say, the way it was written, it suggested it someway else."

"Maybe you shouldn't believe everything you read, Mr. Wright."

Then the voice in the background. "Get him to say where he is."

Walter looked at the phone. He thought of that day hunting the bobcat, how the bobcat had taken herself far away from her den before doubling back, miauling, hollering, leading their group farther and farther afield. And that in her action she was neither lying or telling the truth. She was simply acting as was her nature, taking them in circles closer and closer to her home.

"*Wagli yelo*," whispered Walter into the phone.

"What's that?" asked the woman. "I didn't hear you so good."

"Just thinking aloud."

"You want to talk to someone, Mister Wright?"

"Well, I guess I just did."

"You sound like you got some worry you want to get off your chest. Maybe we can come over and pick you up? If you want to speak to Dad, well, that would be okay."

"Well, I'm over in Minden at the pharmacy now, if you're interested," Walter lied. "Thinking of getting some breakfast."

"Minden, you say?"

"Yep."

"Well, I must be mistaken. I had the impression you might be somewhere else."

"Nowhere near, I'm afraid. Kind of a real long drive, to tell you the truth. I don't expect you'd want to come that far."

"No, I don't expect we would. That is a long drive," agreed the daughter.

"Two hundred miles," said Walter. "And I'm planning on heading east."

"Well, that is a long way," said the daughter.

"So I should be getting on."

"Hang on, Mr. Wright, I have someone here who wants to talk to you."

"Mr. Wright, is that you?" asked a man's voice.

Walter recognized the tone of the man. He'd heard it before. The way a man asks if it's you and he already knows. The police.

"Yep, I guess it is."

"Can I speak to you for a moment? Seems you got into some trouble with some boys. Seems like you shot up their car, committed a few felonies."

"*Wagli yelo*," said Walter.

"What's that?"

Walter hung up. *Wagli yelo*. I'm going home.

Walter stopped at a diner on the Interstate, had a mix-up of ham, sausage, and eggs. He read a day-old newspaper and thought of all the things he was supposed to tell Clyde F. Briggs. But he knew from the start it was a bad mechanism. And why was he calling anyway? He sipped his coffee, worried, wondered why he'd chosen to live by this lie. Clyde F. Briggs killed wolves. He killed horses. Only he would see it as the same.

A tourist came into the diner with his wife and children. The man had on a pressed shirt and Bermuda shorts. The boys wore teeshirts with beer labels printed on them. The wife hid her face behind a pair of oversized sunglasses, looked distant. The man saw Walter at the counter, strolled on over with ministerial authority.

"Say, is that your horse you got saddled outside?"

Walter said, "Yep."

"Well, maybe you ought to have that rifle placed somewhere else. I got kids around. Something like that is likely to get people upset. You know the danger of firearms."

Walter gave the tourist a look-over. An out-of-stater, a guy from Omaha with his wife and kids, probably driving around in a station wagon.

"Well, sir, maybe I should," said Walter. "I appreciate the advice. But I couldn't very well carry the rifle inside."

The tourist said, "I didn't want to bring it up, but I thought I should point it out."

"No problem, sir. I see how it might bother you," said Walter. "I'll be sure to keep that in mind in the future."

"You know, guns can be a dangerous thing," the man went on.

"I suppose they can."

"The wrong things happen when people get a firearm in their hands, especially young children."

Walter wondered how long the tourist had been cooped in his car, preaching to his family as they drove along the Interstate. He said, "Well, sir, you have a good day."

"I will. I will have a good day."

The man departed. Walter watched the family settle in a booth, the kids climbing all over, making noise.

The waitress brought his check, said, "Bunch of do-gooders."

Walter saw the lines on the woman's face. About the same as him. He smiled. Like Eve. All old now. "They've lost the art of keeping their opinions to themselves."

"Yes, they have. But you don't got to worry, Mr. Wright. You're okay with me."

"You know my name."

"I sure do. I read about you in the paper this morning. An old cowboy out on his horse. They made you out as some kind of monster, shooting up those kids' car."

"I'm in the paper?"

"Yes, you are, hon. Front page. Got a picture of you too. Looks pretty dandy. It says you aren't right, riding out here on your own, but you're about the rightest person in this whole place. War hero. Rodeo cowboy. Horse broker. Not bad."

Walter sipped his coffee. "Hm."

"Well, I got news for them. My sister lives over in Winnemucca. She knows the family. Says those boys are about the worst juvenile delinquents that ever came to town. They're the sons of a judge. So what can you do? They get in trouble, he presses folks to let them be. Makes monsters of them. Spare the rod. Why, last Fourth of July, someone stole a dog from a farmhouse, did some bad things to it, so bad it had to be put to sleep. I don't have to tell you what they did. You can guess good enough on your own. Well, you know where I'm going with this. No arrests were made. But all the signs pointed to those two boys. My sister says if you come down to Winnemucca, they'll give you a parade. I'll tell anyone in here if they ask. You're a real hero. And that judge, he's a fool for what he does for those boys."

Walter stood, put a hand in his pocket.

"You okay?"

"I guess I sure am."

"You look a little pale."

"I got me some slow-flowing blood."

"You just sit right here as long as you want, hon. I don't want you passing out on me."

"I'm fine. Just a little tired."

"Let me get you some fresh water."

The waitress left for water. Walter put a five-dollar bill on the counter, went to the door. His legs felt spindly under him, and his heart beat hard in his chest. He sat down on a flower box, put his hands on his knees, took a breath. The sun squeezed under the brim of his hat, blurred his vision. He blinked, his eyes watering up so much he felt just like he was looking through a bottle of Karo syrup.

"Goddamn, goddamn," he muttered.

A highway patrol car passed in front of the diner. Walter wiped his face. The car went slow down the highway, going east.

The waitress came out the door with a paper cup full of water. "Here you go, hon. You drink that."

"Thanks."

"You want me to call your family? Maybe say I saw you up this way?"

"No. I'm good. Just a little banged up."

"That's a fine-looking horse."

"He's getting old like me."

"We're still young, hon, you and me. Leastways, that's how I think."

"Well, I still got young thoughts."

"Sure you do."

Walter stood, climbed up on Lucky. And then the guarded silence, Walter looking at the waitress, her at him.

"You be careful, Walter Wright."

"Thanks, I will."

Walter clicked the horse to a start. Lucky stumbled on a fault in the pavement.

Walter fell forward in the saddle, came down on the reins, his arms around Lucky's neck. The appaloosa pulled up.

"Oh, Jeez," said Walter.

"You come right back if you need some help, Mr. Wright," said the waitress.

"Will do."

Walter kicked Lucky to a trot. He knew if he turned he'd see the waitress going inside and picking up the pay phone.

"Goddamn," said Walter, pushing himself into his stirrups, heels down, feeling his weight on the saddle, the roll of the big horse under him. "Here we go."

West of the Known

Chanelle Benz

My brother was the first man to come for me. The first man I saw in the raw, profuse with liquor, outside a brothel in New Mexico Territory. He was the first I know to make a promise then follow on through. There is nothing to forgive. For in the high violence of joy, is there not often a desire to swear devotion? But what then? When is it ever brung off to the letter? When they come for our blood, we will not end, but go on in an unworldly fever.

I come here to collect, my brother said from the porch. If there was more I did not hear it for Uncle Bill and Aunt Josie stepped out and closed the door. I was in the kitchen canning tomatoes, standing over a row of mason jars, hands dripping a wa'try red when in stepped a man inside a long buckskin coat.

I'm your brother, Jackson, the man smiled, holding out his hand.

I did not know him. And he did not in particular look like me.

I'm Lavenia, I said, frantic to find an apron to wipe upon.

I know who you are, he said.

I put my hands up.

Dudn't matter, he said, and the red water dripped down his wrist, We're kin.

With the sun behind him, he stood in shadow. Like the white rider of the Four Horsemen come to conquest, and I would've cut my heart out for him then.

Jackson walked to the stove and handed me down an apron from a hook, saying, I reckon we got the same eye color. But your shape's your ma's.

I couldn't not go. Uncle Bill and Aunt Josie saw me fed but were never cherishing. I did not dread them as I did their son, Cy.

What comes in the dark?

Stars.

Cooler air.

Dogs' bark.

Cy.

Always I heard his step before the door and I knew when it was not the walking by kind. I would not move from the moment my cousin came in, till the moment he went out, from when he took down my nightdress, till I returned to myself to find how poorly the cream bow at my neck had been tied.

In the morning, when Cy was about to ride into town and I was feeding the chickens, we might joke and talk, or try. I had known Cy all my remembered life. We had that tapestry of family to draw upon.

The night Jackson came for me, I heard Cy's step. My carpetbag, which I had yet to fill, fell from my hands. Hush said the air, like a hand in the dark coming for your mouth. Cy came in and went to my bedroom window, fists in his pockets, watching the ox in the field knock about with its bell. Drunk. Not certain how, since no one at dinner had any spirits but Jackson, who'd brought his own bottle and tucked in like it was his last meal.

You gonna go with him, huhn? Cy spoke through his teeth, a miner having once broken his jaw.

He is my brother, I said.

Half-brother, Cy said, turning toward me.

He's older'n me so I guess I best listen, I said, suddenly dreadfully frightened that somehow they would not let me leave.

Jackson an me're the same age. Both born in '50. You remember when he lived here? It was you and Jackson and your ma.

I don't remember Ma and I don't remember Jackson, I said.

It were a real to-do: your pa joining up to be a Reb, leaving us his kids and squaw. She was a fine thing tho. That Indian gal. They lost you know ...Cy sat me down on the bed by my wrist... The Rebs. His hands pinching the tops of my arms, he laid me back. You know what kind of man Jackson is? I heard Cy ask. He was a damned horse thief. Old John Cochran only let him go cause of my pa.

You done? Jackson leaned in the doorway, whittling a stick into a stake.

I jumped up. I'm sorry I'm just getting started, I said, kneeling to pick up the carpetbag.

Get a wiggle on, girl, Jackson said, coming in.

Cy walked out, knocking Jackson's shoulder as he passed.

Jackson smiled. Hey now, I don't wanna put a spoke in your wheel, but how you think you're gonna load all that on one horse?

I'm sorry. Is it too much? I whispered and stopped.

Why are you whispering? he asked.

I don't want them to think we're in here doing sumthin bad, I said and lifted open the trunk at the bottom of my bed.

Look here, Jackson said, You're gonna come live with me and my best pal, Colt Wallace, in New Mexico Territory. And Sal Adams, if we can locate the bastard, so pack as little as you can.

Jackson made like he was gonna sit on the bed, but instead picked my bustle up off the quilt. I got no notion how you women wear these things, he said.

I don't need to bring that, I said.

You know, Lavenia, you weren't afraid of nuthin. When I was here you was a game little kid. He spun the bustle up and caught it.

I disremember, I said.

He looked at me, the tip of his knife on his bottom lip, then went back to whittling. When I'm with you, I won't let no one hurt you. You know that? he called back as he walked toward the kitchen.

JACKSON THREW ME up on the horse, saying, Stay here till I come back. An don't get down for nuthin. Promise me.

Yessir. I promise, I said, shooing a mosquito from my neck, I swear on my mother's grave.

Don't do that, he said.

Why? I asked.

Cause she weren't a Christian.

Wait.

What?

Nuthin.

The dark of the Texas plain was a solid thing, surrounding, collecting on my face like blued dust. The plain and I waited in the stretched still till we heard the first gunshot, yes, then a lopsided shouting fell out the back of the house. The chickens disbanded. A general caterwauling collapsed into one dragged weeping that leaked off into the dogs the stars and the cool.

Jackson opened the door and the horse shifted under me.

Please, I asked, What did you do?

Jackson tossed the bloody stake into the scrub and holstered his pistol. I killed that white-livered son of a bitch, he said, jerking my horse alongside his.

And the others? I asked.

You know they knew, don't ya? Aunt Josie and Uncle Bill. He let go and pulled up ahead, They knew about Cy. Now you know sumthin, too, he said.

Through the dark I followed him.

A FEW MORNINGS after, we rode into a town consisting of a general store, two saloons, and a livery. We harnessed the horses round the back of one of the saloons. Jackson dug a key out from under a barrel and we took the side door. He went behind the empty bar and set down two scratched glasses.

You used to be more chipper, he said. Don't be sore. An eye for an eye is in the Bible.

There's a lot of things in the Bible. Thou shalt not kill, for one, I said, sitting up on a stool.

Waal, the Bible is a complicated creature, he said, smiling. And you and I're living in Old Testament times. He poured me a double rye. I can't warn a trespasser with no sugar tongue. I have to make it so he don't come back and you don't go bout that cordially, minding your manners. No ma'am, I have to avenge the harm done upon me. But I can tell you that I don't kill wantonly.

And I don't drink liquor, I said, pushing the glass back across the wood still wet from the night.

Truth is, he clinked my glass, I shouldn't have left you. When I run away

I mean. It's jest being you was a girl, and so little, a baby almost, I figured Bill an Josie'd take to you like you was their own, especially after your ma and our pa went and died. But those folks didn't do right. They didn't do right at all. We can agree on that, can't we?

I don't know I guess we can, I said and a rat run under my feet.

Those folks, they weren't expecting me to come back. But no one's gonna hurt you when I'm around–that there is a promise.

I picked up my glass. We'd run out of food on the trail the morning before and as we broke camp, Jackson'd made me a cigarette for breakfast.

But I didn't know what you were fixing to do, I said, running my tongue over the taste of ash in my mouth.

You didn't? Let me look about me for that Bible cause I'd like you to swear on it.

Can you even read?

Enough. Cain't spell tho. He refilled my glass, Look, it ain't your fault this world is no place for women.

But us women are in it, I said.

Have another, he said. Don't dwell.

A bare-armed woman appeared in a ribboned shift, breasts henned up; she went into Jackson and said Spanish things. He smiled, giving her a squeeze, Go on then, he said to me. Go with Rosa, she'll take care a you. Imma go get a shave and a haircut. Should I get my mustache waxed and curled?

I laughed despite myself. The whore held out her hand, Come with me, Labinya.

Upstairs, she poured water in a washstand. Some slipped over the side and spilled onto the floor; she smiled then helped me take off my clothes heavy with stain. Her nose had been broken and she was missing two top teeth on either side. I stood there while the whore washed me like a baby. I wondered if this was something she did to men, lingering on their leafless parts for money.

On the bed, divested, I could not care what next would befall me. There was no sheet only a blanket; I covered my head with the itch of it and cried. I cried cause as sure as Hell was hot I was glad Cy was gone, cause I could not understand why when first Jackson took my hand I had known he was not good but bad, and I knew that right then I was good but would be bad in the days to come, which were forever early and there as soon as you closed your eyes.

The whore was still in the room. But when I grew quiet, the door shut, and I could not hear her step, for the whore was not wearing shoes.

SINCE I WAS between hay and grass, my brother dressed me as a boy. It only needed a bandanna. I's tall for my age and all long lines so it was my lack of Adam's apple he had to hide if I was gonna work with him and not for the cathouse, since my face was comely enough tho never pleased him, it looking too much like my mother's (he said and I did not know).

In the back of the saloon, the bandanna Jackson was tying bit the hair at the nape of my neck. Lord, I think you grew an inch these last few months, Jackson said then turned my chin to him. Why're you making that face?

Cause it pulls, I said, playing with my scabbard. Jackson had gotten me a whole outfit: a six-shooter, belt and cartridges.

Waal, why didn't you say so? Needs to be shorter, he whipped the bandanna off, Hey Rosa, gimme them scissors again. What d'ya mean no por favor? She said you got pretty hair, Lav. Rosa, why don't you make yourself useful and get us some coffee from the hotel–Arbuckle if they got it–and have that barkeep pour me another whiskey on your way out. Lavenia, I am gonna cut it all off if that is all right with you.

I shrugged as Colt Wallace of the white-blond hair who could speak Dutch and play the fiddle came into the saloon with Sal Adams who always wore a big black hat and had told me when he taught me three-card monte that his father had one lung and ate only turnips.

Hey boys, you ready for a hog-killing time tomorrow? Sit down here, honey. See Rosa, Lavenia don't mind! Jackson shouted to the whore who was going out into the night and across the street in her trinkets and paint.

Jackson, said Colt, dragging a chair to our table away from the games of chance. What are you doing to the fair Lavenia Bell?

Keeping her from launching into a life of shame, an helping her into one of profit, Jackson said, and my black hair fell down around me. Sal, gimme her hat. Lavenia, stand up. Go on. There. She looks more like a boy now, don't she?

Sal smiled and said, A boy with a woman's heart.

Colt gave an old-fashioned Comanche yell, he said, Sure she looks like a boy cause she's flat as an ironing–

Jackson had both hands around Colt's throat. The table tipped and Sal stepped in the middle of them, steadying it. Fall back, Jackson, Sal said. Colt misspoke. Didn't you? You understand, Colt, how such words might offend?

Choking, Colt tried to nod.

Please don't, Jackson! I ain't hurt none by it. Truly, I said. Listen, I don't even want breasts.

Why not? Jackson turned to look at me.

I don't know–guess they'd get in the way of shootin?

Jackson laughed and let him loose.

Sure Sal, coughed Colt. I mean, I didn't mean nothing by it, Jackie. I meant to say they'll think Lav's a boy long as they don't look at her in the eyes.

What the hell you mean by that? Jackson asked, rounding on Colt again.

He means she's got long eyelashes, Sal said, taking our drinks from one of the whores.

Shoot Jackie, aren't we friends? Here, Colt toasted, To good whiskey and bad women!

IT WAS A day's ride. Sal stayed to guard the town square and watch for any vigilant citizens with guns, while Colt and I went with Jackson into the bank, the heft of worry in my bowels. There was only one customer inside, a round man in spectacles, who Colt thrust into and said, Hands up, with his loud flush of a laugh, as Jackson and I slid over the counter, six-shooters out, shouting for the two bank tellers to get down on their knees.

Open up that vault, said Jackson.

We can't do that, sir, the older teller said. Only the bank manager has the key. And he's not here today.

Get the goddamn money. This whole town knows you got a key.

Sir, I would if I could but—

You think I got time for this? Jackson hammered the older teller in the face with his pistol, and the man thrashed over, cupping his nose. Jackson straddled him as he lay on the ground, saying, Now you open that vault right quick.

The older teller blinked up at him through bloody hands, I won't do that. I refuse to be . . .

Jackson thumped the older teller's head with the butt of his right pistol and that older teller began to leak his brain. There was a sting in my nose as I watched him drip into the carpet. Until then, I had no notion that blood was child-book red. Jackson turned to the younger teller, who looked frantic at me.

Son, you wanna live? Jackson asked.

I willed him to nod.

Gesturing to me, Jackson said, Give this boy here all the bonds, paper currency and coin in these bags.

Hurry it up back there! hollered Colt, forcing the customer to his knees and peeking out the front door, Sumthin's up! Sal's bringin the horses!

Me and the younger teller, Jackson's pistol cocked on him, stuffed the burlap sacks as Jackson climbed backward through the bank window. That's enough. Now get on your knees, he said.

As I tossed Jackson the first sack, the young teller rose up and grabbed me from behind, snatching my gun, waving it at us, shouting, You cowardly bushwackers, attacking an unarmed man! You're a whore herder—this girl is a girl!

Jackson shot the young teller in the chest, dove through the window and got back my gun. He slapped it into my stomach. Shoot him, he said.

Who? No, I pushed the gun away.

Hey! Colt shouted, What in hell is goin on? They're gonna have heard them shots!

I looked to the young teller rearing in his blood. Please Jackson, don't make me do that, I said.

Put him out of his misery, honey. He's gonna die either way.

I raised the gun then just as quick lowered it. I cain't, I said.

You're with us, ain't ya? Jackson was standing behind me, the warm of his hand went on the meat of my back, After all Lavenia, you just done told that boy my name.

Colt's gun sounded twice from the front.

And so I shot the young teller dead through the eye and out of that bank we rode into the bright forever.

ALONE, JEST US two, in what I had by then guessed was her actual room, tho it had none of the marks of the individual, the whore put the whiskey between my fingers.

Èl no debería haber hecho esto, she said, locking the door and loosening my bandanna.

Leave it, I stared in her mirror. Make me drunk, I said. I want the bitter of that oh-be-joyful.

Drink. She put the glass to my lips, then took it back and topped it off, asking, How old you?

Fifteen. Sixteen in June, I said. The whiskey tore a line down my stomach to let the hot in. Wait. If you can speak English, then why don't you?

She shrugged, handing me back a full glass, Is more easy for men to think the other.

And I ain't a man, I said.

She nodded. Why you brother dress you like one?

So when we ride no man messes with me and I don't mess with my bustle. Is it hard being a-a soiled dove? I drank. It's awful hard on one being a gunslinger.

She smiled with her missing teeth, took off my coat and shirt then sat down inside the bell of her ruffled skirt. My husband die when I you age, she said. I make good money this place.

Money . . . I repeated, and took the whiskey off her bureau where it sat next to a knife and a small bottle of Best Turkey Laudanum. I got money now I guess, I said and laid a few dollars down. If you don't mind, I said and droppered laudanum into my whiskey, I hope this will stupefy me. I drank it and flopped back on the bed.

Where you mama?

Dead. When I was three. My pa's sister raised me. Aunt Josie.

You papa?

I shook my head, Dead from the war.

Solo Jackson, she said.

Hey Rosa, what if sumthin bad happened that I did?

The door handle turned, then came a knocking and my brother: Hey Rosa, lemme in there. I gotta see her. Lavenia?

I scrambled up.

Rosa put her finger to her lips, Lavenia no here.

She's gotta be—hey, Lavenia, Lavenia! C'mon now. Come out and jest let me talk to ya for a minute, honey.

I swallowed more whiskey'd laudanum. Hey Rosa, I whispered, holding out my free hand.

No now, Jackie, Rosa said, taking it.

If you did a bad thing but you didn't mean to? Cause he was gonna die anyways either way. I pulled till her head went under my chin. But he was alive and then he wasn't and I did that, I did.

Jackson no good.

No, no good, I said.

You have money? You take and go. Far.

But I'm no good, I said.

Open this damn door! Jackson pounded. Listen Rosa, your pussy ain't worth so much to me that I won't beat your face off.

Hush up! I shouted, Shut your mouth! The shaking door stilled. I don't want you, I said.

Lavenia, I heard him slide down the door. Hey, don't be like that.

I leaned my forearm and head onto the wood. Why? I asked.

Baby girl, he said, don't be sore. Not at me. I cain't.

Why did you make me? I asked.

Darlin, those men seen our faces. What we did we had to do in order to save ourselves. That there was self-defense. Sure, it's a hard lesson, I ain't gonna falsify that to you.

But I'm wicked now, I said, feeling a wave of warm roll me over. I slid.

Hey, I heard him get to his feet, Hey you lemme in there.

Rosa put her hand over mine where it rested on the lock. The augury of her eyes was not lost on me. As soon as I opened the door, Jackson fell through, then tore after her.

Jackson don't, I yanked him by the elbow as he took her by the neck. You–she didn't do nothing but what I told her to!

He shook me off but let her go. Go on, get out, he slammed the door and galloped me onto the bed, tackling me from behind and squeezing until I tear' d. I did not drift up and away but instead stayed there in what felt to be the only room for miles and miles around. He spoke into my hair, saying, We're in this together.

Jackson, I sniffed and kicked his shin with the back of my heel, Too tight.

He exhaled and went loose, The fellas are missing you down there.

No, they ain't.

They're saying they cain't celebrate without the belle of the Bell's.

I rolled to face him, pushing the stubble of his chin into my forehead, Why do you want to make me you?

Would you rather be a daughter of sin?

I am a daughter of sin.

You know what I mean. A . . . Jackson searched his mind, A frail sister.

I could not help but laugh. He whooped, ducking my punches till he wrestled me off the bed and I got a bloody nose. You hurt? he asked, leaning over the edge.

Lord, I don't know, I shrugged in a heap on the floor, sweet asleep but awake. I cain't feel a thing. Like it's afternoon in me, I said.

Jackson glanced over at the laudanum bottle and backhanded me sharp and distant. Don't you ever do that again, you hear?

My nose trickled doubly but I said, It doesn't hurt. I tried to peel Jackson's hands off his face, Hey it truly truly doesn't!

I laughed and he laughed and we went down to the saloon drinking spirits till we vomited our bellies and heads empty.

THE NEXT NIGHT two deputies walked into the saloon and shot out the lights. In the exchange of dark and flash, a set of hands yanked me down. I'd been drinking while Jackson was with Rosa upstairs. I got out my six-shooter but did not know how to pick a shadow. A man hissed near my head and I crawled with him to the side door.

Out of the fog of the saloon, Colt stood, catching his breath, saying, There ain't nothing we can do for Jackson and Sal. If they take them to the jail, we'll break them out. C'mon.

No, I said, getting up.

A couple bystanders that had been gawking at the saloon were now looking to us.

Lavenia, Colt took me tight by the shoulder, and swayed us like two drunkards into the opposite direction. In the candlelight of passing houses, Colt's hand, cut by glass, bled down my arm.

At the end of the alley, Colt turned us to where three horses were on a hitch-rack. We crouched, untying the reins, and tho my horse gave a snort, it did not object to the thievery, but we were not able to ride out of town unmolested. The sheriff and his deputy were waiting and threw us lead. Buckshot found my shoulder, and found Colt, too, who slid like spit down his horse and onto his back, dead.

HEY THERE DEPUTY, said Jackson through the bars, How much for a clean sheet of paper and that pen?

The men outside the jail began shouting louder. The silver-haired sheriff sat at his desk, writing up a report, ignoring us all.

This un? the deputy stopped his pacing.

I'll give you twenty whole dollars, Jackson said. I'll be real surprised if I make it to trial, so least you could do is honor my last request.

There were a few scattered thumps on the door.

Won't we make it to trial? I asked.

Well darlin, there's a mob out there that's real upset bout me shooting that bank teller and that marshal and that faro dealer and that one fella–what was he? A professor of the occult sciences!

I laughed. The men kicked at the door. The sheriff checked his Winchester.

Jackson chuckled, I'm writing against the clock. The windows smashed as if by a flock of birds. Jackson didn't look up from writing.

Now sheriff, you won't let them hurt my baby girl will ya? You gotta preach to them like you was at Judgment Day. Gotta tell them that this young girl here was jest following me, was under a powerful family sway. Deputy, would you kindly give this to her.

The deputy took the letter.

The sheriff said, Son, there are about forty men out there with the name of your gang boiling in their blood. By law the two of us must protect you and that child. I jest hope we don't die in the attempt.

Thee Dream-

Dremp't I was with you, Lav,
near yur breth so dear.
I never new no one lik you
and I wisht you wer near.
No Angel on earth or Heven,
could rival your Hart,

no Deth or distunce can Us part.
If any shud tell you
they love you eternully,
there is no one you tell em
who Loves you lik Me.

Fare well! My sister and frend,

Allso my Bell of Bells,

Yors I Hope,
Jackson Bell

The forty exited the street and entered our cells.

They dragged Jackson and I into the dogs the stars the cool and the night. Their hands in what hair I had; my hands underbrush-burned and bound together in bailing wire.

In an abandoned stable somewhere behind the jail, they made Jackson stand on a crate and put the noose hanging from the rafters round his neck. They were holding down the deputy and the sheriff, who looked eyeless cause of the blood, having been beaten over the head.

I was brought to Jackson and saw the rope round his neck weren't even clean.

Hey gal, my brother said, You're my final request. Now what do you think? Don't you think I kept my promise to you? You'll be all right. If you cain't find Sal, Rosa will take care a you.

I nodded and the men pulled me back.

Hey you ain't crying, are ya? Jackson called out, swallowing against the rope. C'mon, quick–you got any last thing to say to me?

The men brought me to a crate and tied a noose around my neck.

What the hell's going on? Jackson asked.

You all cannot murder a woman without a fair trial, the sheriff started up.

Now fellas, it ain't s'posed to go like this. Listen to the sheriff here–Jackson said and the men walloped him in the belly.

Lavenia Bell, the men asked, crowding me, What is your final request?

Sometimes I wish I were just a regular girl, not a whore or an outlaw or playacting a man. I had a father for two years and a mother for three, but I cannot remember what that was like, if they care for you better or hurt you less or if they keep you no matter what it costs them.

The girl first, the men said.

I am not afraid, I said. You kept your promise good. Thank you for you.

Have you no wives, no sisters or daughters? shouted the sheriff.

I felt the thick of hands on my waist.

Wait! Don't y'all see? She would never done nuthin without me not without me–

The noose tightened.

The sheriff was struggling to get to his feet, hollering. Boys this will weigh heavy on your souls!

Hey I'm begging you to listen–look boys, it weren't her that killed them tellers it was me–only me!

Up on the crate, it was that hour before sun, when there was no indication of how close I was to a new morning. I waited for the waiting to break, for the dark of the plain in my face to bring me to dust.

You Owe Me

Shelley Blanton-Stroud

One September night after picking, arms sticky yellow, tomato-leaf smell of piney, bitter sunlight under her fingernails, Jane walked home along the river, which was finally slowing after months of running fast and clean with melted Sierra snow. In Indian summer, when the grass bleached white and the blue burnt out of the sky, Jane looked down as she walked, even at night, in case a rattler stretched fat across the path in the heat.

That may be why she didn't see at first what was happening right in front of her as she approached her family's cardboard and canvas home, just off the levee where the Sacramento and American Rivers converged, an easy walk from pick-work and canneries and the soup kitchen.

Uno Jeffers's headlights shone on the dirt between his Ford and their lean-to, Cotton Boll Brothers loud on his radio—If the old Ford stops, and you gotta get gas, it's gotta come outta them beans.

His car was loaded with the Hopper family things—shovel, mattress, blankets, pots, crowbar, washtub, Jane's hope chest of books and awards, everything they'd carted from Sweetwater to Sacramento in the great west-bound caravan of Okies. Everything they'd collected since.

Daddy's banjo and hat were on the dirt, not in the tent, not in the car.

Momma stepped out of the tent, full belly first, squinting into the headlights, black hair frizzing like thoughts shooting out her scalp.

"Where's Daddy?" Jane asked.

Momma spit out a toothpick. "In town. With Elthea."

ELTHEA WAS MARRIED to dumpy Leroy Lathrop, editor of a skid-row newspaper, *The Valley*. She herself owned Do or Donut Shop, a base from which she was able to meet up weekly with Daddy, who seemed to like her Sunday morning maple smell.

Just a week before, for what seemed like the hundredth time, Jane had walked to donuts with Daddy and witnessed it.

"Abraham Lincoln Hopper," Elthea said, coming out to the counter from the back room.

Daddy smiled, putting off heat. Neither of them said anything for a good minute while Jane focused her eyes on the display case, thinking, Order the damn donut. But instead he started singing, as if Elthea were the only person on earth who might understand just how misunderstood he was—Big man stoopin' so low, hasta stand up one day. He sang it hoarse, hitting some notes off key, lingering a beat long on words you might not expect. He made the air quiver around him like heat waves that distract you from your blisters while you walk. Daddy was like that.

He could play just about anything on the banjo. He could make it funny—wolves howling, trains roaring, babies crying—the kind of stuff all the kids liked. He could make it beautiful too, with haunting tunes he'd make up on the spot, tunes that made the women cry and sometimes the men. He also used the banjo for angry music.

His voice was full of feeling and intelligence. He tended to scratch out the sound on the most emotional words. Often, he wrote his own. He was a poet. Everybody knew he had that in him. Folks would hear where the Hoppers were camped and show up, circling around him while he played in front of a fire, staying up all night to listen to Abraham Lincoln Hopper. Jane was proud of that.

He delivered this particular performance in a dingy donut shop for a chubby counter woman on a Sunday morning with no less style than he conjured every Saturday night for paying customers—scab-armed pickers, sitting on dirt, tilting beer, tithing a dime each to Abraham.

When he finished singing, Elthea clapped, real slow, and rocked her curls back and forth in appreciation, the crepey flesh around her collar turning pink. Momma didn't react that way to his talents anymore.

He smiled, teeth white under a scruffy mustache.

"Do you need some help with the boxes, Elthea?"

"I always need help with the boxes, Abraham."

"I'm gonna help Elthea in the back with the boxes, Jujee." He followed Elthea to the back room, eyes on her wide hips in a tight white uniform.

Jane moved without a donut to the front booth under the window and watched people pass on their way to market. She licked her finger and pressed it on each donut crumb left behind on the table, one at a time, bringing it to the tip of her tongue. Like she was trying to stay calm.

Just the day before, she'd dropped a fat envelope of her Sacramento High *Daily Dragon* clippings on the corner of Leroy's desk. She'd told Daddy about her plan to get on at that paper. He knew about her plan. It would ruin things for her if Leroy showed up wanting to see Elthea and found her in back with Daddy.

Jane went up to the counter for a napkin and cocked her head at the coffee mugs jiggling on the back-wall shelves, at the backroom breathing, like a pierced heart and lung, that burbling release of liquid and steam. Her eyebrows lowered.

She sat at the counter and wrote on a napkin to the beat of the jiggling mugs and the flow of their breath. When she finished, she went behind the counter and used a wax paper square to pick up a maple old-fashioned, took one bite, and set it back on the shelf. She also took a bite of a sprinkle and a bear claw and a cinnamon roll, carefully turning the bite marks back to the wall when she was done. Then she returned to her seat at the front table.

A few minutes later, Daddy came back, flushed and messy. Elthea waved goodbye, dimpled fingers close up to her eyes, waggling like lashes.

It must have done something for Daddy to leave Jane alone at that table while he went off to rut with Elthea every week and then came back to find her waiting there. It may have been a test of Jane's loyalty or taste or of Daddy's appeal. It may even have been his idea that it was a gift to Jane to include her in his life this way. For some months, it looked like a donut would pay for this behavior–she was, after all, a hungry girl. But it wouldn't anymore. Didn't he care what she was trying to do? He was putting something important for Jane at risk. She didn't like this feeling, when two things she wanted conflicted. It made her want to choose one fast and forget the other, make the confusion go away. Clarify things.

Back at the tent, she wrote up the napkin story in her notebook and called it "Donut Ass." That didn't change anything, but it made her feel better to write it, scratching an itch.

UNO LIFTED THE tent's sheet flap with an Indian basket table tucked under his good left arm and a jelly jar Momma used as a vase in the shriveled right hand he'd caught in a thresher as a boy. He sneered at Jane. "Evening, beauty queen."

Though Jane was tall, coming up on six feet, she only weighed 125 pounds—all vine, no taters, according to Momma. Not much of a beauty.

She looked at Momma, scowling, then back at Uno. "What're you doing with our stuff?"

Momma said, "Don't be rude to Mister Jeffers."

"Mister Jeffers?"

Momma stepped out of the headlights' glare, closer to Jane. "Our names were drawn for a cabin. We're back in."

Uno was the Tumbleweed Labor Camp manager. The wait list was long and the Hoppers had a black mark next to their name.

"You musta bent some rules," Jane said. "Does Daddy know?"

"Well, he should know," Uno said, "but he probably don't."

Momma nodded, looking up at him through thick black lashes.

Jane said, "He knows plenty."

Momma pinched the skin on Jane's arm, twisting it. "I said not to sass."

Jane pulled her arm away, rubbing the red spot. "Daddy won't like this."

There'd be a blow-up, everybody talking—white-trash Hoppers, all that. Worse still, if Leroy learned Daddy had cuckolded him just when Jane was aiming to get on *The Valley*, Jane would need a new plan. Her parents required a lot of managing so as not to botch up her life entirely, beyond what was already messed up by nature, economics, and ruinous government policy.

But Jane was optimistic and liked to control what she could, believing her effort would make a difference.

Uno set the basket and jar in his Ford's front seat, and when he and Momma went back in the tent, Jane started unloading what they'd packed, even the mattress, almost everything but the hope chest, making a pile on the dirt.

Jane had always kept the family together, stealing money from Momma's bean can when Daddy asked her to, though never as much as he wanted. She bought him whiskey from the Watkins tent down the levee with the bean-can money, topping off a three-quarter jug with water. She lied for him about how he lost the Studebaker, keeping the card game a secret. And the personal stuff with Elthea and the others before her. She protected herself and Daddy from Momma's knowing the details of his behavior. Momma's opinions were strong and persuasive.

Even if a person knew Momma well enough to fear her, that person could often be seen moving closer to her spot at the side of a field, offering to share a sip of water out of a lidded mayonnaise jar, mimicking the way she stretched her back and arms, the way she laughed loud at a joke. Though she was only five-one, she was powerful and real and completely herself, not a fake. And when a person stood near enough to her, he had a good chance of hearing the truth about his life—Baby oughta be crawling by now. Stop howling and get off the porch. Don't like the shape of that mole.

Jane heard a lot of such truth.

Still, she figured, any type of family was better than no family at all.

When Momma and Uno came out of the tent again, carrying stools, Momma's eyes bugged at Jane's boldness. She threw her stool down, crossing the space between them, gripped both sides of Jane's jaw with one hand and squeezed hard. Though Momma was small, she was bulldog sturdy, Jane's opposite.

Momma let go and Jane rubbed her second red spot. "We can find some place better." Daddy wouldn't move back to a camp they'd been kicked out of by Uno Jeffers for no good reason. Wouldn't even do it for hot showers and an outhouse.

"Give us a minute, Uno." Momma tilted her head toward the levee, and he put down two stools and walked off in the dark, lighting a cigarette. She waited until the glowing tip was a distance off. "I won't drop this baby on dirt. Daddy'll risk it, but I won't."

Jane looked up toward a rustling in the bushes. Must have been the collie dog.

"You owe me," Momma said for the millionth time, rolling both fists into her lower back. Jane had taken too much space being born, blocking her twin brother Ben's path into the world. Preventing it, in fact. She did owe Momma. "We're moving to Tumbleweed, the doctor'll come, and he'll get this baby out of me, live. Uno–Mister Jeffers–has fixed it."

Maybe this would make up for Ben. But still, people would talk about Momma and Uno and Daddy if this happened. And Jane was too low around here already to get the things she wanted.

Momma wiped the palms of both hands against the feed-sack dress stretched over her middle. "Moving back to Tumbleweed'll put us ahead."

"Won't put Daddy ahead." Jane didn't mention herself.

"He won't be around forever, Jane."

This was something Momma said when it would further her argument, when it was more useful to be alone than leashed to Daddy, who tended to lurch after every fresh scent. It was true he wandered in and out of their lives, but in spite of his flaws, he never crossed the line to hurt Jane in a way she wouldn't forgive. She was a practical girl, knew what mattered and what didn't. Daddy wasn't good, but he was good enough. Even if they didn't have some government document proving it.

The bushes parted on the other side of the car, and Daddy came around it into the glare of the headlights–thatch of blonde hair, tiny-lined, sunburnt face with a scar on his left upper cheek matching the curve of another guy's shovel. The air buzzed when he stepped into their circle.

"Don't act like I wouldn't give you no license. You never wanted it. Not from day one. Day one. It would interfere with your plans."

Momma's face brightened. "You want to be tied down? Ha!" Her belly jutted between them. "If you won't provide, I'll find a way." Her eyes sparkled at the insult.

"What way is that?"

"I got us another cabin."

"How'd you get it? What'd you have to sell?" His mouth twisted up, contemptuous.

Jane's hands opened and closed, blood flooding her extremities.

"Well, it wasn't the car. I believe you sold that cheap for town tail."

"Got yourself a scheme? Working with Uno?"

"Least he works. Like a man."

"You ain't too big to slap."

Jane's head rattled, lid on its pot, thoughts boiling. She'd heard this talk before but never heard it escalate so fast. She surveyed the campsite for options.

Momma laughed, like she didn't know how he would react, or like she was ignoring that knowledge. Or counting on it.

He said, "You're a disrespectful woman."

"Man's got to earn respect."

Earn money, is what she meant.

Uno returned, stepping back into the headlights, next to Momma. "Get back to town, Abraham."

Time slowed, Uno's words drawn out—Towwwwwn, Abrahaaaaam. He inched up taller. "I'm driving their things to Tumbleweed."

Daddy pointed his long arm at Jane. "You think I'll let you steal from me? My woman? My child?"

"They don't belong to you. Kate's chosen someone who can provide."

"Chosen you?"

Uno puffed out his chest, a barrel-chested chihuahua. "You think you're a musician? Haw! Show me two dimes you ever earned by music."

Daddy's face changed all the way to ugly. This wasn't going to stop itself.

Both his clenched fists rose and he exploded, punching right, straight at Uno's head, left and right again, knocking him to the ground, silent, bleeding.

But this time his fists didn't end it. Momma, in her eighth month, came at Daddy with a stool—lifted it up and cracked it on his back, like in the movies. Brought it down with enough power to burst it into tinder all around him.

Daddy turned, roaring, shoved Momma to the ground with two hands, and everything stopped. Jane's feet, hands, and head were still. She'd worked so hard to keep something like this from happening. But now she did nothing, couldn't see a path.

"Come on then, finish us off. Don't starve us to death. Do it fast, like a man."

"Momma, stop!" She had to pull things back.

"Shut up, Kate. Have you got to always push?" Daddy said.

"Do it! Such a man. If you're such a man, do it."

He unbuckled his belt, started to remove it.

"Daddy, no!" Jane yelled, but it looked like he didn't even hear her.

Momma was still on the ground, propped up on her hands, knees spread wide, yelling.

Jane cried, "Momma! Why do you have to do this?"

He flicked his belt back and forth, walking circles around her.

Jane reached in the Ford's open door and grabbed the crowbar.

Then he did it, swung that belt at Momma from the side, so it made a wide, whooshing arc, slapping her skin with a crack, releasing her scream.

Momma looked straight at Jane, her eyes saying, Do it.

Daddy's face was lit up, arm muscles popping like a cartoon bully. Not finished.

Jane had to keep this train from making its next stop.

She felt a great surge, a sparking, an ignition.

She swung the crowbar the way Daddy taught her to swing a bat, loose in her hands, stepping into it, aiming for his shoulder, connecting, maybe with his shoulder, maybe higher.

He fell in stages to his knees, his bloody hands, then his face to the dirt.

Jane dropped the crowbar, looked at Momma, wondering, Is this it?

"We don't have much time," Momma said. "Take him up Jiboom, to I Street, down 99." Momma waved her arm toward the Golden State Highway, half the north-south double barrier, along with the Southern Pacific tracks, separating them from the nice people. "Go south of Galt. Leave him on the shoulder. We'll say he's gone for a job." Her idea was so complete.

The sheriff would be coming for Jane and Daddy, the criminals in this situation.

Momma got a rope from the car and tied his hands in back. She was good at knots. She grabbed a quilt from the pile and spread it next to Daddy–"C'mon."

Jane had to choose, really choose, so she did, because this was who Jane was, the kind of person who decides, in or out, and then closes the damn door on the decision, at seventeen years old, at twelve, even at nine. That's who she was.

So she bent with Momma to roll Daddy onto the quilt, grabbing its short end so they could drag him to the car. He was heavy and they struggled, had to stop and rest over and over, laying the blanket down in the dirt and then picking it up again. They left Uno passed out where he was.

When they got to the Ford, Momma unwrapped him and told Jane to sit him up, reach under his armpits and grab his wrists, which she did. Momma crossed his ankles and put both legs over her shoulder. One, two, three, she said, and they stood and lifted him at once–they'd done this before–into the back seat, their joined breath making the car's air thick. They draped him over Jane's hope chest.

The radio played Tex and His Brothers–This game, ain't for losin'. I'm fixin' to win the next hand.

Momma got out and pointed at the wheel, panting.

"Ain't you coming with me?" Jane asked.

Momma rolled her left fist on the side of her belly, looking pained. "I'll handle things here. Go on."

Jane had only ever driven a car two hours, two years before, when she was fifteen, when they still had the Studebaker. Daddy narrated instructions the whole way. He didn't repeat that driving lesson after she ran off the road into a tree stump outside Marysville, requiring two days' labor to fix the front end. He said she drove like a girl, like he forgot what she was. She could kill him this night just by putting him in the back seat of a car she was driving. But she got into the driver's seat and laid her hands on the wheel.

Momma came around to her window and passed her the bloody crowbar. "Just in case," she said. "Go on." And Jane dropped it on the floorboard.

Jane closed her eyes and then opened them before doing what Daddy said back then—"Pull back on the emergency brake, Jujee. Now push the spark control all the way up, all the way. Pull the hand throttle halfway down. That's it. Now turn the gas valve open. Turn the choke control valve full clockwise, wait . . . Now back off a quarter turn. Okay, turn the ignition switch on. Push in the clutch and put the transmission in neutral. Now pull the choke control out. Almost there. Turn the engine over three revolutions—choke in on the third."

The engine started.

"Push the throttle lever up, Jujee, and the left lever all the way down. Push the accelerator pedal. Now turn the choke control."

A hot breeze blew through the window, sprinkling ragweed pollen on the front seat, making Jane cough.

She backed up in a jerk, stalling. Then she started over, did it all again, finally turning Uno's car around, off the levee, onto Jiboom, then to I, then to the two-lane highway, gripping hard when a truck passed, headlights shining on roadside trees, branches reaching overhead to grab at each other.

Thirty miles. Pull him out of the car. Untie his hands. Drive home. She whispered it over and over as she drove past vinegar-smelling canneries, tomato fields, ripe tangy cattle, orchard stumps like headstones.

When they were nearly to Galt, Daddy's head popped up in the rearview, causing her to jump, and the car swerved off the road onto gravel before she could straighten it out again, back onto asphalt.

"Stop the car. I gotta throw up." His voice was rough and slurry.

She couldn't stop.

"Go ahead, Daddy."

He doubled over, gagging onto the floorboard.

"Stop the car," he repeated, craning to wipe his mouth on the seat back. "I'll drive."

"I'll stop soon."

"Jujee, I don't blame you, what happened back there."

She saw in the rearview there was blood all over his neck and face and shoulders, and under the blood his skin was white. She felt something strong but didn't know what to call it. She wasn't in the business of naming feelings. She named goals.

"You was acting out of instinct. I know that. But we gotta get back there now, Jujee, before Uno steals everything."

His eyes looked loose, like each one saw something different.

"I don't think we'd better."

"Don't take this on yourself, girl. I got this. I'm in my right mind now. I can fix things up. Your momma shouldn't have put this on your shoulders."

Everything was always on her shoulders. Didn't he see that?

"Let's get back there, fix it up."

He was sweating and his mouth looked wrong, his flexing jaw muscles, his flaring nostrils. A melted mask of his face.

The skin near Jane's ear pulsed. "I don't think so, Daddy."

"What's that?"

"I don't think it's a good idea."

He waited before answering. "You talking like that to your daddy?"

He wasn't acting like a daddy. What kind of family would they be if she took him back? She couldn't fake that hard now.

"Jane Hopper, I mean it. If you're my girl, you need to untie me now and let me drive us back to that camp and get our things."

His girl.

"I ain't going back, and neither are you."

He was quiet again. Then, "You ain't going back to Momma?"

When she didn't say anything, he went on. "You're right. She thinks she's got us under her thumb, making out like her money is everything."

"This ain't about money."

"It's always about money," he said. "Keeping me on the chain, working, that's it. She has no appreciation for beautiful things. She doesn't understand what I do, what I'm capable of, though I've stayed with her all these years, all those fields and tents."

"This is about a cabin." Jane yanked it back to the matter at hand, but she knew Daddy was right. It was about money. Momma always talked about climbing up off the bottom rung, where they'd been stuck for four years, living in that tent, cordoned off by river, tomato fields, train tracks, and highway. She told everybody how she got them out from under an Oklahoma bank's boot-heel, all the way to Sacramento. If Momma wanted more power over her fate, she needed money for leverage, and she'd do what it took.

"You think moving to Tumbleweed's about improving our situation? Yours and mine, Jujee? You think that baby in her belly's part of our family?"

She didn't answer, wondering if it mattered who the daddy was. In her experience, it was the momma that mattered.

"Okay, then. You're right. We'll head down to San Luis. Get us some pea work. There's some nice little bars there that like a good singer. You untie me, and I'll drive us there."

That wasn't going to happen. She said, "I'm not going with you," and began to cry. She'd stood between them so long, holding them together.

"What are you saying?"

"Momma's moving to Tumbleweed, you can go to San Luis and I'll . . ." –what would she do?–"I'll go to San Francisco." There was no reason for her to say this other than a poster at the movie theater downtown, which always reminded her of Uno's daughter, who'd run off there some time ago, and somehow it glowed in her mind like the far-off horizon.

Daddy laughed hard at that, longer than he should, mean look on his face. "Sounds like you got a bona fide plan. Yes, ma'am. Whole lot of picking work in Frisco, acres and acres of tomatoes. Yes, ma'am. Who am I to interfere with a girl's bona fide plan?"

He thought she was stupid. Had he always thought that? Her, stupid?

She slowed for the Galt stop sign–dark Texaco station, butcher, feed-store, depot. A spotted dog ran across the road. Daddy looked left and right, and she shifted and pushed her foot on the pedal and the car lurched forward.

Galt was in the rear view now, nothing but road and sky and the SP tracks and Tokay grapes near harvest, glowing on the vine.

"You can't leave me bound up at the side of the road."

"I'll untie you. You can catch a ride to Stockton."

She pulled the car over, crunching onto gravel, front wheels stopping just at the shoulder before it dropped into an irrigation ditch. Then she got out and opened the back door.

He stood, five inches taller than her.

Up close she saw the slick black blood, and the skin on her face felt cold. He turned his back so she could untie him. It took a while, as her hands were shaking and Momma's knot was good, but then the rope dropped and he turned back around.

They stood there a minute, his face looking scrambled—the parts familiar, the whole unknown. Was his left eye higher than the right? Had it always been?

Water rushed in the ditch behind him, past and future both flowing by.

Then he grabbed her right wrist, twisted it, making her drop to her knees.

"Wrong choice, girl."

Jane's face contorted in pain from his twisting, but she didn't drop the car keys. He wouldn't go further. He couldn't do that to her. He didn't have any people—Granny died back in Sweetwater. He wasn't going to sever the last real connection he had. This is what Jane thought.

But he twisted harder. "Disloyal," he said. "I thought I could trust my girl."

He thought only of himself. Not about her. No one would think of her but her. No one ever had.

Everything went white-blue, the color of a high whistle shrieking, and Jane's head wanted to split with pain and anger, like something new had entered her, or something old wanted out. In her head she heard so many words and cries, but loudest of all she heard, Hit him. She saw the truth that she would do anything to survive. She punched Daddy in his groin with her left fist, felling him again.

He lay there moaning and clutching himself.

Scrambling up to get away, she dropped the keychain.

Though he was doubled over, he reached and grabbed it.

She snatched the blood-sticky crowbar off the floorboard—"I'll do it again!"

Daddy threw the keys into the dark and she could nearly see them flipping through the air. It took so long before she heard the triple clank, metal on metal, before the keychain hit, up near the car's front end.

Why'd he do that? Why didn't he want her to get away from all this? His throwing those keys seemed like the worst thing he did that night, the worst thing any of them did that night, proof of the idea that had been nibbling her brain those past few months—that her people were chaotic, untrustworthy. They weren't for her anymore, if they ever were. She was better off on her own. And seeing she had to go, had to break from these people, at the very same time when that river of anger rushed through her, her stringy muscles took over and she brought the crowbar down on his hip, this time like a pick, not a bat, releasing some essential Jane that had never gotten out before.

He bellowed and then he grabbed her feet, knocking her down, and she fell into the ditch. Her face hit cold water and she sputtered and rose up coughing. She struggled to stand, the water waist high. She stepped on something sharp—a branch?—tearing right through her shoe into her foot. She pulled it out, screaming. The pain moved in a wave all the way up through her body, into her head, pounding to get out. Then she crawled up the edge to the muddy bank.

He was standing over her now—"I thought you were different."

"I am," she yelled.

You are, raged the voice in her head.

Different than anybody knew. Different than she was a few hours before.

Her fingers sank in the mud, inches from moonlit metal, the crowbar. She reached and gripped it again, raised up and swung, hitting him hard on his knees.

He cried out and tumbled into the ditch himself, splashing, yelling.

Her foot hurt so bad, and she'd used up all her physical power. Her skull felt brittle, like it might explode from the pressure. He was going to climb up and get her, throw her in the water, drown her. She knew it. She was going to end right there, in the muddy water. Not be a writer in the papers, or on the radio. Just a dirty, ugly girl, white trash, dead, alone in a ditch. She waited, sobbing, her face muddy, streaked, red, brown, white. She'd fought, but it was over.

When finally she stopped crying, the only sound left was the rushing ditch water. Still she waited, heart pounding, but nothing happened–something should happen. She waited longer. Still nothing. No one. An empty space between then and now.

She breathed–one, two, three, four, one, two, three, four, one, two, three, four. When her breath no longer rasped, she thought maybe he swam off, climbed out of the ditch down the road, was hitching a ride to Stockton. He wouldn't come back. She waited some more, but still nothing happened.

She thought, He can't come back. He's dead.

Her ears filled with a sizzling, her thoughts on fire. She sat on the dirt and waited until they'd gone all to ash.

Then she got up and threw the crowbar in the ditch, limped to the car and opened the glove box, finding what she wanted, a matchbook. She struck one match, pushing too hard, breaking it. She struck another but couldn't make it light, scratching it over and over before tossing it. Then one smoked and lit right up but by the time she held it out in front of her it burned her fingers and she flung it away. Next one she got a little light from. Finally, she struck one that shone onto the keychain, lying against the front tire.

She got back into the driver's seat and started the car, without Daddy's voice in her ear, and turned the car around, toward home, toward the confluence of rivers.

When she got to camp, the tent was gone, Momma and Uno too. Even Daddy's banjo. Just trash, empty cans, a broken plate, spilled nails. She felt a burst of pain in her forehead and fingered an almond-sized lump there, like a third eye, which worried her, aware as she was that fatal wounds were often bullet-small.

Did Momma expect her to join them at Tumbleweed?

You've paid your debt, said the voice in her head.

Jane sighed, shoulders slumped.

She kicked the dirt, looking for any small thing that belonged to her—book, bag of marbles, comb—but found none of it. Near where Daddy hit Uno, she found seven pennies and a card hand-printed in pretty letters—Sweetie Jeffers, 3528 Clay Street, San Francisco. Uno's run-off daughter.

Jane put the card, like a charm, in her pocket, got back in Uno's Ford, her hope chest filling half the back seat, and started the car.

Your Call Is Important

Linda Lenhoff

Here's what I know, I tell myself each morning as I walk: There's a little boy four doors down chained to a doghouse in his backyard. There's a little boy chained up behind a house in my neighborhood. I let the sentences repeat in my mind as I take each step, the way children repeat rhymes as they jump to the next square in hopscotch. As if it will propel me forward. As if saying it does anything for anyone at all.

I start my walk to campus down a hill of broken sidewalk, a reminder that this is earthquake territory. I count the houses as a kind of mantra—one, two, three, four—as if it will bring luck, which sometimes it does. Sometimes I don't see him. But what do people in houses two and three think? What kind of comforting rhymes do they tell themselves? Is it possible they haven't seen him, or that they know something I don't? Am I making this whole thing up?

But no, there it is. House four: a sickly light green, shades always drawn, the dog run along the side leading no doubt to a backyard filled with overgrown weeds, mangled tree limbs, swirls of silt leading upward but not in any optimistic kind of way. Sometimes I make out his little legs, ending in a pair of imitation Keds tennis shoes.

There's a little boy chained to a doghouse in my neighborhood. And I've done nothing about it, I whisper to the stop sign at the corner.

I'm the kind of person who's done nothing about it, I say silently to the crossing guard, who's too busy to notice me anyway.

But I'm pretty nearsighted. I once mistook this very stop sign for that very crossing guard when some kids put an orange jacket over it at Halloween. With my vision, the figment of my imagination on the dog chain could well be a German shepherd. A smallish one.

A German shepherd in imitation Keds. A German shepherd playing with imitation Keds. The pictures in my mind do not soothe me.

PLUS, THERE'S THIS weather. San Diego's annoying, smoggy mornings; afternoons that can heat up beyond expectation. The dryness—it causes hallucinations, fantasies. Drought and destruction and cracked-up sidewalks. Face it, it's a desert, a mirage in itself. I once saw such wavy lines in the road that I got distracted and headed onto the freeway ramp—the off-ramp—headed the wrong way. And there were a couple of near-misses with bicyclists by the beach, plus that guy crossing the road in Carlsbad by the big tree—but that could have happened to anyone, couldn't it? These are not happy thoughts—certainly not anything I've ever admitted to anyone. It's not like I'm one of those people who think they're always right.

That's right, Patty (I say this to myself a lot, along with, Wake up, Patty; It's good for you, Patty; and, Just don't think about it, Patty). That's right, Patty: there's (maybe) a little boy chained to a dog run on the side of a house. In this heat. A little boy imagining mirages, dreaming fantasies, trying to escape his leash in imitation Keds.

Or not. Just another mistake in the road.

No wonder I'm always so sweaty by the time I reach school.

I SIT IN my teaching cubicle—not an office, just a couple of closely placed partition walls, a desk, and a highly valued window—watching unexpected rain fill up the library pit. It's not really a library pit, of course, but a construction ditch for what's known as the new Library Center. No one's announced when it'll be finished, just as they haven't announced why it's called the Library Center instead of just the Library. The rain isn't that hearty, but it's increasing its presence—although I'm not sure how weather can change so quickly and if it means we've done something indefensible to the environment. There's a coolness in the air that wasn't there four hours ago, something not entirely unwelcome but still a little alarming. The rain taps against my window like a shy student who needs to ask a question but is worried I'll remember how badly he's doing in class. This rain (and any rain is unexpected here) has begun to muddy most of the campus. If it doesn't let up in a few hours, the streets will be flooded, and traffic accidents will be in the double digits. Plus, it's slowly, hypnotically, putting me to sleep.

I've fallen asleep before, after teaching my back-to-back freshman English courses. Most of the graduate teachers come into our shared area all springy and wired, babbling of peer editing groups and issues debated: abortion, euthanasia, racial integration. As for me, I tend to go straight to my cubicle, look out the window at the pit, checking to make sure no progress has been made, and fall into dreamy sleep. I have probably failed to find my proper calling, and not for the first time. More than once, students have had to wake me to ask questions, but often they just leave little notes on my desk. "Came by to see you!" "Hope you feel better!" "Need help with essay when you're well!" I find these touching. Although sometimes I do have a headache, sleeping is just my natural reaction to teaching.

But today I'm not just tired from classes. I've gotten a disturbing memo, although you'd think it would get my heart pounding. It announces that the Samsons, both English teachers, both about sixty, with his-and-hers short gray haircuts (the kind of cut that's so short it looks prickly, like one of those things you wipe snowy boots on) have taken early retirement. The Samsons, my sometimes advisors (I never ask for much advice), my all-the-time landlords, have no doubt been forced out. They love it here, decorating the place each Christmas with sprigs of fir, each Easter leaving little chocolate eggs for all their students. In the autumn they go out to the mountains and bring in fallen leaves, then scatter them through the halls for us to crunch our way through. They even clean up afterward.

I hold up my memo until the words start to blur. A voice wakes me.

"So much for Grandpa and Grandma," says a fellow graduate student, a dark, curly-haired guy several years my junior (they all are). I think his name is really Mark, but for some reason, he's always referred to as Anti. He's part of the group known as neuro-postmodernists around here. Their name for themselves, but many of us consider it a euphemism.

"I'm very fond of them," I say. "They've always been nice to me," which is true. They've hinted at wanting to sell me the house when I get a real teaching position, which they've hinted they want to make sure I get right here. It's the most natural, familial gesture anyone's made to me in years.

"You're just buying into the sappiness of the status quo," the Anti-Mark says.

"You're just young and don't know anything," I think but don't say. Age is relative, of course, and I am old to be a graduate student, but I can't take seriously a twenty-two-year-old with neuro-postmodernistic tendencies—whatever they may be, and I do have a feeling something sexual is involved—and sneakers that cost over a hundred dollars, although I'm estimating.

"I run toward sap," I say, turning away. The rain picks up outside, rattling the windows. I wonder if the neuro-postmodernists have thought up some progressive, advanced way to get home in this rain without an umbrella, but I doubt it.

I walk home quickly, a *San Diego Union Tribune* over my head—I picked it since it's a little thicker than *USA Today*, which of course is also in color and might run onto my clothes. I pass by house number four without looking up, afraid of what I'll see, or what I might think I see. I do slow down and listen (my hearing is far better than my eyesight), but all I hear is rain—drops hitting the ground, the deeper sound of drops hitting that doghouse. My grandmother used to say that not knowing was worse than knowing, and she may be right, unless what you find out is that there's a muddy boy in a splintering doghouse waiting for something else you can't imagine. I try to picture my grandmother's face, what she might say to this, but for some reason, she won't look up.

Patty, you may need another nap.

But no, today something different is planned for me. I get home and change my wet clothes, then get in my car and head for the local Hilton hotel. I've never done this before, and I can't be sure why I agreed to do it now.

You may already be a winner, Patty, I tell myself, driving carefully so that (a) I don't hit anyone and (b) the windshield wipers don't put me to sleep.

I'm headed for a perfect rainy-day activity, I tell myself, although I'd be embarrassed to tell anyone else.

The invitation came in a phone call, the kind you get at dinnertime, the kind you know better than to answer, but when you live alone, you don't always have your best long-term interests at heart. Besides, I told myself, it's bad to eat dinner in front of the TV. Much better to eat while talking on the phone, which means you can talk to strangers with your mouth full, breaking two parental prohibitions at once. I surreptitiously took bites of chicken as the guy talked, telling me that I'd filled out an entry form to win a new Camaro, reminding me (of course) that I hadn't won the new Camaro but was a prizewinner nonetheless. Something electronic. Something electronic and new and free, if only I'd come to my choice of breakfast or late-afternoon lunch and listen to a presentation on a new planned community. Or a planned new community. I probably swallowed at this point and missed the real order, but it may not really matter. As any underemployed graduate student knows, the words *lunch is included* have a certain appeal.

The hall is warm and cozy at this Hilton, something I hadn't expected. It's the kind of room that's usually freezing with air-conditioning, but somehow they've one-upped the weather, and this place is toasty without being too warm. I settle into an overly cushioned blue chair—there must be hundreds of them—and discover that it rocks slightly and is the kind of soft I must have always been looking for in a chair, without even realizing it. I now know how Goldilocks felt.

I'm almost too comfortable to get up for the buffet, but the sweet smells of Danish, warmed turkey, mashed potatoes, and steaming chicken soup lure me. There's something to admire in a place that serves you chicken soup. Maybe they know more about me than I think. It's not even Campbell's, but something someone has chopped and stewed personally. The meal embraces me and those around me as we each eat in our slightly rocking seats pulled up to tables covered in deep blue cloth. The napkins are orange—real fabric, not paper. I realize that this moment is everything I've always wanted from Thanksgiving. Whatever has led me here, I'm thankful.

I snap out of it only a little as the lights dim. Somehow, I expected an old-fashioned slide show, someone clicking away at a rickety projector, the occasional slide turned upside-down. But welcome to the information age, Patty, where everything you need is digital. (Unless you're a graduate teacher. We're still using mimeograph machines.) No distracting clicking here, just the sounds of Windham Hill—like music behind a soothing woman's voice, the kind of voice that would anticipate your every need, offering you a second Danish before you'd finished the first. The kind of voice you'd want to accept from. Yes, thank you so much. I do want a second pastry, a warm cinnamon roll. I hadn't even realized how important one could be.

And I want to live in Santa Vallejo, I tell the voice, of course I do. Now not only does the room contain all the scents of home, the presentation fills our eyes with visions of needs fulfilled, needs met by the new community of Santa Vallejo. Parents hug little children and send them to play on the shiniest of swing sets. Grandparents cook up a stew in the kitchen of a house that could be yours, Patty, although it's been cleaned by someone a little more attentive. In the kitchen's background I see the same pastries we've just consumed. Freshly baked. Smelling of cinnamon. Seconds and thirds. Back in the town center, low tiled office buildings blend into the community. "Community," the woman's voice repeats at us, "community," although I'm not really registering the words as much as waiting for Grandma to reappear, waiting to see what lies beyond the next playground. Teachers lead bands of children dressed in clean primary-colored clothing, some holding balloons. Malls greet you and fit into the architecture. Cleanliness. Godliness. All the comforts of home. Not too big, not too small. This place is just right.

After the show I find I've been asleep in my chair, the room quieted. Others are asleep, too, but not out of boredom. We've been rocked to sleep by the grannies of our dreams, by those with the power to say yes, yes, you may. As I rise, a person hands me a brochure, entitled "Santa Vallejo–the Promise of Community," and a little black-and-white traveling TV. As she hands me the TV, I feel like I've been given an assignment, but then I remember that I had won a prize. For a brief moment I'm unsure which I value more, the TV or the brochure with its promise. It's a nice brochure, four-color, thick, serious. With my arms full, I feel fulfilled, as if I've gone home for a visit to a loving family and they've loaded me up with packages to take home. And promises they intend to keep.

The feeling lasts all the way home. I take my treasures into the house and put them on top of a bunch of stuff that I collected from my school mailbox and haven't looked at much, as it's usually just advice about rhetoric. I'm convinced no one really needs this. There I find a letter I must have missed. It's from the Samsons, my somewhat adoptive family and sometime advisors, sharing their thoughts with me. I feel truly full, sated. I want to hug everything that is mine. Oh, the power of the written word, Patty. Savor it, Patty.

Dear Patty,

You've probably heard that we've accepted the Golden Handshake and are retiring. Well, life does hold its surprises. We've loved teaching and are so glad it has brought so many people into our lives, and we include you among our most treasured students. We're so sorry to say that we're going to need the house back. We'll need to consolidate our finances for our retirement, and we plan to move back into our small house that you've been so kind to care for. We've loved having you as a tenant and, we hope, as our friend. We wish you luck in every endeavor. Won't you please be out by December fifteenth?

Love, Elizabeth and George Samson

December fifteenth. Two days after the end of the semester. One week from yesterday. I remember: how long has it been since you checked your school mailbox, Patty? A month? Longer?

I think about all these numbers and passages of time as I go into the living room–with its nice old-fashioned moldings and working fireplace–and put all the wood I've collected into the fireplace. It's not really cold enough for this, but I don't care. I light the fireplace and watch the flames overcome the logs. On top of the fire, I place their letter. Warm as the room gets, I can't completely regain the feeling from this afternoon. But I still feel a little something hopeful. I can still picture the grandparents from the video, their arms open, offering sweets and something deeper. They look nothing like the Samsons.

IN THE MORNING I stop at door number three. The dream house, the color of strawberry Häagen Dazs, as clean and tidy and welcoming outside as the cottage Hansel and Gretel approached. The front doormat has bluebirds on it.

I knock softly, even though it's 8:45 and the neighborhood is up and hopping. I can hear the crossing guard down at the main intersection. She sings "Do Re Mi" today. It makes me glad I don't live nearer to the intersection. No one answers at the pink door, so I knock a little more forcefully, although I can't get the picture of Julie Andrews spinning around on that mountaintop out of my head. I know it's not even the right scene for the song. Finally, through a small square window centered high on the pink door, I see the top of an older woman's head. Many of my neighbors, I've been told, have lived in the area for years.

"Yes," the gray top says through the door.

"Hi," I say, "I'm Patty Grant. I live in the Samsons' house two doors down?" I point in my direction then circle my hands over my head as if describing my house as a large mushroom.

"Yes?"

"I'm your neighbor?" I wait. Nothing much happens. "I was wondering if I could talk to you about the child next door?"

"Oh?"

"Could you open the door, just maybe a crack?"

"No, dear, we don't do that."

"Well, have you noticed the child? Does it seem mistreated to you?" I lower my voice slightly at the word *mistreated*. I'm not sure if the whisper makes it through the door.

"I'm sorry, dear, we really prefer not to buy anything door-to-door."

"I'm not selling anything." I raise my voice and stand on my tiptoes so I can see better into her small window. I can only make out to about her eyebrows. I've seen the woman before, of course, gardening. But she's never waved or greeted me. I don't know her name.

"The child next door?" I put my hand above my head and point in the doghouse's direction. "Have you seen one?"

She shakes her head. "Sorry, dear. I can't say that I have." And she's gone.

All's quiet at house number four, but from the street I can see the chain that leads to the doghouse. Swaying. I cannot bring myself to knock at house number four's door, partly because I can't imagine what I'd say.

"Excuse me, is your child chained to the dog house?" What if they answer *Yes*? What if they answer *No*?

Them: Yes, that's our [boy/girl] by the doghouse.

Me: Shall I come by after school and take him [her] for a walk?

No, of course I wouldn't say that.

Them: No, there's no child by our doghouse.

Me: Oh. (The door slams here.) Or . . .

Them: He's just playing. You know how children are. Or don't you have children? (Slightly accusatory voice here.)

Me: Playing with a leash on him?

Them: Safety first.

Me: What about the splintering wood, the rain?

Them: Children enjoy being outdoors. It's better for them than television. (The door slams here.)

But wouldn't a good neighbor find out more? Someone living in Santa Vallejo, say, in the midst of the closely knit community with its shiny swing sets, wouldn't a neighbor there be bound by some sort of community pledge to take matters into her own hands?

What if they don't open their door, Patty? What if they do?

When in doubt, consult a text. Like the good graduate student I am, I head for the bookshelf in the TA offices. Actually, consulting the research librarian might be the thing to do. I approach her in my mind. "Hello, one of my neighbors has his or her child tied to a doghouse. Can you recommend a book or books to consult on this subject?" Instead, I grab the phone books. Yellow or white? Is this a case for 911? Is it an out-and-out emergency? Is it a time-crucial matter? How could I explain that I'm calling only after noticing this for weeks, maybe longer?

The White Pages. A to Z. I try the Easy Reference List at the beginning of the government pages. And it really is easy. I only have to go to the C's—Child Abuse Reporting—the county social services department. I dial the 800 number and wait for the recorded message. The voice asks me to consider which button I want to push for which service. Please press One to report a probable case of child abuse in your area. That sounds like me.

Please hold, the voice says. On comes some music I used to work out to at aerobics, back when aerobics seemed necessary and wise. All she wants to do is dance, the music says, dance, dance. I'm not sure it's appropriate music, but it does have a strong bass.

Every few seconds I hear a click that sounds like someone's coming on the line. I get prepared to tell my story (Should I mention the rain? The heat? The shoe?), but it's just another operator's voice telling me to please stay on the line and that my call is important. Your call is important, Patty. Finally, as the song plays for the second time, I get transferred back to the main menu. I'm a little alarmed at this. If I want to report a probable case of child abuse, press One. If I want to inquire about adoptive services, press Two. If I want information on an existing case, press Three. To speak to a representative, press the star key. I press the star key.

Your call cannot be completed as dialed. Please try again.

Silence.

But I do try again, because my call is important.

I press Two this time. I get the same song. I find it annoying that all she wants to do is dance. I put the phone down on my desk, where I can still hear the music, and try to read a student's paper about the similarities and differences between lesbianism and Judaism. The bass pounds. Toward the end of the song, I pick up the phone again. With the last beat, the recording hangs up on me. If a recording can do that.

I try a few more times, trying to keep track of which buttons I've pushed and which I haven't. The student paper has completely misrepresented Judaism, but all the words are spelled correctly. I dial 911. A real voice answers, surprising me, as I'm waiting for a recording to tell me which number to press.

"What is your emergency?"

"Yes, I'd like to report a possible case of child abuse in my neighborhood?" I've written the sentence down by now so I can just read it.

"You need to call child social services at 800-455–"

"Yes, I've tried, but their recording seems broken and won't transfer me to anyone."

"They might be busy and you have to be patient."

"I think the recording's broken, though."

"Then you can call the local office directly." She gives me the number.

Progress. I thank the real voice.

"Use 911 only for emergencies," the voice says, then hangs up, confirming my fear that a little boy in a doghouse is not considered an emergency.

I dial the new number. A different computerized voice answers, instructing me to please wait and my call will be answered in order. It doesn't say in what kind of order. It doesn't mention that my call is at all important. A different song by the guy from the Eagles starts to play. It's slower and doesn't have anything to do with dancing but makes me wonder if someone got a Best of the Eagles CD on sale. Maybe each county agency takes one song. Still, I refuse to listen to the words–I don't want to memorize them inadvertently like I did the last song. So I stare at my watch and try to hum randomly, fill my ears with a kind of blurriness. The song plays four times for a total of fourteen and a half minutes. I start pushing buttons, which has no effect, but the push-button sound does at least drown out the music. After the fifth version, I hang up.

I check the phone book for the downtown office address and get my papers together. I give the Judaism/lesbianism paper a C+. It does occur to me, looking around the office, that I wish I could confide in someone. I've seen other TAs gathered round one another, chatting about penmanship and boyfriends, and I've even joined into a few discussions on the values of plus and minus grades, whether a topic sentence is overrated, and how to properly tone down your enthusiasm for the really cute boy students. But I don't feel I can confide something like this to any of them. I'm older–it's how they see me. Thirtyish, over the hill, but not wise beyond my years. I keep a low profile; I don't make waves. So, this seems more the kind of thing to tell a total stranger, for me at least.

I leave the campus and walk as quickly as possible back to my house for my car. The crossing guard yells at me to slow up, although I think she means slow down. For some reason, I listen to her, as if she were an authority figure instead of just a woman in orange. She has one of those forceful kinds of voices, I have to admit, especially when she isn't singing show tunes. Once out of her sight, I run again, directly past house number four, and get my car going. I head in the direction of the local child abuse office. I will not be intimidated by any more answering machines. I prepare to be intimidated one-on-one.

But a sign on the door informs me that the office is closed until further notice. Other offices can be found in San Ysidro (this is far from here) and Riverside County (this is farther). Our local office may reopen if the new state budget is passed. It says this in professionally printed letters, as if trying to persuade me to take some political stance, some political action, which I might consider if I knew what could possibly help. I just have no idea. I try not to think about any of this.

On my way home, I stop at Ralph's to get some good packing boxes, even though I still have a few in the garage, having moved too many times. I have boxes from my days in Mission Viejo working for the Letters to the Editor section. I may even have a few boxes from old family days in Los Angeles, the brief visit to Orange County, the mistaken journey back to Los Angeles, although I don't always like to see the old markings. Kitchen, bedroom, living room. The words seem ambiguous enough, but they bring back memories. I prefer my boxes unmarked.

Next to the big trash bins behind the store I find some really good boxes –they're from canned goods, bottled water. No stains, no rips, no funny smells. I probably look a little odd standing there smelling boxes. I pick up a nice smallish V8 box but something scurries out of it and runs behind the bin, startling me so that I throw the box back as fast as I can. It was something's home, I berate myself. I step back and feel a little dizzy.

Get a grip, Patty. Tell yourself what a nice set of boxes this is. Altogether I've got five really good boxes, maybe more than I need, given my previous collection, although you never know what will become of cardboard left too long in the garage. I fumble with the boxes, like a clown juggling items never intended by nature to be juggled, and try to load them into my car. My very old Toyota wagon, beige fading to a sickly skin color. I look up to see a woman in a bright blue car slowly approaching me.

"You can ask for boxes inside!" she yells at me angrily. She gives me a sneer as I lift two of my boxes from the ground. The woman's about my age, although her car is much nicer and she's wearing noticeable makeup, pink lips and cheeks, although not the same shade. Complementary shades, if you like pink. She drives away with this look of disgust, her car eerily making almost no noise at all. I guess that's an attractive quality in a car these days, stealthiness, but I find my thundering old Toyota comforting. I like to hear it roar as I press the gas, whether it's supposed to or not.

At home, I find myself sorting and stacking belongings, unearthing long streams of dustmite-ridden material. When it gets dark, I stand out in front of my house, looking out into the street. The neighbors are all inside, so the only sounds are cars from the distance, plus the rattling sounds of animals rustling through bushes. Occasionally, a skunk will come up to the back door, brave and fat, hunting around the garbage cans. The possum are far less attractive—I tend to make a lot of noise in hopes they'll run off, but they're fearless and dumb. Creatures braver than I pad around the trees as I examine my street, not looking in that certain direction of that certain green house. I turn to look back at the house I'll be leaving, wondering how long before the skunks need to move on too. Something that lives out here ate my tomatoes right off the vines last summer, waiting until they were a perfectly ripe, deep red. I can't see the Samsons putting up with this, although there might have been a time when I'd have thought they would.

I spend the next days packing and grading final papers, writing little comments in the margin for the students who've been nice, and turning in my grades. Taking breaks, I go room by room evaluating my belongings: Little of the furniture is mine, just books and blankets, mostly. Clothes, a few of my grandmother's pots and pans. The dishes belong to the Samsons, along with the silverware. Even the computer is theirs—old, the screen fading on one side. I have my aging small TV and its new little traveling TV offspring from the presentation, plus my tiny stereo. Folders and folders of schoolwork that I don't want anymore. Throwing things away at a time like this may come back and haunt me, I know. But I load up a few garbage bags anyhow. There's not even much in the fridge to part with. Living alone means I don't have much that's too heavy for me to carry by myself, that everything I have seems condensed enough to fit into the compact car. Even my TV seems oddly light, as if it were made out of Styrofoam. When I'm through packing up the car, the house looks pretty much the same, so that I wonder whose life I've been living. I don't even like the pictures—flowers painted in periwinkle, not even a real flower color. It makes me wonder if I ever liked it here. I thought I did.

On the fourteenth, I open my mail to find a package from the presentation. A full-color notebook filled with Santa Vallejo postcards, bumper stickers, and a ten-page brochure. I go to put the brochure from the presentation lunch inside this one, but find it's gotten itself lost in the moving mess. It may be trapped inside a garbage bag, soon to be nibbled by skunks of various weight, heft, and aroma. It may turn up five years from now in a box with no markings.

Late that night I stand outside, since inside seems like a house that I might have once lived in. The air feels as if it desperately needs to rain, but some other element won't let it. Something angry bites me. I trip walking along the sidewalk as I have dozens of times—I've always thought that it's my nearsightedness that makes me trip, but these cracks would attack anyone. Tripping makes the right side of my head threaten to ache, but it decides against it. I turn up the street, but not with a great sense of purpose. It's a little surprising how purposeless I feel, unless I'm just hiding it from myself. I think back to Goldilocks—now, did she have a certain determination, looking from bowl to bowl, bed to bed? Was she actively pursuing that thing that would be just right? Or was she just wandering? No, Goldilocks was starving, exhausted, desperate, not just for food and sleep but for the right food and sleep. The loving sense of food and sleep, rest, warmth (community, the presentation's voice echoes in my mind, nodding, urging me on).

Outside house number four I hear yelling. It's coming from way inside the house. A bathroom, maybe, because there's that funny reverberating you get from tile all around you. I can just picture the tiles—green with bathroom mold and crud blackening the spaces between them. The porcelain tub with orange drippy-looking rust stains. I hear an odd woman's voice, slurring words—just garbled sounds without meaning. The way dogs supposedly hear us. But these are angry sounds. Threatening. And outside, I see the chain leading into the doghouse.

Wake up, Patty.

It's after midnight. There's a little boy chained to a doghouse after midnight, bitten by angry insects, definitely without the right kind of food and sleep. I let myself into the dog run—it's locked, but the lock is so dilapidated it springs open in my hands. It's not much bigger than the cheap lock you keep on a diary. I see an old dog bowl next to the house as I approach, and this bowl, with its dirty white outside and scratched up inside, this bowl is, I think, the worst thing I've ever seen. I once saw a woman with her head cracked open in a car accident, but this is worse. This one ten-inch bowl is worse, and I want to tear it apart, bludgeon it with a hammer, blast the hell out of it. But I can't move. The stupid bowl has me paralyzed.

I finally turn to look. A light from the side of the house shines directly into his eyes. What's around his neck isn't a dog collar, as I'd imagined, but a thick piece of rope, like a curtain sash, tied to the chain. Double-knotted. He looks at me sleepily, sucking on one hand, the other grasping one of those blankets people take to picnics or football games, only they wouldn't take this one. They wouldn't give this one to a dog. I'm a little afraid to approach, as if he were a scary stray dog. But he's a little boy, three or four, I can't tell. Curled up on an old pillow. This is a little boy, Patty. There's no such thing as a stray little boy.

Getting the rope off is hard—I finally have to cut at it with the doll-size scissors from the Swiss Army knife I have on my keychain. Although I worry briefly about him striking out, he stays still as the rope binds and pinches his skin. I hear a few squeaks that must come from him, but he continues only to grasp at the filthy blanket. When I take it from him I expect a little fight, but he lets go of it easily, as if he had no claim to it at all. I pull him out of the doghouse, his ripped imitation Keds hanging half off. He's so light. I carry him and try to figure out how heavy he is in comparison to other things, but I can't really imagine the weights of the usual standards. A sack of potatoes? I'm one person—I don't buy a whole sack. They'd go bad.

He fits perfectly into the last free space in the car. I place him next to a soft blanket and my unused guest pillow. The look on his face confirms what I already suspected, something about the vast difference between greed and desperation. He sinks into the thickness of the blanket and that plumpness I'd found so annoying in my extra pillow—I can tell they feel just right. I place the Santa Vallejo notebook between the front seats—there's a little map inside—and start driving my way out of this storybook.

Publisher's Note

Baobab Press

This Side of the Divide, an anthology from Baobab Press, hopes to reflect the diversity and complexity of the *real* American West's landscapes, peoples, lifestyles, successes, and issues. In this volume, twenty-five authors engaged with settings from Alaska to Arizona, rural Montana to San Francisco. They write with keen perception about the lives, work, aspirations, fears, and ethnic roots of a diverse population. They tell their stories in voices and styles as varied as the region they examine. These writers—some of them well established, others less known but no less gifted—are proof not only of the diversity of the contemporary West but also of the wealth of its literary culture.

Based in Reno, Nevada, Baobab Press and its editors live in close proximity to this great writing. We see and hear it daily at local venues and in national publications. It only seemed inevitable that Baobab Press would in some way attempt to harness, promote, and launch a celebration of these voices. *This Side of the Divide* is that celebration in the form of an anthology. Here is our humble attempt to tap into that golden vein of contemporary American Western literature.

The University of Nevada, Reno, MFA Program in Creative Writing has played an essential role in developing this anthology. Baobab Press offered students hands-on experience in acquisitional editing, reviewing submissions, selecting a list of finalists, and contributing suggestions for revisions. Students also identified and contacted established writers whose work they felt would serve the overall aesthetic vision for the book. Without their efforts, this book would still be in process. Baobab Press is deeply grateful for the contributions of each of the UNR MFA students: Matthew Baker, Raluca Balasa, Casey Bell, Rachel Chimits, Linzy Garcia, Molly Gutman, Isabelle Lang, Danielle Mayabb, Scott McFadden, Logan Seidl, Olivia Soule, Natalie Turley, Laura Valenza, Michelle Wait, as well as the non-MFA student volunteers Zachary Campbell, Rachel Sosh, and Peter Zikos. *This Side of the Divide* is especially indebted to Christina Camarena, who managed MFA operations and involvement in the creation of this compilation.

Christopher Coake, director of UNR's MFA in Creative Writing Program, mentored the students and provided Baobab Press with valuable insights and contacts in the literary community. The vast knowledge, exquisite taste, and endless energy and patience that have made him such a valued member of UNR's faculty also made him an essential member of the editorial team. We thank him for his generous participation in this project.

We received several hundred submissions from writers all over the country. Space constraints allowed us to publish only a small percentage of these stories, but we thank everyone who submitted work to us, especially those longlisted in "Submissions of Note." We were profoundly impressed by the variety of themes and styles reflected in these submissions and inspired by the talent these writers showcased. As these authors demonstrate, the art of the short story is thriving in America.

We are also deeply grateful to the established writers who have allowed us to include their work in this anthology, and to their publishers for giving us permission to do so. Their generosity has helped to make this book possible.

Submissions of Note

The editors of Baobab Press would like to recognize the considerable talents of the following writers and thank them for submitting excellent work:

Cathleen Calbert — "Blood"

Daniel Corfield — "My Father's Hands"

Clinton Craig — "Tell Penny I'm Sorry/ I Love Her"

Richard Dokey — "Manlius Laughed"

J. S. Kierland — "Lessons Unlearned"

Annie Lampman — "Honeysuckle"

Nathan Alling Long — "Anything That Moves"

Laura Jean Schneider — "Offside"

Sandy Smith — "Ghost Towns"

Derek Updegraff — "The Bull from Kelp Forest"

Anna Villegas — "To Forest Lawn and Back"

Contributors

BEIDEMAN, C. R.

C. R. BEIDEMAN writes and teaches writing in Bozeman, Montana. His fiction has been published by *Every Day Fiction, Stonecoast Review, Yellow Medicine Review, Riverfeet Press,* and others. @CRBeideman

BENZ, CHANELLE.

CHANELLE BENZ has published short stories in *Guernica, Granta.com, Electric Literature, The American Reader, Fence,* and *The Cupboard*, and is the recipient of an O. Henry Prize. Her story collection *The Man Who Shot Out My Eye Is Dead* was published in 2017 by Ecco. It was named a Best Book of 2017 by the *San Francisco Chronicle* and one of *Electric Literature*'s 15 Best Short Story Collections of 2017. It was also longlisted for the 2018 PEN/Robert Bingham Prize for Debut Fiction. She currently lives in Memphis where she teaches at Rhodes College.

BLANTON-STROUD, SHELLEY.

SHELLEY BLANTON-STROUD teaches college composition in Sacramento, California, and coaches writing in economics and engineering at the Independent System Operators. Her stories have appeared in such online journals as *The Brevity Blog, Cleaver Magazine*, and *Eunoia Review.* Others are forthcoming in print in the anthology *Waves: A Confluence of Women's Voices* and *Aethlon: A Journal of Sports Literature.*

CASPERS, NONA.

NONA CASPERS'S most recent book, *The Fifth Woman* (August 2018), was awarded the Mary McCarthy fiction award and was listed as one of the books to watch out for in 2018 by *The Masters Review* blog. She has authored other four books, including *Heavier Than Air,* which received the Grace Paley Prize in Short Fiction and was a *New York Times Book Review*

Editors' Choice. She has received a NEA Fellowship, San Francisco Arts Commission Cultural Equity Grant, Joseph Henry Jackson Literary Grant and Award, and an *Iowa Review* Fiction Award, among others. Her stories have appeared in *Kenyon Review, Glimmer Train, Cimarron Review,* and *The Sun*. She co-edited with Joell Hallowell a nonfiction book, *Lawfully Wedded Wives: Rethinking Marriage in the 21st Century*. She teaches creative writing at San Francisco State University. www.nonacaspers.com

DAVIDSON, ASHLEY.

ASHLEY DAVIDSON'S fiction has been published in *Nashville Review, Shenandoah, Five Chapters, Copper Nickel,* and other journals. She received an MFA from the Iowa Writers' Workshop and lives in Flagstaff, Arizona.

EVENSON, BRIAN.

BRIAN EVENSON is the author of a dozen books of fiction, most recently the story collection, *A Collapse of Horses,* and the novella, *The Warren*. He has been a finalist for a Shirley Jackson Award five times, for the Edgar Award once, and has won the International Horror Guild Award. His novel *Last Days* won the ALA-RUSA award for Best Horror Novel of the year. He is the recipient of three O. Henry Prizes as well as an NEA fellowship and a Guggenheim Fellowship. A new collection of stories, *Song for the Unraveling of the World,* will be published in 2019. He lives in Los Angeles and teaches in the Critical Studies Program at CalArts.

EVERETT, PERCIVAL.

PERCIVAL EVERETT is the author of nearly thirty books, including *Half an Inch of Water, So Much Blue, Percival Everett by Virgil Russell, Erasure,* and *I Am Not Sidney Poitier*. He has received the Hurston/ Wright Legacy Award and the PEN Center USA Award for Fiction. He lives in Los Angeles.

GILLETTE, DAVID.

DAVID GILLETTE was born in rural Colorado and has lived most of his life in small towns, which often serve as the basis for his fiction. He studied creative writing and broadcasting at the University of Iowa and published his first short stories while traveling and working overseas. He has taught writing and media studies at universities in Florida, Japan, and Australia, and he now teaches interactive narrative at Cal Poly in San Luis Obispo, California.

GRIESMANN, LEAH.

LEAH GRIESMANN has received grants and residencies from the MacDowell Colony, the Elizabeth George Foundation, the Swatch Art Peace Hotel in Shanghai, the Key West Writers' Workshops, the *Virginia Quarterly Review* Writers' Conference, the DAAD (Berlin), the Writers in Paradise Conference, and a Steinbeck Fellowship in Fiction. Her Las Vegas-based fiction has appeared in *Union Station*, PEN Center USA's *The Rattling Wall*, *The Boiler*, and *The Weekly Rumpus*, among other publications, and has been read or performed at The Center for Literary Arts, PEN Center USA, Lit Quake San Francisco, Sacramento Stories on Stage, Why There Are Words, the New Short Fiction Series in North Hollywood, and the Shanghai American Center. Her linked Las Vegas-based story collection, *Stripped*, was named a finalist for the Hudson Prize in Fiction and the St. Lawrence Book Award at Black Lawrence Press.

GRIFFITHS, SIÂN.

SIÂN GRIFFITHS lives in Ogden, Utah, where she directs the graduate program in English at Weber State University. Her work has appeared in *Georgia Review, Cincinnati Review, American Short Fiction* (online), *Ninth Letter, Indiana Review*, and *The Rumpus*, among other publications. Her debut novel, *Borrowed Horses* (New Rivers Press, 2013), was a semi-finalist for the 2014 VCU Cabell First Novelist Award. Currently, she reads fiction as part of the editorial team at *Barrelhouse*. www.sbgriffiths.com

HUA, VANESSA.

VANESSA HUA IS a columnist for the *San Francisco Chronicle* and author of the forthcoming novel *A River of Stars* and the short story collection *Deceit and Other Possibilities*. For two decades, she has been writing, in journalism and fiction, about Asia and the Asian diaspora. She has received a Rona Jaffe Foundation Writers' Award, the Asian/Pacific American Award for Literature, the San Francisco Foundation's James D. Phelan Award, and a Steinbeck Fellowship in Creative Writing, as well as honors from the Society of Professional Journalists and the Asian American Journalists Association. Her work has appeared in numerous publications, including the *New York Times*, the *Atlantic*, and the *Washington Post*. She lives in the Bay Area with her family.

LANI, ANDREA.

ANDREA LANI'S essays and short stories have appeared in *Orion*, *Brain, Child Magazine*, *Zoomorphic*, and *SaltFront*, among other publications. She's a senior editor at *Literary Mama*, a Maine Master Naturalist, and a freelance writer and editor. She lives in Maine with her husband and three sons. www.andrealani.com.

LENHOFF, LINDA.

LINDA LENHOFF is the author of *Life à la Mode* and *Latte Lessons*. She has published short stories along with nonfiction articles on food, travel, books, and other topics. She lives in the San Francisco Bay Area. lindalattelessons.wordpress.com.

LEVY, AHARON.

AHARON LEVY'S fiction, nonfiction, and poetry have appeared in various journals. He has received fellowships from the Macdowell Colony, the Anderson Center, the Vermont Studio Center, and La Napoule Art Foundation. He lives in Brooklyn, New York.

MADRID, L. L.

L. L. MADRID lives in the desert with the other feral creatures. She is the 2017 recipient of the Luminaire Award for best prose. When L . L. isn't writing, she edits a journal called *Speculative 66*. @LLMadridWriter; www.llmadridmakes-thingsup.com.

MAYNARD, MARK.

MARK MAYNARD is an English and creative writing instructor at Truckee Meadows Community College in Reno, Nevada. His linked short-story collection, *Grind*, was published by Torrey House Press, and was chosen as the 2017-18 Nevada Reads Book. He has an MFA in creative writing from Antioch University, Los Angeles, and his work has appeared in *Lunch Ticket, Nottingham Review, Tahoe Blues*, and *The Films of Clint Eastwood: Critical Perspectives* (University of New Mexico Press, 2018). Maynard was the recipient of the 2015 Nevada Writers Hall of Fame Silver Pen Award. He lives in Reno with his wife, Molly, and their five children.

MELOY, MAILE.

MAILE MELOY is the author of the novel *Do Not Become Alarmed*, the linked novels *Liars and Saints* and *A Family Daughter*, and the story collections *Half in Love* and *Both Ways Is the Only Way I Want It*, which was named one of the Ten Best Books of the Year by the *New York Times Book Review*. She has also written a trilogy for young readers, beginning with *The Apothecary*. She has received the PEN/Malamud Award, the E. B. White Award, and a Guggenheim Fellowship. She was born and raised in Helena, Montana, and now lives in Los Angeles.

MILLIKEN, DOUGLAS W.

DOUGLAS W. MILLIKEN is the author of the novel *To Sleep as Animals* and several chapbooks, including *The Opposite of Prayer*.

MOUSTAKIS, MELINDA.

MELINDA MOUSTAKIS was born in Fairbanks, Alaska, and raised in California. She is the author of *Bear Down, Bear North: Alaska Stories*, which won the Flannery O'Connor Award, and was a 5 Under 35 selection by the National Book Foundation. She is the recipient of an O. Henry Prize, the Hodder Fellowship, the NEA Literature Fellowship in Fiction, the *Kenyon Review* Fellowship, the Jenny McKean Moore Writer-in-Washington Fellowship, and the Rona Jaffe Cullman Fellowship at the New York Public Library.

SCHMIDT, MIRANDA.

MIRANDA SCHMIDT is a writer, editor, and teacher. Her work has appeared in *TriQuarterly, The Collagist, Electric Literature, Orion, Phoebe*, and other journals. She teaches at the Loft and Portland Community College and has edited for *Phantom Drift, Sun Star Review, Seattle Review*, and other publications. She is a 2017 Lambda Literary Fellow and graduate of the University of Washington's MFA program. She lives in Portland, Oregon, with her wife, two cats, and many trees.

WARNER, CATHY.

CATHY WARNER is a California native who relocated to Washington's Puget Sound in 2011. She is the author of the poetry volume *Burnt Offerings*. Cathy's fiction, memoir, and essays have appeared in dozens of print and online journals and several anthologies. She has received the Steinbeck and SuRaa fiction awards and has been nominated for the Pushcart Prize and *Best American Essays*. cathywarner.com.

WILLMS, MICHELLE.

MICHELLE WILLMS'S work has appeared in the joint bilingual issue of *Scrivener Creative Review, Lieu commun, Black Dandy, In/Words, The Writer's Block*, and others. Michelle is a creative writing MFA candidate at the University of British Columbia through the Optional-Residency program. She lives with her husband and children in Ontario, Canada. www.michellewillms.com

WILLY, E. G.

E. G. WILLY is a West Coast writer. His stories in English have appeared in *Conjunctions, Zyzzvya, J Journal, Berkeley Review,* and *Redwood Coast Review.* His stories in Spanish have appeared in *Azahares* and *Acentos*. Anthologies that have included his writings are *The Breast* (Global City Press, 1995), *Stories from Where We Live* (Milkweed Editions, 2001), *Creatures of Habitat* (Mint Hill Books, 2015), and *Lock and Load: Armed Fiction* (University of New Mexico Press, 2017). "Wagli Yelo" is an excerpted chapter from Willy's novella *Two Horses*.

WILSON, KIRK.

KIRK WILSON is an NEA Fellow whose work in poetry, fiction, and nonfiction has been widely published in literary journals and anthologies. He is the recipient of the *New Millennium* Award for Nonfiction, a Pushcart nominee, and a finalist for the *Crazyhorse* Nonfiction Prize and the Machigonne Fiction Award. A chapbook of his poems, *The Early Word*, was published by Burning Deck Press. His true crime classic *Unsolved* has been published in six editions in the US and UK.

WOLFF, TOBIAS.

TOBIAS WOLFF'S books include the memoirs *This Boy's Life* and *In Pharaoh's Army: Memories of the Lost War*; the short novel, *The Barracks Thief;* the novel, *Old School*; and four collections of short stories, *In the Garden of the North American Martyrs, Back in the World, The Night in Question*, and most recently, *Our Story Begins: New and Selected Stories*. His work is translated widely and has been recognized with numerous awards. In 2015 he received the National Medal of Arts from President Barack Obama.

Permissions

BEIDEMAN, C. R. "Upstream Vertigo." Copyright © 2019 by C. R. Beideman.

BENZ, CHANELLE. "West of the Known" from *The Man Who Shot Out My Eye Is Dead: Stories* by Chanelle Benz. Copyright © 2017 by Channelle Benz. Reprinted by permission of HarperCollins Publishers.

BLANTON-STROUD, SHELLEY. An early version of "You Owe Me" was published in *Soundings Review* (Summer 2016) as "Wrong Choice Girl." Copyright © 2019 by Shelley Blanton-Stroud. Reprinted with the permission of the author.

CASPERS, NONA. "The Fifth Season" is reprinted from *Heavier Than Air: Stories*. Copyright © 2006 by the University of Massachusetts Press. Reprinted with the permission of the University of Massachusetts Press. All rights reserved.

DAVIDSON, ASHLEY. "Thirst" first appeared in *Hawai'i Review*, Number 81 (2015). Copyright © 2015 by Ashley Davidson. Reprinted with the permission of the author.

EVENSON, BRIAN. "The Intricacies of Post-Shooting Etiquette" was first published in *Chicago Review* (Winter 2000) and then in his story collection *The Wavering Knife* (Fiction Collective 2, 2004). Copyright © 2004 by Brian Evenson. Reprinted with the permission of the University of Alabama Press. All rights reserved.

EVERETT, PERCIVAL. "Graham Greene" from *Half an Inch of Water.* Originally published in *Callaloo*. Copyright © 2015 by Percival Everett. Reprinted with the permission of The Permissions Company, Inc., on behalf of Graywolf Press, Minneapolis, Minnesota, www.graywolfpress.org.

GILLETTE, DAVID. "and drop" was published in *Summerset Review* (Summer 2016). Copyright © 2016 by David Gillette. Reprinted with the permission of the author.

GRIESMANN, LEAH. "Desert Rats" appeared in *Union Station* 6 (Summer 2012). Copyright © 2012 by Leah Griesmann. Reprinted with the permission of the author.

GRIFFITHS, SIÂN. "Sk8r" appeared in *Georgia Review* (Fall 2015). Copyright © 2015 by Siân Griffiths. Reprinted with the permission of the author.

HUA, VANESSA. An earlier version of "Harte Lake" appeared in her story collection *Deceit and Other Possibilities* (Willow Books, 2016). Copyright © 2019 by Vanessa Hua. Reprinted with the permission of the author.

LANI, ANDREA. "Confluence." Copyright © 2019 by Andrea Lani.

LENHOFF, LINDA. "Your Call Is Important" was previously published in the *Tishman Review* 1:4 (2015). Copyright © 2015 by Linda Lenhoff. Reprinted with the permission of the author.

LEVY, AHARON. A version of "Sasquatch Seeks a Mate" appeared in *Ecotone* 4: 1 and 2 (Winter 2008). Copyright © 2019 by Aharon Levy. Reprinted with the permission of the author.

MADRID, L. L. "The Casita on Flower Street." Copyright © 2019 by L. L. Madrid.

MAYNARD, MARK. "Last Call at the Smokestack Club." Copyright © 2019 by Mark Maynard.

MELOY, MAILE. "Kite Whistler Aquamarine" from *Half in Love* by Maile Meloy. Copyright © 2002 by Maile Meloy. Reprinted with the permission of Scribner, a division of Simon & Schuster, Inc. All rights reserved.

MILLIKEN, DOUGLAS W. "A Thirteenth Apostle's Star" originally appeared in *Camera Obscura* 4 (2012). Copyright © 2012 by Douglas W. Milliken. Reprinted with the permission of the author.

MOUSTAKIS, MELINDA. "Miners and Trappers" was previously published in *Kenyon Review* 33: 4 (Fall 2011) and then in the collection *Bear Down, Bear North: Alaska Stories*, Flannery O'Connor Award Series (University of Georgia Press, 2011). Copyright © 2011 by Melinda Moustakis. Reprinted with the permission of the University of Georgia Press. All rights reserved.

SCHMIDT, MIRANDA. "Aquarium." Copyright © 2019 by Miranda Schmidt.

WARNER, CATHY. "Impressions of a Family" was first published in a slightly different version online at *A Lonely Riot Magazine* (May 2016). Copyright © 2016 by Cathy Warner. Reprinted with the permission of the author.

WILLMS, MICHELLE. "Old Car." Copyright © 2019 by Michelle Willms.

WILLY, E. G. "Wagli Yelo." Copyright © 2019 by E. G. Willy.

WILSON, KIRK. "The Goat's Eye" was published in *Meridian* (Spring 2012). Copyright © 2012 by Kirk Wilson. Reprinted with the permission of the author.

WOLFF, TOBIAS. "That Room" first appeared in different form under the title "In the Hay," in *New Yorker* (June 19, 2000), and as "That Room" from *Our Story Begins: New and Selected Stories* by Tobias Wolff. Copyright © 2008 by Tobias Wolff. Used by permission of Alfred A. Knopf, an imprint of the Knopf Doubleday Publishing Group, a division of Penguin Random House LLC. All rights reserved.

The body of *This Side of the Divide* is set in Vendetta OT, designed by John Downer for Emigre Fonts. Vendetta unites roman type design with contemporary concerns for the optimal display of letterforms on computer screens.

The headers are set in Summa, developed for Delve Fonts by Don Sterrenburg. The classic roman spirit and bracketed, cupped serifs together with the narrow width and elevated x-height of Summa give it a lofty, elegant appearance and an economic use of space.